PRAISE FOR *SWEET LITTLE LIES*

"Remarkable."
—*Minneapolis Star Tribune*

"Frear keeps the reader riveted."
—*Newark Star-Ledger*

"Astonishingly assured. . . . A stellar crime fiction debut by an author to watch."
—*Crime by the Book*

"[A] taut, psychologically twisted debut."
—*Publishers Weekly* (starred review)

"A truly satisfying—and gritty—mystery."
—*Kirkus Reviews* (starred review)

"An intense page-turner. Admirers of the police procedurals of Tana French and the thrillers of Clare Mackintosh will welcome Frear's dramatic debut."
—*Library Journal*

PRAISE FOR *SWEET LITTLE LIES*

Named a Top Debut by the *South Florida Sun Sentinel*

One of *Crime by the Book*'s "Best Debut Crime Novels"

A Book of the Month Club Main Selection

"Frear creates as fascinating a character as readers are likely to encounter this year. . . . A study in the damage that falsehoods inflict, a meditation on the grievances and grief of family—and a thumping good read." —*Free-Lance Star* (Fredericksburg, Virginia)

"Outstanding. . . . *Sweet Little Lies* is a confident first novel that succinctly melds the police procedural with the psychological thriller." —Oline Cogdill, *South Florida Sun Sentinel*

"A smart page-turner that you'd never guess was written by a first-time novelist." —AARP, "Summer Fiction Preview"

"Impressive. . . . Will also work as a way of keeping Tana French fans happy while waiting for French's next book."   —*Booklist*

"An assured debut. . . . All the characters—minor or lead, living or dead—are well crafted. Frear also makes an impression with her vivid dialogue and prose. . . . It's no secret that *Sweet Little Lies* is an engrossing read."   —*Shelf Awareness*

"One of the best debuts I've read in some time."   —*BookPage*

"A tremendous debut. Caz Frear delivers on a compelling premise with taut prose, snappy dialogue, and a fresh, confident voice. Highly recommended!"
—Alafair Burke, *New York Times* bestselling author of *The Wife*

"I read *Sweet Little Lies* in one sitting; it is a terrific debut."
—Lynda La Plante, creator of *Prime Suspect*

"Brilliant! Unputdownable and great writing. Recommended."
—Marian Keyes

"Outstanding. . . . Frear has an astonishingly confident voice for a new writer and there's a dark humor that lifts the storytelling to a different level."
—Ann Cleeves, creator of the Vera Stanhope and Shetland Island mystery series

"Kick-ass feminist, as well as laugh-out-loud funny."
—*The Independent* (London)

"A superb page-turner, packed with impressive police procedural, a fascinating, festering, twisting mystery that weaves tantalizingly between past and present, and a plot that thrills and confounds to the final showdown. A remarkable debut from an exciting new author."
—*Lancashire Evening Post* (London)

SWEET LITTLE LIES

A Novel

Caz Frear

HARPER

NEW YORK • LONDON • TORONTO • SYDNEY

HARPER

Originally published in Great Britain in 2017 by Bonnier Zaffre Publishing.

FIRST HARPER PAPERBACKS EDITION PUBLISHED 2019.

Library of Congress Cataloging-in-Publication Data has been applied for.

ISBN 978-0-06-282327-4 (pbk.)

19 20 21 22 23 LSC 10 9 8 7 6 5 4 3 2 1

For Alex, Chessy, Fifi and William,
and Mick

I recall the day we heard about Maryanne with high-definition clarity, although I know nothing about what happened to her, nor the manner in which she left.

I don't offer this by way of an alibi. Neither is it a well-practiced defense. After all, it's not as if I've ever had to explain myself—on the scale of likely suspects I was always nestled firmly alongside Gran, hovering somewhere between "laughable" and "nigh-on impossible"—and yet in order to understand the demons that hound me, and indeed in the spirit of the police oath I claim to hold so dear, I feel it's necessary to make clear that I know nothing about what happened to Maryanne Doyle, the girl who went to Riley's for hairspray and never came back.

I have my suspicions, of course.

I speculate plenty, especially after white wine.

But when it comes right down to it, I actually know nothing.

The same cannot be said of my father.

1998

It was 31st May 1998 and we'd been kicking around Mulderrin for over a week. I was eight years old, podgy, with a head full of greasy curls and a mouth full of wobbly teeth, and I was almost certainly wearing my Poke-mon T-shirt. Back home in London, my friends were getting ready to go back to school after the half-term holiday but Dad had just announced, between mouthfuls of toast, that we had "special dispensation" to stay on at Gran's for another week, earning him a high-five from my big sister Jacqui and a slap across the face from Mum.

Trying to diffuse a tension I didn't understand, I looked up from my Pop-Tarts. "Mum, what does 'dispensation' mean?"

Mum rolled her sleeves up like a yobbo about to start a pub fight. "Look it up in the dictionary, sweetheart. You'll find it near 'dishonest' and 'dis-grace.'"

Jacqui stretched across the table for a yogurt, her tangled blond hair shielding her cocksure grin. "It means Dad told the school to go fuck them-selves."

Mum eyeballed Dad like a piece of rotten meat.

Dad, not Jacqui.

But then everything was Dad's fault. Jacqui's gob. Noel's grades. My podginess. Even the good stuff, like the presents that kept appearing at the foot of our beds, and the new hi-fi—a real top-of-the-range one, accord-ing to Dad—ended up tarnished by the stain of Mum's disapproval. Even this trip to see Gran, the first holiday we'd had in three years: "Call this a break?" she'd said, as we'd queued for the boat at Holyhead. "It's just cook-ing and cleaning in a different house. A house that doesn't have a dryer or a decent hoover."

Weighing up the scene before me like the shrewd little politician I'd learned to be, I stuffed a Pop-Tart into the band of my leggings and made myself scarce, figuring it was only a matter of time before the spotlight shifted and I'd be switched from passive observer to sitting target. When Mum was like that, it was always a fine line to tread.

Other things I remember.

I ate malt loaf for lunch that day. Four fat wedges slathered thick with real butter. Gran loved to watch people eat, always complaining that the only person who ever called to the house was that scrawny one from the Department of Social Protection and you'd be all day trying to get her to eat a biscuit. "Not like you," she'd say, cheerleading me through a plate of ham sandwiches that you wouldn't give to a wrestler. "Now you wouldn't get blown down in a strong wind, my Catrina."

Later, because I'd behaved at Mass (and hadn't told Mum about the stop at the phone box on the way back), Dad gave me two pounds to spend at Riley's on stickers and sweets.

It was also the day that Geri left the Spice Girls.

With loved ones and family pets all still alive and kicking at this point, Geri's departure was the first sense of loss I'd experienced in my eight short years. The first stab of betrayal. It was Jacqui who broke the story—a fantastic coup for an English girl abroad—and I can still see her now, hurtling toward me across Duffy's field, her voice breathless with scandal, completely betraying the cool-as-ice image she'd been emulating since meeting Maryanne Doyle earlier in the week.

"Can you believe it, the bitch! The fat ginger Judas. So much for friendship never ends! Are you OK, little one?"

I wailed into her armpit with all the power and persistence of a colicky baby.

"There's a helpline you can ring," Jacqui said, hugging me in the way that only big sisters can, smothering me in a cloud of menthol cigarettes and CK One. "I'll walk you to the phone box later, if you like. Or I think I saw that Maryanne girl with a mobile? She might lend it to us if we give her something. Do you still have that two pounds?"

I didn't have the two pounds, and I didn't have any stickers or sugary things to show for it either. No sooner was it in my hand than Noel, my older brother and monumental shitbag, had snatched it away, warning me I wouldn't see my ninth birthday if I even thought of grassing him up. While I was fairly sure he wouldn't harm me—he was way too scared of Dad for a start—the mere threat of Noel's presence with his red sniffy nose and jagged dirty nails was enough to render me silenced and frankly, most days I wished he was dead.

So what with Mum slapping Dad, Geri turning traitor and Noel stealing my hush money, May 31st 1998 hadn't exactly been a great day for me. In fact, I wrote in my diary that it was the "Worst Day Ever in the Entire History of the Whole World Ever." Even worse than the day I'd been sick on the escalators in Brent Cross and Noel told everyone I had AIDS.

It was so bad I hadn't even noticed Maryanne was missing.

Maryanne was Jacqui's friend, so Jacqui insisted anyway. I never saw them exchange anything other than the odd funny fag and backhanded compliment. If I had to sum it up, I'd say Maryanne was oblivious to Jacqui, who at just fourteen was three years her junior and still in her training bra.

I'd looked up the word "oblivious" after Jacqui had stomped into Gran's one night, raging about Maryanne and her mates going off with some "bog-boys," which meant she'd had to walk home in the dark.

"I'm telling you, that Doyle one's oblivious to anyone's feelings," Mum said, stirring a pan of hot milk for Gran's brandy-laced cocoa. "The mother was the same, though God forgive me, I shouldn't speak ill of the dead."

I certainly wasn't oblivious to Maryanne. From the second I clapped eyes on her, I'd been dogged in my pursuit of this glittering creature in her baby-doll smocks and hoops the size of Catherine wheels—trailing behind her and her crew, mute with reverence and pained shyness, looking to get involved in literally anything they'd let me. Not that they ever did let me. In fact, she only ever deigned to acknowledge my existence once, at the farmers' market that was held every Friday in the town square.

It was two days before she disappeared.

"Hey, I like your Tinkerbell," she said, touching the tiny pink pendant that hung around my neck—a Holy Communion gift from an aunt who wasn't big into Jesus. "Where'd you get it? It's gorgeous! Look, it matches my belly-button ring, dead-on!"

She inched up her top and a group of tanked-up lads, wolfing chips out of cones, requested loudly that she get more than her belly-button out. Maryanne wasn't ruffled though. She just gave them the finger and turned back to me.

But then Maryanne wasn't exactly short of admirers. With her licorice-black curls and blossom-pink pout, most boys turned into cartoon clichés around her—eyes out on stalks, steam billowing from ears, blood-red hearts pumping outside their puny adolescent chests.

And it wasn't just the boys either.

It was the men.

The husbands.

The dads.

Dad told a lie that holiday. A big snarling monster of a lie. The kind that grown-ups always say you should never ever tell.

The kind that always comes back to haunt you.

There was only one person who knew it was a lie but eight-year-olds don't count, do they? Eight-year-olds are too busy with their stickers and their sweets and their Pokemon and their Spice Girls to ever have a clue about what's really going on.

Dad made lots of mistakes that holiday but his biggest was to equate being eight with being stupid.

Because I know he told a lie about Maryanne Doyle.

I know it truer than I know my own name.

1

Four p.m. Every Monday. For one hour. For the next eight weeks.

In roughly the same timeframe I could achieve something tangible, left to my own devices.

I could learn to code like every good little Millennial, or master the perfect soufflé.

But what I can't do is change the past. I can't redraft the god-awful ending or whitewash the dirt. These cozy, weekly, early-evening chats, well-intentioned as they are, can never obliterate the memory of tiny red footprints on cream kitchen tiles, nor wash crusty dried blood out of baby-fine hair. Nothing we discuss in this room can ever change what happened, and so it makes it all rather pointless in my book. Just a weekly invitation to my own private pity-party.

"Why are you here, Catrina?"

Dr. Dolores Allen, playing beautifully to type, glances furtively at the clock—the signature move of her profession. I follow her gaze and see I've got eight minutes left.

I keep it brief.

"Because DCI Steele needs to tick a box so she's outsourced the problem to you." The window's open a crack and in the distance I can hear a group of toddlers chirping "Little Donkey," out of tune and out of rhythm. The sound soothes me and then savages me with each jarring note. "Basically, she thinks I need my head sorted and, lucky old you, she thinks you're the woman to do it."

"And what do you think?"

"*Little donkey, carry Mary. Safely on her way . . .*"

"I think she might be right." I nod toward a wall peppered with achievements. "I mean, master's from Queens, BPS, BACP. Very impressive. A BA in Textile Design, that's me. Or a BA in Coloring In, as Steele calls it."

She smirks. Or at least I think it's a smirk. Dr. Dolores Allen has one of those Mona Lisa mouths, the kind that makes you think that you're not quite in on the joke. It's an unfortunate mouth for a psychologist to have when you think about it. Wry smiles rarely win deep trust.

"Catrina, I'm interested that you referred to yourself as a 'problem' just now. Is that how you see yourself?"

I shift awkwardly in my chair and the scrunching of the leather fills the silence while I try to work out how to answer without digging myself in deeper. "Everyone defines themselves by their problems, don't they?"

"They do?"

"Of course. Everyone beats themselves up: 'I'm fat,' 'I'm single,' 'I'm broke.' Take my sister, Jacqui, for example . . ."

"Your sister didn't walk into a prostitute's bedsit to find a blood-soaked child brushing the hair of her horrifically mutilated mother."

Emotional bushwhack.

Dr. Allen's face is blank, her tone entirely neutral, but her words are like spears prodding me back into that room with all the blood and the piss and the cheap, slashed-up furniture. I stare her down while desperately scrabbling about in my brain for something vacuous to focus on. Anything just to block it out. I settle on a puerile joke DC Craig Cooke sent me this morning. Something about his penis and a Rubik's Cube but I can't remember the punchline.

She leans forward and I instinctively lean back, an animal scolded. "I'm sorry to provoke you, but you have to think about what happened. You have to confront it."

"Don't give up now, Little donkey. Bethlehem's in sight . . ."

I pull my coat tight around me, a textbook defensive stance. "The only thing I need to *confront* is how to stop Steele shipping me out on secondment. Have you heard the latest? The Financial Intelligence Unit! I may be many things, Dr. Allen, but 'financially intelligent' isn't one of them."

"You should keep an open mind. Maybe Murder isn't right for you?" It's a loaded statement dressed up as a question. Fair play to her. "Why do you view a move as a negative thing? My understanding from DCI Steele is that it's quite the opposite. A secondment could be . . ."

"Beneficial? Good for my development? I see you got the same memo."

"Cynicism is a common state of mind for people who've experienced a traumatic event."

I laugh quietly into the collar of my coat. "Cynicism is a common state of mind for a police officer, Dr. Allen. In fact, I'm fairly sure it's part of the entry criteria. That, and the ability to lift thirty-five kilos."

She reaches for her coffee, eyes locked on mine. "Do you believe I can help you?"

I stare at my palms, pretend to mull this over. A clairvoyant once told me that the curve of my heart line means I only ever open up in one-to-one situations. I'm not sure Dr. Allen would agree.

Eventually I look up. "Honestly? No. But that isn't a reflection on you. I've had counseling before, for other stuff. That didn't help either."

She keeps her voice casual. "Anything that feels relevant to discuss here?"

"Not really. Some cognitive behavioral stuff for a minor eating issue. Family mediation after I keyed my dad's Audi TT and he threatened to break my arm."

She doesn't react. "Do you think you're beyond help, Catrina?"

"It's been said."

"Oh yes? By who?"

I resist the urge to start counting people off on my fingers, aware that it might look a tad neurotic. I don't want to add "paranoid personality disorder" to my school report, after all. Although it'd almost be worth it for the look on Steele's face.

"So this is what I'm paying ninety pounds an hour for? To be told something I already fucking know. Cat Kinsella came out of the womb thinking the midwife was looking at her funny—anyone will tell you that . . ."

"My dad," I say. "Repeatedly. And DCI Steele, obviously."

She sidesteps the Dad thing again—different therapy, different hourly rate. "Surely the fact you're here shows that DCI Steele believes you're worth helping?"

"Oh *come on*. You don't get all those letters after your name for being gullible. Steele's covering her arse, plain and simple. She's worried I'm going to start wailing 'PTSD' if someone has so much as a nosebleed, so she's dumped the problem on you." I know I sound snide and disrespectful and a whole host of other things that I try hard not to be, but I'm a work-in-progress, what can I say. "Sorry, no offense . . ."

"None taken, Catrina." She waves away my apology with a bony, jeweled hand and I notice a small gleaming Peridot, similar to the one I used to steal out of Mum's jewelry box so I could pretend I was married to Gareth Gates.

"By the way, no one calls me Catrina. I prefer Cat, if that's OK."

"Of course. Although you didn't need to wait three sessions to tell me." She rests her hands in the nook of her lap and I sense she's about to go all *counselor* on me. "Do you often find it difficult to say what you want?"

Et voila.

"Nope," I say, draining the dregs of my coffee. "Although while we're at it, I much prefer tea."

She smiles, jots a few words down. I suspect it's something along the lines of "uses humor to deflect discomfort" rather than "remember to pick up some PG Tips."

Outside the toddlers have stopped singing.

"Look, honestly, I'll be fine," I say, a bit *too* full of beans to convince anyone. "It's the little girl I feel sorry for." I slow my breathing, steady my voice. "Tell me, will she remember everything that happened or could she forget, given time?"

I call her "the little girl" so Dr. Allen doesn't start bleating about "*over-empathy*" but her name is Alana-Jane and her favorite song is "Five Little Ducks." I know this because she told me she sang it to her mummy to try to wake her up, and I know that she ate dog biscuits for two days because it was all she could reach, even when she stood on the pink bucket. I also know she wore a "Daddy's Little Girl" vest under her blood-spattered hoodie and I *absolutely* know that her daddy killed her mummy, even if the CPS ruled that we'd face an impossible task proving it.

"My only professional interest is in what *you* remember, *Cat*. What you might forget, given time." She closes her pad, signaling the end of our *tête à tête*. "You mentioned in our first meeting that you weren't sleeping very well? Any improvements?"

"Nah. But then I've never been one of life's great sleepers."

She shifts position, briefly energized by this admission. "Any ideas why?"

I shrug. "I lived above a pub until I was eight—it doesn't exactly cement regular sleeping patterns. Or maybe I eat too late? And then there's the cheap, crappy pillows . . ."

Dr. Allen stands up and walks slowly toward the door. She doesn't exactly look annoyed by my flippant response—I'm not sure "annoyed" is licensed for use on the "Counselor's List of Appropriate Faces"—but there's definitely a flash of something human. A silent scream of *"why do I do this fucking job?"* that we're all probably entitled to by the twelfth month of a hard year.

"So, er, the little girl?" Determined to get an answer, I stall for time, making a huge, almost slapstick performance of buttoning up my coat. "Do you think she'll definitely be affected by it, long-term?"

"At three years old, it's very difficult to predict," she says eventually. "She's unlikely to remember the details. She might even forget or block out the 'event.' But it's likely she'll remember the feelings. And she'll carry those feelings through life, into her relationships, her work and so on. Strong, innate feelings of fear, anxiety and insecurity, that she may never fully understand."

Spikes of deep discomfort when you least expect them.

The constant low-level dread that taints everything you do.

"And of course at three years old, she's not really old enough to understand the finality of her mother's death. The irreversible nature of it. That concept will add a whole new complexity in a few years' time."

I picture my nephew, Finn—six years old and struggling with the concepts of broccoli, backstroke and three-digit sums.

"I've bought her a Christmas present," I say quickly, just to stop the flow of her gloomy predictions. "One of those Frozen dolls. It's Anna, I think. They'd sold out of Elsa."

Dr. Allen says nothing. In our fairly limited time together, I've come to realize that "nothing" generally means "bad" and that I'll be held to account for the *"over-empathetic"* Christmas present at a later date. Probably when I least expect it. But then maybe I've got her all wrong? Maybe she just has to get on. Maybe she has another soul to save, or Christmas shopping to do. Maybe she actually doesn't care once the sixty minutes are up. I have no idea what drives her to do her job. She probably feels the same about me.

"Merry Christmas, Cat." She flicks the catch on the door and a whoosh of relief shoots through me. "Look after yourself. You'll be with your family, yes?"

"Of course," I lie. "Twelve hours of rich food and poor conversation, same as everyone. Merry Christmas to you too, Dr. Allen."

The assumption that "family" equals "nurture" seems a little utopian coming from someone who deals in the science of dysfunction, especially after my "family mediation" remark, but then a frosty Christmas week in a twinkly, bustling London can do that to a person and I'd feel mean-spirited not playing along, even though I'm not sure I've got the stomach for Christmas with my family.

Come to think of it, I'm not sure I've got an invite.

2

Fevered and ghoulish, like Satan's little imps, we sit and wait in darkened rooms, aching for death to bring us to life.

Welcome to a slow nightshift with Murder Investigation Team 4. Where the only crime under investigation is "Who ate the last of DS Parnell's mince pies?" and the only questions come courtesy of Chris Tarrant on three a.m. reruns of *Who Wants to be a Millionaire?*

You see, when you work for the dead, you're stuck with a notoriously unreliable employer. Sometimes they're all over you, screaming their need for justice at every cursed turn. Conscripted by tortured ghosts, your need to serve them never goes away, not even when you sleep. It ferments in your stomach like a late-night curry, waking you at godless hours and leaving you queasy and exhausted for days.

But other times there's nothing. Nothing new, anyway. Just an avalanche of paperwork and quiz show repeats.

They can never prepare you for the downtime, for the sedentary stage that follows the kill. When you're holed up at Hendon—the Met's training center for new recruits—and you're being dazzled by mock courtrooms and flashing blue lights, you can never quite believe that admin will soon become your god. Data, your religion. I certainly couldn't anyway, although in fairness I might have been warned. There's every chance I just didn't hear it over the sound of my pounding heart every time a murder detective, *especially* the fabled DCI Kate Steele, took to the hallowed stage.

The slack-jawed child swooning over the prima ballerina.

"OK, for thirty-two thousand pounds, who is the patron saint of chefs?"

DS Luigi Parnell—nightshift's lead imp, and incidentally about as Italian as a bacon sandwich—jabs his Arsenal mug in my direction and winks at me like we're old allies from the trenches, even though it's less than six months since he alighted the Good Ship Gang Crime and took up with Murder. "Come on then," he says, "you and Seth are supposed to be the brains around here. Lowest rank, highest IQ, that's what the boss reckons. Enlighten me and Renée?"

DC Seth Wakeman looks up from a textbook, surreptitiously brushing pie crumbs off his sweater. "No idea, Sarge."

"Nor me," I tell him. "I'll Google it."

Parnell looks pseudo-disgusted and swivels back to the TV, muttering something about private-school educations and Google being the death of independent thinking. DC Renée Akwa laughs and offers me a crisp. I mindlessly grab a fistful even though I'm not keen on the flavor and it's only been an hour since we stank out the squad room with a garlicky pizza.

Awesome Renée Akwa. Twenty-five years a DC and as constant as the sun. I'd have sneered at that once, back when I had notions of progression but it's amazing what a flip-out in a prostitute's bedsit can do to pour concrete on your glass ceiling.

I squint at my screen, too lethargic to reach for my glasses. "So St. Lawrence is the patron saint of chefs. St. Michael's the patron saint of coppers, if you're interested. He's the patron saint of the sick and the suffering too."

Parnell doesn't rise to it, choosing to nag Seth instead. "Here, Einstein, are you ready for another test? Fat lot of use Google will be when you're trying to remember 'Revisions to PACE Code G' for your boards next month."

Seth groans, pretends to hang himself with a strip of tinsel, and the laugh that breaks out goes some way to dissolving the twisted ball of angst I've been ferrying around since I left Dr. Allen's introspection chamber earlier this evening. Later, as Parnell argues with Chris Tarrant that the Nile is *definitely* longer than the Amazon, and Seth gives us his rugby club's slightly un-PC rendition of the "Twelve Days of Christmas," the urge to do a Miss Havisham, to bolt the doors and stop the clocks and cocoon the four of us in our cozy-as-fleece squad room for-ever, overwhelms me.

And then a desk clerk clutching a bottle of cough syrup spoils every-thing.

"Luigi, you're wanted," he croaks from the doorway. I struggle to hear the details as they huddle together—Parnell's shot-putter bulk blocks out all soundwaves—but I get the gist.

A body. A woman. Leamington Square, by the entrance to the gar-dens. Just at the back of Exmouth Market.

It looks suspicious. Islington police have secured the scene. DCI Steele has been notified.

Exmouth Market.

Not strictly our patch, but when the other two on-call Murder teams are up to their eyeballs in bodies and you're just sitting around eating crap and procrastinating about paperwork, you don't start quoting boundaries and grid references. I don't anyway. Parnell gives it a try.

And with a creeping sense of unease that strips away all the notions of sanctuary I held just two minutes ago, I think to myself that it is my patch really. In the umbilical sense, at least.

I spent the first eight years of my life there.

Last I heard, my dad was back there, running our old pub.

Mixing with his old crew again.

Living the Bad Life.

At ten p.m. every evening, as punctual as a Swiss clock, Dad would ex-cuse himself from whatever barroom brawl he'd been refereeing and walk the few hundred yards up to Leamington Square Gardens to smoke his solitary cigarette of the day. Whether he was dodging Mum—an evangelical ex-smoker—or whether he did it for reasons of solitude and sanity, I never really knew, but I'd watch him most nights from my window, quickly throwing down whatever book I'd been reading by the light of my Glo Worm as soon as I heard his steps crunching across the gravel. Eventually he'd become just a dot in the distance, a flash of a phone or the flare of a lighter, but I felt comforted by it somehow. Happy that he had five minutes' peace.

He took me with him once. I was only six. Mum was at Auntie Carmel's so Dad warned me it was "a special treat" which generally meant "secret," along with everything else that happened when Dad was left in charge (crisps for dinner, a very loose diktat on brushing teeth, and illegal poker nights in the back room with the men Mum didn't like). It was the first time I'd been to the gardens at night—I'd been there often during the day, playing shops in the bandstand, hopscotch on the path— and after we'd been there awhile and we'd chatted about *Toy Story* and my new puffer jacket, Dad asked me if I was frightened being out so late. He said most kids my age would crap themselves and start bawling to go home.

I told him I wasn't scared of *anything* when he was with me and he'd ruffled my curls and said that was right.

Tonight I feel scared though, and even with Parnell at my side, as solid as the plane trees that line the perimeter of Leamington Square, I can't seem to shake the feeling that no good will come of being back here.

Not quite a sense of doom, but one of nagging disquiet.

As soon as we're parked up by the outer cordon, I walk over to Parnell's side and let his genial grumpiness soothe me.

"Forty lousy minutes and it'd have been changeover. Some other sod's problem, and a hot shower and a cuddle with the wife for me. Jinxed we are, Kinsella, bloody jinxed."

"Doesn't bother me," I lie. "No one to cuddle up to or switch the hot water on. Might as well be freezing my arse off with you."

If I say this enough times, I might convince myself. Then I might also be able to convince myself to tell Parnell and Steele that I grew up less than a football pitch away from here. That my dad runs a pub so close you can hear the jukebox on a warm summer's day when the main doors are open. That I lived above that pub until I was eight years old.

Before everything changed.

But I *can't* give Steele any more reasons to ship me out of Murder, not after *Bedsit-gate*. Not that this is the same, mind. There isn't anything procedurally wrong with having once grazed your knee on the same spot as a dead body. But then you don't get to DCI level, with no fewer than four commendations under your belt, without knowing how to exploit an opportunity, and therefore any admission that I've got the slightest personal connection to this case and Steele will have me counting beans with the Financial Intelligence crew before I can say "Excel spreadsheet."

As Parnell continues his mournful dirge, I weigh this up one final time, staring at my reflection in the car window. All I see is someone who needs her job in MIT4 as desperately as she needs a haircut and a big dose of vitamin C.

It's simple. I'll say nothing.

Steele's here already, forensic-suited and booted, chatting to two SOCOs, Scenes of Crime Officers, as they bob up and down placing evidence markers on the floor.

"Jesus, she got here quick," I say. "Doesn't she live over Ealing way?"

Parnell rummages in the boot, his voice is muffled but the square is convent quiet. "I keep telling you, she's not human. She doesn't take a shower and get dressed like you and me. She regenerates, like the Terminator." He straightens up and waves over to Steele, tossing me a pair of shoe covers and a protective suit with the other hand. Steele signals for us to hurry up, pointing at a hunched figure standing by the entrance to the forensic tent. "Oh brilliant. Is that the back of Vickery's head?"

"Not in the mood for being patronized in sub-zero temperatures, no?"

Joking aside, I don't have an issue with Mo Vickery. Hats off to anyone who can stand in a ditch for eight hours collecting maggots and call it a vocation. And when you're twenty-six, rosy-cheeked and you've hitched your wagon to one of the most hierarchical organizations in British society, being patronized is kind of par for the course, really. A rite of passage you can either embrace or ignore.

We suit up in silence. Parnell struggles with his zipper while I scrape every last strand of my hair into a bun before Mo Vickery tells me *again* that she'd sooner I "piss on her porch" than come anywhere near her crime scene with my thick Celtic thatch.

"So what do you reckon?" I say, nodding toward Steele. "Must be bad to get her out of her jim-jams."

Parnell grabs his e-cig out of the car door and takes a fast, deep draw, his face etched with longing for a big-boy cigarette. "Chief Super gets twitchy around Christmas," he says. "Joe Public doesn't like the idea of someone's presents going begging under a tree while they're being carved up in the morgue so he always brings the big guns in." He blows out a plume of something sickly, apricots maybe. "Although it could be a tramp for all we know. Some old dosser who's shuffled off to the great cardboard box in the sky, right at the end of my bloody shift."

"All life is sacred, Sarge." I grin the grin of the lapsed Catholic.

"Yeah well, so are my testicles, and Mags will be using them as baubles if I end up working another Christmas."

He slams the car door and the noise has a finality to it, like the hammer at an auction. We walk across the square and duck down under the inner cordon. Parnell's knees click loudly and he groans even louder.

I suppress a laugh, almost.

"Yeah, all right, never get old, kiddo." I nod toward the tent, a reminder that not everyone gets the chance. "OK, never get fat then," he adds, sheepish. "And take your cod liver oil every day—the liquid, though, not the tablets. There's more vitamin D in the liquid, it's better for your joints." He looks satisfied, his good deed done for the day. "Don't say your uncle Lu doesn't teach you anything . . ."

"Masks," booms Vickery, not bothering to turn around. "*He's* already handled her. We can do without any more contamination, thank you."

I aim a sympathetic look toward "*he*," the young PC manning the cordon, but he doesn't look fazed.

"Preservation of life was my priority," he says, in a way that must make his mum really proud. "I had to check for a pulse, I'm afraid. The witness was a bit . . ." He makes a drinking gesture with his right hand. "Well, she wasn't sure she was actually dead."

Vickery shoots a deadpan glance toward a young girl perched on the back of an ambulance wearing stripper heels and an emergency foil blanket, and then looks back at our unmistakably dead body. I want to point out that there's a whole world of difference between being politely informed of a body over the telephone and literally stumbling over one when you're brain-fried from Jagerbombs and panicking about train times, but I keep my own counsel.

Steele flicks her head toward the ambulance. "Have a word afterward, Kinsella. You're more her age. You might get more out of her."

I nod and we step into the forensic tent. Vickery leads the way.

Outside it's about as pitch-black as London ever gets but inside, with the all the LED lights and flashing cameras, the full Technicolor horror of this woman's last hours takes centerstage. I hesitate to look down for a few seconds, silently counting one, two, three, in small sharp breaths before I clock Steele looking at me. Irritated or concerned, I'm not sure. It's usually a blend of both. On the count of four I give in to the inevitable and lower my gaze to see something you couldn't really call a face anymore, more a tawdry Halloween mask—blood blanketing the head, hair completely matted, apart from a few blond tufts that seem to have survived the flood, throat scored with long thin slashes as if someone was sharpening a knife. I crouch down and closer to the body I smell something. A fruity, floral perfume that must have been sprayed in the not-too-distant past, and a whiff of something like fabric softener on a well-cared-for coat.

Scents of a recent life.

More depressing to me than the acrid stench of death.

My stomach revolts and I stand up quickly. Too quickly. I try to cover myself by pretending to offer Parnell my slightly better vantage point but Steele sees through me. I'm not usually that deferent.

She slips her mask down. "You OK?"

Define OK. I haven't cried, vomited or momentarily passed out, which is more than can be said for what happened at *Bedsit-gate* but OK? Far from it.

A stint with the Bean Counters flashes before me.

"I'm fine, Boss." I even manage a small smile, hope that it reaches my eyes.

"Do we have an ID?" asks Parnell, cocking his head this way and that, trying to make sense of her face.

"No, but there's a receipt in a pocket so we've got that photographed and sent over. Renée's onto MISPER already but frankly they're going to need a bit more than 'female' and 'blond' to go on." Steele wafts a hand in front of her face. "And with all the blood, it's hard to give them anything approaching a precise age at the mo. Hands look youngish but then so do mine I'm told, and I'm no spring chicken."

"She might not be a missing person as far as anyone's concerned," says Vickery, peering closely at the woman's neck. "She hasn't been dead that long."

I swallow hard, will my voice to come out normal. "So how long do you reckon, Mo?"

We're not exactly on "Mo" terms but it's got the right air of casual.

Vickery cranes around, addressing Steele, ignoring me. "What I *reckon* is that she certainly wasn't killed here. There isn't enough blood to suggest an attack took place here and the faint lividity is patchy which confirms she's definitely been moved. Unfortunately, what this also means is that without knowing the conditions of the primary crime scene, it's very hard for me to estimate exact time of death."

"Educated guess?" says Parnell.

Vickery lets out a well-practiced sigh then gently prods the woman's jaw as we all peer closer. "As you can see, rigor is in its very early stages. There's a little stiffening around the facial muscles that would suggest two to three hours perhaps, but it all depends on whether she's been outside from the get-go or whether she was kept indoors for a while and then dumped. Rectal temperature is thirty-four degrees, but again this doesn't tell me anything definitive unless I know where she's been.

Stomach contents should narrow it down a bit. And lividity is still quite faint which suggests we're looking at less than four to five hours."

"Cause of death?" says Steele, sarcastically hopeful.

Vickery gives a wry smile. I'm not sure she's capable of any other type. Every facial expression seems to be undercut with either contempt or bemusement.

"Take your pick. We have a nasty wound to the front of the head. Possible petechial hemorrhaging which might explain the circular contusion around the neck, but I won't be able to get a proper look until we clean up the slashes to her throat—which incidentally, I don't believe *will* be the cause of death. They're nasty but a bit too shallow. No way they've gone through to the larynx."

"Hesitation marks?" I suggest. "Someone trying to pluck up the courage?"

A begrudging nod. "Possibly. Or could be old-fashioned torture."

"*Possibly*" and "*could.*" The watchwords of every crime scene.

Steele sighs. "I'll take a guess on cause of death for now, Mo. Educated or wild-as-you-like."

"As you wish, but I won't be held to anything."

As if we'd dare. Even Steele treads carefully around Mo Vickery, which is pretty telling given that, rumor has it, Steele once told a Deputy Assistant Commissioner to "take a chill pill."

Vickery steps outside the tent and Parnell and Steele swiftly follow, instantly gulping in the Arctic air. Something keeps me rooted though and for what seems like a moment but can only be a few heartbeats, it's just me and her—this blood-drenched everywoman in her sensible winter coat and low-heeled Chelsea boots.

I move when the tone of Steele's cough reminds me Vickery's patience isn't so much thin as emaciated.

"My guess would be she was strangled," Vickery's saying as I join them. "Struck on the head with a blunt instrument, then strangled while subdued. I say subdued because people fight like hell when they're being strangled and there doesn't appear to be any obvious defensive wounds. Also"—she hinges forward at the hips, a yoga pose I recognize for stretching out the spine—"this girl has long nails so I'd expect to see marks on her palms if she was conscious at the point of death. Clenching is very common during strangulation."

"She could have been tied up, drugged?" offers Parnell.

Vickery hinges up, loses her balance slightly. We pretend not to notice. "Drugged, possibly. Tied up, unlikely. There's no obvious marks to the wrists but I'll know more once I get her on the table."

The thought of taking her to the morgue seems to deflate Parnell, as if keeping her here under the pre-dawn stars and the promise of a new day makes her somehow less dead. Similarly deflated, and conscious we'll soon have an audience—a few bathroom lights are already flickering along the west of the square—I go to speak to the witness.

Close up, she's even younger and twice as drunk.

A paramedic with a slight overbite intercepts me. "Tamsin Black, nineteen. We're not getting much sense, I'm afraid. Think she might have imbibed a bit more than just booze, if you catch my drift."

I like the way he says "imbibed," like a Jacobean aristocrat, so I give him a warm smile that just about stays within the boundaries of "crime scene appropriate." "When will I be able to talk to her?"

"You can try now, love, but I wouldn't bother. She's puking more than talking."

On cue she retches, a futile little jerk that produces little but amber-colored bile.

I glance at the paramedic's name badge. "Well, I don't know about you, Phil, but I'm impressed she had the wherewithal to phone it in, in that state."

Phil looks nervous, rubs his overbite. "Looks like she had the wherewithal to post it on Facebook too. I saw it flash up on her phone. Sorry."

I groan inwardly. "Not your fault. Thanks for letting me know. I'd better try to get that deleted before her mates log on for the day."

I start to walk over, but then someone says something about a panic attack so I back off and watch while the experts try to explain the basics of diaphragmatic breathing to someone struggling with the basics of bladder control. Tamsin Black looks so listless and pale through the layers of fake tan—and so painfully young—that I have to fight the urge to stride over and take her hand. To tell her I understand and that she can talk to me. To tell her the brutal images will fade.

Essentially to lie that it gets easier.

Then I realize I'm being *"over-empathetic"* so I walk back over to Steele and grass her up immediately. Steele does the requisite amount of eye-rolling but honestly, it's a battle we conceded long ago. Facebook helps more cases than it ever harms so we live with it.

Parnell yawns. "So what's the plan then, Boss?"

"I need to wait for them to finish, give them permission to remove the body," says Steele, nodding toward the SOCOs. "Then I'm heading straight over to HQ to get things set up. You pair stay here for a while. House-to-House should be here soon so can you brief them, Lu? *Hopefully* we'll get something from CCTV but for now we're working on the assumption that she must have been driven here, so someone might have heard a car?"

"Funny place to dump a body, don't you think?" I say. "There's got to be easier places than the middle of central London."

"Panic maybe? Listen, Kinsella, have another crack at the witness before they whisk her off to hospital, OK? I know we can't rely on the detail too much but at least it'll be fresh and I want to get some sort of statement out of her before Mummy Dearest gets here and starts saying her little angel's been through enough already."

Exactly what my mum would have said. Once she'd ripped me a new hole for staggering around London half-comatose and half-naked at half-four in the morning.

God, I miss my mum. To the rest of the world you're just a living, growing mass of cells. Your brain fully forms and your bones start to lengthen and before you know it, you're a card-carrying grown-up who's expected to drive cars, pay bills and remember to buy tinfoil. But to your mum, you'll always be a bit gormless. The girl who sneezed in her porridge and ate it anyway.

And I miss that. I miss being a half-wit and being loved for it.

Lately I've been obsessing about what Mum would think of twenty-six-year-old me. What she'd say if she could see me now, out of bed and being productive before lunchtime.

In all honesty, she probably wouldn't recognize me. It's fair to say I wasn't the easiest of adolescents. Dad often said that it took an iron fist and a will of steel to discipline me—not that he ever tried, of course, preferring always to claim that there was no point in *him* disciplining me when he just couldn't work me out. Couldn't "get on my level."

I'd worked him out though. I knew exactly what he was.

I saw the way he'd looked at Maryanne Doyle, and I saw a lot more too. Heard a few things as well.

Not that I ever told him, or anyone else for that matter. The silence of childhood fear gradually morphed into teenage rebellion—a far more fun way to vent my hate than raking up history and throwing accusations—and lately, in recent years, we've slipped into a kind of venomous stalemate. A white-hot apathy.

You stay out of my way and I'll stay out of yours.

Mum knew I loved her, though, I'm sure of it. I certainly told her enough times. Every morning and every evening and several texts in between.

"Luv U," "Ur the best, Mum! xxx"

And *apparently* she can see me now. According to the same clairvoyant who mumbled clichéd statements about my heart line, Mum's always with me and she's proud of me. She enjoys watching me dance *apparently*. It assures her I've moved on from her loss. I didn't have the heart to tell the lousy charlatan who was charging me sixty pounds an hour for this heartwarming slice of hoodoo, that the *only* time you'll ever find me dancing is when I'm paralytic-drunk and Mum definitely wouldn't enjoy watching that. Who would enjoy watching their last-born child twerking in front of a rabble of baying IT consultants while trying not to vomit peach schnapps?

Mother's Day 2013.

They haven't got any easier or any less shambolic.

"You look bloody shattered, girl." As if reading my mind, Steele comes over all quasi-maternal, laying a hand on my arm. "Initial briefing at one p.m., OK, but in the meantime, go home and get a few hours shut-eye. That's an order, both of you." She says "both" but she's looking at me. "I mean it. Stay here for an hour, tops . . ."

We stay three hours.

Three hours where we learn very little.

I speak to the witness again but you couldn't exactly call it a statement, just a few random proclamations of *"So much blood"* like a bizarrely reimagined Lady Macbeth, and repeated requests for her mum. As instructed, Parnell briefs the House-to-House crew—a team of six men and women dedicated to fighting crime with questionnaires and clipboards—and we even do a bit ourselves, flashing our IDs at confused-looking people with morning breath and bed hair. It yields zilch though. A whole load of "nothings" and one dubious "maybe" which doesn't really fit with our timeline anyway.

After three hours of spreading hysteria, Parnell announces that he's going home to have sex, bacon and a steaming hot bath. He doesn't mind in what order.

I don't announce where I'm going.

3

McAuley's Old Ale House. Maccers for short.

My dad's pub.

Home.

Home right now is a ten-by-eight in the eaves of the Dawson family residence in Vauxhall, where I've got my own sink and toilet, two shelves for my food, and the gnawing guilt of knowing a child was evicted from her bedroom in favor of £500 a month because Claire Dawson lost her job and they needed a lodger.

Home, from the age of eight, was a five-bedroom detached new-build in Radlett. A *"cul-de-sac,"* Mum proudly announced, as if a dead end was something to aspire to. I'd had to look up what it meant.

But to me, my real home, the place where I was formed and where I was at my most happy, will always be McAuley's Old Ale House.

As I was just a child when we left the pub, my sister Jacqui insists that the only life I've ever known has been one of en-suite shower rooms and Sky TV, but she couldn't be more wrong. I remember every madcap minute we lived above McAuley's. The peeling paint and the knock-off furniture. Dad cashing up while Mum was mopping down. I was so bloody content there. A proper little pub kid, rushing down the stairs on Saturday morning, gathering up the coins that people had dropped the night before, nicking crisps, skimming pints. Learning the word "cunt" and how to play snooker.

It's changed, though. Duck-egg blue, no longer brick-and-pollution-colored. *"Aspirational,"* I bet Jacqui calls it, meaning hipsters drinking whiskey sours out of jam jars. Less "boozer," more "gastro-pub." When we lived here in the nineties, you either microwaved it or you battered it; if you were being particularly cosmopolitan, you might have put a sprig of parsley with it, but now there's a chalked sign outside offering *"Potted Prawns, with apple and radish"* and *"Slow Cooked Porchetta."* Not a deep-fat fryer in sight.

There's a few lights on but it's too early to be open so I walk around the back and up the fire escape to what we used to illogically call the front door.

What am I doing? Why have I come? It's not even ten a.m., Dad probably won't be here.

The sound of my steps on the fire escape reverberate in the way they always used to and the door opens before I get a chance to look for the bell. But it isn't Dad standing there, it's the cut-price version. The man whose bitter failure to be Dad left him skulking off to Spain to pull pints in a strip club. Or at least so I thought.

My brother Noel stands in the doorway, rubbing sleep out of his eyes with thick, scabby fingers. We've got the same cupid's bow and the same allergy to shellfish but apart from that we could be strangers. We certainly try to be. He's chunkier than the last time I saw him, with ridiculous pumped up arms that haven't quite got the right ratio of muscle to fat. He leans his bulk against the doorframe and the squashed fat of his biceps turns from pink to puce as we stare each other out.

I break the silence first. "Well, if it isn't the prodigal son returned. What are you doing here?" The question's entirely rhetorical as I know it'll be about money. "Is Dad here?"

"'Fraid not," he says, heavy on the "t." He doesn't so much invite me in as walk away from the door and the sight of him retreating tempts me to do the same.

Curiosity wins out though and I step inside.

The hall smells of frying. Pork on the cusp of charcoal. I follow Noel into the kitchen and wait while he prods sausages around a pan, swearing at a space-age hob that has more functions than a cockpit. I look around but there's nothing to recognize. Not one single memory evoked. There's no hand-sketched growth-chart on the back wall by the trash bin. No sandwich toaster shaped like a cow. No stain from where I split my chin and dripped blood on the welcome mat. Nothing to say I ever lived here at all. It's all clean lines and brushed steel.

It reminds me of the morgue.

I talk to Noel's sun-damaged back. "So when did you arrive?"

There's a black hold all on the floor with its contents spilling out. There isn't enough to suggest a long stay but with Noel you'd never know. You travel light when you're doing a midnight flit.

"A while ago." Ever cagey.

"You're obviously not big news, Noel, I hadn't heard."

He smirks and spears a sausage, brandishing it across the floor like a weapon. The fat drips onto the tiles, pooling like petrol.

"Still doing that veggie bollocks? Or was that Jacqui?"

Jacqui. For about four months in 2001. And even then it was only veal.

I push the fork away. "So why'd you come here then, not Radlett? Hertfordshire not gangster enough for you?"

"Radlett?" He looks confused, which confuses me. "God, you really aren't a regular visitor, are you? I mean, Dad said it'd been six months since he'd last seen you but I thought he was exaggerating, getting his months mixed up. I should be calling you the prodigal daughter, really. At least I've got the excuse I'm in a different country. Where are you living these days?"

"Why do you want to know? Planning to burgle me again while you're back?" I pull a mock-contrite face. "Oh, I'm sorry, that wasn't you, was it? It was pure coincidence that a mate of yours found out my address and knew *exactly* where to find Mum's jewelry without disturbing anything else."

He barely flinches. Doesn't deny or defend himself. Just rummages in a cupboard, tutting at the lack of brown sauce.

Eventually he sits down at the table. "Dad seemed pretty upset, you know—about not seeing you in ages. Bit slack of you, really . . ."

Shit-stirring is Noel's favorite pastime. His undisputed key skill.

"Yeah well, I was pretty upset about him bringing that bimbo to Finn's sixth birthday party. How long had he known her? A fortnight?"

He nods. "Oh yeah, I forgot, Dad's supposed to live like a monk. From what I heard, Jacqui wasn't the least bit bothered so what it had to do with you . . ."

"'Course Jacqui wasn't bothered, Dad was paying for the party. A private room at the Rainforest Café. Very nice."

"I know. I saw the photos." He trickles ketchup over his blackened breakfast in thin, jagged lines. *Slashes across a throat—shallow but nasty.* "Didn't see many of you, mind. Sulking in the toilets, were you?"

I really don't know why I'm getting into this.

"A body's been found on Leamington Square," I say, cranking a major gearshift. "A woman. A youngish woman."

Clearly I don't know she's youngish, except on some wispy, intuitive level.

Noel shrugs, he couldn't be less interested.

I shake my head, ask again, "So what are you doing here then? Are you broke? In the shit with someone bigger than you?"

He doesn't look up, just keeps working away at his breakfast. "You know, given you haven't seen Dad in six months, it rather precipitates the more pertinent question of what *you're* doing here, little sister, not what *I'm* doing here."

Precipitates. Pertinent. A barbed reminder of an intelligence gone to waste. Noel's convinced that if he'd had the same private education as me, he'd have found a cure for cancer by now, or at least bought a Porsche, and the very fact he hasn't is always somehow laid at my door. For coming along seven years later. For my schooling falling in line with Dad's eventual coming into money.

Money that was never really explained, or questioned.

"I told you why I'm here, were you even listening? A woman's body's been found up the road from here."

He pauses, a piece of white toast hangs in mid-air. "And that's what you came to tell Dad?"

My mouth's dry. I need a glass of water. I spot tumblers through a frosted glass cabinet but there's no way I'm helping myself. This is a stranger's home.

I should go.

"Look, do you know whether he'll be here soon or not?"

"Haven't a fucking clue. I'm not his keeper." Noel pushes his plate away—two thousand calories in two minutes flat. "I think he's shagging that sweet-ass with the lip-stud though, the one who comes in here, so as soon as he's bored doing that he'll surface, no doubt. Can't give you an exact time though, sorry."

My insides scream. Lip-stud suggests young, and young suggests nothing ever fucking changes with my father.

I head toward the door. "Just tell him I called, OK?"

"Sure." Noel opens the dishwasher, tosses the pan in. "Any message I can pass on?"

I almost laugh at this. Truth is, I've no idea what I came to say.

Yeah, tell him I know he lied about Maryanne Doyle.

Tell him it's OK though, I was too scared to ever squeal.

But tell him I've been punishing him for it for the past eighteen years.

Instead, I say, "Yeah, tell him not to put non-stick pans in the dishwasher. It strips away the coating."

Noel laughs and trails me down the hallway. The morning's changed in the short time I've been inside and a low wintry sun dazzles my face as I walk back down the fire escape.

"Don't be a stranger, sis," he calls after me. "We'll have a drink sometime, yeah? Bring a colleague. Preferably one in uniform."

I stick my middle finger up then instantly wish I hadn't. It seems too flippant a gesture to be aimed at Noel, too matey; the kind of thing I reserve for Parnell when he's whinging about my driving or the weakness of my tea.

The door slams shut and I take out my phone. Ten fifteen a.m. Hardly worth going home now. However, in the interests of dodging Steele's wrath, I wander down to Exmouth Market to buy toothpaste, a lemony-stripe top from one of the many cutesy-kitsch boutiques and some cod liver oil, and then I head straight to the public loos to transform myself into someone who looks like they've been home. Afterward, to kill more time, I amble slowly toward Spa Fields, drawn to the sounds of shrieking children hurling themselves around the adventure playground—part of the regeneration of Exmouth Market, or the gentrification, if you're being snide. When I was a child, Spa Fields had been known for much darker adventures and I'd never been allowed to play here. Noel used to frequent it though.

Drink, smoke, fight, repeat.

Once when I was six years old, the police brought Noel home from Spa Fields. Something about a girl and a smashed bottle. I sat on the stairs listening to Dad raising hell about Noel bringing coppers to his door. Screaming that "Uncle" Frank would do his nut, and had he even thought about the effect on takings if "certain people" got wind that the Old Bill had been seen sniffing around McAuley's? Mum had just wanted to get to the bottom of it. To understand if there was another side to the story, or if she really had given birth to such a nasty piece of vermin.

I don't know if she ever got her answer. It was certainly never mentioned again. Like so many things within our family, it was glossed over or blocked out. Dad managed to smooth things with "Uncle" Frank, who incidentally isn't our real uncle—he's Dad's "blood brother." His *"brother from another mother"* he insists when he's drunk too much Bushmills.

Dad has two brothers. Real ones, those of the shared DNA kind. Uncle Jim and Uncle Kenny. I haven't seen them in a long time and I don't know too much about them, but what I do know is that, unlike "Uncle" Frank, neither of them ever beat Dad up with a pool cue for talking out of turn to a rival outfit. Neither of them ever remarked that Jacqui had "a bankable body" or offered her a job in their nightclub the night before she sat her A-levels.

Sitting on a bench beside the winter remnants of a foxglove tree, I wrap my coat tight around me and watch the children for a while, giddy with excitement that it's only a week until Santa comes. Then I fiddle with my phone for a bit, fire off a few emails. Obsess about who this "sweet-ass with the lip-stud" could be.

There was a Latvian girl who worked in our pub one Christmas. A student. She'd had a lip-stud too. Her name was Alina and she was supposed to be making her English better but she ended up making my Latvian better.

"*Mans vārds ir Cat un es esmu septiņas.*" (My name is Cat and I am seven.)

"*Man ir brālis sauc Noel un viņš smaržo maziņš.*" (My brother Noel smells of wee.)

I liked Alina. She used to make me laugh by saying that her other job was dancing to pop music in her pants in "Uncle" Frank's nightclub. I don't know what happened to her though. She was there one day and gone the next.

A bit like the snowman in that sappy cartoon me and Dad used to watch.

Dad had liked Alina too.

4

I slip back into the station just before one p.m., the chill in my marrow fending off punch-drunk tiredness for the time being. Violent death makes restful sleep seem like a rather shallow privilege of the living anyway, and it's not as if the Sandman and I are great pals at the best of times.

It occurs to me that I could ask Dr. Allen for something to help me sleep. To date, I've generally relied on wine, weed and a whole ton of emotional eating to numb me into eventual slumber but maybe a chemical crutch might be nice, although I'm not sure of the protocol.

Do you wait to be offered?

Does asking for something sound the "not-coping" klaxon?

More importantly, do I even care?

Right this second, probably not. With Leamington Square and my encounter with Noel trawling up long-buried memories and black tarry thoughts, the idea of some state-sanctioned oblivion buoys me more than it should.

"DCI Steele?" Parnell's just ahead of me, slumped against the front desk, interrupting the custody sergeant's flow as he checks the dietary needs of some goon in a "Gangzta" hat about to be booked in.

The sergeant glowers at Parnell. "Third floor. Door with the broken handle."

In reality, we don't need directions as the gravitational pull of an incident room is Herculean in strength. Stepping out onto the third floor, we instinctively turn left and follow the corridor to the end, straight and purposeful like darts, ignoring all the early-afternoon hustle of a central London station. From a few steps away, I clock Steele through the doorway looking sharp and match-fit, bouncing on her stockinged feet, all five feet three of her—shoes indiscriminately discarded somewhere, no doubt. *"I can't think straight with sore feet."*

Prepping the incident board are man-mountain DS Pete Flowers and blade-thin DC Craig Cooke—aka the Feast and the Famine. Both are solid coppers, without question. Diligent types. Flowers could probably make inspector if he wasn't so charmless, while Craig's a good guy to have around, a one-man-band of dad jokes and contagious optimism. I give a thumbs-up to Seth, still beavering away thanks to three cans of Red Bull and the lure of a gold star from Steele, and I smile vaguely at a stunning girl in a mustard duffle who I've worked with before—although when I say "worked with," I don't mean in the Cagney-and-Lacey sense—just that we shared the same kettle, copped the same flak.

But I'd know that duffle coat anywhere.

Given my job, I should feel blessed to have a good memory for pointless prosaic detail. Truth is, it's more of a curse and it's one of the reasons I find it hard to sleep. In a matter of seconds, my dead-of-night thoughts can sway from the consuming, feral agony of Mum's final days to the saltiness of the pork at Jacqui's wedding, while images as banal as driftwood and duffle coats rub shoulders with suspicions about my dad that are so black and unmentionable, I have to keep them locked in a box at the center of my frontal lobe.

In my mind, this box has always been purple. A deep Catholic purple with a heavy black lock. Despite the lock there's no key to open the box, to do so would be catastrophic, but occasionally a thought seeps out through the tiny space where the base meets the lid. It's already happened several times today.

"Righto folks, let's make a start." Steele hushes the room in two seconds flat. "Now contrary to popular belief, I'm not completely in love with the sound of my own voice so here's the drill. I'll go through the basics, answer any questions, get everyone up to speed, and then I'm throwing it out to the floor for a bit of audience participation, all right?"

A horseshoe of fresh-faced DCs sit up, synchronized in gutsy ambition. For a second I long to throw myself into the heart of their competitive clique and leave Parnell to his quiz shows and arthritic knees. But it's a quick spark of sentiment, gone before it can take root. I never seem to shine with people of my own age. I just never feel that relevant.

"So, quickly, let's talk about me, shall we?" Steele hops onto a desk, shuffling to make herself comfortable. Her legs don't quite touch the floor and with her flowery print dress and swaying feet, she looks like a child about to recite a nursery rhyme. "For those who don't know, my name's DCI Kate Steele and I'm the Senior Investigating Officer leading this investigation. You can call me Boss, Guv, whatever you like. You can call me Kate if you sense I'm in a good mood, but you run that risk at your own peril, m'dears. Behind my back, you'll no doubt call me Cardigan Kate, on account of the fact that my upper arms haven't been seen since 1989 but that's fine, I'm used to it. Christ knows, I've been called worse. Just don't let me hear you or you'll wish your mother had had a headache the night you were conceived."

A smile spreads across the faces of those who've worked with Steele before. We know this script verbatim.

"Now, there's a few of you I don't know so if you have something to say, put your hand up and state your name. I probably won't remember it but don't take offense. It doesn't mean you're not a remarkable human being, it just means I'm a batty old woman who can't remember where she parked the car half the time, never mind a load of new names every time I head up a case, so if you can just play along if I get your name half-right, I reckon we'll all get along fine. OK? Everyone happy?"

The horseshoe constricts, one or two allow themselves a cautious smile.

"Wonderful." Steele turns to face the incident board. "So, victim's name is Alice Lapaine. Thirty-five years old. A married, part-time pub chef from Thames Ditton in Surrey."

A point to her bloodied corpse followed by a quick reverent pause. Just enough time for us to contrast the normality of her life with the savagery of her death. *There but for the grace of God go I* . . .

"Vickery's in court this afternoon, maybe tomorrow, so there's a delay on the post-mortem, but in layman's terms—possible strangulation, a blow to the front of the head, slashes across the throat—not fatal. Other bumps and scrapes, mainly to the legs and chest. She was fully clothed, no obvious signs of sexual assault. No obvious defense wounds either. Vickery estimates she'd only been dead a few hours, four to five hours max. She was found on Leamington Square at approximately four forty-five a.m., however Leamington Square is *not* the primary crime scene. We have her on CCTV being dumped there at five past four in the morning. Benny-boy, you're up."

DC Ben Swaines, boyband-handsome in a tedious, steam-cleaned kind of way, steadies himself for the spotlight with one last run of his hand through his sandy-blond hair, but unfortunately not even his sterile loveliness can detract from the fact that it's a pretty depressing tale of stolen cars, poor-quality CCTV, tinted windows and balaclavas.

Basically, nothing a good lawyer couldn't make mincemeat of.

Parnell visibly sags with each blow, however Steele looks on, totally at peace with Ben's litany of disappointments. All part of the game, she reminds us, especially at the start of the case before the grunt-work kicks in.

"The car, a Vauxhall Zafira, belongs to a Richard Little." Ben looks relieved to have at least one tangible thing to offer. "A piano teacher from Tulse Hill. He's been in Malta visiting his parents since the eighteenth so he's in the clear. Didn't even realize his car had been stolen. He parks it outside his flat—it's off-street residents' parking but it's easily accessible. It'll be a lump of ash by now, no doubt."

"We're talking to the neighbors, right?" says Steele.

Ben nods. "The car was definitely outside at nine thirty p.m. A neighbor, Mr. Spicks, got home around then, remembers being narked that 'Liberace' had parked it in his usual space before buggering off to Malta. Seemed happy it'd got nicked, to be honest."

"Run the CCTV again." Steele balls her hands into fists and leans hard on the table, knuckles taut and pearly white. "Watch this and store it, folks," she says, tapping her temple. "Brazen is not the word."

We sit in grisly silence and watch a figure get out of the driver's seat, stretching their back slowly, almost luxuriantly, as if they've just finished a long, arduous drive. There's a quick glance away from the car, a last look up to Farringdon Road, perhaps—the only realistic source of interruption at that time of the morning—and then they open up the back seat and haul Alice Lapaine out by the shoulders, tossing her onto the tarmac and making every one of us flinch as her head smacks the road. The figure stands over her briefly, composed and stock-still, before getting back in the car and driving off. Nothing at all to suggest a crime of panic.

I've seen more signs of stress on someone illegally dumping a mattress.

"Judging by build"—Steele brings us back into the room—"I'd say we're looking for a man, but we can't completely rule out a strapping sort of woman."

Craig smiles nervously. "Here, it's not my Karen, is it?"

There's a murmur of a laugh but it doesn't take flight.

"Cameras have the car heading east for a few miles but they lose it when it turns off the Romford Road," says Ben, looking apologetic, as if the fallibility of CCTV is his own personal failing. "I've alerted relevant CID—Barking, Dagenham, Hornchurch, Stratford, a few others. They're going to keep their eyes out, but you know . . ."

"Kids or dog-walkers. It'll turn up somewhere. What's left of it," says Parnell.

Steele hops back on the desk and flicks through her notebook, which is pink, leather-bound and embossed with *Keep Calm and Nick Villains*. A present from me for her fiftieth last year.

"So, we don't have the car and we also don't have her bag, her purse or her phone. No surprises there. POLSA are down on their hands and knees combing the area but let's just say I'm not holding my breath." POLSA—Police Search Advisers, or in other words, Hardy All-Weather Heroes. "*However*, and I'll have a drumroll for this please, we did find a receipt stuffed in one of her pockets. It's for an espresso ristretto, whatever the hell that is. Bought at a café in Wandsworth on Friday, paid for by credit card, and thanks to the wonderful Seth Wakeman's persistent stalking—and OK, maybe the small matter of Chief Superintendent Blake's early morning intervention—Visa coughed up the details quickly." Seth takes a small bow. "The bad news is, and can you believe the utter Sod's Law-fulness of this, the café's closed until Thursday. The two owners are on some Christmas market jolly in bloody Dusseldorf, so bang goes our chance of finding out if Alice met with anyone until then. It's a bit off the beaten track so no CCTV either."

A chinless DC rises up but I get there first. "A receipt's hardly foolproof ID. How do we know it's definitely her? She could have picked it up randomly, stuffed it in her pocket."

"It's her. We need formal ID, of course, but Renée's at the Thames Ditton address with the husband now and they've scanned through a photo and it's definitely our girl. Actually, we need to get that up on the board, pronto. Kinsella, it's on my desk. Do the honors."

I walk into Steele's office, a kaleidoscopic blur of box-files and dry cleaning, and quickly start moving papers around, tidying as I go. Under a coffee-stained memo from the Borough Commander, Alice Lapaine stares up at me through a clear plastic folder. Unbloodied and intact, she looks familiar somehow, although it's more of a feeling, a vibration, than cast-iron recognition.

It's an odd photo, I think, to sum up a life. Off-guard and out-of-focus. The kind of throwaway snap you'd take to use up the last of a film. Sitting on a garden chair, Alice's lips curve upward in an attempt at a smile, but something about her body language, the hunched shoulders and the crossed arms, looks off. Like she's shrinking from the lens, trying to make herself small.

She doesn't feel small to me, though. This blue-eyed, blond-bobbed vision of complete-and-utter ordinariness is making my skin itch and my skull pulse.

I give myself a shake and walk out.

Steele's still holding court.

"So, the husband's being driven in for formal ID in the next couple of hours. Once we have that, I'll decide what exactly gets released to the media."

"The proper media, you mean," grunts Flowers. "It's all over social media, thanks to the numpty who found her."

I bristle at this, contemplate saying, *"You mean the numpty whose life has been irrevocably tainted? The numpty who'll have to relive this horror over and over in exchange for nothing more than a cup of tea and a Victim Support number?"* But Flowers has a prickly ego sometimes so I stay quiet, focusing intently on the floor instead until I'm sure the last remnants of pissed-offness have left my face.

Steele shrugs, crosses one leg over another. "Not a lot we can do about that now, Pete. So, the husband, Thomas Lapaine." She holds up a finger. "One: he claims he hasn't seen his wife in four weeks—she took off, not an unusual occurrence, apparently. Two: there was no one in when Renée got there around ten thirty a.m., so she had a quick chat with a neighbor, and she hadn't seen him for days. Which doesn't mean he'd gone AWOL, of course, just that their paths hadn't crossed . . ."

"His car?" asks Parnell.

"She couldn't be sure because—get this—the Lapaines don't live on a street or in a flat, or under a bridge like Benny-boy"—a nod toward her current favorite stooge—"they live on a private island on the Thames. Twelve houses, a population of about thirty, and to get back to my point, they all have to park in the village so the neighbor wouldn't know if his car was there or not."

Flowers whistles. "Private island, eh. There's money then?"

Steele nods. "And three: when Thomas Lapaine did arrive home fifteen minutes later, he said he'd been out all morning. *Walking.*" An alien concept to a woman who lives in four-inch heels. "Again, not unusual apparently. Three miles along the Thames Path, from Hampton Court to Kingston Bridge and back again. Takes a couple of hours. Obviously, Renée's going softly, softly at the moment, but to my mind, it's suspect. Bloody *walking*? When all the forecasts are warning, 'Don't take a shit in case your arse gets frostbite?'"

"He could be telling the truth," I say. "Of course, what we'd have then is a potential suspect and an early-morning walk along a river path? Disposing of evidence, maybe?"

As a detective, I'm more fueled by the mysteries and the "what-ifs" than the verifiable truths but I've sat in enough of Steele's first-day briefings to know that I'm about to get my snout slapped for ruining her Festival-of-Irrefutable-Facts.

"Not a bad theory, Kinsella. One that has absolutely no basis at all at the moment, but not a bad theory."

We are nothing if not consistent.

Duffle Coat's hand shoots up. "DC Emily Beck, ma'am. So is Thomas Lapaine a serious suspect?"

I cringe as Steele swats the question away. "Husband's always a suspect. Ask me another."

"Was he dressed for walking?" I ask. "I mean, you'd want more than your winter woollies in this weather. You'd want decent boots, for a start. A flask. A waterproof, maybe?"

Steele raises an eyebrow. "Never had you down as a rambler. Honest answer is I don't know. I've had two minutes on the phone with Renée all morning and she's obviously having to play nice. Until we've got evidence that Thomas Lapaine is anything other than a grieving husband, I don't want him feeling like he's a suspect. The last thing we want is him turning against us before we've had the chance to interview him properly."

Seth shouts over from his desk. "Bad news, Boss. He might already be against us, I'm afraid. The PNC check has thrown up something."

Parnell makes a praying gesture. "Tell me it's for offing an ex-wife, Seth. Make it easy on us."

"Alas no, Sarge. Section 5. Public Order Offense. He climbed on top of a van at a Reclaim the Streets March in 1996. Usual hundred-yard-hero, calling us 'pigs' and 'wankers' from a safe distance. He got six months suspended and an eight-hundred-pound fine. He's been squeaky clean ever since. However, and this is the interesting bit, he made an accusation of police brutality."

Steele's smile is acidic. "Did he really? Him and the rest. Anything in it?"

Seth shakes his head. "Doesn't look like it. He got a tiny bit of gravel rash when they forced him to the ground. It went to the PCA. They rejected it. He didn't appeal."

"Could make him touchy though," says Parnell. "We'll have to build that into our interview strategy."

Steele nods. "So what can you pair bring to the party? By the way, this is DS Luigi Parnell and DC Cat Kinsella for anyone who doesn't know. They were both at the scene this morning. Lu and I go way back, back before some of you were on solids, so if he tells you to do something, do it."

Parnell looks at me expectantly and I realize I'm being offered up as spokesperson.

"We don't have a great deal really." *When will I learn the art of positive spin?* "Girl who found her was too wasted to tell me anything. Just kept asking for her mum and her inhaler. We'll have another crack when she sobers up but I don't think she's going to be much help. It was forty minutes between our victim being dumped and found. Whoever dumped her was long gone."

"And it's quiet around there," says Parnell, hands raised. "Leamington Square's off the main drag and yes, I know it's residential, but it was four a.m. Not too many residents wandering about at that hour."

He's right, of course. If you had to pick a time when even the most decadent of deviants would be tucked up in bed, you'd probably pick four a.m. on a hypothermic Tuesday morning. But I still think there must be easier places to dump a body.

Steele called it brazen. I call it significant.

Parnell continues. "House-to-House are working the square and all the access roads but it's not throwing up much. It's up to you, Boss, but you could think about widening the parameters? Open it out toward Exmouth Market, maybe?"

No. Not Exmouth Market. Not my family.

The thought of Dad being questioned about a dead woman, no matter how peripherally, stirs something in me. Something dizzying and destructive.

"Could do," I say, heart hammering. "Personally, I think it'd be a waste of time at this stage. People are too preoccupied before Christmas to be that much help. And they're jumpy as hell too. We'd spend more time giving reassurance than we would gathering information."

It feels like a lifetime before Parnell speaks again. "Maybe, maybe not." He looks to Steele. "Kinsella's right about one thing though, people *are* as jumpy as hell. They're either going away and leaving their houses empty, or they've got family visiting, and obviously neither's ideal when there's, and I quote, 'a madman on the loose.'"

Steele groans. "Magnificent. That's all we need. I hope you warned the residents not to talk to reporters. If they get a sniff of a 'madman,' they really will think it's Christmas."

A silence falls over the room. Just the white-noise drone of technology and Flowers' stomach rumbling in low, melodic tones.

Steele breaks the lull with a weak laugh. "Look, I think we're just about done here. The Feast needs feeding, don't want him keeling over, do we?"

Flowers licks his lips in a way I think we're supposed to find grotesquely erotic.

"Usual drill," says Steele, voice raised. "DS Parnell and DS Flowers are your first ports of call, but my door is always open. Unless it's closed, of course." She walks over to her discarded shoes, a pair of emerald suede courts that cost more than my rent. "So, final call. Anything else? Anyone?" She turns on her heel, dropping a hand to Parnell's arm as she passes. "Lu, be a love and sort out assignments. Kinsella, a word, my office."

"Now I know we're in the age of 'female empowerment' but I've got to tell you, Kinsella, you look like shit warmed up." Steele gestures for me to sit down, picks up a lipstick and applies it perfectly without the aid of a mirror. "I mean it, you look awful. Washed-out. Although maybe it's that top—yellow's definitely not your color." She pauses. "Did you buy it in a panic? I'd take it back if I were you."

Her face is the very picture of authoritative benevolence, but it's all in the voice.

She knows.

I don't know how she knows, but she knows.

"Good sleep?" she adds with a pinched smile.

"Oh, you know, on and off." I jerk a thumb toward the incident room. "Parnell's not looking too rosy either."

"Parnell! Christ, it'd take more than a bit of beauty sleep to save Luigi Parnell. He's a lost cause. There's still hope for you."

Harsh but fair. Unashamedly overweight and sometimes a little under-groomed, Parnell's the kind of detective who makes you forget Sonny Crockett and Fox Mulder ever existed.

She drums her nails on the desk. Expertly manicured. I can never imagine her sitting still long enough to have them done. After a few seconds, she stops and leans forward. "Look, I'm not going to beat around the bush. Are you absolutely sure you're ready for this one?"

Be calm. Be rational. Stay classy, Kinsella.

"Of course," I say, feigning cool surprise. "Why? Have I done something wrong?"

"No." She lowers her head, mutters *"for God's sake,"* then glances up again, trying to look like she doesn't want to throttle me. "I just think it might be too soon after . . . well, you know."

"Alana-Jane. It's OK, you can say her name. I won't have a meltdown."

"I was thinking of the mother, actually."

"Dafina Tolaj. You can say her name too."

She points the lipstick at me. "Listen you, I'm less bothered about her name and more bothered about the fact that she was another blond, thirty-something woman covered in blood." *She looks familiar somehow.* "I think you can do without that again so soon, don't you? Especially while you're still seeing Dolores."

Dolores, not Dr. Allen. Visions of them dissecting me over a nice bottle of Merlot does them both a disservice, but I have a tendency to catastrophize when I'm cornered. Another counselor told me that.

"You don't want me on the case, is that it?"

Full-volume. "For God's sake, Kinsella, I'm not picking the netball team. You're not the fat kid in PE so quit with the doe eyes. I need everyone at the top of their game at the moment and I'm just not convinced you are."

"Based on what exactly?" It sounds stroppy, confrontational. I mumble a quick "*sorry.*"

Steele shoots me an arch stare. "Based on the fact I saw you at the crime scene this morning. You never used to be that queasy."

I try humor. "What can I say? We got pizza from Big Jimmy's again last night." I rub my stomach. "Seriously, Boss, they should close that place down."

She smiles and I sense a tiny victory. "Look, I'm not sure Dolores would advise you being involved, that's all."

"Has she said something?"

"No." *Of course she has.* "So how are the sessions going?"

"Am I still batshit crazy, you mean?"

"I mean are you finding them helpful?"

I could tell the truth but it's easier and ultimately to my benefit to play along. "I am, surprisingly. I'm actually feeling pretty good. *She's* pretty good. I definitely feel a lot calmer. And come on, be fair, no one's at the top of their game at five a.m. Not even you."

No reaction so I change tack. Less front, more fawning.

"Please, Boss, I feel a connection to the victim now. A responsibility. Please. I really want to work this case. Work for you," I add.

Steele purses her lips and sits back. Her chair's the cast-off of an ex-DCI, a man of Hulk-like proportions, and consequently it makes her look like a pixie. On her desk there's a mug quoting Shakespeare. "*And though she be but little, she is fierce.*"

"OK," she says finally but there's a threat in her voice. "But you report direct to me, OK, and you tell me the second you feel wobbly. Parnell's your everyday supervisor, but I want to know *everything* you're up to, right? *Everything.* If I ask when you last had a bowel movement, you tell me, is that clear?"

"Crystal, crystal," I say, smiling and nodding, almost to the point of bowing. "So, er, who's interviewing the husband?"

I figure I might as well push my luck.

"I'm doing the formal ID with him but I'm going to arrange for him to be interviewed at home. We might get more out of him in familiar surroundings."

"Absolutely, Boss. Absolutely." I keep smiling and nodding, nodding and smiling. "So, er, can I be in on the . . ."

"Yes," she snaps, impatient but with a glint of humor. "Parnell actually requested you, if you must know. I think he's quite smitten." She laughs at my horrified face. "Relax, Kinsella, don't flatter yourself. He's got four sons, that's all. I think he's always fancied a surrogate daughter."

This stirs something inside me too complicated to name, although "nice" might be an uncomplicated way to describe it.

Steele reaches for her internal phone, nods toward the door. "Right, *hasta luego,* Kinsella—or bugger off, whichever you prefer. Get prepped with Parnell, OK, and grab Renée when she's back, see what she makes of the husband." She points the receiver at me. "And just so we're clear, Parnell leads the interview."

I stand up and give a small salute. Message received, over and out.

Or "*si, yo comprendo,*" whichever she prefers.

5

Thames Ditton Island glistens as evening falls, and despite the reason for our visit, it's hard not to feel a little festive when faced with the constellation of Christmas lights flickering red, green and white among the dense canopy of trees, illuminating the river and the spectacle of Hampton Court Palace just beyond.

"God, it's so pretty," I say as we walk across the narrow footbridge. Parnell treads tentatively, as if he doesn't quite trust it.

"It's an insurer's wet dream. Look how high the water levels are! Must cost an arm and a leg in premiums."

When we reach the Lapaine house (small, white, timber-clad in the style of a Swiss chalet and to Parnell's relief, mounted on stilts), we find we're not the only visitors. The SOCOs have landed, and boy, they're not happy. Unlike Parnell, the island seems to have inspired in me a home-spun dream of sharing my breakfast with a kingfisher before heading out for a mid-morning sail, but even I have to admit that it's an inconvenient way to live. Certainly not ideal for forensic work, with the poor sods having to lug Alice Lapaine's personal effects—her laptop, diaries, address books, bank statements—from the house, across the river to the mainland, and all against the backdrop of a skin-cracking December chill.

In the midst of this, Thomas Lapaine stands in an open-plan living room looking out onto the water, bereft and confused, a stranger in his own home. A home that hasn't been decorated since the seventies if the swirly carpets and woodchip walls are anything to go by.

The man himself strikes a stark contrast to the time-warp house. Slick and urbane with a top-dollar haircut, he looks like the lead in a time-traveler romcom. As Parnell taps the living-room door softly, he turns his head. Red-rimmed eyes bore into ours, begging us to say something that will make him feel just one percent better.

Parnell begins. "Mr. Lapaine, I'm Detective Sergeant Luigi Parnell and this is my colleague Detective Constable Cat Kinsella. On behalf of the Metropolitan Police Service, may I offer you our sincerest condolences." In the absence of any other appropriate response, Lapaine nods. "Following the formal ID you made earlier today, I can now confirm that we're treating Alice's death as murder."

He blinks twice, quickly. "Thank you for letting me know." There's a rich, formal tone to his voice. Accentless.

"Mr. Lapaine, can you think of anyone who would want to harm your wife?"

"Can I think of anyone who would harm my wife?" he whispers, quietly exasperated by the question, shaking his head at a fixed point on the floor. "No one. No one at all. She was so kind, so . . . *harmless*. I don't understand how this has happened."

I'm about to attempt a consoling response when he has a better idea. "God, I need a drink." He walks toward the kitchen. "Would you like a drink? If your *friends* haven't emptied the cupboards, of course."

I'd gladly sell a kidney for some wine right now—250 ml of pure anesthesia. Parnell shakes his head so I grudgingly mouth the words, "Not for me, either." Thomas Lapaine shrugs, grabs a bottle of scotch and a glass and invites us to sit down.

"We're sorry about the intrusion, Mr. Lapaine," says Parnell. "However, your wife's personal effects are crucial to our investigation. You mentioned to DC Akwa, the officer you met this morning, that you hadn't seen your wife for nearly four weeks, but that this wasn't a cause for concern. Can you tell us when you last had any sort of contact with her?"

"December 5th. Two weeks ago. It was my birthday." He takes a sip of scotch—not the kind of slug I'd be taking in his position—then drops to the armchair opposite Parnell. "Although, strictly speaking, I didn't have contact with her. She left a message to say 'happy birthday' on our home phone."

"You weren't in?" I say gently.

"No," he says, barely a whisper. "I always have dinner with my mother on my birthday. Claridge's. It's become something of a tradition."

"Didn't she try your mobile?" asks Parnell.

"I'm guessing she wanted to get away with leaving a message. She knew I'd be out, you see." He answers before we can ask. "Look, Alice was quite complex. Sometimes she just wanted to be alone and I respected that. We respected each other."

Parnell nods. "You told DC Akwa that Alice had a history of disappearing for short periods."

"I'm not sure I put it exactly like that. Alice liked her own space, that's all. There's a little cottage in Hove she liked to rent sometimes. I told the detective that."

"An officer took a statement from the landlady just half an hour ago and she says that Alice hadn't booked the cottage in well over a year."

He shrugs. "There's a place near Paignton too. She just liked a week by the sea occasionally, I can't always get away because of work and . . ."

Parnell narrows his eyes. "So you weren't concerned that she was gone for longer than a week this time?"

"No. I knew to let her get things out of her system."

"What things?" asks Parnell, verging on testy.

Lapaine picks up the bottle again and swills the liquid around, momentarily mesmerized. He could be formulating his lie or he could be locked in his own private hell, contemplating how the dice might have rolled if he'd been home when Alice had called, but when he looks up again, he looks sharper. Hardened.

"Life, Sergeant. Don't you ever want to run away and be by yourself? Step out of the daily grind once in a while?"

"Absolutely." Parnell nods emphatically. "Where do I sign? But I'd tell my wife where I was going, when I'd be back and how often she could expect to hear from me."

He gives Parnell a sardonic look. "Well, that rather defeats the object of going it alone, wouldn't you say? If your every move can be monitored?"

Parnell stands up and walks across to the window, throwing me a look of *"I can't get a handle on this one."* In fairness, Parnell isn't exactly known for his lack of empathy—he's the kind of guy who always tries to find common ground, whether it's discussing the "pop charts" with Ben or short skirts with a suspected rapist, anything to get the other person talking. But I can see he's struggling with Thomas Lapaine and this curiously modern marriage. Maggie Parnell classes her monthly cut and blow dry as precious time away.

I put my notepad down, take over. "Mr. Lapaine, believe me, I understand the need to go it alone sometimes but four weeks is a long time. Didn't you once think about calling her?"

"I did a couple of times, she didn't answer, I didn't leave a message . . ." He shakes his head, his own inadequacy dawning on him. "I should have been firmer, shouldn't I? I should have kept calling her and insisting she come home but . . ." His voice cracks and the tears come. Not exactly a flood but the trickle seems genuine.

I leave it a respectful few seconds before jumping back a few beats. "How did she sound on the answering machine, the evening she called? Normal?"

He pushes his hands into his eyes. "I suppose so, yes."

"We'll want to listen to that message," says Parnell, sitting back down.

"You can't. I wiped it."

Parnell's knee jigs. "Sounds a tiny bit callous, if you don't mind me saying? Your wife leaves a message, the first time you've heard her voice in two weeks, and you wipe it?"

"I was angry." He realizes what he's said, removes the edge from his voice. "I was *annoyed* that she hadn't tried my mobile."

"But you said you respected her need for personal space?"

Lightning quick. "Respected, yes. I didn't say I liked it."

Parnell concedes the point and moves on. "Mr. Lapaine, obviously we'll be going through your wife's personal effects, her online activity etc., but it would save a lot of time if you could give us the names of all the people your wife knew in London, who she might have visited or stayed with. In particular, anyone in the Wandsworth area."

"There's no one. No one at all." There's something about his face, not so much flummoxed as dumbfounded, that makes me inclined to believe him—inclined to believe there's no one he knows about anyway. "I just don't understand it. I assumed she'd gone to the coast like before. She loved being by the sea, whereas she *hated* London. Absolutely hated it."

"*A city full of rats and chancers,*" Mum used to call it. She couldn't flee London quick enough for the bourgeois mystique of Radlett.

"Seriously, Alice never went to London. *Ever.* I booked a dinner for our anniversary once, at the Landau—she loved the chef, Michel Roux, you see. We used to watch him on that show. God, what's it called?"

"*Masterchef,*" offers Parnell. I raise an eyebrow.

"Yes, yes, that's it," he replies, animated, eager to open up for the first time. "I had it all planned out. Cocktails in the bar, dinner in the restaurant, a suite at the Langham." He pauses, screwing his face up in fresh confusion. "But she just wouldn't go. Refused point-blank. Said it was a waste of money, she didn't like the crowds, or the tube, or fancy restaurants for that matter, which was news to me, as we'd eaten in plenty when we lived overseas. And the waste of money comment, well, that was just nonsense. God knows how much she spent on food every week, buying rare ingredients for recipes she'd seen on the TV." He lets out a brittle laugh. "Do you know what she said in the end? '*Buy Roux's cookbook instead and I'll make dinner at home.*' Can you believe that?"

Keen to keep him in full-flow, I say, "Mr. Lapaine, how did you and Alice meet?"

"Please, call me Thomas, Tom even. We met in Brighton, late 2001. Alice lived there and I was on a Stop-the-War march. I think she liked that I was principled." A shy smile. "I just fancied her rotten."

I scan the room for a wedding photo but there's none. None of them at all, in fact. Just one small photo on the windowsill of an older couple sagging in the heat standing next to two camels.

"And when did you marry?"

"In 2003," he says, twisting his wedding ring. "Young by today's standards, I suppose."

Parnell interjects. "You mentioned earlier that you lived overseas?"

He nods. "Yes, we lived in Brighton for a while after we married, but then I got a job offer in Sydney and after that, Perth. Then Hong Kong for quite a while. Cape Town, for nine months." Parnell opens his mouth but Lapaine second-guesses the question. "I know a lot about boats."

"When did you come back to the UK?" I ask.

He slumps back in his chair, exhausted. "In 2010. My parents were getting older. My father was struggling with the business and he was keen for me to take over. It just felt like time to come home. Alice wasn't keen at first, but we wanted to start a family and she understood that it would be nice to have grandparents close by—Alice's mother died when she was a teenager and she never knew her father—so we agreed to move near to my parents. I said she could choose the house, that was the deal. She chose here."

He sweeps a hand toward the shimmering river, presenting it like Alice's own personal masterpiece.

"The location obviously made it rather expensive so we haven't done much to the house, but it's quiet and it's by water and that's all she wanted." He thinks on this, briefly. "Sums Alice up really—'quiet and always by water.'"

Parnell tackles a tricky observation. "So, er, you didn't end up starting a family?"

There's a silence for a few seconds while Thomas Lapaine pushes his sleeves up and leans forward. Legs spread wide, forearms on thighs. It's a staunchly masculine pose that tells me everything before he even says it. "We tried for a few years but it didn't happen. We had all sorts of tests and then we started IVF. Several rounds of IVF. It was tough. We'd actually just decided to give—" He stops suddenly, pulled up sharp by a memory he's not sure whether to share.

I keep my voice gentle. "Tom?"

He stares at me, slightly baffled. "Well, it's just, I'm so sorry—I've been telling you how she never went to London but—how could I have forgotten—we *did* go to London, once, a few months ago. But it really was the only time. It was to see another consultant, someone who'd been recommended to my mother. The price was sky-high, about fifteen thousand pounds per go plus extra for blood tests and all the other indignities you have to go through, but he claimed to have a sixty-five percent success rate. Alice found that hard to resist, even if it meant going into London."

I nod, not sure what this tells us. "You must have been excited?"

That brittle laugh again. "*I* was. But shortly afterward Alice said she wanted to give up, just like that. She said she'd come to the conclusion that it wasn't meant to be." He scratches at his wrist, frowning. "She seemed quite philosophical about it really."

"When was this?" says Parnell.

He thinks for a minute. "We saw the consultant around the end of October. I'm sure you'll find the exact date when your colleagues rifle through my wife's things."

"What exact date did Alice leave?" I ask.

"Thursday 19th November. I came home from work and she was gone. She'd left me a note. A note and some home-cooked meals in the freezer."

"Do you have the note?"

A deep slug of scotch. "No."

Parnell resists the urge to roll his eyes. "Can you tell us what it said then?"

"Just that she needed some time alone and that she'd call soon." His voice wavers. "And that she loved me, very deeply."

And that she was heading into space with Elvis on a solar-powered unicorn. That's how much credence we can give this note.

I throw him a bone just to see how eagerly he takes it. "Do you think she needed time away to come to terms with the IVF decision?"

"Perhaps," he says, sadly. "I honestly don't know. Maybe."

"Had you come to terms with the decision, Tom?" Parnell, fierce-proud father of four and unashamedly gooey when it comes to all things babies, softens his voice a little, surprising both Lapaine and me.

"I was disappointed, I can't deny it."

"Did you row about it?" I ask, before Parnell does.

"We didn't row."

"Oh, come on, Tom," Parnell cajoles. "Everyone rows."

He gets up, tosses the now-empty bottle of scotch in the trash bin. "I'm aware of that, Sergeant. I'm not averse to a row myself with business associates, or my parents from time to time. But Alice wasn't like that. You couldn't row with her. She was too sweet a creature."

The martyrdom of the dead is the bane of a Murder detective's life. It's hard to pinpoint the truth when people are too busy polishing the halo.

"OK," says Parnell evenly, "you didn't row, but you must have *enquired* about the sudden change of heart?"

He sits down. Hurt flashes across his face, still raw. "She said it was the money. Basically, where would it end? We'd been through so many rounds already and in the cold light of day, she felt even a sixty-five percent success rate seemed too big a risk for such a large amount. We're not exactly churchmice, Detectives, but look around, we're not rolling in cash either. We'd had to make sacrifices to fund the IVF. We'd spent savings, taken out loans, borrowed from my parents."

"How much?" asks Parnell. "In total?"

He puffs out his cheeks. "Around fifty thousand, I'd say. Still, I told Alice it didn't matter, it was only money, but she'd made her mind up. She said we'd forced it enough and the disappointment was killing us. I had no choice but to accept it. Even though she was so sweet-natured, when she dug her heels in about something you had to let her be. Same with our anniversary trip to London . . ."

"That was about wasting money too? Well, partly," I add, before he corrects me. "Did you and Alice have differing views about your finances?"

"Not especially."

I check my notes. "You told my colleague this morning that Alice worked for a few hours each day at a pub in the village."

"That's right."

"Why only a few hours?"

He shrugs but there's a wariness in his eyes. "That's all they could offer, I believe."

"OK, but there must have been other jobs Alice could have done?"

"I'm not following, Detective." I'm not sure Parnell is either.

"Well, it's just that if Alice was conscious about money, and if money was tight, I don't understand why a fit, able woman wouldn't find a more lucrative job." Lapaine stays silent, uncomfortable with the line of questioning if his pursed lips are anything to go by. "Hey, look, it's not a judgment, Tom. I'm just trying to understand as much as I can about Alice—her values, her . . ."

"I was against her working full-time, OK." *So it's not just the house that's stuck in a time warp.* "And yes I know how that sounds, but you have to understand that working full-time in hospitality means regular evening work, weekend work, and I didn't want that for our marriage. Alice agreed."

Controlling, or kind of understandable? Is wanting to be at home at the same time as your partner really so primitive or simply pragmatic? Necessary for the health of any long-term relationship?

I decide that I can't decide. Murder skews your view of how the normal world operates.

Parnell picks up the baton. "We'll obviously be looking at your wife's bank records—any activity helps us to build up an idea of her movements. Did Alice have her own account or is it a joint one?"

"Joint. Her salary wasn't much but it covered a couple of monthly loan payments. She did have her own credit card, although she hardly used it. The limit was only a few hundred pounds." He looks to me, the perceived softer option. "Our joint account won't tell you much though so I wouldn't waste your time. She mainly withdrew cash from the ATM. She always preferred cash."

I smile apologetically. "All the same, we'll need to take a look."

His answer isn't quite instant. "If you must."

Parnell keeps his tone steady. "How did you feel about her withdrawing the money?"

Lapaine shrugs. "I didn't expect her to live on thin air."

Parnell nods. "Well, no, but she says IVF is a waste of money and then weeks later she's swanning around taking money out of your joint account. I think I'd be annoyed."

A blanket of near-silence. Just the sound of the river rushing outside.

"I did not kill my wife, Sergeant."

Fair play. It's exactly what I'd do. Expose the elephant in the room and you control it.

Parnell doesn't flinch but the admission switches him back into formal mode—no more "Tom" for a start. "I'm afraid we have to ask these questions, Mr. Lapaine, and while I regret any discomfort this causes, it's crucial we eliminate you as quickly as possible. Do you understand?"

Lapaine says nothing. Parnell carries on. "You'll also understand that I need to ask where you were last night and the early hours of this morning."

He stares at Parnell, dead-eyed—tiredness or loathing, I'm not sure. "I was home. From seven thirty p.m. until I left for my walk at about eightish this morning."

"Ah yes, your walk. You're committed, I'll give you that. Pains me to walk to the car when it's this cold."

"It's not a labor of love, I assure you. I hurt my back earlier in the year and walking and swimming are the only ways I can keep active, and I find swimming so monotonous. The back and forth repetition of it."

"Did anyone see you this morning?" I ask.

"I don't recall meeting anyone. There's occasionally a few people following the same route in the opposite direction, but as you say, it was cold. Fairweather walkers."

"Can anyone verify your alibi for last night?" says Parnell. "It's an entirely routine question, I assure you."

"I'm not in the habit of spending evenings with anyone but my wife, I'm afraid."

"Did you make or receive any calls then, send any texts?"

"No, I don't believe I did." He grips the arm of the chair to steady himself but his shaky voice betrays him. "You can't honestly think that I hurt my wife?"

I could quote the statistics now. I could lay it on the line just how hard he's going to have to work to convince us that he's not just another depressing tick in an all-too-familiar box.

I could reduce his marriage to yet another arbitrary percentage.

You had a sixty-five percent chance of fathering a child with your wife.

There's a sixty-three percent chance that you killed her.

But like a good little note-taking, nodding DC, I say nothing.

6

Steele rockets out of her office carrying a bulging makeup bag and plonks herself down in my chair. I sag against the wall, ready to drop.

"Right, I've got twenty minutes before I need to shoot over to Kensington to charge a few nasty little scrotes with joint enterprise so a) ignore me while I put my slap on and b) cut to the chase, is the husband a viable suspect?"

Parnell has his feet up on the desk, a KFC bag rests on his stomach. "Well, it's not a happy marriage, however he dresses it up."

"Do a straw poll in this station, Lu. You won't find too many happy marriages, or too many murderers, I hope."

"Twenty-three years in February. Quite happy, thank you."

Parnell looks as smug as a man can look with chicken grease on his chin.

"Good for you," says Steele, applying eyeliner with the steadiest of hands. "But the fact the Lapaines don't match up to the standards of Mr. and Mrs. Luigi Parnell doesn't constitute reasonable suspicion. Anything else?"

"They'd been having IVF," I tell her. "They'd just seen another consultant in London but she wanted to give up. He said he accepted it but . . ."

Flowers sticks his head above his screen. "A man finds out he's a jaffa? I can see that tipping into something nasty." Emily Beck looks confused. "A jaffa, you know? Seedless."

"He means infertile, Emily." I turn back to Flowers. "Anyway, who says he's a jaffa? The issue could have been hers?"

Flowers points a chewed Biro at me. "Well, there's your motive then?"

"To kill her!" I can't keep the scorn out of my voice even though he's a sergeant and I really should try harder. "Maybe to leave her, if you're a particularly cruel bastard. But to kill her? Behave."

Flowers grins, which throws me. Sometimes I think he hates me, from my perceived closeness to Steele to the fact I always forget to put sugar in his tea, but other times I wonder if he thrives on the banter.

Steele isn't grinning though. She doesn't have time to contour her face, profile a suspect and referee an argument in twenty minutes flat. "Button it, Kinsella," she says. "Lu, anything else?"

"He doesn't have an alibi. He was at home all night, alone."

I unbutton it. "Which isn't provable, but is completely feasible."

Steele stops mid eye-flick. "Come on then, you're obviously not convinced. Spit it out."

I don't feel ready but what the hell. "Well, look, I don't know, Boss, what are we saying? 'Something' tipped him over the edge, he killed her, and then he dumped her body twenty miles away in the middle of central London? I dunno, I'm just not feeling it."

A quick nod. "Well your concerns are duly noted, but right now he's the only possible suspect we've got, bar some random stranger, and it's not feeling like that to me. We need to speak to that consultant in London—see how they came across at their appointment." Parnell gives Emily the nod to get on it. "Do you like him for this, Lu?"

In just a few words, two decades of trust, respect and grueling late nights pass between Steele and Parnell.

Parnell sighs. "Honestly? Not as much as I'd like, no."

"Do you know what's niggling me," I say to Parnell. "This 'Alice hated London' thing."

And her eyes, I realize then. Almond-shaped, ocean-blue.

Flowers, Barnsley born and bred, pipes up. "We weren't all born within the sound of Bow Bells, Kinsella. Some folk think London's a bit up-itself and overpriced, if your cockney ears can believe such a thing."

"Bow Bells? That's East London, Sarge. I was born in Islington—makes me a northerner, like you. What I'm saying is, she hated London with a passion but they'd also lived in Sydney, Cape Town, Hong Kong, so it's not a case of the country bumpkin being frightened of the big smoke. I mean, I can understand her not wanting to live in London, but she point-blank refused to even visit, even when he'd planned nice surprises for her."

A "*tsk*" from Flowers. "She sounds like a bloody nightmare. I'd have strangled her years ago."

I don't bite, nor does anyone else. It might be because the clock's ticking on Steele's twenty minutes, or it could be that we all quietly agree.

"OK," says Steele, blotting her lips, a rich petal-pink. "We've just about managed to get her photo in the *Standard* this evening. We'll try for the nationals tomorrow if we don't get any solid sightings in London, but with any luck we should have some idea where she's been for the past month within the next twelve to twenty-four hours."

Flowers rubs his eyes. "My bet's with a boyfriend."

"It'd explain the IVF change of heart," says Parnell.

Steele shouts over. "Any joy on the phone records, Benny-boy?"

"Still waiting. And yep, I've said it's urgent."

Steele raises her voice another decibel. "Also, we need more photos of Alice Lapaine. Better ones, to be blunt. Press office reckons the one we've got is a bit dreary. They want happy, smiley ones to pull on the public's heartstrings."

"I didn't see any at the house," I say looking toward Parnell. "Not even a wedding photo."

Parnell screws up his KFC bag, pats away the heartburn. "Doesn't mean anything. I haven't got a clue where my wedding photos are. Probably in the garage covered in mold and white spirit."

"Well, the husband must have some, somewhere," says Steele, "or how about Facebook? Seth, anything from her laptop? Any photos of her cuddling bloody kittens, or whatever it is the Press Office wants? Any evidence of a secret boyfriend?"

Seth shakes his head while exhaustion strips his voice of its usual public-school jollity. "I only had it briefly before Forensics took it, but there wasn't much to see. She has a Facebook account but she hardly uses it. A measly sixteen friends in total, mainly from Hong Kong and Sydney. We're obviously tracing them. Ben's made a start."

A raised hand from Ben Swaines. "She's got a Hotmail account, but again, it looks like she rarely checks it. It's mainly junk and online shopping receipts. Of course there could be lots of deleted stuff that I'm not seeing. Digital Forensics will obviously take a much deeper dive, but . . ."

"But on the face of it, she wasn't exactly Bill Gates." Steele sighs. "It's never easy, is it? Renée—what are her friends saying? Her real three-dimensional friends."

"What friends?" Renée yawns, puts a hand up in apology. I hadn't even noticed she was here—fatigue is making us all muted, invisible. "I talked to a few people at the pub where she worked. They said she was very quiet, kept herself to herself. She worked eleven a.m. till three p.m. which are their busiest hours, so she just tended to crack on when she got there, no time for small talk like there would be if you were opening or closing up. They were obviously wondering where she'd disappeared to four weeks ago, but then it isn't all that unusual in the pub business. They were a bit annoyed but not particularly bothered, was the impression I got."

"They didn't call Thomas Lapaine?" I ask. "He must have been down as her next of kin?"

"Nope," replies Renée. "They tried her mobile a couple of times, couldn't get through so they thought *c'est la vie* and hired someone else."

"Well, I'll be damned," says Steele. "It's dog-eat-dog in the Shires these days."

"Neighbors didn't have a lot to say either," Renée continues, stifling another yawn. " 'Nice enough,' 'quiet.' Same about him. The only friend Thomas Lapaine could point me to was a Debra Pulis who works in the deli on the high street. To be honest, she seemed a bit surprised to be classed as a 'friend.' Alice popped in there most days and they'd chew the fat about the weather, TV, cooking, what-have-you, but she didn't really know her."

"I think that's sad," says Emily. "Imagine having no girlfriends to confide in. Nobody interested in what you're up to."

Imagine.

Sounds ideal to me.

While I'm not quite Alice Lapaine on the Billy-No-Mates scale, I tend to steer clear of the soul-sister sorority types. The kind who want to know everything about you, from your menstrual cycle to your relationship with your parents. Don't get me wrong, I have a life, of sorts. I've got a few mates I sporadically get drunk with, there's a couple I occasionally stay sober with, but all they know about me—all they really need to know—is that I drink anything but Chardonnay and my family aren't close. They've no idea that my menstrual cycle's patchy and I've wished my dad dead.

Steele stands up abruptly, eager to get going. "Right, home-time, the lot of you. We've got fresh blood arriving in the next half hour to manage anything that comes through from the *Standard* so go home and get a proper night's sleep. Maybe eat a few vegetables," she adds, staring at the junk-food detritus littering our desks.

"Quick pint?" suggests Flowers.

"Why not?" says Parnell, heaving himself out of the chair. "Just the one though and then home. Man cannot live on two hours sleep in twenty-four hours. Not this old man, anyway."

"Or this youngish man," says Seth, wrapping a stripy scarf around his neck—Oxford or Cambridge, I can never remember. "In fact, I think I'm starting to hallucinate. Is it just me, or are Emily and Ben having sex?"

Our heads snap toward the corner where Emily's bending down sniggering at something non-work related on Ben's PC, her chin resting on his shoulder, their hands touching as they tussle over the mouse. It's about as intimate as anyone's ever been within MIT4 so they may as well be having sex.

Close-knit comrades, we are—touchy-feely we are not.

Which is a shame as, after the day I've had, I could really do with a hug.

I settle for a glass of wine. OK, two. A tepid drop of the house white when I'm paying and a nice citrusy Sancerre when it's Flowers' round. I think about staying out, numbing myself into a harmonious stupor, but I change my mind as soon as Emily starts talking about Fat Cats, a god-awful bar where people go to get mauled when their self-esteem's just about hit rock bottom. While I'm not exactly a stranger to that kind of soul-crushing setup, tonight I don't fancy being that girl.

I don't fancy a row with my sister either, but I can sense it's heading that way as I trudge to Leicester Square tube with my phone glued to my ear.

"Look, hold on a minute, Cat," Jacqui says, "I need to . . ." She runs to the front door and shouts something about de-icer before hollering up to Finn to switch his night-light off.

Typical Jacqui, always in the middle of a domestic maelstrom. Always making you feel that your presence is one big interruption, even when it was her who called you.

"I'm back," she says, breathless. "So, Christmas Day. Will you be here for breakfast, or just lunch? By the way, I'm not bothering with Christmas pudding this year, it's only Ash who eats it."

"Er, I'm not sure, Jacqs. I wasn't aware I'd been invited."

She laughs, hyper and high-pitched. "You're family, of course you're invited."

Jacqui does this. Erases all memories that don't fit with the image of the shattered nuclear family, stoically soldiering on in the absence of the dead matriarch. I could remind her that I wasn't there last year because two Christmases ago, Dad caught me in a grip that left an angry mottled bruise on my arm when I suggested he was glad Mum was dead. While I'm not exactly proud of my outburst, in my defense he'd just answered a text at the table—*Mum's table*—from someone called Chloe and I'd instantly seen red. A chile-hot, combustible red.

"Look, I'll try to come but I can't promise. A big case has just broken."

"I know, Leamington Square. Noel texted me."

I try to keep the edge out of my voice. "Yeah, you kept that one quiet. Is he lying low, is that it? Who's after him this time?"

"He's visiting his family, Cat. It's normal this time of year."

"It's normal for him to be after something."

She ignores this, parasitic brothers don't fit the "happy families" image either. "Anyway, I didn't keep anything quiet. If I'd seen you I'd have told you. You can't be all elusive and still expect to be kept up to date on everything."

"Elusive? Come on, that's not fair. You know my job's a bit mental . . ."

"Yeah yeah. You know Sadie, who I work with?"

"Vaguely?" I reply, confused where we're heading.

"Well, she's got three kids and her sister's a single mother of two, who also happens to be a firefighter, but they still manage to meet for martinis once a week, *every* week without fail."

Yes, but they probably get on. "No point in us doing that, you don't even like gin."

Jacqui sighs down the phone. "We haven't seen or heard from you since fireworks night. That's what, six weeks ago?"

A nice evening, I have to admit. I turned up with a hundred-shot firework called an *"Atomic Warlord"* and Finn told everyone I was the "bestest."

And Dad was in Marbella for "Uncle" Frank's sixtieth. It was the only reason I went.

"How's Finn?" I ask.

There's a pause, the kind of pause that makes my heart twist inside out. "He's OK. He had a bit of a seizure last night. It scared me more than him though, he didn't even wake up. We're seeing the pediatric neurologist again after Christmas."

"I read up about them. Lots of kids grow out of them as they get older."

"Exactly, he'll be fine."

Jacqui's refusal to look worst-case scenarios in the eye usually makes me want to strangle her, but when it comes to Finn, I'm happy to play along. If I'm honest, Finn's the only reason I still see Jacqui on a semi-occasional basis (I call it "semi-occasional," she calls me "elusive.") It's not that I don't love my sister, we're just markedly different people, and I find it hard to stomach her blind—*the bitch in me would say, "mercenary"*—allegiance to Dad.

"Listen, I'd better go, Jacqs, I'm nearly at the tube."

"Hey wait, tell me about Leamington Square," she says, excitedly. "God, that takes me back."

I wonder if it takes her back to drinking Bacardi Breezers in the gardens and being fingered by half of St. Hilda's, or if she's erased that part of history too. No doubt she has herself picking daffodils in a floaty gingham dress, singing sweetly to fledgling birds as they come to land on her shoulder.

I reach the tube, edge inside the brightly lit entrance for warmth. "Look, I'm really going to have to go now. I'll let you know about Christmas in a few days, is that OK?"

"Well, no actually, it's not. Would it hurt you to be a bit more organized, Cat?"

It's the strict maternal tone, not the criticism, that ignites me. "Jesus! It's just a few roasties and a bit of dry meat that no one likes anyway. And it's not like you're tight for space, your dining table could seat a UN summit."

"We're not having it at mine. Dad wants to host for a change. I'm doing the cooking but he's—"

"Paying?" I interrupt. "Good work, sis. Nicely done, as always."

Little bitch. I regret it the second it leaves my mouth.

"And what are your plans for Dad's check this year?" Sneeriness doesn't suit Jacqui but I deserve it.

My plans are the same as always—half to the nurses who looked after Mum, half to the Sally Army. A few years ago I bought some Jimmy Choos and an Apple Watch—a one-off litmus test to see if I could own anything without feeling squalid and corrupt.

I sold them both on Ebay, new and unused.

I don't tell Jacqui this, though. I also don't ask how a part-time florist and an IT support engineer can afford to send their son to one of north London's leading pre-prep schools. Instead, I gloss over the dig and get back to logistics.

"Look, if Dad's hosting then I'm really not sure . . ."

"Oh for heaven's sake, Cat. Please, can't you try to . . ."

"No, no, it's not that," I say quickly, not wanting to go there. "It's just that with this new case, I could be called into work any time so I could do without being all the way out in Radlett."

Jacqui laughs. "Dad rented Radlett out months ago, Cat." *Did he?* "He's living at the pub full-time now. We're having Christmas lunch at the pub. Nightmare, I know."

A prick of happiness spars with a stab of angst. It's hard to call a winner under the effects of two large glasses of wine.

Christmas at McAuley's Old Ale House.

Home for Christmas.

There's no one in when I get back to Vauxhall, which comes as a blessed relief. It's not that I don't like the Dawsons, I do, I just don't have the energy for their kids this evening—their constant demands to be turned upside down, to French-plait my hair, to sing songs from *The Jungle Book* for the hundredth time. I could be firmer with them, I suppose, try to shake them off on the grounds of having "grown-up stuff" to do. But when you're paying £500 a month for a small double room in Zone 1, with your own sink and toilet, you're wise to make yourself indispensable.

My stomach bellows. I should probably make dinner.

The kitchen's a bomb site as usual, as if the Dawsons were kidnapped partway through a cook-off. Claire Dawson's always cooking with her girls. Cooking and crafting and painting and swimming and a whole host of other "ings" that mean that there wouldn't be any need for a lodger if they'd only pick cheaper hobbies. Jacqui insists that Mum used to cook with me but I don't remember, although I know we made jelly once. Lemon and lime jelly for a "tropical trifle." We gave some to Dad but he fed it to the dog.

I sit by the fridge. Eat a bag of grated cheese like a packet of crisps.

"*Disordered eating,*" a counselor called it. "*Often the result of an aloof or aggressive relationship between a father and daughter.*"

"Aloof" is definitely off-base. Dad rarely did anything that didn't mark me out as being special, as being the only one who ever got under his skin. Sometimes that manifested itself in material things—toys, sweets, clothes as I got older, basically everything I ever asked for and plenty I didn't.

Sometimes it manifested in the threats he'd make. The barely concealed aggression when I'd pulled one of my "stunts" again.

The scratched Audi TT.

The vodka blow-out at a christening (age fourteen).

The fleeting engagement to a complete loser (I was seventeen, he was a thirty-eight-year-old "street poet").

All these things designed to goad Dad into hurting me so that everyone would see just how dangerous he could be.

I take the cheese, an overripe kiwi and a can of cherry Coke and walk up the two flights to my bedroom, feeling an enormous sense of relief to be back in my ten-by-eight with just Alice Lapaine's case notes for company and a Bowie documentary playing low on the TV. I turn it up occasionally when I know the song, looking for patterns of deceit in Thomas Lapaine's statement as I sing along to "Starman."

In my lowly experience, murder's rarely a mystery. It's hardly ever the subterranean labyrinth of red herrings and OMG! twists that you see on the TV and most of the time it's depressingly straightforward—a knifing in a nightclub, a partner flipping their lid, a pimp marking his territory, each motive stark in its simplicity. But already, Alice Lapaine's murder is making my head scratch. I'm still scratching at eleven p.m. when my phone rings. Parnell.

"Sarge," I say with an involuntary smile.

"Steele just called." He sounds pin-sharp and pumped-up, the complete opposite of earlier. "Big news, kiddo. This case just got a whole lot weirder."

I sit up, galvanized by the thought of more brain-ache. "Come on then, don't be a tease, what's the story?"

"A call's come in. Some Irish fella, living in Mile End. Saw the picture in the *Standard* and reckons Alice Lapaine is his sister. Only she's not Alice Lapaine. She's a MisPer from the west coast of Ireland."

She looks familiar somehow . . .

A roar fills my head, a hellish cacophony.

"Could it be a crank? What's the boss think?"

"Seems to think it's legit. He's coming in to give a DNA sample ASAP but he's adamant, apparently. Same mole on her clavicle. Says she's also got a birthmark between her shoulder blades, a bit like a bruise."

"And Alice Lapaine does?"

"Maryanne Doyle does. Looks like our girl is called Maryanne Doyle."

The world tips.

Everything I've ever known tilts to a forty-five-degree angle, taking me with it. I stutter a goodnight to Parnell then put my head between my knees, trying to breathe deeply but the shock doesn't subside. Instead it seeps into my lungs and makes my breath even more desperate.

Maryanne Doyle. Two words, four syllables skewer every layer of my skin.

I reach under my bed for the shoebox and take out my red fluffy notepad—the place where I write the unspeakable things when my head can't contain them.

"*Journaling*," a counselor called it. "*A safe place where you give voice to your fears until you feel you can share them.*"

And I write. Fast, uncensored but as methodical as I can be. This is no time for jumbled thinking.

WHAT I THOUGHT I KNEW:

~~In 1998, Dad was involved in the disappearance of Maryanne Doyle?~~

In 1998, Maryanne Doyle disappeared and Dad knew <u>something</u> about it??

Maryanne Doyle was never seen again—~~murdered???~~

<u>WHAT I KNOW</u>:

Maryanne Doyle <u>wasn't</u> murdered in 1998. She was alive until yesterday.

Maryanne Doyle has been found a few hundred yards from Dad's pub.

In 1998, Dad lied about knowing Maryanne Doyle—<u>**THIS IS FACT**</u>

So you see, some fears can never be shared. Some fears are so cataclysmic that to share them would be tantamount to suicide.

Life as I know it, obliterated.

1998
Tuesday 26th May

Scary's dark curls, Geri's big boobs, Baby's blue eyes. My three fa-vorite Spice Girls rolled into one, stood at the top of the road with her thumb out.

"It's called hitchhiking," Dad said, starting the car. "There's no buses or tubes around here, poppet, so you have to drive or hitch a lift if you want to go anywhere."

"Hitchhiking," I repeated, swilling the word around. "Can we give her a lift?"

"Ah, I don't know," Dad said, like he didn't really mean it. "Mum wouldn't like it."

"But Mum's not here."

"That's my girl."

He grinned at me in the rearview mirror and I grinned back but I in-stantly got the bad feeling. The one I always got when we lied to Mum—nervy, like I had bats in my tummy. Normally Dad would buy me treats and the bad feeling would pass. Cheese and onion crisps always did the trick.

We turned left at Gran's gate, toward town. "I suppose Jesus taught that we should always help strangers?" Dad said.

Dead right. Matthew 25:35–40. I'd learned it in Holy Communion class.

Not that she was a complete stranger. I even knew her name: Mary-anne. She worked in the Diner where Jacqui hung out and once when we'd picked Jacqui up, she'd served me a banana split and told a table full of boys that her favorite ice cream was "cock-flavored."

Jacqui'd found this hilarious. Dad pretended not to but I'd clocked a smile as he'd counted out the two pounds fifty. He'd smiled at her again when we left.

Back in the car, Dad peered up at the sky, reading the clouds. "Mmmm, you know it looks like it could rain. Maybe we should pick her up." He turned his head. "But not a word to Mum, sweetheart, you know what she's like."

I didn't actually. All I knew was that if I wanted to share a car with the next best thing to a Spice Girl, I'd have to promise to keep the secret.

If I'd known she'd completely ignore me, I wouldn't have bothered. She didn't cast one single glance back. Didn't even say hello. Stuck-up like Posh Spice, I decided.

She wasn't stuck-up with Dad though, firing question after question at him for five solid minutes. Who? Where? Why? What?

Was he here with his wife? Did he mind if she smoked?

Dad said she'd better not. "The wife wouldn't like it."

"Do you always do what your wife wants?" I could see her smirking in the wing mirror.

When we dropped her off just outside the town, she asked Dad one final question.

"So will you be out this evening, Mike?"

It was Padraigh Foy's sixtieth, she said, and there'd be free beer and fierce craic in Grogan's if he fancied it. I shouted from the back that he didn't fancy it because he'd promised to watch Spice World with me, but I don't think she heard because she just walked away. Not even a thank-you or a quick wave. It made her less pretty being that rude.

We didn't watch Spice World that night, or any night after. Every time I asked, Dad said he had to meet a man about Something Important and that Jacqui would watch it with me instead, but she never did. Jacqui only ever wanted to watch Friends or The X Files (or "her own reflection," Gran would say when she thought we couldn't hear).

Dad must have been meeting a man about Something Very Important as he didn't come home until gone two, not once. I'd hear the bing-bongs ring out on Gran's grandfather clock.

He did bring me back a pack of cheese and onion Taytos though, to make me feel better.

Nothing says sorry like a pack of cheese and onion crisps.

7

The next day, our cozy little crack squad turns into a full-scale jamboree with twice the number of people chasing up leads and striding about looking determined. I spend my time intermittently throwing up in the toilets and smiling at new faces, intently staring at my laptop in the short bursts in between, desperate to avoid direct eye contact with Parnell and Steele. Luckily they've both been squirreled away in Steele's office all morning alongside Chief Superintendent Blake and a couple of other Big Knobs—I know they're Big Knobs because Steele told me to use the decent mugs when she sent me to make coffee. It's the only interaction we've had all day.

Around three this morning, I'd entered an almost altered sense of consciousness where I convinced myself that I had the backbone to walk into Steele's office at nine a.m. sharp and come clean on everything I knew about Maryanne Doyle. It was the right thing to do, I'd reasoned, burning with a righteous professionalism I never knew I had; in fact it was the *only* thing to do if I ever wanted to face myself in the mirror again, and crucially it was the timing of my epiphany that sealed it.

Three a.m., known as "Dead Time"—the hour when the barrier between the living and the dead lifts and the ghosts start to move between realms.

So it was Mum telling me to come clean, basically. Or so I'd believed until the marijuana haze wore off and the clarity of daybreak returned me to a far more basic instinct—self-preservation—and a far more pragmatic perspective.

What exactly do I know anyway? That my dad definitely didn't kill Maryanne Doyle in 1998, but that he'd lied about knowing her?

It's barely a line of inquiry, never mind a smoking gun.

"So what are we calling her then?" Flowers sticks a photo of Maryanne Doyle to the incident board, wholesome and dewy with those cushiony pink lips and blue eyes twinkling like helium stars. "It's going to get bloody confusing now. Is she Alice or Maryanne?"

"Hard to believe it's the same person," says Craig, shaking his head. "I mean, I'm sure we all looked different in the nineties—you wouldn't have called me The Famine back then for a start, I was a bit of a porker, if you must know—but this Alice, Maryanne, whatever we're calling her, she looks completely different. Like the life's been sucked out of her."

Renée gives a sideways glance. "I think it's called age, Craig. Stress. Modern life."

"Stress?!" says Flowers. "Living on a private island and cooking scampi and chips in the local a few times a week?"

I exchange a "dickhead" look with Renée who passes it on to Ben.

"Well, I think we should go with Maryanne," says Seth, "inside these four walls anyway. If that's who she was born, that's what we should call her."

"No." It bursts out of me, loud and vehement. "She changed her name to Alice so that's how she wanted to be known. We owe her that courtesy, surely?"

Kinsella's my mum's maiden name, you see. I was born a McBride but I changed it to Kinsella after she died. A memorial to the only person I've ever really trusted and an irrefutable "fuck you" to my dad.

Although, I am starting to trust Parnell, I think. It isn't anything he's done as such. We haven't been in any life-or-death situations together, unless you count the time we arrested a suspect outside a supermarket who tried to attack us with a frozen leg of lamb. It's just his presence I trust, his relentless steadiness.

It shores me up, somehow. Makes me steadier.

Seth shrugs a "whatever" and looks toward Steele's office where the Chief Super and the Big Knobs are filing out. Steele's in the center and Parnell walks behind in his best shirt-and-tie combo, the tie bobbing on his hillock of a stomach. If it wasn't for his nose hair, I'd say he looked cute. The Big Knobs leave but Blake stays behind, smoldering by the back wall like an aftershave model. Not yet forty, Chief Superintendent Russell

Blake's the poster boy for the Met's High Potential Development Scheme. A politician through and through, all PR, Policy and sharp Prada suits.

This is pure rumor, of course. I've never actually spoken to the man, although I did once hand him a napkin in the staff canteen.

Steele bangs a desk with a stapler and we all come to heel.

"Right, folks, I trust you've all made friends and I don't need to make introductions. Couple of things—firstly, I just want to extend a big thanks to Chief Superintendent Blake for"—she looks around the room—"giving us the extra resources because clearly this case has just got a lot bigger." Blake gives a somber nod. "Secondly, *because* it's now bigger, I'm going to be taking on more of a coordinator role—the brains of the operation, if you like—and DS Parnell will be stepping up to Acting Detective Inspector, so all roads lead back to him, OK?"

A murmur of "fair play" rings around the room. I'm obviously pleased for him but I can't help getting a pang of new sibling syndrome. More people to manage means less time steadying me.

"So the brother's ID'd the body and he's confirmed it's his sister, Maryanne Doyle."

"The moron brother," as Jacqui used to call him.

"Maryanne went missing from Mulderrin, a small village on the west coast of Ireland, in 1998. Not a call or a letter or a proverbial sausage since. We're obviously waiting for a DNA comparison before we go public but basically, it's her. He was able to tell us several distinguishing features."

"So might the killer," I say.

"What? He kills her then draws attention to himself?" muses Seth. "He'd have to be supremely confident, or supremely mad."

"It's not unheard of."

"And confident fits with the relaxed dude on the CCTV," adds Ben.

Steele picks up the stapler, tosses it from hand to hand. "Mmm, I think the brother's a bit taller than CCTV man, although it's hard to say for definite so I wouldn't rule him out. Anyway, look, the file's been sent from Ireland but I've been warned it's a bit thin on detail, and I'm not sure how much attention we should be paying it, in any case. It was eighteen years ago, people go missing all the time, and 'Maryanne Doyle' was alive and well and living as Alice Lapaine until yesterday so there may be absolutely no relevance at all."

I cling to Steele's words yet feel sick at their implications.

Could I have been wrong about Dad all this time?

But then why? Why did he lie?

In the cold light of day, with doubts flooding my head, this question starts to seem naïve at best. OK, Childhood Me might have allowed herself to believe in the steadfast honesty of Grown-ups, but Grown-up Me knows that people lie all the time, and for an abundance of reasons, not all of them sinister.

But he knew her.

He flirted with her.

She disappeared.

Then he lied.

Pieces of a puzzle I completed a long time ago. *Could I have been wrong?*

However, now isn't the time for regret or introspection. Now is the time to get hold of that file.

"I'll go through the Ireland stuff," I announce, maybe a little too eager. "Let you know if I think anything needs following up."

Steele looks to Parnell, formally passing the crown.

"No, I want you to interview the brother," says Parnell. "He's coming back in, *after work*." He refrains from adding "*the heartless git*." "Go easy, but see if you can sense any motive, because if we're looking for reasons for why she might have been in London, the brother's a reason, isn't he?"

I nod, there's nothing else I can do. It's an instruction from a senior officer and a favor from a friend. A patronage of sorts. But rather like the Mafia, Parnell's public show of faith means I now can't let him down without bringing him down, and yet I'm letting him down just by sitting here with my memories—*Maryanne serving ice cream, rolling fags, putting my Tinkerbell pendant into her denim jacket pocket.*

Flirting with Dad. Calling him the Diet Coke man.

Acting Detective Inspector Luigi Parnell deserves far better than me.

"Right, back to the grindstone folks," shouts Steele, waving ta-ta to Chief Superintendent Blake as he slips out. "Parnell's off to the post-mortem later so news from that very soon."

"Lucky me," says Parnell, who after nearly thirty years' service still shudders at the sound of the rib shears.

Renée picks up her bag. "Think yourself lucky, Boss. I've been lumbered with telling Thomas Lapaine that his wife had been lying to him about her identity for the past fifteen years. Wanna swap?"

He doesn't. Most of us would take stomach contents and rib shears over the awkwardness of emotional pain any day.

"I'll tell you who is lucky though—that one, there." Renée points at me, grinning. I'm confused. "Ah, of course, you didn't see Aiden Doyle when he came in first thing, did you? Well you're in for a treat, lady, the man is an absolute D.I.S.H."

"Sexist!" shouts Flowers, and for the first time today I crack a genuine smile.

Much later, I walk into the "soft" interview room—the squishy, pastel sanctum we preserve for children, vulnerable people and now smokin'-hot brothers of dead Irish colleens—to find Aiden Doyle tapping on his smartphone, left knee bouncing. Six feet something of pure crackling energy and cheekbones you could cut turf with.

I can't fault Renée's taste. The moron brother doesn't look so moronic now.

I half expect to recognize him but there's nothing, not one single recollection. I'm not sure why I'm so surprised as I didn't really register boys when I was eight. Boring, non–pop star boys anyway. To me, every teenage boy was just another superfluous version of Noel—spiteful, monosyllabic and unwashed—whereas teenage girls embodied everything I thought was good about life—giggling, glitter and clip-cloppy high heels.

Maryanne was wearing candy-pink peep-toes the day we gave her a lift.

I offer my hand. "Detective Constable Cat Kinsella."

"Kinsella. There'd be Irish in you then?"

His west-coast accent curls around my heart like an old blanket. Gran, cousins, aunts, old men with old sheepdogs. Nice people I never saw again after that holiday.

"There would indeed," I say, sitting down. "Thanks for coming back in, Mr. Doyle—and thanks for sorting a photo so quickly. I'm sure this has been a huge shock and I'll answer any questions you have the best I can, however I'll warn you, we have far more questions than answers at this stage."

"No problem." He stands up, dwarfing me. "And call me Aiden. Mr. Doyle makes me think of my old fella and believe me, it's not a happy thought. Do you mind if I help myself to tea?"

"If you don't mind that it tastes awful."

He smiles and goes about his business. No obvious signs of distress. Although in fairness, eighteen years is a long time. Maryanne's been out of his life longer than she'd been in it.

He sits back down, sighs. "Well, yeah, it's been a shock, all right. Not that she's dead, I mean, I kinda assumed she was dead. It's more that she was alive all this time, you know?"

You and me both, mate.

"I looked out for her for years," he goes on. "Like, I went to Galway once for a piss-up, celebrating the end of exams, and I thought I saw her in the queue for the Alley." He smiles. "As if Maryanne would have been seen dead in the Alley, of all places. Always thought she was a class above, you know." There's no scorn in his statement, only fact. "Then I thought I saw her at a football match. Mayo versus Roscommon. Spent hours and hours rewinding and pausing the tape, convincing meself it could be her from a certain angle, if you added a few kilos. I suppose I just wanted to think that she was out there somewhere, having a good time, going to nightclubs, watching the match. She was football mad, you know. Well, footballer mad."

I let him talk, tactically and for pure enjoyment.

"I stopped looking after a while, though. Then after seven years, this woman from some new setup, Missing in Ireland Support Services, rings up and says we can apply to have her declared dead if we want." He raises an eyebrow. "'*If we want,*' she says, like it's a great fucking option." Then, "Sorry, I shouldn't swear."

"Swear away. You're not in confession."

"Ha, not in a long time, Detective. Same as yourself, no?" I smile. "Anyways, we didn't have her declared dead. I mean, what would be the point? She didn't have an estate or anything, unless you call a crate of shit CDs and more shoes than Imelda Marcos an estate." He scratches at his head like he's tearing at his brain rather than tending to an itch. "Jesus Christ, I just can't believe she was right here in London, right under my fucking nose."

He doesn't apologize this time.

"We think she was only in London for a few weeks. She lived in Thames Ditton, in Surrey."

A quick hunch of the shoulders. "Don't know the place. Don't know London that well, to be honest. I've not been here long meself, got transferred from the Dublin office two months ago, and it's been non-stop work, work, work. I need to get out more."

I want to ask what type of work allows for distressed denim jeans and threadbare gray T-shirts but it's not exactly relevant. We're not on a date. "Aiden, we're trying to find out why Maryanne was in London in the weeks prior to her death. We've spoken with her husband . . ."

"Yeah, your boss said she was married. Fair play to her. I'd like to meet him."

One suspect meeting another suspect? I don't think so.

"Now's really not the best time . . ."

"O' course. Jesus!" He gives me a look that says, "*What do you think I am?*" "I meant when the dust settles a bit, maybe . . ."

I nod vaguely, bring things back on track. "Her husband tells us she wasn't the greatest fan of London."

"Sure, who is? You can't get a pint for less than a fiver."

I can't help but bite. "Christ, I don't know where you're drinking? The tourist traps, I bet. You're right, you definitely do need to get out more."

If it sounds like flirting, I'm not. Flirting implies a certain amount of effort and guile and I'm capable of neither today.

Still, I overcompensate by going in for the kill.

"Aiden, Maryanne's husband can't think of any reason why she would have been in central London. Maybe you can?"

If he's annoyed, his face gives away nothing. "I haven't seen my sister in nearly two decades, she could have had an appointment with the feckin' Queen for all I know."

I lean forward. "Or maybe she was visiting you? You could be the reason?"

His chin lifts. "I'm not following."

"Well, it just strikes me that here we have a woman who, by all accounts, can't stand London, who never visits London, who seems content living her very quiet life in a sleepy village in leafy Surrey, and then her brother arrives in the capital two months ago, and all of a sudden London isn't such a bad place?" I leave it hanging for a second. "So can you see where I'm coming from? Can you see why I might make a connection?"

"I can," he says, nodding, completely agreeable. "But there is no connection because I haven't see her, and God knows I'd have been easy enough to find if she'd wanted to. She might have reinvented herself, but I'm still plain old Aiden Doyle. Same bloody haircut since time began. Same great big scar on me cheek where she slammed me with the hurley stick. Same cringy picture on the company website for years with the same bloody email address and contact number. If she'd wanted to find me she could have. She obviously didn't."

He glances at his watch, almost certainly trying to give the impression that if she'd hadn't the time to care, then neither does he.

"Can you confirm where you were on Monday evening/Tuesday morning between the hours of say, eleven p.m. and five a.m.?"

I get the expected *"are you having a laugh?"* look but that's all. No gaping mouth flapping about in outraged protestation. No demand to see "who's in charge of this investigation," right before Steele makes them wish that they'd kept their mouth shut and stuck with little ol' me.

"I was at home, in bed."

"Can anyone verify that?"

"Sadly not." He swipes his hand across his mouth, suppressing a tiny smirk. "I've been working like a dog since I got here and I haven't had time for much *verification* in the bedroom department." A little laugh. "And that's going to go against me, is it? Here was me thinking I was being a good lad, not stringing some young one along for an easy ride when I haven't time to wipe my arse most days."

"With regards to your alibi." He laughs again—most innocent people do when an evening's ironing suddenly becomes sworn testimony. "Did you speak to anyone on Monday night, between the hours I mentioned? Even a text could help rule you out. That's all I'm trying to do here, Aiden, rule you out, so we can get on with finding whoever did this."

He thinks about this. "I texted a mate in Oz at some point during the night, will that do? Bloody text from him woke me up and I gave him shite for it. Guess I owe him a pint now, eh?" He scratches at his head again. "I suppose it must have been about oneish, I'd been in bed awhile, anyways. I usually turn my phone off before bed but me old fella's not been well so I've been leaving it on."

A flash of Jonjo Doyle. A ratty little man who hated kids in pubs, "filthy" foreign lager and all things English.

"I'm sorry to hear that."

"Not sure I am. He's not got long left, I reckon another clean shirt would do him, as we say back home." He stares into his mug for a few seconds and then looks up suddenly. "He was a cruel, useless man, Cat, the cruellest of the cruel, but he's still me dad, you know? I'd have preferred he'd gone to his grave not knowing this . . . Ah sure, maybe I won't tell him . . ."

I nod my understanding, enjoying the sound of my name from his mouth. The familiarity.

"There were rumors he'd killed her," he says, almost amused. "Well, not exactly rumors, just pub talk. Gobshites making up stories 'cos they've got nothing better to talk about."

"That must have been very hurtful. For you and your dad."

He doesn't milk the sympathy. "Oh, don't get me wrong, he was handy with his fists, all right. He'd clumped her once—in public, too—so don't go feeling too sorry for the bastard. But murder? No. No way. It hit him hard enough when Mam died. He'd never have *harmed* Maryanne, no way. Well, I mean, *proper* harmed, you know."

The west coast lilt, the cheekbones and now a dead mammy. If I could marry him here and now, I would.

"What do you think happened, Aiden? Why do you think your sister disappeared?"

Answer me the most significant question of my life.

He puffs out his cheeks. "Sure, you wouldn't know what to believe. Some folk were saying—when they weren't saying that me old fella had killed her and set fire to the body—that she had a bit of a thing for older blokes. There was talk of some married one in Galway, a doctor, but I never went for that." A tiny laugh. "Not that I wouldn't believe it—Christ knows she'd make eyes at the pope himself—but it didn't explain why she never got back in touch. With me, anyway. I mean, we weren't dead, dead close, but still . . . you'd think . . . well . . ." He stops talking, wipes a thumb at an imaginary mark on his face. "Ah, d'you know what, fuck it."

Hurt swathed in layers of front. Boy-hurt.

"What about her friends? Teenage girls talk. Did they have any theories?"

"*Friends*," he says, sourly. "She was joined at the hip with these two bitches, Manda Moran and Hazel Joyce. God forgive me, but they were a right pair of wagons."

Manda Moran draws a blank but Hazel Joyce steps forward. Red hair clamped back in a tight ponytail. Imitating Jacqui's accent, making her sound like Eliza Doolittle.

"I did think to meself that if anyone knew anything, it'd be them, so I pounced on them one night coming out of Grogan's. Thought I'd put the frighteners on them. Play the big man, you know." He almost smiles at the memory. "Ended up making a proper tool of meself, I did. Hazel Joyce had these two big brothers coming up the rear and they knocked seven shades of shite out of me. And do you know all they said, well the Joyce one said, as I was lying on the ground coughing up a lung—'*If you hear from Maryanne, tell her she still owes me twenty quid.*' Can you believe that? She was always mad jealous of Maryanne, though. Maryanne was good-looking, you know, and Joyce had a face a dog wouldn't lick . . .'

He reaches for a glass of water, pours me one too.

"When did you stop believing Maryanne was alive?"

"I don't know, after a few years, I suppose. And then when that one started going on about declaring her dead, well, it just kind of confirmed that something bad *must* have happened. And she was always hitching into town, you know? Jumping into the first car that stopped, not a bother on her. '*Too fucking lazy to walk,*' me old fella used to say. From him! A man who'd been on the dole his whole bloody life."

"What did the Guards make of it?"

"Bog all, really," he shrugs. "Me old fella wasn't exactly on great terms with them so that didn't help. Although to be fair, she was seventeen and she was known for being a bit wild. She'd ran away before, you see— only to Ballina for some festival but she was gone a few days, so I don't think they paid much mind. Maybe I should have pushed them more but I was only fourteen. They'd have laughed me out the station."

"No other siblings?"

"We've an older brother. He'd left home years before Maryanne went missing though and he's in Canada now. We haven't spoken properly in years. I get the odd Christmas card, pictures of his kids—well, they're not kids now, they're in their teens. I suppose I'll have to give him a bell now . . . tell him about Maryanne, me dad . . .'

"He doesn't stay in contact with your dad?"

"Nope. Let's just say my folks weren't really cut out to be parents. Both too fond of the sup. Mam was a happy drunk, at least. That's how we saw it anyway. When the old fella was pissed, he'd dole out punches and rebel songs, but me mam, she'd be all kisses and promises. You know, things she was gonna buy us, places she was gonna take us. You knew it was baloney, but it was nice baloney. I miss her."

"How old were you when she died?"

"I was twelve, Maryanne was fifteen. Cirrhosis of the liver. It wasn't a nice death." A pause. "The women in our family don't have much luck, do they?" He reflects on this for a second but he's not a wallower. "Come here, you said you'd answer any questions I have and I do have one. My question is, 'What's with all the questions?' What has Maryanne doing a runner out of Dodge all those years ago got to do with her being murdered yesterday?"

I steel myself to answer in the entirely politic, noncommittal way that I'm paid to do.

"We're not sure at the moment. We're just trying to get an idea of who she was. It could be the key to everything or it could mean absolutely nothing. I'm sorry, but that's the most honest answer I can give you."

And because screaming, *"Wouldn't I like to fucking know?"* in your face really wouldn't benefit either of us.

"Fair enough," he says—genuinely, I think.

He looks around the room, dwelling a beat or two on a canvas of pink poppies that I think he's supposed to find soothing.

"You know, Maryanne was a pain in the hole from the minute she got up in the morning until the minute she went to bed but she was my big sister, you know? She didn't deserve . . . this. She wasn't a bad person." He drags his eyes away from the poppies, plants them on mine. "Ah, would you listen to me, Cat. I haven't set eyes on her in eighteen years, I've no idea what type of person she was. She could have been some gangland crime boss for all I know. The Don Corleone of, where'd you call it, Thames Ditton." His smile gets broader. "Yeah, I could imagine that. Totally. Always had big plans, did Maryanne. Always so sure she was going to be someone. Be famous, like." A sharp rueful laugh. "She's famous now, isn't she?"

The office is quiet as I slink back in. Not exactly empty, but empty of anyone who'd have the remotest interest in what I'm up to. Seizing my chance, I breeze toward Steele's office, smiling at people as I pass, even hovering for a few minutes to give my dishonest opinion on a pair of fleece pajamas some Romeo has bought his lucky Juliet for Christmas.

Cool. Calm. Collected.

Just a lowly DC walking into a mighty DCI's office and raiding her desk like a junkie scavenging for a fix.

Nothing to see here, folks.

I find the featherweight file under a pile of overtime sheets and there's not much to see there either. They definitely weren't joking when they said it was light on detail. I quickly scan the pages, all three of them— one standard Missing Persons form and two faded sheets which I'm loath to call witness statements as they read more like a sketchy *Who's Who of Mulderrin*—a Sergeant Bill Swords' private census, complete with withering observations and snippy little asides.

Martha Higgins–neighbor. Nothing relevant, couldn't get any sense out of her, not playing with a full deck.

Manda Moran–friend. Hasn't seen MD in days. Suggested some fella in Galway? Colette Durkin told her about him (Hazel Joyce told Durkin). Durkin a fierce liar though and M. Moran would believe the moon was made of cheese.

Colette Durkin–friend. Saw MD in the Diner on Sat morning (30th). Said MD was in bad humor. Denied knowledge of any fella in Galway. Wouldn't know what to believe. Slippery as the day is long.

Pat Hannon–neighbor. Scuttered, uncooperative. Says MD has a "dirty mouth" but a harmless old soul.

I find what I'm looking for three-quarters down the final page.

Jacqui McBride, fourteen, visiting from England (Agnes Kinsella's crowd). Doesn't know MD well, last saw her Thursday 28th sitting on St. Benedict's wall. Spoke briefly with parents. No relevant info.

So Jacqui had told the truth. She'd admitted she was a bit-part player and hadn't tried to plant herself firmly in the thick of things like she normally did, back then more than ever.

In total it looks like Sergeant Bill Swords spoke with around twenty people. Not quite the "bog all" that Aiden Doyle suggested but perfunctory at best. A pass-muster B minus. Even the official Missing Persons form has a whiff of ticked boxes and jaded indifference.

Is the person suspected to be a victim of a crime in progress, e.g, abduction? NO	
Is the person vulnerable due to age, infirmity, or any other factor? NO	
Are there inclement weather conditions which would seriously increase risk to health? NO	
Does the missing person need essential medication or treatment not readily available to them? NO	
Does the missing person have any physical illness, disability or mental health problems? NO	
Is there any information that the person is likely to cause self-harm or attempt suicide? NO	
Has the person previously disappeared AND suffered or was exposed to harm? NO	
Are there any indications that preparations have been made for their absence? Brother says bag is gone but nothing else obvious	
Are there family and/or relationship problems or recent history of family conflict? Jonjo Doyle well known to Guards for petty violent incidents	
School, college, university, employment or financial problems? NO	
Drug or alcohol dependency? NO	
CONDUCTED SEARCH OF PREMISES AND ENVIRONS 1 June 1998 Sgt B Swords	

> **RECENT PHOTO OBTAINED 01/06/98 Sgt B Swords**
>
> **DETAILS SUPPLIED TO MISSING PERSONS BUREAU**
> 1 June 1998 Sgt Tom Lennon
>
> ---
>
> **INITIAL RISK ASSESSMENT**
> **LOW – MEDIUM RISK**
> No evidence to suggest a crime has taken place.
> Bit of a wild one. Several friends/colleagues suggest flighty behavior isn't out of character.
> Stayed away in Ballina before.
> Likely a runaway.
> Voluntary missing person – **<u>will review as appropriate.</u>**
>
> **SERGEANT BILL SWORDS**
> Sgt B Swords
> 1 June 1998

There's part of me—the painstaking, zealous part that makes me tailor-made for Murder, despite what Steele thinks—that's sick to my stomach at the thought of a teenage girl vanishing off the face of the earth and it warranting no serious follow-up. Yet tonight, as I crouch in Steele's office, I could kiss Sergeant Bill Swords for his slap-happy half-job. For doing no more than what was absolutely required.

"Spoke briefly with parents."

And for his interpretation of the word "briefly."

Because that's not how I remember it. I remember two pots of tea drunk. A whole plate of fig rolls and half the coconut creams too. I remember the "Angelus" ringing out at six p.m. and a big fat man, presumably Supersleuth Swords, leaping out of his chair, shocked that they'd been gassing for well over an hour when he had crimes to crack on with and cows to bring in.

But then, time always flies when Dad's on good form.

And he was on sparkling form that day.

8

When I was fourteen I dyed my hair to look like Maryanne. Mousy-brown to licorice-black in the time it took to wreck Mum's newly tiled en suite. I knew straightaway it didn't suit me—it was less Maryanne, more Morticia—and I knew I'd pay dearly for the unholy mess I'd left behind, but it was worth every punishment that Mum could mete out just to see the look on Dad's face, sucker-punched and speechless at the bottom of the stairs.

Sucker-punched, that's how I'd describe him now. The shock of my face seems to flatten him. He looks pale and transparent. Only the beams from the halogen lights that criss-cross the ceiling give him any kind of color. Any kind of humanity.

He'd been laughing as I'd walked in. Hunched over the bar, snickering at a video on some city boy's phone.

He's not laughing now.

"Catrina, you came back."

I psych myself for a stilted hug—want one even, in some bone-deep, primeval way, but there's nothing. Just a glass of white wine foisted across the bar and a slightly belligerent look.

"I have to speak to someone quickly," he says, grabbing my arm—more proprietorial than paternal. "Do not move, do you hear me?"

I shrug like the fourteen-year-old I always revert to and hoist myself onto a bar stool, pushing the glass of wine away. Across the bar, to the side of a tasteful but utterly joyless Christmas tree, Dad argues with a tall girl in a black backless dress. They're too far away and I can't see her face but as there's tribal tattoos snaking all the way down her back, I work on the assumption that bad-ass body art and facial piercings often go together and I figure this could be Little Miss Lip-Stud. Dad's current *shag du jour.* The sight of her bare skin twinkling diamond-white in the glare of the tree lights makes me feel like a maiden aunt, sat there on my bar stool, straight-backed and sweating in my buttoned-up parka, but I refuse to undo even one notch.

Not stopping.

I watch as Dad says something and *Shag du Jour* stomps for the door, throwing back one final insult and one pointed finger, like a witch casting a hex on the place. At least this one's feisty, I think. He usually goes for giggly and saccharine. Curves in all the right places but all the personality of a crash-test dummy.

As he walks back over, he pulls at the back of his neck, releasing tension.

"Upstairs."

He lifts the bar hatch and beckons me through but I walk straight past and into the nearest booth. There are two half-eaten burgers on rectangular slate slabs and some sort of spillage but I sit down anyway, picking up a napkin and wiping up the worst. Dad slips in across from me. The king in his castle, almost regal on the velvet padded seat.

"Trouble?" I say, smiling, prickling with animosity. "That's the problem when you go young, Dad. Us Millennials can be a bit demanding. A bit entitled. I think it used to be called 'high maintenance' in your day. Maybe a nice little Doris your own age might be less hassle? More grateful?"

He grins. I get a sudden urge to swipe his face, quick and vicious like a cornered cat.

"She's not *that* young. I thought you'd have better observational skills in your line of work." He stops, flags the attention of a minion and waves him over. "She's in her thirties, actually, and anyway she's just a friend."

"Didn't look too friendly."

He ignores this, turns his head toward his little fiefdom. "So what do you think?"

I shoot a bored stare in the same direction. "I think the Christmas tree sucks."

"Oh yeah? Pray tell?" He looks genuinely wounded. I almost laugh.

"It's a bit . . ." I struggle to find the right word. I'm tired and my brain feels doughy—a big flabby lump of contradictory thoughts. "There's just not many decorations, that's all. It's a bit spartan."

"A bit spartan, eh? Good word." He digests it for a moment. "Tell me, is that the same as 'a bit shit?'"

"*Exactly* the same."

I suppress a smile. Smiling at Dad always feels like defeat.

"So to what do I owe the pleasure? I like the hair, by the way." It's only an inch shorter and half a shade darker but Dad's the type of man who notices these things. "You look a bit tired though," he adds, throwing his arm wide across the back of the seat. "Are you eating properly? Tell you what, I'll get chef to make you something. Anything you want. Peach and honey pancakes, maybe? You could never resist them."

Some things never change. Dad trying to manipulate me with sugar is one of them.

"Peaches are rank this time of year. I've gone off honey."

His jaw tenses but with the arrival of the minion at the table, he softens in a flash and the affable gaffer takes center stage. All backslaps and banter and loud effusive laughs.

"Hey, Xavier, meet my daughter, Catrina. My baby girl." He taps the side of his head. "She's the one who got all the brains."

The implication being that Jacqui got all the beauty.

I let that sit for a minute, ride out the hurt until I arrive at a place of "*Who-the-fuck-cares.*"

Dad's voice comes back into focus, that cockney-boy lilt that the punters lap up. "So yeah, Xav used to work at Artesian, sweetheart. We nabbed him eventually, though, didn't we, mate? Got big plans, me and Xav. Big plans . . ." "Xav" smiles vaguely, as if he was hoping for a far simpler plan that just involved being handsome and perfecting Negronis. "Anyway, a Peroni for me, chief, and anything my girl wants." To me: "He does a mean Mai-Tai, sweetheart. Ex-Trader Vics, you see."

"Just tap water. Please."

Never let it be said that I got all of the brains and none of the manners.

I wait until he's gone. "Artesian, no less. No offense but isn't this place a bit of a comedown? You must be paying him well. In fact, Frank must be paying you well. I wouldn't have thought the pub trade's as lucrative as your other sidelines, or are your 'big plans' just a cover?" A wave of nausea, then a tiny jolt of nostalgia, washes over me. "I mean, is this place really just Frank's nerve center again? His countinghouse, like before."

A step back in time to the 1990s. To iffy-looking men talking in low voices in the back room. Iffy-looking packages piled high in our airing cupboard.

Dad chews the side of his cheek—a habit I've inherited for riding out anger. "It was nothing to do with money. I just fancied a change. Radlett felt too big after a while. Too many memories and not enough visitors."

I brush off the dig. "Seriously, I thought barrel changes and blocked loos would be a bit beneath you these days? Don't you miss lording it around Hertfordshire in your Jag?"

He grins at this. "Oh come on, Cat. It was never really me, was it? All that gardening and golf club guff. Radlett was never my dream. I never really . . ." He tails off, picks at a nonexistent thread on his cuff but we both know where he was headed. *I never really wanted the straight life.* "So yeah anyway, Frank mentions he's looking for someone for this place again. Says he knows it's been years, but do I fancy it? He'd spent a load on the place, you see, but it was going down the tubes—usual story, a couple of managers don't know their arse from their elbow and boom—suddenly the place gets a reputation." He takes a packet of Marlboros out of his shirt pocket, bats them between his hands. "Basically, Frank wanted someone to put a bit of heart back in the place." A coy glance up. "I don't know what you think, but I think I've succeeded."

What I *think* is that Frank needs to rinse more dirty money than Mr. Arse and Mrs. Elbow were prepared to turn a blind eye to, and he knows there's none more blind than Michael McBride when it comes to a nice fat earner.

This all goes unspoken, of course. Instead I focus on the cigarettes. "What's this? I thought you'd packed up? A bit stressed out at the moment, are we?"

I don't know why I'm goading him but it's a habit set so hard, it's Pavlovian.

He shrugs. "I tried. I failed. As my old man used to say, you've got to die of fucking something."

"Right before he dropped dead at the age of fifty-six. What are you now?"

"Fifty-five." He sits up, puffs his chest out. "Anyway, it won't happen to me, I'm at the gym most mornings."

I'd rather cut my own tongue out than admit it but it shows. While a lot of men wither and stoop under the weight of spousal grief, Dad's stock seems to have appreciated year on year. He's certainly never looked stronger or fitter than he does now.

But then, Dad was always good-looking. Problematically good-looking, some would say. Eyes glinting green-gold and a smile like a solar flare. Even now, with his hair peppered gray and his jawline slightly softer, he's still got that catch-all appeal that makes teenage girls want to grow up faster and elderly ladies reverse the clock.

Our drinks arrive along with a bowl of something birdseedy. "So I assume you're not here to test the tap water?" he says, eyeing my glass with disdain.

I'm here because you lied about Maryanne Doyle and now she's dead.

"Jacqui says you've rented out Radlett. What've you done with my stuff?"

His eyebrows shoot up. "And that's what you're here for? Honestly? You're worried I've thrown out your old board games?" He lets out a deep sigh. "Well, panic over, sweetheart. I haven't actually rented it out." He casts me a warning glance. "And that goes no further than us, by the way."

"But Jacq—"

He holds up his hands. "Shoot me, I lied. Look, I couldn't bring myself to have strangers moving in but you know as well as I do that the minute I said I was moving out, that'd be Jacqui's cue to move in. She's always dropping hints about how it's more of a 'family home.'"

"There's only three of them, what do they need a five-bedroomed house for?"

"Trying for another baby, I think. I don't ask much, it's their business."

"Really? Finn will be seven by then, at least."

He looks at me, confused. "So? Same age as Noel was when you came along. Only a year older than Jacqui."

Mum banged out her first two in quick succession. I came later—a happy accident, apparently. They joked they'd been hoping for a new kitchen that year, instead they got me.

"Yeah, and look how that turned out. They both hated me for getting all the attention, spoiling their fun."

"Jacqui didn't hate you." He doesn't have a leg to stand on with Noel. I don't have one happy memory of him playing with me, except the time he said we'd play hide-and-seek and he locked me in the pub cellar.

"Jacqui tolerated me because I was a toy she could show off." Her living breathing Tiny Tears.

"You're too harsh on that girl."

"Am I? It's not me lying to keep her out of her family home!"

"Oh I need this, I really fucking need this." He tilts his head back, aims a long, labored breath toward the ceiling. "Look, I love the bones of Jacqs—and Ash's a good bloke and Finn's a dote—but I might want to move back in again at some point, you know, and the idea of living with them full-time . . ."

"As opposed to Noel who's the perfect house pet?"

He rolls his eyes. "What do you want me to say, Cat? He's my son and I worry about him. I worry about all my kids. Jesus, you have no idea how much I worry about you." I try to tell him not to bother but he railroads on. "I mean, did you hear about that young copper? Shot dead, somewhere in America. Pennsylvania, I think." A sad shake of the head. "She was only twenty-four. Just a child."

A child unless you're fucking them and then anything post A-levels is fair game.

"Save your prayers, Dad, it doesn't happen a lot here."

He raises his voice. "It's still a dangerous job, and you're still my baby."

This is new. Danger's never really come into it before. He usually prefers grandiose speeches about "us" and "them" and "never the twain" blah blah blah. Pithy little statements about blood ties and trust.

"It makes me happy though," I say, which is partly true. "And you once said I could be anything I wanted—*even a Tory*—if it made me happy. I bet you don't remember, do you?"

Straight back at me. "I bloody do. Six years old and you announce you want to be a plasterer after we'd got all the work done in the hallway. Noel and Jacqui were laughing at you."

"Yeah, and you said if it made me happy, then why not? You even bought me my own set of trowels."

This gets me, gut-level. I see it in his eyes too but he wards it off with a laugh. "I don't think anyone ever got shot doing a day's plastering. And trust me, sweetheart, when you have kids of your own you'll realize that 'safe' trumps 'happy' every time."

And yet I haven't felt safe with you in years.

"They found Maryanne Doyle's body." There's a roar from across the bar. A last-minute penalty. An eleventh hour reprieve for someone. "Near here," I say, louder over the cheering. "Leamington Square."

Dad's eyes flick to the commotion. He hunches his shoulders as if bracing himself against an invisible storm. It can't be more than a few seconds before he speaks again but it's time enough for him to make a decision.

"They found who?" he says, cocking an ear toward me, squinting in irritation at the noise.

"Maryanne Doyle." My mouth feels full of grit. "You know, the girl from Mulderrin."

A slant of the head. A search through his mental rolodex, then suddenly, enlightenment. "Jonjo Doyle's girl, you mean? The one that ran away?" His voice goes up a notch higher. "What, they found her here, in London?"

I nod. "Yep. Murdered. You must have seen it on the news. Heard about it?"

His face clouds over but it's not what I think. "I haven't been able to watch any frigging news. Noel did something to the TV and now it won't 'initialize,' whatever the hell that means. Do you know what 'initialize' means? I can't find the manual . . ."

Classic stonewalling.

I don't let him off.

"It's just, well, it happened pretty much on your doorstep. The old grapevine mustn't be working like it used to."

"To be honest, I haven't been here much the past few days." He takes a slug of his pint, a third in one swallow. "I mean, yeah, now you mention it, I think I did see some yellow tape flapping about up the road but that's hardly big news around here."

My heart bangs. "So what do you think?"

He looks at me quizzically, like he doesn't quite understand the question. "Well, it's terrible, of course. Bloody terrible. Tessie Doyle—wasn't that the grandmother's name? She was one of your gran's cronies. We should send a mass card, at least. What do you think?"

I slap down the sentiment. "The granny's probably dead by now. She was practically dead then."

"The father then. Don't get me wrong, he was a prick of the highest order but I wouldn't wish that on my worst . . ."

"He'll be dead soon too."

His eyes narrow. "I must say, you're very well informed."

"I'm working the case."

And for that second, the world shrinks to just us. Just his face and mine. Every smell seems to evaporate. Every color ceases to exist. And there's a silence. A silence so laden with fear and mistrust that it turns everything else abstract and us both to stone.

Dad recovers quicker though, lets out a low whistle and a sarcastic tut.

I wait for a few seconds as the room comes back into focus. "What?"

He tries to do casual but there's a flush creeping up his neck. "Ah, nothing really. Just thought there'd be some petty coppers' code about personal connections and all that jazz . . ."

I try casual too but my shoulders are locked. My neck's coiled like a helix.

I plump for confusion. "And what's my personal connection, Dad? That my gran played bingo with her gran?"

His hands lock tight around his glass. "Is that how your boss sees it?"

"Since when have you been so concerned with police ethics?" I say, bristling.

He picks up a napkin with the other hand, a grease-stained white flag. "Hey look, work away, Detective. I mean, what would I know? But if memory serves me right, Jacqui had a few words with the Guards at the time."

I stare at him, blankly, pretend I don't get the point.

"Well, that'll be on some system somewhere, surely?"

Top marks.

"Tell you what, Dad, how about you let me worry about that? And anyway, she was killed on Monday night, thirty-five years old and a long way from Mulderrin. I doubt there's a connection."

I'm about five bottles of wine, sixty sleepless nights and seven hundred dark thoughts away from knowing whether I believe that or not.

Dad seems to take it at face value.

"God, that Mulderrin holiday, that takes me back," he says, forearms on the table, all slumpy and relaxed now. "Good-looking kid, weren't she, the Doyle girl. Jacqui will remember her, I bet."

I remember her, Dad. I remember every little lie you told too.

"Do you know what I remember about that holiday?" I tell him. "You disappearing all the time. Mum putting me to bed every single night so I never got a story."

"Christ, and you reckon Noel knows how to hold a grudge!" His laugh is short, sharp and hard. "Aw poor little Catrina. Do you want me to read *The Three Little Pigs* to you now? Make up for it, like?"

I refrain from *"Go fuck yourself."* Convey it with a death-stare instead.

"Do you know what *I* remember about that holiday?" he says. I switch the stare to "impassive" but I'm ravenous for what he'll say next. "I remember you didn't want to go. Got yourself in a bit of a state about it. We were taking you out of school a few days early and you were stressing your class rabbit wouldn't get fed. And you were worried about Reg. Do you remember Reg?"

I remember Reg. One of the pub's regulars and a lovely old man. He lost his wife to cancer and his dog to the number seventy-three bus in the space of three weeks but he rarely lacked a smile or a poorly ex-ecuted joke.

I say nothing though, just nod.

"So I said you shouldn't worry so much about everything—Reg and Bugs-fucking-Bunny would be fine, but that it was lovely you were such a thoughtful little girl and that I was proud of you." My face feels hot. I press my lips together, blink three times. "And you were, back then. You were such a little belter. So kind. A bit on the lively side sometimes, but never naughty, not like Jacqui, and well . . ." He leaves Noel's name hanging. "I mean, I know parents aren't supposed to have favorites, but there was never any contest. What happened, Cat? Why are you so de-termined to be miserable?"

"I'm not. Why are you so determined to convince yourself you're happy? Is that what the Jag and your women and this stupid place do? Make you forget that life's essentially shit?"

He reaches for my hand, managing to graze the tips of my fingers be-fore I snatch it away. "I know I'm not happy, Cat. How can I be? *'You're only as happy as your unhappiest child.'* Ever heard that saying?"

My eyes prickle and I know I'm going to cry, or capitulate, if I don't shift the tone of this conversation and do something drastic.

I pull the pin out of the grenade.

"Did you sleep with Maryanne Doyle?"

He shifts. The light throws a shadow across his face and I lose his eyes for a crucial second. When they reappear, I swear he looks different. There's an icy serenity about him. About as far away from sucker-punched as an accused man can be.

"Well, did you? It's not a trick question, Dad. It's not multiple choice."

"Are we really going to do this?" He almost sounds amused—like he's heard the corniest joke ever for the hundredth time but still can't help smirking. "I mean, don't you ever get bored of this, Cat?"

Bored, no. Bone-weary, yes.

"So tell me I'm wrong. Tell me I'm crazy, like you always do."

"I don't think I've ever used the word 'crazy.'"

He hasn't in fairness. "Maddening," "antagonistic," and on one occasion, "pure poison," but never crazy.

"I notice you haven't used the word 'no' either." My voice is shaky. I've been shackled to this narrative since I still had my milk teeth but now that I've said it—now that it's out there—it sounds fantastical, or at the very least, flimsy. "Say it, Dad," I urge him. "If you didn't sleep with Maryanne Doyle, say 'no.' Just answer the question."

"No." His eyes flare as icy serenity gives way to quiet fury. "No, I didn't sleep with Maryanne Doyle. Just like I didn't sleep with your auntie Brona. Or Katy Keilty's mum. Or your Irish dancing teacher. Or Cathy Hammond from the Flag. Or basically half the women you seem to think I did."

Half? I very much doubt that. I'll admit I was never one to discriminate when it came to accusing him—Auntie Brona still makes me boil with shame—but I know I was right about a lot of them. Just not the rank outsiders he's been clever enough to name.

I steady my voice. "Then why did you lie about knowing . . ."

He grabs my hands across the table. "Enough, Catrina." I open my mouth but he puts a finger up to halt me. Another to my lips, shushing me. "I mean it now. *Enough*."

Strong, calm, commanding. As if pacifying an angry dog.

But I won't be pacified, not yet. "Because you did know her. We picked her up . . ."

He jerks his hand up and catches me by the jaw. It doesn't hurt but the grip is tight and it stops me speaking. My skin hums underneath. To the rest of the bar it probably looks playful.

"Is this ever going to end, Catrina? All this bullshit? You'd think you'd never put a foot wrong in your life. Can't you accept that everyone has"—he chooses his word carefully—"failings?"

"Failings," I sneer. "There's no such thing, Dad, just bad decisions."

He triggers the "M" word. "Mum always forgave me, why can't you? God knows you always followed her lead on everything else."

Deliverance comes in the form of beautiful Xavier—incensed, and I mean Spanish incensed, about some woman claiming she gave him a twenty when he knows she gave him a ten. Dad stands up heavily, walks over to the bar, hands out, chin high, all ready to sort out the *obvious misunderstanding*, using nothing other than that iridescent smile and a touch of the McBride charm.

I pick up my bag and leave.

I should have told Dad that this isn't about Mum. It's not about forgiveness. It's not about sleazy affairs or bunk-ups in the bar. It's not about Katy Kielty's mum or sexy students pulling pints.

It's about murder.

It's about the lie—the litany of lies—he told about Maryanne Doyle eighteen years ago and the fact she's turned up dead just a short walk from his door.

But fear muzzled me, far more than his clasp on my jaw ever could. The fear of what he might unload if I kept pushing and the fear of losing him forever if I'm wrong.

Because what if he's not who I think he is? I can't ignore the fact I've spent most of my life, not exactly sure in the belief, but certainly toying with—then blocking out—the idea that Dad might have killed Mary-anne Doyle in 1998. Now that's been proved impossible, can I trust my own instincts any more than I mistrust him?

Because what if he's not a Bad Man? What if he's just a liar? A wom-anizer. A run-of-the-mill arsehole. Just an aging matinee idol with a moody, over-inked girlfriend and a complicated TV system he can't work out.

What if I've spent the past eighteen years tormenting him—*tormenting myself*—for what amounts to nothing more than a few grubby white lies?

9

Seven a.m.

I wake up late, late for me anyway, twisted and practically mummified in my sheets with a cold sheen of sweat coating my body and a dozen family photos scattered across the bed. I don't recall dreaming last night, although I must have done. The experts say that you always dream. That your dreams act as safety valves through which you live out unconscious desires, free from the hindrance of consequence or the shame of taboo.

I've never actually dreamed of killing my dad, although I did once dream that he'd killed me.

I sit up quickly, grateful for the late hour. Wake at seven a.m. and I'm thrown straight into focusing on real things, safe things—showers, vitamins, turned milk, tube delays—whereas at five a.m., my usual rise and shine, I've got two hours of lying in the half-light to grapple with. Two hours of thinking about all the things I could have done better and all the people I never see. Sometimes I use the time more effectively. I read lamebrain magazines by the light of my phone, doping myself with articles like "Change Your Face Primer, Change Your Life!!" Other times I whisper affirmations into the silence, soothing myself with sad little cheerleads—advice from just about every self-help book I've ever been dopey enough to buy.

I am enough.

I am *more than* enough.

I love and approve of myself.

I am a good person.

It's the last one that shames me. This notion that *good* somehow equals *protected*. Anyone would think I'd spent the past two years jazz-handing my way around Disney, not wading through the relentless grime of MIT, where despicable, unthinkable things happen to good people every day. Just last year I worked a case where a sixty-two-year-old dinner lady, well known in her local community for her charity fun runs and history of fostering disabled children, was fatally stabbed in the head four times in broad daylight, all over a piece of dropped litter.

She'd been a good person. One of the best by all accounts. I bet she never felt the need to affirm her goodness into the silence at five in the morning.

Fat lot of good *being* good did her.

Alice Lapaine had been a good person too.

"Right, I've skim-read the report and I'm giving Vickery eight out of ten for crystal-ball accuracy." At nine thirty, Steele sweeps into the office balancing files, a bucket of coffee, a paper bag containing something greasy and the thing she calls her handbag that most people would take on a minibreak.

Parnell, moving quicker than I'd have given him credit for, grabs the coffee as it threatens to capsize. "Cheers, Lu," she says, puffing and panting, dropping everything onto the nearest desk with a heavy thwack. "Chaps and chapesses, listen. I've literally got fifteen minutes for a quick catch-up and then I'm out all day—meetings with Blake, the Press Office, the bloody Dalai Lama for all I know. I'm assuming you've all had a chance to read through the PM reports? Well, you better bloody have, put it that way. Benny-boy, be a love and get the photos up on the big screen." To Parnell, "Lu, you lead. I need to eat."

Ben busies himself being technical while everyone else dives into last-minute revisions in case Parnell decides to play Ask the Audience.

"So folks, Thomas Lapaine." Parnell walks over to the incident board and lands a meaty paw on his picture. "We need to get him back under this roof again because the PM threw up something very interesting—Alice had given birth to a child at some point. The shape of the cervix and pelvis confirms it. It's hard to say when exactly, and I'm not even sure what this means, but it's something he neglected to mention."

"Well, leave me out of that discussion, please," says Renée. "I think I've burned my bridges there—the first time we met I told him his wife was dead, the second time I told him she'd been lying through her teeth about who she really was."

"Bad, huh?" I ask.

"As bad as you'd expect. A few tears. A lot of shouting. He threw a glass at the wall as well—his mum shooed me out then, told me I was 'impudent' and that she didn't like my *tone*." Renée grins and I know what's coming. "Didn't like my skin tone, more like. I don't think Mother has a very diverse social set, if you know what I mean. It was a big enough shock learning her daughter-in-law was a hundred percent Irish."

Emily stops chewing a hangnail, straightens up. "Boss, I met the IVF consultant yesterday and I saw the patient registration form they both filled out. There was nothing on there about a prior pregnancy."

"Maybe Thomas Lapaine had no idea," I suggest. "It could have been before they met?"

Ben points to the screen. "Come on, stretch marks across the abdomen, faint ones on the breasts. He must have realized, even if it was from before."

Our female contingent shares a pained grin. I think about hoicking up my top and parading my silvery lines right in front of his innocent little face but I settle for embarrassing him instead. "Ben, have you ever actually seen a naked woman? A real one, I mean, not one that lives in your laptop or on your iPhone. Ever heard of a thing called a growth spurt, or a bit of weight gain?"

"Maybe they had a stillborn?" says Renée. "You'd kind of understand him not wanting to revisit that, not when he's only just found out his wife's dead."

Parnell considers this but he's not convinced. "Mmmm, I can see him not volunteering the information, but he talked to us *a lot* about kids. You'd think it would have come up somehow if there had been a child and, well, now there wasn't."

Steele steps in. "Renée, check records—adoption, birth, deaths, everything for a child born to either Alice Lapaine or Maryanne Doyle, here and in Ireland."

"'Course you know what this means," says Renée. "If she'd given birth in the past, the chances are Thomas Lapaine was the problem."

"Which means what?" I ask. "Last time I looked there wasn't a direct link between male infertility and homicidal tendencies."

Renée nods. "No, but it's a very emotive subject, just saying."

"Didn't I say being a jaffa could tip into something nasty? Didn't I?" Flowers sounds elated.

Much as I know it'll pain Parnell, he agrees. "Could be that Alice wanting to stop trying tipped him over the edge. Snuffed out any chance of proving to himself that he's a real man." He puts a hand up, bats away my protest. "I'm not saying that's what I think, Kinsella, I'm just trying to put myself in his shoes. Think how he might think."

Truth is, there aren't many in this room with any real idea of how an insecure man staring down the barrel of childlessness might think, certainly not Seth and Ben, who'd rather be saddled with colostomy bags than babies at this point in their lives, and definitely not MIT4's resident stallions—Parnell, Flowers and Craig Cooke—who've got about a hundred kids between them.

Steele looks at her watch. "OK, can we move on from the contents of Thomas Lapaine's scrotum and see what else we've got? I haven't got long."

Parnell continues. "Time of death. Vickery's still being a bit cagey but we're going to work with somewhere between one and three a.m. Cause of death is manual asphyxia, *however* there are virtually no signs of struggle so she was almost certainly unconscious when she was strangled, probably from this blow sustained to the front of the head—picture five."

We've all seen the crime-scene photos, the worst of which burn onto your brain like asphalt, but post-mortem pics allow for a bit more professional distance. Flowers flicks through the pages like a man choosing a main course—and that's not a criticism, I can't wait to get there myself.

"Now—and pay attention because this is important—her skull wasn't fractured by the blow. There's no real damage to the brain so Vickery's a bit on the fence about this. She says it *could* be classed as inconsistent with what you'd expect to see in your average beating and so it *could* mean that rather than being hit on the head with something in a deliberate attack, she might have just hit her head accidentally."

"Or a fall?"

Steele points at me, animated. I can feel myself glowing. "Yeah, good, Kinsella, a fall's definitely a possibility. It fits with the mild bruising on her legs—pictures eight and nine." She doesn't even have to look at the report to know the layout. "But as we're dealing in '*coulds*,' for a second let's imagine that the wound *could* have been caused by a deliberate blow. What does that tell us?"

She doesn't give us time to answer.

"Well, it tells us it wasn't particularly frenzied or there'd be more damage to the brain. And then if you add that to the fact that the cuts to the throat were also very tentative, very shallow, what we seem to have is a rather reluctant, albeit, fairly determined killer."

"Reluctant but determined?" says Seth, wistfully, doing that Sherlock thing that either amuses or irritates me depending on my mood. "Bit of an oxymoron, don't you think?"

Parnell jumps in. "I think what the Boss means is he meant to kill her . . ."

"Or she," says Flowers, thinking he's hilarious. "Can't discriminate these days, remember."

Craig punches the air. "Right on, sister!"

Parnell explodes. "Shut it, everyone, this isn't a joke." This jolts me, scares me a bit, even. It's the first time I've heard Parnell properly lose his rag and I don't like it. "Anyone finding this the slightest bit funny, I suggest they go down to the morgue and take a look at what's lying in the fridge, OK? A young woman with her whole life ahead of her, snuffed out, and we have absolutely no idea why."

I get what he's doing. You have to shapeshift a little when you're acting up in a role, otherwise everyone thinks you're still their mate. You're still Papa Parnell who loves a laugh and a joke and an arse-about as much as the rest of us.

Parnell continues, calmer now. "What the Boss means is whoever *they* are, *they* meant to kill her, all right—the hyoid bone was fractured so we're talking considerable force—they just seem to have taken a few gos to choose their weapon, as it were."

"So they're inexperienced then rather than reluctant," I say.

Steele snaps. "Jesus! Can we just forget I said 'reluctant.' Wrong choice of word, my bad. Inexperienced, yes, Kinsella. Indecisive. Shitting bricks. How am I doing? Any other oxy-whatsits I need to be aware of?"

Steele, with her first-class degree from Durham and her Masters from LSE isn't immune to dumbing down if it buoys up the troops.

I do have one more oxymoron though, or a contradiction at least.

"Sarge," I say, turning to Parnell. "Or is it Boss, now? Anyway, don't you think it's odd that the manner of death's so jumpy but the manner of disposal's so, well, brazen? Remember the CCTV? Our guy, or girl"— a quick nod to Flowers—"stretching out their back like they're doing flipping sun salutations, not dumping a body."

"Yoga," says Renée before Flowers asks.

"OK," nods Parnell, happy to run with it. "So what do you think that could mean?"

"That it's less stressful dumping a body than actually killing some-one?"

Seth gets in on the action. "Maybe the person on the CCTV isn't our killer? Just someone tasked with dumping the body?"

"Easy," warns Steele. "I don't even want to think about that without evidence."

Parnell raises a hand. "Speaking of which, we don't have much. Fo-rensics have a few footprints . . ." This gets a communal groan. Foot-prints don't hold a candle to fibers, or blood, or skin, or semen, unless they're stamped across the victim's chest and we get to play Cinderella with an actual foot. "Yeah, yeah. Don't shoot the messenger."

Renée chips in. "Sounds like they could be forensically aware then?"

Parnell shrugs. "Not necessarily. The primary crime scene could be awash with lots of lovely stuff but until we find it, we're stuck with footprints, I'm afraid."

I've got other things on my mind. "No semen at all then? So definitely no unprotected sex in the past seventy-two hours. Might make the 'secret boyfriend' theory a bit less likely? I mean, sure, they could have been using condoms but . . ."

Parnell's on it. "We've asked for a vaginal swab, see if they can get traces of condom lubricant. It won't tell us anything definitive, but it'll tell us *something*, at least."

"We can't rule out a boyfriend based just on that," says Flowers. "Maybe they just hadn't mattress-danced in a few days. I know, I know, folks, it's hard to believe that I go without for any length of time, but it happens, kids."

Parnell nods along. "I hear you, Pete, but there's no other obvious signs of sexual activity, and if there was a boyfriend, I reckon it'd have to have been a red-hot affair to lure Alice Lapaine into London, not the kind that abstains for three days. Anyway, we'll see. Lab couldn't give us any timescales, *obviously*."

Steele mumbles into the PM report. "Not so reluctant to give us costs though."

"Talking of money," says Parnell. "What've we got on her transactions so far?"

"Bank records have her in London from Thursday 19th November," Renée confirms.

"Which backs up Thomas Lapaine's story," I say, not in any way championing him, just stating a fact.

Renée lifts a warning finger. "Yeah, but hold your horses, I'm coming back to him in a minute. So she used their joint account to pay for two nights in a hotel—if you can call it a hotel—it's a grotty little outfit off Gray's Inn Road. Still managed to relieve her of two hundred fifty pounds for two nights' bed and board though. For a single room that someone on Trip Advisor called, what was it, Ben?"

Ben cranes his neck. "'Cold, tired and eminently depressing.'"

I can't resist it. "Sounds like your last girlfriend, Seth."

"Cruel, Kinsella," he replies with a grin.

Seriously, the shifts I spent counseling Seth over his ice-queen ex—a Finnish vegan with an allergy to everything, a reluctance to give head, and in my opinion, an ill-conceived pixie cut.

Renée continues, half-smiling—she'd played agony aunt too. "So we've talked to reception at the hotel and someone remembered her vaguely. Nothing out of the ordinary though. Never saw her with anyone."

Parnell rubs his eyes. "And then what?"

"Nothing. From November 19th, there's no more credit or debit card transactions we can trace. All we've got are cash withdrawals from the joint account—all over central London, maxing the limit every time—two hundred fifty pounds every four or five days but—and this is the interesting bit—that stops last week. Last withdrawal was 13th December. She . . ."

I interrupt, not my finest habit, but this is a brainstorm, not a formal brief, and there's no prizes for diffidence. "Two hundred and fifty pounds every four to five days? That's not enough to live on in London, including accommodation. She *must* have been staying with someone."

"So why'd she stop fleecing the husband?" says Flowers, his voice thorny with experience.

I shoot him a dirty look. "Er, do you want to look up the meaning of the word 'joint?'"

Renée rolls her eyes but she's past arguing with him. "She had no choice. I've just had it confirmed that Thomas Lapaine cleared out their joint account at the beginning of last week. Left her high and dry, the rotten sod."

"Can he really do that?" I ask, shocked. "Empty the account without her knowledge?"

It's genuinely news to me. And to think Steele's got me pegged as Financially Intelligent.

"Hmm-mm," nods Renée. "Not a very nice thing to do, but completely his right. Either account holder can clear it out at any time."

I'm not sure whether to pity or envy couples with this level of faith. It seems absurdly naïve on one hand, but then the whole point of intimacy on the other. Literally putting your money where your mouth is when it comes to the word "trust."

"Right, get him back under this roof today," says Steele to Parnell. "Just for another 'chat' of course. Try to avoid any tears, or shouting, or glasses hurled at walls, please. In any case, there's not a whole lot we can hurl at him at this stage, not until we've got more forensics, but just get him to quit with all the 'we understood each other' bollocks, OK? There's something rotten at the core of that marriage and we need to know what it is."

Parnell nods. "Ben? Anything come back on the phone records?"

Ben's edgy. "Well, yeah, kind of. We've got the call she made to Lapaine on his birthday and then various unanswered calls to her phone— a few from Lapaine and then a couple from someone at the pub the day after she left, probably just seeing why she hadn't turned up for work, and then there's your usual junk calls, etc." He takes a breath. "But most interestingly, we've got six calls *from* Alice to two different pay-as-you-go numbers over the past few weeks. First one, November 23rd. Last one, December 12th. Problem is, both phones are switched off. We need to wait for them to be switched back on before they ping the mast and we get a location. And if either person is somehow involved, that might never happen, of course."

"Can we trace where they bought the top-up?" I say. "Pull the CCTV?"

Ben nods. "We're on it, but if they bought the top-up in a tiny offy in the arse-end of nowhere, forget about it . . ."

"All fun and games," someone grumbles. I think it's Flowers.

Parnell does his best to rally everyone. "Right, good work, folks. We *are* making progress even if it doesn't feel like it."

As everyone starts to disperse back to their desks, Parnell grabs me. "I want you to get over to Wandsworth. That café she bought the coffee in on Friday, it reopens today."

"Righto."

Steele appears. "And take Emily with you. Let me know if she's good for anything other than picking her nails and looking at ASOS."

Poor Emily Beck. It's a novelty we all fell for. The freedom to be fashionable again after two years in uniform.

"Boss, can I have a word." Parnell and Steele both turn around. "Big Boss?" I say, and then, to my shame, "Lady-Boss?"—aware I'm making Steele sound like a cheap market-stall perfume.

"Sure. We'll have to walk and talk though." She holds out two box-files. "Here, carry these for me."

I wait until we're outside the room and halfway down the corridor. I suspect she's not even listening properly but at least I can say I told her. "Er, I just wanted to let you know, I took the Ireland file off your desk yesterday. Had a quick shuftie." A tiny flash of *"oh, did you now?"* crosses her face but it could just be the dodgy strip lighting messing with me. "I knew you were busy and well, after meeting the brother, I was curious. There's nothing much in there, nothing relevant, I think."

We get in the lift. "What did you make of him then, the brother?"

"I sent you my report," I say, instantly defensive. "One for Parnell, one for you. I emailed it to you last night."

She hits the button for the ground floor. "Whoa, Kinsella. I wasn't checking up on your paperwork, I was just asking. Making conversation."

My face burns. "Oh right, sorry. Well, it's hard to know what to make of him, really. He's not exactly grief-stricken but it's been eighteen years. He's moved on with his life and then, this. If you're asking if he's a serious suspect, my gut says no. He says he hasn't laid eyes on her since 1998 and we've nothing to contradict that. No contact between them on Maryanne's Facebook or Hotmail, etc."

She lets this sit as the lift descends. When the doors open into reception, we're greeted by a teen with a busted eye socket and a woman raising hell over a lost coat.

"He could still be the mystery pay-as-you-go," says Steele, signaling *"one minute"* to her driver outside.

"He could. And he was home alone, so yeah, it's about as reliable as Thomas Lapaine's alibi, but he did have a text exchange with a friend at around one a.m. and Tech are looking into it now. If that comes back kosher, and the phone masts bear him out, we've got him tucked up in bed in Mile End around the time of death so . . ."

"So we go again. We dig deeper."

"Yup."

"You OK?" she asks, eyes fixed on mine. In her stiletto suede boots, we're about the same height.

Petty cynic that I am, I wonder why she's asking.

She's on to me though. "It's just a question, Kinsella. A fairly common one in polite society. If it helps the most common answers are, '*I'm fine thanks*,' '*Not too bad*' and '*Can't complain*.'"

"All those things then," I say, smiling.

"Mmmm." She scrutinizes me for a few seconds which makes me feel twitchy and exposed. However, just as I'm starting to think about my next move, about what I might have to deflect next, a car horn sounds and she bolts suddenly for the door. "Yes, yes, I'm coming, all right! Keep your knickers on. Jesus!"

I'm waiting for the lift when I feel the draught again. Steele's standing in the doorway, eyes already watering from the barbaric cold outside.

"Hey, Kinsella, just to stress again—even though I'm not here, what we talked about still stands, you hear me? You report everything to me. You check everything with me. *Everything*, OK?"

Everything except the thing I can't tell you. The thing that's forced me to pick sides.

And I haven't picked you.

Not yet, anyway.

10

There's no Donatella to be found at the Donatella Caffé, just two squawking pensioners called June and Bernie who can only seem to agree on two things. The first being that we really *must* try the stollen cake, the second being that I have lovely hair. The issue of Maryanne Doyle is proving a little more contentious though, with June insisting she'd only been in a few times, while Bernie's adamant they could near enough erect a plaque to her.

I honestly don't know where to hedge my bets as they're both as dotty as each other and equally ancient. Not that old means unreliable, of course. Far from it. Give me an eagle-eyed pensioner over a self-absorbed Gen Y any day of the week. Nosiness trumps narcissism every time.

These pair are breaking the mold though.

"Well, she was definitely here Friday morning," says Bernie, pointing at the receipt, stating the obvious.

"But do you actually remember seeing her?" It comes out a bit snotty so I quickly make amends. "Go on then, give me a bit of that stollen. I'm useless. I've no willpower at all."

Bernie looks appeased and hands me a slice the size of a car battery. "Well, I'm not sure," she says. "I had a lot on my mind on Friday. I've got to have an operation, you know."

June looks up from a tub of tuna mix and mouths "*Gallstones*."

"And it's chockablock on a Friday, always is. There's a Zumba class up the road who come in here afterward. Sit for hours, they do." I offer her money for the cake but she shakes her head. "No, no, it's on the house, I insist. I've always been a big fan of the police, haven't I, June? Dangerous job, especially for young girls like you pair. Call it repayment."

I smile. "Repayment comes out of your council tax, Bernie, but thanks all the same. I'll be needing a few Zumba classes myself after this."

Emily takes over as I tuck in. "Did you ever see her with anyone?"

They eye each other nervously, like the wrong answer could get them life without parole. It's June who eventually braves it.

"No, I don't think so. Nice looking girl, weren't she? Classy, I mean. Had one of those fancy brown coats. We used to call them flasher macs back in the day but they're all the rage now apparently."

I hoover up another forkful, dutifully faking a cake orgasm. "Any chance of the other dates she came in, ladies? Apart from Friday. I appreciate it's not easy."

"Well, we don't sell many of those ristretto things," offers June. "I could go through the till roll for the past few weeks, see if I can find another."

"We *do* actually," says Bernie, all superior. "That fat man with the cap, he always has one. And that lady with the Down's syndrome lad, not that she gets a minute's peace to drink it, the poor creature."

June looks smug. "Ah, but the police can cross-reference to see if they were here on a particular day, and if they weren't then it must have been this dead girl. It's called 'process of elimination,' Bern."

"It's called watching too much bloody Inspector Morse."

"Did you ever talk to her about anything?" I interrupt, breaking up the spat.

Bernie frowns. "Such as?"

"Well, where she'd been? Where she was going? Why she was in the area?"

Baffled expressions. Customer engagement clearly isn't their forte.

It's June who pipes up again. "I think I saw her over there once, if that's any help." She points across the street. "Some time last week. That gated road where the posh houses are. It might have been her, anyway. Same sort of hair, same browny coat." She adds a hint of warning to her voice. "But I was going past on the bus and he doesn't take any prisoners when he's behind schedule so I didn't exactly get a good look, and I wasn't wearing the right glasses. I'd had to borrow our Eileen's because I'd left mine at the harvester." A small shrug. "Anyway, whoever it was was bending down talking into that walkie-talkie thing."

"The intercom, you fool," snaps Bernie.

I hand my card across the counter, give another thumbs-up for the cake. "That's very helpful, June, thank you. And anything the till roll throws up would be great."

"Waste of time," says Emily as we stand outside, shuddering against the shock of the cold, our shoulders huddled up around our ears.

Most investigative work is, I should tell her. However I'm taking a surprising amount of pride in my prefect role so I do my best to strike a positive tone.

"Not necessarily. Let's check out this gated road. If it was Alice Lapaine, someone must know her."

Emily curls her lip. "Yeah, if it even was her. I'm not sure anything those two said would stand up in court."

"True. But if you want your murders sewn up in the space of two hours, go and binge-watch Morse with the lovely June in there. Otherwise, get your arse over the road with me."

Keeper's Close is a pronounced curve of nine houses, the kind of street a child would scrawl, with gravelly paths meandering between perfectly manicured lawns, primary-colored front doors decorated with pine cones and Christmas wreaths, and white picket fences sectioning off the Haves from the Have-Mores. At the top of the close, a Waitrose van is parked outside what is clearly the best house—a three-story period property that makes the other million-pound drums look a bit pedestrian and naff. Like plain and frumpy bridesmaids forming a guard of honor for the far more elegant bride.

Emily tries not to look impressed but when £50,000 of Range Rover pulls up to the gates she practically goes cross-eyed with envy.

"You're in the wrong job," I say to her, signaling to the driver to wind down his window. "If it's fancy cars you're after, you're going to have to make damn sure you marry well. And you're *definitely* barking up the wrong tree with Ben Swaines."

She feigns outrage. "Get lost, I don't fancy Ben. It's just flirting, livening up the . . ."

I'm spared the girly chat by a frail old man leaning out of the car window, waiflike in his behemoth of a car. "Can I help?" he says in a quiet, raspy voice.

I flash my ID. "Do you live here, sir?"

"Yes. Well, no. I do at the moment, most of time anyway. What's this about?" His face clouds. "God, it's not that arsehole, Bingham, again, is it? She'll go mad."

I file Bingham for later and pull Alice's photo out of my pocket. "Do you recognize this woman?"

A quick but curious glance. "No, sorry. But you'd be better off talking to my daughter." He points toward Keeper's Close's very own Taj Mahal. "The house at the top."

He pulls off and we follow behind slowly. By the time we reach the barn, the elderly man isn't looking so fragile, berating the Waitrose driver for some barely noticeable scratch on a pillar while behind him, a good-looking woman wearing skinny jeans and a poncho-cum-granny blanket-type-thing, looks ready to commit murder. We wait a few seconds for her to acknowledge us but she's too busy pacifying her father and pleading with a small child to stop tormenting the cat.

"Hello," I shout, over the racket of alpha men and cranky kids.

The elderly man looks around, momentarily confused, like he's completely forgotten his encounter with the law in the time it took to drive up the pathway. "Oh sorry. Gina, these officers want a word."

Gina looks at us unmoved, as if somehow resigned to yet another drama. "Oh, OK." She scoops up the cat-tormenting child. "Can you bring the shopping through, please? I've rather got my hands full."

I figure the instruction's aimed at the Waitrose man but I make myself useful anyway, hauling a case of Pouilly-Fumé off the van and following her into a cavernous hall—all stone floors and timber beams and a Christmas tree to rival Rockefeller's.

"So what's this about?" she says, craning her neck around, trying not to be strangled by the clinging toddler.

"We're investigating a murder, Mrs. . . . Sorry, I didn't catch your name."

"Hicks. Murder?" The usual blend of alarm mixed with macabre delight.

We follow her into the kitchen where an identical toddler is slumped on a beanbag in front of *Paw Patrol*, and a neighbor, who introduces herself as Tash Marwood, is wrapping ham around figs. I lean against the Aga and blow Tash Marwood's mind with the "M" word while we wait for Gina to bribe the toddlers out of the room with Fruit Shoots and Pom-Bears. Eventually negotiations cease and she closes the door.

"Murder, you said? Good God! Who? Where?" She looks toward Tash Marwood. "God, it's not someone on the close, is it?"

"No. Central London. The victim went by two names, Alice Lapaine and Maryanne Doyle." I wait a beat to see if there's a flicker of recognition from either of them. Nothing. "We're following a line of inquiry that she was seen at your main gates recently, talking into the intercom. We'll need to speak to all the residents."

Gina lets out a long breath. "Well, the names mean nothing, I'm afraid. Tash?"

Tash shakes her head, eyes full of appalled excitement. "Do you have a picture?"

Emily offers the photo. Tash offers an instant "No, sorry." Gina's just about to say something when her father staggers into the room, legs buckling under the weight of two cases of wine. She bolts toward him, furious.

"Dad, I told you not to lift those. Go and get Leo to help. Jesus!" She hoists the wine onto the marble island and sighs deeply. "I'm sorry, my father's not well so he's staying with us, and I'm trying to get ready for a party and all in all, it's a bit of a madhouse today. Christmas drinks with the neighbors," she explains with all the enthusiasm of someone facing the firing squad. "We did it the first year we moved in. It was my husband's idea—basically, he extends the invite and I put in all the effort. Anyway, unfortunately it seems to have become rather a tradition."

"I'll bet it has. People love a tradition that involves drinking someone else's booze."

She smiles—perfect straight teeth, well-cared for rather than manufactured. "Anyway, what I was about to say was that the Chapmans at number four have an au pair who looks a *bit* like this woman. The au pair's younger, of course, and well, she's not exactly her double, but there's definitely a similarity. It could have been her at the gate? What do you reckon, Tash?"

Tash looks up from her canapés. "Wouldn't surprise me. Mine's always forgetting her keys, forgetting the gate code, expecting to be buzzed in at all hours. It's like having another child to look after half the time. Absolute nightmare."

Emily shoots me a look. "*Can-you-believe-this-broad?*"

Gina smiles again, embarrassed by her friend. "I know, I know, first-world problems and all that."

I smile. "Hey look, you deserve a medal as far as I'm concerned. Twins, right? My sister has one and she's permanently on the edge of a breakdown."

"Try four. Twins and two teenagers."

"Blimey," is all I can think to say, then, "At least you have babysitters on tap, I suppose."

"There is that. My eldest Leo is good with them. I wouldn't leave them with Amber though. She'd be too busy Instagramming to notice they were drinking bleach."

I pull a face that says, "*Teenage girls, eh.*" "You mentioned your husband before, Mrs. Hicks. Is he in? Only it'd be good to show him the photo too, just to see if it rings any bells."

She sighs the sigh of the put-upon-but-well-compensated wife. "Detective, my husband would struggle to recognize me in a photo, that's how often he's here." A snort of *"tell me about it"* from Tash Marwood. "How long will you be around though? He did say he'd *try* and get home early-ish to help out—if you can call shouting at the children and criticizing my wine choices 'helping'—I can't imagine he'll shed any light though."

I smile blandly and hand her my card. "If we don't manage to see him, could you ask him to call the station and an officer will return with the photo." She nods, compliant but bewildered. "Mrs. Marwood, is there anyone in at your home?"

Tash Marwood doesn't look up this time, too busy doing something intricate with pears. "Not really. Tim's been in Singapore for the past week, he doesn't get back until tomorrow. There's Maria, my au pair, I suppose. Feel free. Although if you get more than five words out of her, I'll be shocked."

"There is another thing, Mrs. Hicks, your father mentioned an 'arsehole' called Bingham earlier. He thought that's why we were here. Anything we need to be aware of when we knock his door?"

"Bingham?" she says, with a twitch of a smile. "You mean our resident grumpy old man? Oh it's nothing, really. Leo had a bit of a party while we were away a few months back and Bingham's convinced that someone well, defecated, on his lawn."

"Charming. I take it he's not invited tonight?"

She laughs. "Er, no."

I have to ask. "And did someone defecate on his lawn?"

She nudges me off the Aga, slides a tray of something almondy onto a shelf. "I wouldn't put anything past teenage boys, Detective. Some of them are filthy pigs. But I know Leo didn't and I also know he won't be having any more parties. Not after his father finished with him."

As if called to the stage, the kitchen door crashes open and a handsome man-boy swaggers in with a case of wine under his left arm and his little sister on his right hip. At first glance, he doesn't look like the type to defecate on a lawn but then I don't have much to compare him to. The only teenage male I've endured at close proximity is Noel and this lad seems like a different species with his confident, easy "*hellos*" and trendy, sculpted hair.

"Mum, the cat scratched Mia again. We should drown that little runt."

Maybe not so different, after all.

"Do you recognize this woman?" Emily doesn't waste any time pulling the photo out again. The man-boy stares for a couple of seconds, biting a fleshy bottom lip before giving a listless shake of the head. He doesn't ask who we are, doesn't ask who the woman in the photo is. Teenage apathy at its best.

The apathy's catching and I suddenly feel bored and underutilized standing in this kitchen. I give Emily the nod, say, "OK, well, thanks very much for your time. And if you do think of anything . . ."

"You know, you haven't picked a great time to come calling," says Tash Marwood. "Most people on the close are at work during the day."

Gina nods. "Shame you didn't come later. You'd have got all the neighbors under one roof. Around the fireplace. Like that program, *Poirot*!"

I laugh because they seem to think it's a great gag and also because I want a favor.

"Actually, it'd be great if you could mention it to your guests. If they're not in, we'll obviously leave details, but if you could encourage them to call us ASAP, it'd be much appreciated."

They both look delighted by this, Tash Marwood especially. "Oh, consider it done, Detective. Anything but the strangled small talk. I mean, who wants to talk about school fees and Brexit when you can discuss murder!"

It's distasteful but it's the truth.

I let it slide.

Tash Marwood's not wrong. We haven't picked a great time to go knocking and all I manage is one harassed-looking au pair with patchy English and the much-maligned Bingham—or Bingham-Waites as he corrects me—a Grade-A cretin wearing a too-short dressing gown and the gait of the perpetually pissed-off.

Bingham-Waites doesn't recognize Alice but suggests she might be a whore visiting one John Hardwich at number six. He's always *"at it,"* he informs me, in a way that makes me want to go home and scrub my skin raw. Next, he suggests she could be one of Lady Muck's skivvies—Gina Hicks can't wipe her arse without bringing in help, apparently. In a nutshell, he has nothing to offer except cheap insults and perceived slights, and I leave his hovel of a lair hoping that someone did defecate on his front lawn. It seems like quite a fitting tribute to this hateful little man.

Emily doesn't fare any better. There's no answer at the Chapmans' so no doppelganger au pair to check out, and the only interaction she has at all is with a deranged Jack Russell, scrabbling at the door of number two, desperate to get out and tear her limb from limb.

So all in all, a fairly futile playdate for the two of us. Alice Lapaine may have talked into the intercom at the gates of Keeper's Close if we're to take the word of a pensioner on a speeding bus as sacrosanct, or we could have just wasted the best part of two hours.

At the moment, I'm prepared to keep an open mind. I just need to stay involved in this case.

As we walk the quarter mile back to the car, Emily stresses about the team's Secret Santa while I zone out and think about Leo Hicks, or more specifically, I think back to a party I once threw like his. It was 2006 and I was sixteen. Mum and Dad were in Cyprus and before the party I'd made sure that *anything* Dad held dear was conveniently displayed for the worst of the delinquents I'd invited to the house. I'd even sold his signed West Ham shirt to some scary-looking dude with "ACAB"—All Cops Are Bastards—tattooed across his knuckles.

I asked for a fiver. We settled on two pounds fifty.

"Not when his father had finished with him," Gina Hicks had said about Leo, and I wonder what punishment he'd faced on their return. Chores? Curfews? Confiscations?

Dad did nothing, initially—discipline was always very much Mum's domain whereas dereliction of all parental responsibility was very much his. It was only days later, when I offered him the two pounds fifty and he realized his precious football shirt hadn't been nicked after all, but sold, by his daughter, for roughly the same price as a Big Mac, that he showed his true colors, slamming me against the kitchen wall and whispering, *"One day you'll push me too far, sweetheart, and it won't end well. That's not a threat, it's a promise."*

Of course, my sister says watered-down versions of this to my nephew all the time.

"If I have to come up there, Finn Hadley, you'll regret it . . ."

"I won't warn you again, young man . . ."

And only the other day, I overheard Flowers telling his wife, *"She doesn't need new Nike Air Zooms, Gill. What she needs is a boot up the fucking arse."*

So as a rule, parenthood seems to be a never-ending issuing of cheap shots, veiled threats and frayed tempers, but still I know—as sure as I knew then—that Dad was only one deep breath away from hurting me that night. And who knows, maybe I'd have deserved it. Everyone has their breaking point and I'd been pushing Dad for a long, long time.

I don't want to think about this anymore so I tell Emily I like her bag just to make conversation. It's black, functional and totally nondescript in every way but the five-minute anecdote about where she bought it (Zara, Cambridge, they didn't take the security tag off and she got stopped on the way out) brings my heart rate back to normal and chases away any residual thoughts about my dad.

Further salvation comes in the form of my ringtone. Parnell.

"Hey Sarge." I fumble for the keys to the pool car.

"All right, kiddo, how'd you get on?"

"Nothing that helpful. Emily's going to write it up when we get back."

Which is news to a scowling Emily.

"How far away are you?"

I throw the keys to Emily, signal for her to drive. "We're just leaving Wandsworth now. Why? Where's the fire?"

"Thomas Lapaine's coming back in. I want you with me."

I pause—to my credit, I pause. It's never my intention to antagonize Steele, far from it.

"So has the Boss OK'd it? I mean, what about Renée? Or Flowers?"

"I *am* the boss. Acting DI, remember? No, I want me, you and Seth to take turns with him. You heard Renée before, she's not exactly flavor of the month with Tom Lapaine, and Flowers hasn't got the finesse for this one. So get your skates on, I need you back here for a quick brief."

If I knew what was good for me, I'd fess up to Parnell that Steele doesn't want me *too* involved in this investigation. Too active at its core. She's fine for me to lean up against Agas asking routine questions to peripheral witnesses. She didn't even mind me being in on the first Thomas Lapaine interview when my role was simply to "*um-hum*" sympathetically and take notes. But now he's a proper suspect? I'm not so sure. And I run everything by her, she said. She couldn't have been any clearer.

I consider this for all of two seconds.

"No problem, Sarge. See you in half an hour."

11

We get our plan together over bone-dry turkey and overcooked veg in the staff canteen—or in "*Santa's Grotto*" as a sign, messily scrawled on the back of a road traffic collision report, informs us. Flowers is on charity bucket duty, lumbering between tables and bullying everyone into digging deeper, which I suppose is the point.

"A tenner, you mean bastard! You've paid more for a blow job . . ."

"Tighter than a nun's chuff, you lot."

Above the clamor of insults and X-rated grumbling, Jim Reeves tries to raise the tone, crooning on someone's iPod about the magic of Silver Bells, and I find myself getting a sharp pang of sentimentality for something I never knew. Christmas was never the most enchanted of times in our house. It was the only time Mum ever drank and although it was never really much—just a couple of G&Ts here and the odd glass of bubbly there—it was always enough to add that extra few degrees of heat to a marriage that somehow managed to simmer along just below boiling point for three hundred and sixty-four days of the year.

"So we start fairly soft." Parnell pushes his plate away, finally admitting defeat in the war of Man vs Heinous Food. "Me and Seth will kick off. We'll say we're just following up, now that he's had some time to digest the news about Alice/Maryanne. Has anything occurred to him that might help? How's he coping . . . appreciate it was a huge shock . . . that sort of thing . . ."

The rest, as outlined by Parnell, is relatively simple. We'll try different approaches to fox him and switch lineups when it looks like he's getting comfortable. Parnell's going to do the authority thing, the wizened old hand trying to dot all the *i*s and cross all the *t*s, and Seth will do the posh thing—I may have had my vowels rounded out at Lady Helen's

School for Girls, but what I know about birthday suppers at Claridge's and boats you could write on the back of a postage stamp.

Which leaves me in the observation room, watching it all unfold on TV—primed to do the female thing, whatever the hell that means.

"So I either glide in and wet-nurse him, if that's what the interview needs, or I burst in like a madwoman and tear his nuts off with my teeth?" I say, biting into a stuffing ball.

"Exactly," says Parnell, only slightly alarmed. "Depends which way it goes . . ."

What we didn't plan for was it going a different way entirely. Parnell and Seth barely have time to do the "sorry the coffee's awful" skit and my arse has barely hit the observation room chair before Thomas Lapaine blindsides us all with an unexpected chattiness. And not the verbal diarrhea that suggests nervousness or guilt. He's entirely relaxed and composed. Like he's settled down into the confessional box for a therapeutic offload. There isn't a speck of red left in those rich brown eyes to suggest he's lost even an hour's sleep, never mind his wife in the most brutal of circumstances. His hair looks different too, coiffured, parted slightly to the left. He's prepared for this visit like it's a business lunch.

This is a different Thomas Lapaine.

Emboldened.

Betrayed.

But not lawyered-up, mercifully. And with no intention of doing so either, despite Parnell's reading of his rights.

"For the benefit of the tape, it is Thursday 18th December, 2016 and the time is six twenty-nine p.m. I am Acting Detective Inspector Luigi Parnell and with me is Detective Constable Seth Wakeman and—"

Lapaine leans in. "Thomas Lapaine. Look, I think I know why you've called me back here. You want to know why I cleared out the joint account. I don't know a lot about the workings of police investigations, Detectives, but I assumed you'd find out."

Parnell does his "disappointed parent" voice. He does it to me sometimes when my language gets a bit sordid or I eat M&M's for breakfast. "So why didn't you just tell us, Tom? You must realize that us finding out the hard way doesn't exactly show you in a great light?"

A tiny lift of one shoulder. "You never asked."

The fact he genuinely seems to think that's an acceptable comeback makes me conclude that Thomas Lapaine possibly isn't the sharpest tool in the box.

Parnell leaves it though, there's no point arguing with true idiocy. "So come on then, why did you clear it out?"

Lapaine's eyes wander but there's nothing to look at. Just walls the color of smog and a carpet that makes the walls look upbeat.

"If I say it was to force her back, I suppose that doesn't show me in a great light either?"

"A piece of advice, Tom, I'd forget your image and concentrate on the facts from now on, OK?"

He nods, stares at the hand where his wedding ring used to live. "I assumed if she had no access to money then she'd have to come back, and I desperately wanted her home for Christmas." If there's a tiny swell of sympathy for the melancholy contained within this statement, it's soon extinguished. "Mother was asking questions already, you see, and she'd have asked a whole lot more if it was just me turning up for Buck's Fizz and Classic FM on Christmas morning." He lets out a cruel snort. "*Ten a.m. on the dot, don't be late now.*"

There's an acidity to his voice. A mockery of all that he and Alice were. Their traditions, their in-jokes, their shared frustration at not being able to stay in bed eating Quality Street because they had to gather around the radio at "*Mother's*" every sodding Christmas morning. All of that seems risible now, tainted even, by the words "*Maryanne Doyle*" and the revelation that his wife was not who he thought.

We can use this anger though. The martyrdom stuff gets you nowhere. As long as it stays on the right side of demonization, this could be good.

"And what about when she didn't come back?" says Parnell, crossing his arms. "Weren't you concerned about how she'd survive? Weren't you worried when she didn't call to ask what the hell you were playing at? Didn't you call her?"

"I did, actually." Which his phone records bear out. "But no, I wasn't overly worried when she didn't ask 'what the hell I was playing at' because I thought I knew my wife, Detective, and I thought that wasn't her style. However, it turns out I didn't know my wife, *Maryanne Doyle*, quite as well as I thought I did." He spits her name out like a germ.

Parnell changes tack. "How much was in your joint account, out of interest?"

"Not a huge amount. Ten thousand pounds or so, maybe a bit more. Most of our money is tied up in the business. I was hoping the money in the joint account would see us to the end of the tax year."

Parnell does a mental calculation. "So you had more than one reason to track her down then? She was going through nearly five hundred pounds a week."

A tiny shrug.

"How is business?" asks Seth without the slightest hint of edge. They could be a couple of hedge-funders nursing a single malt at Annabel's.

"How is any small business doing, Detective? It's been a turbulent few years. The uncertainty over Brexit certainly isn't helping, but we stay afloat, if you pardon the dreadful pun."

Seth smiles, shyly. "Do you know, it's always been a dream of mine to own a boat. My grandparents had a Fairline Mirage 29. They bought in the mid-eighties, brand-new. It was blue and white. Absolutely stunning."

"A mid-eighties Mirage?" Lapaine looks impressed. "That would have been one of the last Mirage MKIIs. The blue-and-white color scheme is quite rare too."

Parnell pretends to look annoyed. "Er, ahoy there, shipmates! Could we knock the nautical stuff on the head and get back to business?" Seth looks chastised. They've played it well. "So Tom, bearing in mind we can request to see your business accounts like that"—a quick snap of his fingers—"would it be fair to say your business is failing?"

"I wouldn't say 'failing,' no. 'Troubled' would be more accurate." He crosses his arms, mirroring Parnell. "Can I ask what exactly this has got to do with anything, because if you've found a way that I financially benefit from my wife's death, then honestly, I'd be grateful if you'd share it."

Parnell leans forward. "Well, it's just that viewed from the outside, I see a marriage that was troubled, despite the picture you tried to paint last time. A business that was troubled—your own admission, remember. And frankly, an ability to conceive a child that was—I don't think we can really use the word 'troubled' here—it was failing." He thinks for a second then corrects himself. "Well, it wasn't failing. It had failed, past tense."

I wince at the cruelty of the statement and decide it's probably time to switch places. Big Bad Parnell's unlikely to get anything more from him now. He's got him rattled. Emasculated. Which isn't necessarily a bad thing but I might have to build him back up before we hit him with the phantom baby or he might shut down entirely.

Or worse still, lawyer-up.

I swipe a slick of clear lip gloss across my mouth and push my hair behind my ears, showing off my simple stud earrings. Feminine, uncomplicated and unthreatening.

I knock.

"Excuse me, Inspector, can I have a word?"

Parnell pretends to look peeved again and walks out. We leave the door slightly open and stand in the corridor, earnestly discussing Parnell's acid reflux in serious, hushed tones until Thomas Lapaine practically dislocates his neck craning to see what's going on.

After a few minutes I go in, give him news of the fresh line-up.

"Everything OK?" I say, blithely. Seth and Lapaine break off from some chummy chat, presumably about boats. "Unfortunately, Acting Detective Inspector Parnell has been called away unexpectedly. Really sorry about that, Tom, but it happens." I sit down, dump a pile of papers on the table and pull my chair up close. "I'm afraid you'll just have to put up with me instead. So . . ." I turn to Seth then back to Lapaine, smiling. "Where'd we get to?"

Seth's all casual. "Oh we'd just cleared up that business about the joint account."

"Ah right, OK," I say, nodding. "You know, my dad did it to me once. I had a bit of a blowout, island-hopping across Greece one summer and he went and canceled my allowance, stopped my credit card. It worked though. I was back the next day."

"Unlike Alice," Lapaine says, coldly. Reporting a fact, not lamenting a loss.

"Unlike Alice." I leave it there for a few seconds then turn to Seth again. "Did you ask about the phone numbers?"

Lapaine sits up, confused. "What phone numbers?"

"We hadn't got to the phone numbers," Seth confirms.

"What phone numbers?" he repeats, growing antsy.

I make a bit of a performance of sifting through my papers. Lapaine tries to flash-read but frankly half of them aren't relevant, just whatever I could grab in the squad room, most of it bound for the shredder.

Thing is, paper makes people nervous. Far more than technology, surprisingly.

I find what I'm looking for, slide the piece of paper toward him. "Do you recognize either of these numbers?"

His eyebrows knit together. "No, but then I don't recognize many numbers off-hand. Just Alice's and maybe my parents. Whose are they?"

"That's what we're trying to find out. Alice made several calls to both over the past few weeks."

"Well, I can't help."

I flick my hand. "No worries. We knew it was a bit of a long shot." I draw in a little closer, watch his jaw set as the chair legs make a scraping sound across the floor. "Tom, you said that Alice had initially been very keen to start a family. You sort of implied it was the main reason she agreed to come back to the UK."

Impatient. "Yes."

I take a deep breath, a warning to him that he's not going to like what

I say next. "You see, the postmortem report has confirmed something that may, or may not, come as a shock to you."

That gets a laugh. "My wife turned out to be a completely different person to who I thought she was, Detective. I'm not sure anything can come as a shock anymore so please, say what you have to say."

I take him at his word and don't bother with a preamble. "Your wife had at some point given birth to a child, Tom. Not just got pregnant— that's not what I'm saying—she'd actually delivered a child."

It's subtle, so subtle that I'll probably doubt later that it was ever really there, but there's a momentary rigidity to him—from the set of his eyes to the ram-rod straightness of his spine, that tells me he's thunderstruck.

"What exactly are you telling me?" he says, eyes boring into mine. "That my wife carried and delivered a child and somehow managed to conceal it from me? Clearly Alice's ability to deceive was far beyond what I imagined but still, I think I'd have noticed that."

I answer coolly. "Then it must have been before you met. So can you tell us, did she ever speak to you about it? Or did you ever suspect that she'd had a child?"

"Did I ever suspect she'd had a child?" He repeats it back, seeming to consider the question, and for one bright moment I think he might be gearing up for a revelation. A little nugget to bring this case into some sort of focus.

"Yes, she had a child when she was a teenager, by an older man who was visiting on holiday."

The thought ambushes me before I can block it out. My head buzzes as it starts to take root. Suddenly, Thomas Lapaine's voice seems echoey and distant.

"Alice always said that she was born to be a mother, Detective. She said it was all she ever wanted, until one day in late October she decided that apparently, it wasn't. And do you know all I suspected then? That she was looking into the adoption route, or maybe surrogacy. I thought perhaps she wanted to do all the research first and get all the facts before suggesting it to me." He leans in close, as if it's vitally important we understand what he's about to say. "Because *that's* how the Alice I knew would have behaved. How this Maryanne Doyle would have behaved, and whether she'd given birth to a litter of children, I honestly couldn't tell you, and if I'm being perfectly straight with you, Detectives, the way I feel right now, I really couldn't care less."

Seth nods. "You're understandably very angry, Mr. Lapaine. Who wouldn't be?"

"Angry," Lapaine muses. "It doesn't seem strong enough a word but yes, I am angry. I've felt more anger toward Alice in the past thirty-six hours than I ever felt in our entire relationship. And I've got nowhere to direct that anger. I can't speak to her. I can't ask her any of the questions that have been running around my mind ever since your colleague walked into my sitting room and told me my wife was a completely different person to who she claimed to be."

I figure he might as well direct his anger at me. Anything to distract from the anxious knots clustering in my brain, in my stomach, in my whole being.

I go for broke. "Did you ever suspect Alice had boyfriends?"

"Boyfriends!"

I'm not sure if he's shocked by the accusation or the word.

"Lovers," I say, holding his gaze. "A bit on the side?"

"You must have considered it," adds Seth, all man-to-man. "If my girlfriend took off for a prolonged period of 'me-time,' it'd certainly spring to my mind. I'd say it's a fairly obvious conclusion for anyone to draw."

He's unruffled. "Fairly obvious unless you knew Alice. She wasn't exactly the most sexual of people, and before you ask, it wasn't an issue. That side of things was healthy enough. But the idea of her seeking out more sex, is just, well, highly unlikely." A bitter laugh. "Although who knows, *Maryanne Doyle* might have been a complete goer."

"Not all affairs are about sex," I say.

This stirs something. "That's very true, Detective. They're often about looking for warmth when you're not getting much warmth at home."

There's clearly something substantive in his statement but I wait to see if he'll hand it to me.

The silence serves its purpose and he starts rattling within seconds.

"Oh for heaven's sake, what's the point, you might as well know," he says, clamping his hands on the edge of the table, steeling himself. "You'll only find out anyway, I suppose. I've been seeing someone, OK?"

"You were unfaithful?" Seth makes this sound as if it goes against the very tenets of some ancient Wakeman code.

"I suppose I was. Although not physically, until recently. And I felt wretched about that. Although, my deception rather pales into insignificance compared with hers, wouldn't you agree?"

I wouldn't. Maybe I would? I don't know. My head's banging.

I pull a file from the bottom of the stack, open it and quickly refresh. "So when you told us, and I quote, *'I'm not in the habit of spending evenings with anyone but my wife,'* you were lying."

"I'm sorry." He actually sounds genuine, the barbed tone is missing.

"How long?"

"We've been spending time together for a few months."

"And how long have you been getting naked together?"

He looks at me like I've let myself down. "About a month or so."

Seth raises an eyebrow. "So since Alice left?"

I nudge Seth, a bit jokey. "No wonder he wasn't in any initial hurry for her to come home. You must have been having a whale of a time, Tom. When the cat's away and all that. What plays in Thames Ditton, stays in Thames Ditton, eh?"

The words spill out of my mouth but I don't exactly know what I'm doing. Am I being a shrewd detective, goading the suspect into admitting he wanted his wife out of the picture for good, or is it actually *me* talking?

Me misdirecting my anger at another weak man.

I do know that I need to catch hold of myself. I need to make the most of this new information and stop trying to twist it into something personal.

"She's never been to our house," says Lapaine. "I wouldn't sleep with another woman in my marital bed."

My hackles rise again. His bullshit flawed morality sounds achingly familiar.

"We spend time at hers, mainly. I was with her, at her place, the night that . . . the night Alice . . ."

My jaw actually drops. Seth stiffens beside me.

This is big.

"Let me get this straight. You're telling us you were with your mistress the night Alice died?" I throw the file down on the table, a sheet scatters to the floor. "I've got to be honest with you, Tom, I'm a bit confused as to why we're only hearing this now. That's called an alibi. That could have saved you all this bother."

Not exactly, but he doesn't know that.

He pulls his chin up, noble, defiant. "I was protecting her. She has a high-profile role in the community. Two young children. And she's going through a nasty enough divorce already, I didn't want her getting dragged into this."

"Well, she's going to get dragged in now, I'm afraid." I shove a pen and paper toward him. "I want her name, address, contact numbers—" He opens his mouth but I shut him down. "And don't you dare ask us to be discreet because the time for asking favors from us is long gone, Mr. Lapaine. You should have told us this right from the start."

He scribbles, head down low. The top-dollar haircut masks a thinning crown. "It wouldn't exactly have looked great, would it?"

Seth seizes on this. "Oh, so you weren't protecting"—a glance at the page—"Abigail Shawcroft. You were lying to protect yourself."

When Lapaine looks up again, his eyes shine with something. I think it's relief. Relief at having confessed all there is to confess.

"Everyone lies, Detective Wakeman," he says, wearily. "If anything, I'm more guilty of lying to myself than to you." I literally couldn't look more unimpressed. "Oh, you know what I'm talking about, I'm sure you do. Those sweet little lies you tell yourself to make life more bearable— '*My wife isn't secretive, she's just private.*' '*It's not an affair until you get naked,*' to use your words, Detective Kinsella. I'm sure you have a few of your own."

Yeah, a few.

It's puppy fat, not pizza fat.

I haven't lied to my colleagues, I just haven't told the truth.

I don't know with absolute certainty that Dad knows anything about what happened to Maryanne Doyle.

Problem is, while the lie may be sweet as it falls from your lips, the feeling in your gut is always putridly sour.

And almost always bang-on.

When we get back to the incident room, Parnell's already there, pacing up and down giving Steele the lowdown and generally emitting the kind of pissed-off pheromone that ensures no one dares venture within punching distance. While Parnell's not known for being a violent man, he's not usually known for being a sweary man either, but the air's thick with the sound of "fucking alibi" and it feels thickest around me, although that could be my tendency toward self-blame taking hold—my unintelligible need to hold myself in some way responsible for *everything* that goes wrong.

Because Parnell did the first interview too.

He was the senior officer.

And OK, maybe we could have pressed Lapaine harder on his "Home Alone" alibi but did we have any real reason to?

"*Softly softly*" Steele had said. "*I don't want him feeling like a suspect.*"

I only hope Parnell's got the knackers to remind her.

I repeat all of this to Renée in the hope she'll work her Renée magic and say something soothing but she can't seem to find the right words today. She does find a packet of Oreos though and they kind of work the same. Feeling slightly sick but undoubtedly calmer, I go back to my desk and call Abigail Shawcroft, Googling her as I wait for her answer-phone to kick in. It turns out her "high-profile role in the community" involves teaching at a local primary school and according to her Twitter bio, she's *"Mummy to Alexa and Rowan. Loves Glastonbury, netball and cheese lol!!!!"*

I leave a message asking her to get in contact ASAP. I'm just hanging up as Parnell puts the phone down.

"All OK?" I say, tentatively.

Parnell sits down to deliver the verdict. "Seems she's getting philo-sophical in her old age. Ruling him out is as good as ruling him in, ap-parently. At least it's something concrete."

"So we're not on the naughty step?"

"No?" Clearly this hadn't even occurred to him. I definitely need to dial down the self-whipping. "And Lapaine's not in the clear yet either, not until we've spoken to the fancy-woman. And even then . . ."

Even then, starry-eyed lovers, especially those of the secret kind, can't exactly be classed as rock-solid alibis.

"Well, I just left a message." I flop back in my chair. "For the fancy-woman."

"For all the good it'll do," says Seth, sitting with his Barbour jacket on, waiting for the green light to go home. "He's had more than enough time to get his story straight with her."

"He gave it up very easily, didn't he?" Parnell puts a hand to his fore-head with an actor's flourish, "'*Oh what's the point, you'll only find out anyway.*'"

Seth nods. "All that 'I was protecting her' nonsense. Why didn't he keep protecting her then? He's right that we'd have probably found out eventually but it could have taken ages, whereas he handed her to us on a silver platter."

I get their logic, but I'm not feeling it. "I don't think there's anything necessarily sinister in that. I think he's extremely angry, understandably, and trashing the memory of their marriage is the only way he can hurt Alice now. Maybe he wants people to know he was cheating because it makes him look less of a gullible idiot—you know, *'she may have fooled me, but haha, I fooled her too.'*"

"Maybe, maybe." Parnell rubs his hands up and down the sides of his face. "OK, folks, it's getting on so let's call it a day. Kinsella, let me know if Abigail Fancy-woman calls you back but if not, we'll get someone over to the school first thing tomorrow. Surprise her on her work turf, make her feel uncomfortable. With any luck she might trip up, if there *is* anything to trip up. Oh, by the way, Steele's done a piece-to-camera appealing for anyone who might have seen something early Tuesday morning to come forward and"—he pretends to look scared, braces himself for the backlash—"we're going to get an appeal out in the nationals tomorrow for anyone who thinks they might have come into contact with Maryanne/Alice during the 'lost years'—between 1998 when she leaves Mulderrin and 2001 when she turns up on Brighton Beach, making eyes at Thomas Lapaine."

In other words, we're going to hold up a beacon to all the crackpots, crazies and police groupies in Great Britain.

An air of resigned dread settles on the incident room as we start to pack up. Molly, our cleaner, weaves in and out of our desks, giving an extra spruce to those who take the time to acknowledge her every evening, a cursory swipe to those who think they're too important to engage.

I look over at Parnell, hunched and haggard and wrestling with the zip on his Arsenal backpack with a ferocious anger not usually reserved for backpacks.

There's only one thing for it after an interview like that.

"Boss . . ."

12

It doesn't take long to twist Parnell's arm. A quick call to Superintendent Blake to be told he's a good boy, then an even quicker call home to get clearance from Mrs. P, and we're leaning up against the quiz machine in the Bell Tavern, Parnell supping a festively named guest ale (Rocking Rudolph!), and me, the house Pinot. One turns into four alarmingly quickly and it's not long before the photos come out. One hundred and twenty-nine snaps of varying-sized Parnells in varying locations emanating varying degrees of happiness.

One of them pretty handsome, actually, and not too far off my age. A little clean-cut for my hobo tastes but I'm tipsy enough not to care.

"You never created that fine specimen, surely?" I snatch Parnell's phone and hold it close to my face. "We could DNA test him, you know, on the QT. It's not too late to go after the milkman."

"Cheeky cow." Parnell loads another pound into the quiz machine.

"Seriously, can you get me a date? I'd make a great daughter-in-law." I give him a quick poke. "Just think, you could see me all the time then."

"I don't think you're Dan's type. No offense."

"Plenty taken though. Why? What's wrong with me?"

"You're female, for a start."

The Pinot's dulled my brain and it takes me a second to catch on. Parnell rolls his eyes as the penny drops.

"Boss!" I say, punching him on the shoulder. "I didn't know you had a gay son. Well done you," I add, inexplicably.

He spits his pint. "I wasn't aware it was a personal achievement, but thanks." A sideways glance. "You know, a pint of water between drinks wouldn't do you any harm."

"Oh bore off, Dad."

The "D" word pulls me up and I get a surge of affection for Parnell, simply on account of him being just about as far away from my dad as a man could be.

Slightly old-fashioned. Overweight. Decent.

"Seriously though. Why've you never mentioned Dan's gay?"

"I've never mentioned Adam's gluten-intolerant either."

It's a fair point. I don't know why I'm getting so giddy about it. In my defense, I'm feeling off-kilter tonight. Twitchier than usual. The thought of a pregnant, teenage Maryanne Doyle is sucking the air out of my lungs and I'll do anything to block it out, whether that means soaking it with wine or bantering it away with Parnell.

"I've never mentioned the twins are left-handed either."

I gesture for another round of drinks. "Yeah, yeah, point taken."

I could add it's about the only thing he's never mentioned. Parnell talks about six-year-old James and Joe—aka his forty-seventh-year birthday presents—*a lot*, although it's never quite consistent. They're either his later-life miracle or his punishment from God, depending on how early they woke him up that morning.

"So anyway, changing the subject," he says, looking curious. "Why are you drinking with an old duffer like me on a Thursday night? Are there no nice young men you're currently interested in? Straight ones," he adds.

I laugh. "Plenty I'm interested in."

He steps back, sizes me up like a prize bull. "You must do all right?"

"God you're a real charmer, Parnell, do you know that?" He grins. "I suppose *I do* do all right. It's not much to shout about though, is it? 'All right.' I bet Emily does better than 'all right.'"

"I bet Emily's at home right now wishing she made the team laugh as much as you do. Wishing she had your brains."

I give Parnell a flat-eyed stare. "Christ, you can tell you haven't raised women. Trust me, she won't be thinking anything like that. She'll be thinking, *'Oh aren't I lucky to be so princess-perfect and isn't Kinsella lucky that she got a good personality to make up for that unfortunate nose.'"*

It's self-pitying and I don't really believe it but it makes Parnell laugh and that always feels nice.

He pinches my nose between his thumb and his forefinger. "There's nothing wrong with your nose."

"You don't have to be kind, you know. I accept it." I put my hands together in prayer. "I am at peace with my conk, Parnell. Well, unless I'm around my brother and he starts his *'Kinsella by name, Kinsella by nose'* routine."

"Your brother sounds like a prick."

"He is. The prickiest of the pricks. I used to wish he'd die in an accident." Parnell looks horrified so I add a quick laugh. "OK, maybe not die. Just get mangled up a bit, fed through a tube . . ."

"You're bloody dark, Kinsella. I wouldn't go telling your shrink that, she'll have a field—"

"How do you know about that?"

My voice burns with accusation but of course he knows. Of course Steele would have told him. You can't sell a car without the logbook and you can't give someone responsibility for me without mentioning the faulty wiring.

I can't meet his eyes.

"Look, anything to do with kids is tough. Stop beating yourself up."

It's a genuine plea from someone who knows, not a half-meant platitude or a counseling cliché, but I really, *really* don't want to go here with Parnell. I rather liked how I thought he saw me—a bit dark, a bit clever and with a perfectly OK nose. It makes me all kinds of miserable that he knows I can't keep my shit together.

He turns my cheek, forces me to look at him. "Hey, you didn't do anything wrong, Cat."

Cat. Not "kiddo." Not even "Kinsella."

"So everyone keeps telling me but I didn't do anything right either." He waits for me to go on. "I froze, Boss. I threw up. I cried—hysterically.

All in front of a little girl who'd just spent the best part of two days doing jigsaws next to her mum's corpse."

"You have to try . . ."

"No, listen, hear me out, I'm getting to a more positive bit, honest." He doesn't look convinced so I plow on quickly. "Do you know, the only thing I can be, not proud of, just not ashamed of, is that I acted on my gut that day checking on Dafina—that's the mum—ahead of the court case. I mean, if I hadn't, God knows how long Alana-Jane would have been stuck there and the body would have been in a much worse state. Don't get me wrong, she looked horrific—there was so much blood and she'd started to go a bit greenish. But if it'd been a few more days, when the bloating started, and the smell . . ."

Parnell nods. He understands. "Focus on that then. Your natural copper's instinct made an absolutely horrendous situation a bit less horrendous."

I pinch my thumb and forefinger together. "A tiny bit, maybe. I don't think me vomiting through my nose did though."

"I hear the little girl's quite taken with you."

I blink away a tear. "She drew me a picture. Wanna see it?"

"Of course."

I pull it out of my wallet where it's lived for two months, wedged between a photo of me and Mum in a bumper car and a ticket for a live gig I completely forgot about. It's a drawing of me in bright orange outline wearing a spotty pink dress and high heels—one clumpy shoe twice the size of the other. I've only got one ear and my nose is a messy green splodge but I've got a lovely big smile. It bursts out the side of my cheeks and fills the whole width of the page.

It's the smile that gives me comfort that I must have done something right.

"It's uncanny," says Parnell. "She definitely got the nose right."

A quick slap to the head and we stand side by side for a few minutes, silently pressing buttons on the quiz machine, answering questions about everything from country music to past Nobel Prize winners.

Eventually Parnell's appetite for trivia runs out and talk turns back to the inevitable.

"So what about Thomas Lapaine?" Parnell looks frustrated, although it could be the four-pound jackpot we just gambled—and lost. "I haven't got anything personal against the guy but eliminating him puts us one step closer to the 'random stranger' nightmare which is the last thing we all need."

I sip my wine, realize I've sunk two thirds without noticing. "I've got something personal against him. Bloke's a tosser."

"We've met worse."

He's right but I'm riled. "It's just all that 'not getting any warmth at home' crap really winds me up."

"Alice didn't have many friends. Could suggest a cold fish?"

"Nor does he!" I reply, a bit too loud. There's a TV playing in the corner but the sound's turned down. "Tech reckon his social media circle's pretty minuscule."

"Maybe he has real friends. Do they even exist anymore?"

I ignore the question, stay stranded on my own soapbox. "I mean, what even is 'warmth?' Wasn't she putting out regularly enough? He kind of implied that. Or didn't she mollycoddle him enough like *Mother*?"

Parnell shrugs. His position on the fence annoys me, even though it's got no right to, and when you're annoyed and five drinks down, you occasionally say things you regret.

"My dad had affairs."

It comes out as a loaded declaration. A defining statement of sorts. And it is to me, I suppose. It's certainly shaped the person I am and many a counselor has argued that it's the reason behind every neurosis, disorder and general vague oddity that I've been daft enough to admit to. However, to Parnell, I'm just a melodramatic colleague. An emotional drunk admitting her dad did something that a lot of dads do. Mums too.

I try to explain, put my outburst into context.

"And he used to sound just like Thomas Lapaine, that's why I brought it up. Mum didn't love him enough, apparently. She didn't give him enough attention. She was always too busy with us. He was just a cash machine . . ."

"And he said all this to you?" Parnell lands a size nine on my side of the fence. "Not good."

"Yeah well, he wasn't a good husband."

"Clearly. Bad husbands can still be good fathers though."

Bless Parnell, he loves to play the curmudgeon but essentially he's an optimist.

"I dare say some can, he can't."

Parnell takes a long slug of ale. I'm sure he's buying time so he can think of how to change the subject and frankly, who could blame him.

"OK, define a 'good father?'" he says eventually, staying on the same rocky course.

"Someone who puts his kids first. Someone dependable, consistent. You," I add, cringing a bit. "At least from what I know anyway."

"Me?" He takes out his phone again, offers it to me. "Do you think you could call Mags and repeat that. I haven't been home for the twins' bedtime in nearly a fortnight and look at me now, out drinking with you."

"I thought Maggie OK'd it?"

"She did. She's a good woman. The best."

I feel bad now. I have this fantasy that me and Maggie become friends at some point. She tells me stories about a younger and slimmer Parnell while I get her wasted on Glitter Bombs.

"Jesus, you should have gone home, Boss, put your kids to bed. Why didn't you, for God's sake?"

"Because you asked me to come for a drink. And the only reason a young girl like you asks an old duffer like me for a drink is if she's drowning her sorrows. If she's lonely or upset about something."

I say nothing.

"I'm right, aren't I? You're still brooding over the little girl in the bedsit—and, well, it's obvious this case, Thomas Lapaine's affair anyway, has brought stuff about your dad to the surface."

Yeah, just a little.

I don't know whether to laugh like a drain or cry myself dry.

I opt for more silence.

"Look, you can't let it cloud your judgment, kiddo. You've got a long career ahead of you, you're going to meet a lot of cheating slimeballs, I'm afraid. Can't arrest them all."

"S'pose not," I say, after a while. "Hey, unless you become a private investigator when you retire and I help you out with the cheating spouse cases. *Parnell PI*. It's got a ring to it."

"*Retirement*."

Parnell exhales the word but it's not a peaceful exhale. Feeling bad about bringing it up, I draw the conversation back.

"Anyway, I do have one thing to thank Dad's affairs for."

"Oh yeah?"

"Set me on the path to being a detective."

Parnell settles onto a barstool. "Oh, this I have to hear."

"Then you shall." I take a deep theatrical breath. I've never told anyone this before. "OK, I'd have been about nine, maybe ten. Jacqui had picked me up from school and she was supposed to be taking me to Irish dancing but I'd hurt my foot playing rounders so we didn't end up going. Anyway, when we get home I go upstairs to get something and as I walk past Mum and Dad's door, I can see someone in the bed. Well, two people. And I'm confused because Mum and Dad are both supposed to be out somewhere—that's why Jacqui had to pick me up—but I can clearly see two people. So I go a bit closer and peer through a crack in the door and I can definitely make out Dad, but I can't see the other person. All I can see are her feet sticking out the bottom of the bed. And her toenails are this sort of purple color. So I'm thinking 'Is that Mum?' and the idea's obviously grossing me out so I can't knock the door, but I can't phone Mum either because a) I don't have a clue what her number is and b) even at nine years old, I've got the measure of my dad and I'm thinking 'But what if it's not Mum?' So I do nothing, but I decide the next chance I get, I'm going to go through all Mum's nail polishes to see if I can match one to Plum Paws."

Parnell's doing a great job of looking transfixed. "And you couldn't?"

"Nope, all pale pinks and boring nudes. But I decide that's not conclusive proof anyway, because Mum could have just used the last of the purple polish and thrown it away, or she could have left it at Auntie Carmel's or something, so I decide I need another plan." I tap the side of my head. "See, Sherlock Holmes, even then." Parnell grins. "So for weeks, right, I save my pocket money and I beg Jacqui to let me tag along a few times when she goes up to Oxford Street, and I keep looking and looking and eventually I find this dark purple polish in Boots, just like Plum Paws, and I buy it for Mum in the hope she'll at least say, 'Oh what a lovely color, thank you sweetheart' but kind of hoping she'll say—because it'll be more conclusive, 'Oh, what a coincidence, I had one just like this.'"

I pause, but I'm being deliberately melodramatic this time. Parnell's loving it.

"But she didn't," he says.

I shake my head. "No she didn't. She's not exactly rude about it but she says something like 'Good God, it's a bit gothic, poppet'—I didn't know what 'gothic' meant but I could tell it wasn't a good thing. And *then* she says, 'It's not the type of color I'd ever usually wear but maybe I should have an image change, ha ha.'"

"Oh dear."

I nod. "Indeed. Anyway, I had this friend at the time called Katy Kielty and her mum used to take us swimming at Finchley Lido. *She* had dark purple toenails this one time." Another pause. "I'd found Plum Paws."

Parnell laughs. "On one piece of circumstantial evidence! No forensics, no witnesses?"

"Yeah, but she'd always fancied my dad so I had motive."

"Hold up." Parnell stops laughing and looks over the top of my head toward the TV. "This'll keep us busy tomorrow. Forget Plum Paws, it looks like we're on." To the barman. "Turn that up, mate."

Steele's elfin features fill the screen, earnestly appealing for witnesses to come forward to help solve this *"particularly heinous crime."* Her face is somber, unflinching and flawless. Eyebrows perfectly shaped. Lips a deep raspberry red. If Plum Paws triggered my desire to be a detective, meeting Steele stamped it across my heart and I'm willing to bet that I'm not the only female in the force who dreams of being DCI Kate Steele when they grow up.

"Never shy of the spotlight, our Kate," says Parnell, not unkindly. "Do you know what Craig's taken to calling her?"

I cock an ear but my eyes stay fixed.

"Kate Kardashian. You know, because she loves the spotlight . . ."

"Yeah, I get it, Boss." I put a finger to my lips. "Ssssh, I'm trying to listen."

It's a short piece. Just a minute or so of Steele being impressive and of course the two faces of Maryanne Doyle/Alice Lapaine contradicting each other at every turn—carefree and cocksure as an ebony-haired teenager, downcast and diffident by a blond thirty-five.

But it's the last ten seconds that floor me. The panoramic sweep across Mulderrin that captures the roof of Gran's old house, the tilting ash trees lining Duffy's field, the tip of the crucifix standing proud on top of St. Benedict's, where prayers were said for Maryanne Doyle even though everyone was adamant she was nothing but a feckless trollop who'd gone off to find more of her kind.

It has to be stock footage they're using. Just some producer's poetic attempt to contrast the rolling fields of her youth with the urban squalor of her death. Because there's no way the UK media would have descended on Mulderrin just yet. Not without any clear links between the then and the now to spur headlines.

And we have no links to give them.

There's no official links anyway.

Because the fact that one man was in the local area for both Maryanne's disappearance in 1998 and her murder in 2016, is a poisonous seed that's planted so far deep inside my psyche that I'm not sure I could prise it out, even if I had the guts, or the willingness, to try.

1998
Thursday 28th May

How to be a Spy, Rule 1: Learn the habits of your target!

   Dad said he was popping to Reilly's to buy smokes but I knew he'd sneakily bought 200 on the ferry because I'd been hiding behind the Toblerone stand, waiting to jump out on Noel. I also knew he'd only smoked sixty-seven so he had 133 left and no need to buy more. (I'd been keeping count because 200 sounded like a heck of a lot and I didn't want him getting sick like Paige Flannelly's dad who spat blood into tissues and weighed less than her mum.)

How to be a Spy, Rule 2: When you come up against problems, be resourceful!

   Spies should usually wear black but Mum had only packed my blue flowery raincoat with the pink spotty collar so I turned it inside out and hoped for the best.

How to be a Spy, Rule 3: Only carry essential items vital to your operation and survival!

   I packed my diary, a pencil, some smoky bacon crisps and a small lump of cheese, because Mum said it was good for my bones, and I set off on my secret mission, trailing Dad to the bottom of the Pot-Holey Road (because the roads around here didn't have proper names like Oxford Street or Farringdon Road, they were called things like the Long Road Out of Town or the Road Where Pat Hannon Keeps His Cows). Dad turned right by Duffy's gate and I had to quickly duck down in the ditch when he stopped to make a call.

good inteligance intel–dad has a phone!

How to be a Spy, Rule 4: Learn to eavesdrop!

I spied them through a gap in the hedge and she was laughing. Not giggling, like she did with boys in the Diner, but proper wet-your-pants laughing and I'm sorry, Dad wasn't that funny. Even when he did his Homer Simpson impression or told that joke about the chicken and the frog who went to the library.

She sounded like Cynthia, Uncle Frank's skinny wife (we didn't call her Auntie Cynthia, Mum put her foot down about that). Dad always said Cynthia had a laugh like a crow with a machine gun and Maryanne did a little bit too. It was a nasty noise. The sound of someone being mean, not funny.

"That sounds like blackmail to me," I heard Dad say.

"Fuck sake, you're dramatic."

"And you're deluded if you think it's going to happen." Dad sounded angry now.

"You're deluded if you think you have a choice."

How to be a Spy, Rule 5: Store gathered information in a safe and secure place!

I took out my diary and wrote the words down:

black mail. delooded.

I didn't have to write "dramatic" down because I knew what that meant. Mum always told Jacqui she was "dramatic" when she was moaning about having to be home by a certain time or whining that a boy hadn't told her she looked pretty. I didn't know the other two words though. I thought about asking Mum later but the bats in my tummy told me I shouldn't.

I found Gran's dictionary and took it up to bed instead.

13

The next day isn't great.

"That which does not kill us makes us stronger," claimed Nietzsche, or Kanye West, depending on your cultural frame of reference, but exorbitant wine consumption must be the one exception because I certainly don't feel strengthened by last night's two-bottle bender. I feel annihilated.

Which I suppose was my full intention.

Stave off emotional blitzkrieg by destroying myself physically.

I wake on Parnell's sofa with a piece of Lego burrowed deep into my right hip and the memory of me calling him "a boring bastard" when he stopped me going clubbing with a group of bond traders. Issuing him a silent thanks and a more audible "thank God" when I find a pint of water and a packet of Nurofen on the floor beside me, I sit up and take in my surroundings. Sure enough, his living room is everything I'd imagined it to be. Styled by his wife, wrecked by his kids. Like a *Lord of the Flies* stage-set, only taupe and with scatter cushions. I'm not quite sure what to make of the spare toothbrush and the, *God-strike-me-down-dead*, clean pair of knickers on the side of the sofa, but I assume they're Parnell's way of telling me that we're running late already and I don't have time to go home for a spruce-up.

In lighter moments that day, I can just about laugh at the fact I'm wearing my boss's wife's knickers. In darker depths, I pray for death to come quickly.

I work hard though for ten sweaty, nauseous hours. I work especially hard at avoiding Parnell, picking up my phone every time he heads my way or diving headfirst into my bag, scavenging for some unnecessary item. Luckily, I'm not short of reasons to pick up the phone as the public are feeling chatty today following Steele's spot on the news.

The crackpots don't bother me as they're easy enough to spot. Any mention of aliens or Judgment Day, or anyone referencing the decline in Britain's moral fiber can usually be shut down quite quickly. No, it's the genuine do-gooders that take the time. The people who think that they "might" have seen something. The people who want a small slither of the action to take back to the school gates.

I do take one promising call from a man who *thinks* he saw Alice talking to an "older guy" in the Rugged Cross—an odious blot on the otherwise lively landscape of Spitalfields Market—on the Sunday evening before she died.

"Older guy" unsettles me, but half an hour later I'm leaning up against the bar, breathing in booze and BO—and finding the BO more appealing—only to find my man's not quite as sure as he'd sounded on the phone and the barman's only interested in if I've got a fella and what I'm doing Saturday night. I take a description of "older guy" anyway—*"between fifty to seventy, average build, average height, lightish hair, wasn't really paying attention, tell you the truth—Man U had just equalized . . ."* For a millisecond I consider texting Jacqui for a recent photo of Dad but I'm not sharp enough to deal with all her questions, not today, and if I'm honest, I'm not brave enough to deal with the fallout if . . .

If.

I get back to the news that Lapaine's alibi checks out. Abigail Shawcroft is a carbon copy of Alice, apparently—blondish, prettyish in a drab sort of way. We chat this through for a while, come to the conclusion that she doesn't have a lot to gain by lying for him, not with a bitter ex-husband looking for any reason to hammer her through the family courts and an application for Deputy Head still outstanding. After lunch, Emily and I turn our attention back to the Donatella Caffé and the residents of Keeper's Close—the former sparking a frantic discussion about discarded till rolls and tax obligations, for which I'm woefully unqualified to give advice on but give advice on nonetheless. The latter simply spurs more variations of the "No, sorry I can't help" shutdown which is fast becoming the catchphrase of this investigation.

Aiden Doyle checks out too. He was indeed Sleepless in Mile End, having a text exchange with an Aussie mate from one forty a.m. until nearly two fifteen a.m. While it clearly doesn't cover him for the four-hour time period between the murder and the body being dumped, it certainly makes it less likely that he's our guy.

And as the dark gathers at the window for one more day, Renée adds to our cauldron of nothing.

"There's no birth, adoption or death records pertaining to a baby born to either a Maryanne Doyle or an Alice Lapaine," she announces, soberly. "So that adds in the extra complication of a possible missing infant. Or a dead infant, of course."

Dead infants. Dead leads. Deadbeat barmen in dead-end pubs.

Dead on my feet, I head home.

The next few days follow a similar pattern.

Work like Trojans. Feel like losers.

And another trip to see Dr. Allen for me.

At least the "Lost Years" article provides us with light relief, as judging by some of the calls trickling in, the woman formerly known as Maryanne Doyle was one conflicted lady—the kind of lady who sold speed to schoolkids in Hackney while at the same time giving out communion in a church in Porthmadog over 200 miles away.

A couple of callers suggest the same thing—which gets our attention, not to mention our hopes up—that Maryanne was an occasional face on the London dance scene, frequenting the likes of The Cross, The End, Fabric, Turnmills, etc., at the end of the nineties, into the noughties. However, after a short flurry of excitement we have to ask, how does this even help us? No one ever recalls actually speaking to her. Not one person remembers ever seeing her with anyone. By all accounts she was just another anonymous face, bouncing away within the heaving, ecstasy-fueled throng that moved from club to club, looking for the best tunes at the end of another monotonous working week.

Although the idea of her dancing on a podium in the late 1990s, off her face on pills, does give some credence to Sergeant Bill Swords' "likely a runaway" theory.

A theory I'd be only too happy to believe.

"And that's it?" asks Parnell one morning, pained by the knowledge that he's "acting up" on a case that seems to be going nowhere. "I honestly thought we'd get more than this."

"It's Christmas," says Steele, currently gracing us with a few hours face time, free from the demands of Chief Superintendent Blake who'd hold a meeting about holding a meeting. "This time of year, Lu, it's enough to remember where you've left the bloody scotch tape, without trying to think where you were eighteen bloody years ago."

"Anything on the car?" I ask Ben, starting to bore of my own tasks and needing to revel in someone else's failings.

"Absolutely nothing," he says, matter-of-fact. He could do with joining me on *The Art of Positive Spin* course.

"Something on her vagina though," shouts Flowers, putting his phone down. It's tasteless but it gets our attention. "That was the lab. No trace of condom lubricant."

And then with the arrival of Seth bounding into the room, Eureka.

"Ha-ha, I'll see your vagina, and raise you a phone. We've just got a hit on one of the pay-as-you-gos."

"It's been switched on?" asks Parnell, his arm already in one coat-sleeve.

"Not exactly. Silly fool took out the SIM and put it in their regular phone."

"So we've got a location," I say, my heart pounding.

"Better than that, an address. And a name."

Sometimes it just happens like that. Days and days of thankless, arduous nothing and then, boom. All the tenuous leads and the tortuous trips up endless garden paths seem like a lifetime ago, and you can never quite remember why you questioned the purpose of your wonderful, life-affirming job in the first place.

My coat's on and fully fastened before Parnell can even think not to invite me.

14

I've lived in London long enough to know that the suffix "mansion" often lends a false glamour to the most humble of dwellings. However, with a name like Ophelia Mansions, I'm at least expecting to find the odd willow tree or wildflower. What we actually find is a dilapidated six-story eyesore just off the Gray's Inn Road, less than a mile from where Alice Lapaine's body was found.

Predictably, Saskia French lives on the top floor.

We're let in the main door by a man rushing out. His wool over-coat and down-payment-for-a-flat watch mark him out as a "gentleman caller" rather than an occupant and it's obvious Parnell's thinking the same. I see it in his smirk as he flashes his ID, assuring the guy that we're not Jehovah's Witnesses. I hear it in the wicked laugh that echoes all the way up the stairs, in between our puffs and pants.

When we get to the top, the door to 12C flies open and a girl in a nurse's uniform—a real one, that is, not a kinky one—flies out, buckling under the weight of a large gym bag. Her face is blotchy, like it's been freshly scrubbed raw of makeup.

Parnell whips out his ID again. "Saskia French."

"No, I . . . I . . ." She glances back into the flat, looking jumpy. "Are you here about Maryanne?"

Maryanne.

So whatever she was doing in London, she'd reverted to her old name.

"I saw it in the paper. I would have called. Honest, I would have but . . ."

"But what? You were too busy to care?"

"No!" she howls. "I just didn't . . . it's just I don't know anything about, you know . . . and I'm about to qualify, and I just do this to keep my head above water." She looks to us both, backward and forward. "You see, they talk about student grants but they're not enough to live on. I'll stop when I'm qualified, when I'm salaried, I will . . ."

We're almost as thrown as she is. If she didn't expect to be door-stepped by two puffed-out police officers, we certainly didn't expect to be lectured on the state of NHS funding.

"And I thought Saskia would have called. I mean, it's nothing to do with me." A quick glance at her watch. "Oh shit, I'm going to be late for my shift."

A disembodied voice comes from inside the flat—loud, husky and impatient. "Just leave it, Petra. Go. I'll talk to them."

It's an order. An instruction that sends Petra hurtling down the stairs. She'll keep.

"Yes?"

The voice now has a body, and a knock-out body at that. Saskia French stands in the doorway pulling a bulky sweater over a red PVC dress, hopping from foot to foot and blowing her cheeks out at the cold. If it was possible to take your eyes off her legs, which finish somewhere around my shoulders, you'd notice that she's got wide set eyes, heavily kohl'd and a little starey. A razor-sharp black bob with spirit-level bangs. While she's not quite exactly your full-on fetish-queen, there's definitely something of the alternative about her. A certain edginess that propels her from attractive to arresting.

Put another way, she's stop-traffic sexy.

"Saskia, we'd like to ask you a few questions about Alice Lapaine. It sounds like you knew her as Maryanne Doyle."

Several expressions collide but hostility overrides them all. "I'm sorry, I don't think I can help, and I'm expecting someone shortly. A friend," she adds, with a smile more beatific than the Virgin Mary.

Parnell smiles. "No need to be sorry, you can definitely help us. We know Maryanne Doyle—*a murder victim*—made a number of calls to your phone, and thanks to your colleague just now, it's clear Maryanne was known to you so let's not do this pointless little dance, eh? Just a few questions?"

I stick my foot in the door, a preemptive strike that doesn't go to waste when she tries to slam it shut. My foot throbs but I hold her stare. And it's not the easiest stare to hold. Fervent, almost tipping into crazy. The kind of crazy that drives men wild as long as it's at a distance—preferably a one-hour-once-a-week kind of distance.

"Five minutes." She turns and sweeps down a narrow hallway, all five feet eleven of her, pulling doors closed as she passes. "We can talk in here."

We follow her into a small cramped kitchen, the kind of adjunct they build on to an office so people can make tea and microwave porridge but that's about it. There's no washing machine as far as I can see—unless Saskia French's whole wardrobe is of the wipe-clean PVC kind—and even the cooker, a free-standing hob sitting on top of the worktop, looks like something you'd take on a camping trip. The fridge is as dinky as a child's toy.

Still, someone's feeling festive, at least—there's a snowflake sprayed on the window and a sprig of mistletoe dangling from the door.

Saskia busies herself throwing fresh mint into a mug. She doesn't ask if we want anything. While her back's turned, I channel "what-the-fuck?" frequencies across the lino to Parnell.

Why the hell was Maryanne/Alice calling a prostitute?

Parnell cracks on. "How did you know Maryanne Doyle?"

She sighs. Hops up on the worktop and stretches out her legs—bare, unashamedly pale and elegant like a dancer's. "I didn't *know* Maryanne. We shared the same space for a few weeks but I barely saw her. She saw most of her clients off the premises."

I sense the bomb go off in Parnell's head but it's me who reacts. "Clients? You're saying Maryanne was working here."

She looks me up and down, finds me wanting on just about every level and turns back to Parnell. "I've just said, she didn't see a lot of clients here. She was using it more as a base. She left her stuff here."

"Maryanne's stuff is here? She has a room here?" I'm struggling to keep my professional cool, but in the space of half an hour we've gone from laborious grunt work to the revelation that might just light a fire under this case and it's taking me a moment to adjust. To reset my skillset from phone-answerer-cum-form-filler to actual detective.

Parnell doesn't need any time. "Which room?"

"The second on the right, she didn't have much though." Another sigh. "What exactly are you looking for?"

Parnell walks out. I hear a door open and it takes every last piece of my resolve not to burst in behind him.

"Why didn't you contact the police about Maryanne? It's been all over the papers for almost a week."

"Has it?" she says, vaguely. "I don't really read the papers, or watch TV. I'm more of a music fan. Anyway, the less I have to do with the police, the better."

"Your colleague, Petra, seemed to be aware of it. She implied you were too—she was surprised you hadn't contacted us."

"I only found out a day or two ago when I picked up a paper on the tube."

"And you didn't think to call us?"

A shrug. "I had nothing to tell. I *have* nothing to tell."

"Maryanne was staying here and you think that's nothing?"

She bends forward, clasps her hands together like a teacher talking to an imbecile. "Do. You. Understand. English? I hardly ever saw her. I really can't help you."

I change gear, try to ruffle her. "Why do you have two phones, Saskia?"

Her voice takes on a bored, sing-song tone. "It's fairly standard practice. I like to keep my life and work separate. The pay-as-you-go is for work."

"It's been switched off for a week, maybe longer. Why?"

She whispers something I assume to be derogatory, then, "I wanted some R&R, even *tarts* need a week off now and again and when I'm not working, I switch it off. I don't want to be pestered."

I gesture to her dress. "Well, I assume you're working today and it's still switched off?"

"Is it?" A false gracious smile. "Thanks for reminding me."

"You know it is. You took the SIM out and put it in your other phone."

"Look, I needed to check a client's number, OK? The handset had been playing up so I put the SIM in my other phone to save time." She fixes me with a glare. "You know, this really is fucking tedious. How much longer are you going to be?"

I don't respond. "What was Maryanne calling you about, on these dates?" I show her the piece of paper with the calls highlighted but she pushes it away.

"Just house things. Do we need loo roll? Leave the hall light on. That sort of thing."

Annoyingly feasible.

"Obviously I need to ask you where you were on the night of Monday fifteenth, into the early hours of Tuesday sixteenth."

She doesn't seem fazed by the question. "I was here, alone. I told you, I wanted a few days off to get some proper rest, catch up on some admin, spring clean the flat—you know, *normal stuff*. I have the same old boring crap to deal with as anyone else, you know. I'm a human being, not just a whore."

I think I'm supposed to be moved by this plaintive cry but there's something about this woman that inspires minimal sympathy.

"So where exactly did you meet Maryanne?" I say, face completely blank.

"I can't remember."

"Not good enough."

She grips the edge of the worktop and gives me that crazy stare again, eyes wide and threatening. I'm starting to think she might launch herself off at any minute but to my surprise, she starts talking.

"I think it was the Diamond, oh no, hold on, it was Silks." A strip club, basically. "I haven't danced in years but I still go there for a drink, a lot of the girls do. It's good for business and I know the staff. Anyway, Maryanne was there one evening, we get talking—it was actually nice to meet someone English and a bit more my own age for a change—and she mentions she's looking for a room and I think, why not? Earn some extra money and have someone a bit older, a bit more sensible, running the show while I'm away. I work abroad occasionally," she adds.

"Running the girls, you mean?"

She lifts her chin. "I don't operate like that."

"Look, I'm not from Vice, Saskia, I'm not here for that."

And even if I was, this is small fry. As long as no one's trafficked or underage, work away.

She slides down off the worktop, stretches forward for her cigarettes in a long lean pose. "How it works is, not every client can afford to stump up for a hotel room every time he wants to get his dick wet, you follow? So I've got a few trusted girls who use the spare rooms occasionally, and I take a small percentage. I'm saving up for"—to my shame I assume she's going to say "bum lift" or something equally depressing—"a camper van. A fully-restored 1960s VW." She gazes at her surroundings with not quite disgust, but fatigue. "I need to get away from all this for a while."

"What did Maryanne tell you about herself?"

She lights the cigarette. "Nothing. Just what I told you. That she was looking for somewhere to stay."

"And when she was here?"

A deep draw, I recognize it well as the first of the day. "Well, it did seem like she was running from something. We didn't chat much, but we did have a laugh about dodgy clients one day. She mentioned she'd had a few. I got the impression something had happened fairly recently but it was just an impression. I didn't ask for details." A blank look. "I wasn't very interested, to be honest."

I make a note of this. "We'll need a list of all the people she came into contact with while she was living here. We'll be as discreet as we can."

She slams her hand down, raises her voice nought to sixty. "Are you fucking deaf, copper? I. Don't. Know."

I actually jump. There's a jerkiness to her mood that's hard to keep up with. Totally disconcerting.

"Look," she says, a bit nicer, "we weren't 'roomies,' OK. We didn't sit around plaiting each other's hair and talking about first kisses. She dossed here for around three weeks." A thought suddenly occurs to her. "And it looks like I won't get paid for that now, doesn't it?"

I don't dignify that. I doubt she expects me to. "What about you? Any dodgy clients we need to be aware of? Anyone who could have seen Maryanne and taken a shine?"

That sing-song tone again. "No. No one. Contrary to myth, I could count the number of weirdos I've had on one hand. Most of what I do is nothing any self-respecting girlfriend wouldn't do if she could be bothered."

Nice.

"Do you own this property?"

Her nose twitches, a nervous tic. "No, why?"

"So you were subletting the room to Maryanne?"

She mutters *"motherfucker"* and to be fair, I probably deserve it. I only said it to rattle her.

"I don't think the owners would mind that much, actually. I've lived here for years. I'm a very good tenant."

"Why's that? Because you pay them a percentage of your earnings?"

"God, no!" She seems to find this hysterical. "They haven't got a clue what I do. They think I'm a yoga teacher."

She could be, I think. She's got the posture if not the temperament.

Parnell comes back into the kitchen, looks straight at Saskia. "Miss French, we haven't been able to recover Maryanne's bag or phone and it doesn't look like it's in her room either. Can you give us a description?"

She purses her lips, pretends to think. "Er, her bag might have been black. That help much?"

"Immeasurably," he says drolly. To me, "There's nothing much in there, a few items of clothing, a washbag, some cold and flu tablets."

"Yeah, she was a bit under the weather," says Saskia, kicking her feet, suddenly all helpful. "I told her ginseng but some people won't listen."

Parnell looks at her, slightly baffled, then back to me. "Anyway, I've requested a Section 8. We'll need Forensics here ASAP, we need the bedding, her clothes, the lot."

"Forensics!" Saskia flies at Parnell, a whirling dervish of milky-white limbs and red PVC. Parnell steps back just in time which stops her making contact and earning herself a night in the cells, but her eyes are flaming. I think I'd take a punch any day rather than stare down those eyes at close range. "Listen, *mate*," she spits, "I've answered your fucking questions now get out of my fucking flat and take your little helper with you."

Parnell straightens his spine and draws his neck up, just about eye-level. "I need to make another phone call, Miss French, so I'm going to leave my 'little helper' here to explain to you exactly what's going on because I don't think you understand the seriousness of the situation."

She turns back to me, confidence quickly draining, belligerence giving way to panic. "Please. You don't need a warrant. I've given you permission so just take what you want and go. I can't have my flat crawling with your lot."

Technically, she's right. Parnell and I *could* probably get away with a bit of a treasure hunt without a warrant. But Parnell's not in the business of getting away with things. He's a "just to be safe" kind of character.

I try to explain this. "It's not as easy as just taking what we want, Saskia. Forensics will need to go through Maryanne's room with a fine-tooth comb."

"I'd let your 'friend' know not to come over," shouts Parnell from the hallway. "Unless he's a 'friend' you think it'd be worth us talking to."

She moves to the doorway, hands on hips. "Oh, do me a favor and quit the sarcasm, would you? It really doesn't suit you." She draws her eyes downward. "Neither does that tie."

Parnell laughs. "Oh, I'll do you a favor, Miss French. If you say sorry for being rude about my favorite tie, I might just let you get rid of some of the more obvious signs of cocaine use littered around this flat before the cavalry arrives. How's that sound to you? Fair enough?"

She gives an exaggerated shrug and stalks off into a room, presumably her bedroom, to call her "friend." I walk into Maryanne's room, not touching anything, just glancing around at a whole lot of nothing. A small double futon, a cheap-looking nightstand and a clothes rail, that's it.

I turn back to Parnell.

"I'm on bloody hold," he says, tutting,

"What are you thinking?"

He trains one ear on what Saskia's saying, lends the other to me. "Something's definitely off."

I keep my voice low. "Seriously off. I can just about accept that a mousy little pub chef might embark on a double life as a lady-of-the-night. I mean, nothing surprises, right? But there was no semen? No condom lubricant?" Parnell nods, encouraging me to go on. "And this room? I'm not being funny but where's the racy underwear, the sex toys? There isn't even a scrap of makeup, just some deodorant and a few face-wipes."

"The coke's not mine." Saskia walks back into the hallway, her face illuminated by her phone.

"Maryanne's?" I say, surprised by nothing anymore.

"No, no, I mean, it's mine, I suppose. But I don't use it. I don't do drugs," she adds, proudly. "But some clients like it. It, you know, helps . . ."

Parnell raises an eyebrow. "I wouldn't know, actually."

There's a voice down the line and he ushers us away, back into the kitchen. We assume our positions again, her on the worktop, me on the chair. There's so much to ask that I can't think where to begin. Parnell needs to take the lead from here, anyway.

"We're going to need the name of the owners of this flat," I say, just to break the silence. "I appreciate that's going to be awkward but we have to speak to them."

"I'm sorry?" The muscles in her neck tense. "Why?"

"They own the property, Saskia. Out of courtesy we need to reassure them that any damage caused by the search will be put right."

"I'll tell them," she says, quickly. "There's no need."

"It doesn't work like that, I'm afraid." I take out my notepad. "Name, please."

She says nothing. Stares at the back wall. But I don't think it's petulance, it's discomfort.

I let out a long sigh. "Saskia, do you know how quickly we can find this out? This isn't *Scooby Doo*, we're the police. It'd just be a whole lot easier if you'd tell me."

"Nathaniel Hicks," she mumbles eventually, then louder, "His name is Nate Hicks."

It takes me ten seconds to place the name. Five minutes to confirm it with HQ. Ten minutes to arrange for two uniforms to preserve the scene and it'll probably take an hour for us to get over there at this time of day.

Nathaniel Hicks.

Owner of this flat and husband of Gina Hicks.

She of the impossibly perfect life on the impossibly perfect Keeper's Close, where an imperfectly sighted pensioner thought she might *possibly* have seen Maryanne talking into the intercom.

God bless lovely June of the Donatella Caffé.

15

It takes more than an hour. Eighty-five minutes, to be precise. Eighty-five minutes of Parnell getting grief from Maggie about something and crunching his mood out on the gearstick, while I fiddle with the radio, flicking between songs that all seem intent on telling us what a wonderful time of the year it is. What a fabulous time we must be having.

There's no let-up at the Hickses', either.

The door's opened by Santa. A crooked, puny Santa with a rattly chest and slow labored movements who I recognize to be Gina Hicks' father under the synthetic beard and cheap silly hat. He ushers us into the family room where, fittingly, the whole Hicks family is congregating in picture-postcard style. Gina Hicks, nailing "casual chic" again in tawny beige cashmere and brown furry boots, is hanging chocolates on a tree with the elf-suited toddlers, while the man I assume to be Nate Hicks—blondish and brawny, with features just the wrong side of handsome but with the confidence not to care—throws logs and muttered curses onto a smoldering fire that refuses to catch light. On a cream Chesterfield sofa, the eldest lad, whose name escapes me, tunes a violin and quietly hums "God Rest Ye Merry Gentlemen" to himself, while his sister—flat-ironed hair, must be around fourteen—records every twee middle-class moment on her glittery pink phone.

If domestic smuggery could be bottled it would smell just like this. Topnotes of gingerbread and basenotes of cloves.

It only takes two phrases to break the spell though. *"Murder victim"* and *"Your flat."*

I feel like we've walked onto a Bing Crosby film set and pissed on the fake snow.

"That girl was staying with Saskia?" A stunned Gina Hicks drops to the arm of the sofa. "Was she a friend?"

"What girl are they talking about, Mum?"

I clock the bouncy intrigue in the daughter's voice and know where this is heading: Facebook.

"Perhaps we could speak alone?" I say.

Nate Hicks is swift to oblige, scrambling to his feet and throwing the door open. "Right, out, the lot of you. Amber, take the twins. Leo, go and do that elsewhere."

There's a whiny, monotone protest from Amber but an exodus ensues, including the ailing Santa.

"And don't let the twins torment Grandad," Gina calls after them.

As soon as their voices become distant, Parnell clears his throat. "It's been alleged that the victim, Alice Lapaine, aka Maryanne Doyle, had been working as a prostitute."

There's a deep line across Gina's botox-free brow, complete incomprehension in her voice. "And this woman was friends with Saskia? Darling, can you actually believe this?" A quick glance to her husband and then back to us. "I mean, we don't know Saskia that well on a personal level, but she's always been a reliable tenant and I didn't think she'd associate with—" She catches herself, looks embarrassed. "I'm sorry, I know I'm being judgmental and the girl's dead, I'm just surprised that Saskia would be friends with . . ."

"Saskia French is a prostitute," announces Parnell.

"Oh my God!" It's barely a whisper but her eyes are open wide. Nate Hicks looks less surprised, more solemn. Like a grim-faced politician about to make a keynote speech. He walks over to the sofa and attempts to take his wife's hand.

He doesn't succeed. Gina's hell-bent on resurrecting what feels like an old argument.

"This is your bloody fault. I said we should check on the place more often, didn't I? Well, didn't I? Heaven knows you're in London enough, would it have hurt to do a spot-check now and again?"

Nate throws his hands up. "On what basis? You said yourself, she's been the perfect tenant. Rent on time, never a peep. We can't just barge in there inspecting the place on no grounds, Gina. They're not student digs, she's a grown woman."

"Are you sure about this?" says Gina to both of us. "She's been our tenant for years, absolutely no trouble . . ."

I shake my head. "It was obvious from the minute we got there, and Miss French didn't exactly hide it either."

A jubilant child's scream carries through from the kitchen followed by the sound of the Grandad laughing. The laugh quickly gives way to a savage, hacking cough.

"Oh God, they shouldn't be climbing all over him. He's got stage four lung cancer, they reckon about six to twelve months." She puts her head in her hands, sighs deeply. "God, I really don't need this, on top of everything else."

For all her cashmere and clove-scented domesticity, you'd have to be a robot not to feel a stab of sympathy. A sick parent is no fun. A sick parent, a prostitute tenant, and a link with a murder victim must be the absolute pits.

Nate puts his arm around his wife's shoulders, nuzzles her head. "Look, darling, obviously the fact that this dead woman was in our flat is unfortunate, but in terms of Saskia, is it honestly such a big deal? Christ, remember that chap from the Camden flat? He turned out to be some sort of bogus tradesman, a complete fraudster. Saskia's never given us any trouble whatsoever, so is it really our business how she earns her living, distasteful as it is . . ."

Gina's head snaps up. "It is my bloody business if she's turned my property into a knocking shop. You heard what they said, that dead woman was *working* there."

I step in to referee. "If it's any consolation, that's not our concern. You do what you have to do with Saskia, there won't be anything formal from our side." There's a flicker of relief but it's infinitesimal under the heavy mask of worry. "Mrs. Hicks, you said, 'my property' just now. Who exactly is the owner?"

"It's mine."

Parnell takes a seat on the Chesterfield. It's a bit low for his tastes and I see a twinge of regret as he tries to make himself comfortable. "Saskia gave your husband's name," he says. "Why would that be?"

Gina scoffs. "Good old-fashioned sexism, I imagine. I just stay at home raising children and baking organic strudels, don't I, darling? God forbid anyone thought I had a career of my own once. Investments of my own."

The argument fails to ignite when the eldest son walks back into the room carrying a violin case. He gives his parents a bemused stare, as if he hasn't seen them look anything other than wholly composed and efficient his entire life and he senses this might mark some kind of seismic sea change. One that might benefit him if he plays his cards right.

"Not a good time, Leo," says Gina, massaging her forehead with her index fingers.

"So I'm not getting a lift then?" He's dressed like an accountant although I suspect it's a posh school uniform. Sixth form, probably.

Gina gives us a look of *"See, that's all I'm good for."*

"Hey, can I drive myself, Mum?" he says, pushing his luck. "I'm insured on the Lexus."

Nate Hicks pulls out his wallet, rips out two twenties. "Dream on. Walk up to the high street and get a cab, all right?"

"It's like the fucking North Pole out there." He snatches the money anyway.

Nate shoves him out of the door—a little rougher than horseplay to my eye. "Put a hat on then. And watch your bloody mouth, Leo." When he turns around, he's grinning apologetically. "Concert this evening, St. Paul's. Sorry about the gutter language, he's going through a gangster phase at the moment. It's rather grating."

Parnell smiles. "In this game, you meet all sorts of lads on the cusp of adulthood. Trust me, yours isn't doing too badly if he's playing the violin at St. Paul's and not mugging old ladies."

Nate rubs at his jaw. "I know, I know. It's just teenagers and toddlers in the same house, it gets a bit much."

"Been there," says Parnell, "It's tough, especially when you're a bit, well . . ."

A surprising laugh from Gina. "You can say it. A bit older. Geriatric, they call it at the hospital. A geriatric at forty-two. The cheek."

Another smile from Parnell. "Same as my wife."

There's a silence as they wait for us to speak again. It's clear from the way Nate is edging subtly toward the door and jiggling the change in his pockets that he thinks our work here is done.

We sit out the silence, see what it brings.

When he eventually speaks, his voice is stuttery and chummy. Middle-class charm personified. "So, er, obviously we're very grateful for you letting us know, Officers. Is there, er, anything else we can help with? Do you need us to sign anything with regards to taking things from the flat? Do you need keys? Would a spare set of keys help?" A fond glance to Gina. "Although knowing where things are isn't really my forte, is it, darling? Do we even have a spare set? We can certainly get some cut." We let him ramble, let his fawning helpfulness burn itself out. "Aside from that, I don't see what more we can tell you?"

I look confused. "Well, with all due respect, I thought that would be obvious? I'm assuming your wife told you about our first visit?" They nod tentatively. "We need to understand why a murdered woman, who was staying at a property you own, was also spotted on this road—well, at the gates to this road—and in a café just down the way on a couple of different occasions."

I leave out the word *"possibly."* It always spoils the fun.

Nate opens his mouth but Gina cuts in, sounding dazed. Like she's woken up in a dream where everything's back-to-front. "You think we knew this woman? I told you when you came before, I've never seen her before in my life."

"Well, yes, but you can see why we're making the connection, surely? A witness has stated . . ."

Nate makes himself bigger, the classic macho wide-legged stance. "What fucking witness?"

Leo Hicks isn't the only one going through a gangster phase, it seems. Parnell picks up on this. "Could you watch your mouth please, Mr. Hicks. There's no need for gutter language. The identity of our witness doesn't concern you."

He doesn't back down but shortens his stance. "Oh, yes it does, if you're going to come into my house and accuse my wife of being a liar."

"I never said I don't believe your wife. Maybe it's you who recognizes her?"

"I don't, as I told the officer who returned with the photo late last week. Not that I needed a photo, it's been all over the news."

A realization dawns on Gina. "God, we won't be on the news, will we? There won't be journalists on the close? I mean, I'd love to help, I really would. It's terrible what's happened to that poor woman, but honestly, this is just ridiculous. We haven't the faintest idea who she is."

Nate looks at his wife. "Of course we won't be on the news. This is wanton exploration, that's all. There's no credible witness. It's what they call a fishing expedition."

I step into his personal space but keep my tone light. "And under *what we call* the Regulation of Investigatory Powers Act, we can request to see your phone records at any time, Mr. Hicks. How do you feel about that?"

He gives me a thin-lipped smile. "Not a problem, Detective . . . I'm sorry, I forget your last name. I can get them for you now if you'd like. I'm sure I can download a fully itemized bill online. How many copies would you like?"

Parnell stands up, quicker and smoother than I've seen in a long time—less clicky. "We'll retrieve them ourselves, Mr. Hicks, if we decide we need to, but thank you." He nods toward Gina. "Thank you both for your time, we'll see ourselves out."

"The smug fuck," I say. "*Excuse my gutter language.*"

We sit in the car on the pebbled driveway—partly just to unnerve the Hickses, partly so Parnell can have a blast of his e-cig before driving back. He's gone for Green Tea and Menthol this time, and mixed with the quintessential blend of takeaway fried chicken and pine-scented air-freshener that always seems to hang heavy in Parnell's car, I start to miss the scents of middle-class Christmas fairly quickly. I'd wind the window down if there wasn't a chill outside that could bring a tear to a glass eye.

"Could it be pure coincidence?" I ask.

Parnell drums the steering wheel with his spare hand. "What, that she was living in their flat and a completely unconnected looky-likey turns up at the gates here?" He stares through the windscreen, marvels at a gray squirrel attacking a bird feeder. "Could be," he says, eventually. "I'm actually part of a rare breed who believes coincidences *can* happen."

I'm not sure if I am. Conspiracy out-glams coincidence by a country mile.

Still, I'm a pragmatist.

"The kind of lawyers the Hickses can afford will get a hard-on at the word 'coincidence' though, that's our problem."

"Exactly," says Parnell. "So do you know what we do?"

"Give up? Plant evidence?"

Parnell turns his body to face me, the seat belt straining across his bulk. "Are you a James Bond fan, Kinsella?"

The seriousness of his tone tickles me. "Not really. I went through a bit of a spy phase when I was little but it was more Danger Mouse than 007. Why?"

"But you've heard of *Goldfinger*, though? Tell me you've heard of *Goldfinger*?"

I do a little Shirley Bassey which Parnell takes to mean "yes."

"Well, after he comes across Bond for the third time, Goldfinger says—and bear with me, my Latvian accent isn't the best. *'Once is happenstance. Twice is coincidence. Three times is enemy action.'*"

I think about this, nod sagely. "So we find coincidence number three, and when we do, we consider the Hickses to be the enemy." Parnell joins me in the sage nodding. "We might find it in the phone records?"

Parnell puts his e-cig down, holds up two fingers. "One, that wouldn't be a coincidence, that would be us blatantly catching them out in a lie, and two, we won't find anything, he was far too relaxed." Suddenly his head juts forward and he squints into the distance. "Although, hold up. Speak of the devil."

I follow his line of sight and see Nate Hicks jogging toward the car. Parnell gives the accelerator a rev for pure devilment and the jog turns into a lumbering sprint.

"What does he want?"

"You didn't forget your glasses again, kiddo?" I glare at Parnell but it's a fair question. It happens all the time; pub toilets, train journeys, witnesses' homes. I live in fear of leaving them at a crime scene.

Parnell winds down the window. I scowl at the cold and in doing so scowl at Nate Hicks, who's only wearing a thin rugby shirt, making him either rock-hard or panicked.

"Can we talk?" he says. "Quickly."

I look back to the kitchen window. Gina Hicks is framed in early-evening light, nursing a cut knee as one of the toddlers sits on the sink. "I assume you know your wife can see you?"

"I said I was checking you could get out the main gate. The sensor plays up occasionally so it's not a complete lie."

I didn't exactly lie, I just didn't tell the truth.

"Hop in," says Parnell.

He gets in the back, looking completely incongruous. Nate Hicks strikes me as the type of guy who always likes to be at the wheel, metaphorically or otherwise, and there's something satisfying about the sight of him scrunched up in the back of Parnell's Citroën C4.

"I'm sorry I was a bit aggressive back there," he says.

I've an urge to tell him he wasn't aggressive at all, just a pompous oaf, but it's only a thirty-second drive up to the main gates so there's not much time for small talk.

I shift around in my seat. "You know, if you have something to tell us about *'the dead woman,'* your wife is going to find out anyway, and we don't generally take statements from the backs of cars."

"No, no, it's not about her. Well, not really." He drags his hands through his hair, leaving it sticking out at all angles in small fuzzy tufts. "God, this is all so embarrassing. I swear I don't know who this Alice/ Maryanne woman is. Really, I don't." He pauses. "But I do know what Saskia is. I've known for a while now. By pure accident. Despite what my wife thinks, I do listen sometimes and I did check in on the flat . . ." It's paining him to go further.

Parnell lets out a knowing "*Ah*" and pulls up on a verge, a little to the side of main gate. A BMW squeezes through and the female driver gives a confused wave to Nate Hicks. He looks mortified which makes me feel toasty warm inside.

"So you've known your tenant is a prostitute for a while?" I say, acting like I'm just getting it all straight in my head. "But you didn't see fit to tell your wife?"

It's obvious where this is heading but it's fun watching him squirm.

"No, I didn't. I couldn't, we . . . I don't know how it . . . I've never done anything . . ."

Parnell hasn't got time for bluster, he's got the twins' carol concert to-night. "Shall I help you, Mr. Hicks? You had sex with Saskia French, yes?"

He looks at us both, all hunched-up shoulders and hangdog eyes. In his stripy rugby top and cheeks reddened by the cold—or shame—he resembles an overgrown schoolboy. I turn back to the front to hide my disdain.

"Was it a financial arrangement?" asks Parnell.

"The first couple of times and then it became more of a, well, a thing."

"A thing?"

He coughs, awkwardly. "More of a relationship. An affair. In her mind anyway. I wanted to cool things."

I undo my seat belt, swivel a whole 180 so I can face him fully again. "And why are you telling us this?"

It's not a pointed question. I'm genuinely confused. You see, to a Murder Detective, everything is relevant. Every hazy-eyed anecdote, every inconsequential detail, all the way down to what brand of cereal the victim liked to eat at the weekend could prove to be the shiny gold nugget that leads to a break. But to a shyster like Nate Hicks, who clearly has a rather flexible relationship with the truth, everything he reveals is on a strictly need-to-know basis. And I'm not quite understanding why *he* thinks we need to know this.

I get my answer, for what it's worth.

"I'm just trying to make sense of this dead woman thing."

Parnell shoots me a sideways glance. "Aren't we all, Mr. Hicks? So any information you have, let's hear it."

"Well, it's not really information, as such." He shuffles to the middle of the back seat, sits forward, head parked between me and Parnell like a boulder. "I suppose you'd call it more a hypothesis . . ."

1998
Sunday 31st May

It was late Sunday evening when we first heard about Maryanne. Mum was cleaning my ears in front of the fire and Dad was trying, and failing, to teach Noel the rules of poker when the back door slammed and in flounced Jacqui, our resident doomsayer, keen to share her latest scoop.

"Gone. Kidnapped. Kaput." She shrugged, kicking off her Buffalo platforms like she hadn't a care, or a missing friend, in the world.

It transpired, or so the official line went, that Maryanne had gone out the night before to buy hairspray and hadn't been home since. Jonjo Doyle and her moron brother had been searching all around the place but now the Guards had been called and the word around town was that Pat Hannon had killed her.

Gran blessed herself and told Jacqui to shut up. Said she shouldn't be saying such wicked things when Nora Hannon wasn't yet cold in the ground, but Jacqui stood firm, insisting the theory had legs as Maryanne had called him "a wankstain" in the pub and everyone knew he'd killed his wife to collect the life insurance, so maybe he'd got a taste for it?

Maybe he needed younger blood to satisfy his insatiable murderous lust? Fresh meat, she called it.

Mum said Jacqui was banned from watching horror films from now on, and anyway, wasn't it a bit early to be talking of anyone killing anyone? Maryanne was seventeen, for God's sake. Hadn't she and Auntie Brona once gone to Galway to get outfits for a wedding and not come back for two days after latching on to a punk rocker with backstage passes for the Boomtown Rats?

Gran remembered this, which surprised us all because lately Gran remembered less and less, often confusing Mum's name with the dog's and always asking if it was busy in town when you'd only come back from the toilet. But just the mention of Mum's cross-county escapades seemed to ignite a momentary spark.

"Tinkers, the pair of you. You put the heart crossways in me."

Mum welled up at this, probably grateful for the reminder that she'd once been the child and Gran had been the carer, but then Noel killed the moment by saying he hoped Maryanne was dead and fair play to Pat Hannon if it was true. (She'd laughed at his acne and Noel was always one for holding wholly disproportionate grudges.)

And all the time, Dad said nothing.

In the corner of the room, on a relic of a TV, Nick Cotton was back in EastEnders, snarling at the locals and harrassing his mum for cash. I instantly thought of Noel and glared at him across the hearth, channeling waves of pure poison, willing the legs of his chair to cave in so he'd fall into the fire, but most of all wishing that he'd harrass our ma for cash sometimes instead of always taking mine. But then big kids were always taking what they wanted from little kids.

Maryanne Doyle had taken my Tinkerbell and now she'd gone missing.

16

"Well, I'm glad I've got a double shot eggnog latte for this one." Steele shakes her head, exasperated. "So let me get this right, his grand *hypothesis* is that supposed bunny-boiler Saskia French *might* have sent Alice Lapaine to his house to deliver a message because he'd stopped taking her calls and blocked her everywhere?"

"It's a bit teenage," I say. "She seemed perfectly capable of fighting her own battles to me."

Christmas Eve. It's not even seven a.m. and there's already a few of us clamoring for space around Steele's electric heater, thawing out our limbs while trying to get our heads around this mindfuck of a case.

"Oi, budge over." Parnell nudges me with his hip. "You forget I'm older than you, Kinsella. An Arctic chill could finish me off." I laugh. "It's true, I saw a poster in the doctor's."

At least Parnell's trying to be funny. Renée and Flowers clearly haven't had their Weetabix yet if their moods are anything to go by.

"So what does this Saskia say about it?" grunts Flowers.

I wouldn't know. Parnell insisted on dropping me home on the way back from the Hickses' last night, which left him with the happy task of wrangling with Saskia again and me to a night of "normal stuff"—as coined by the woman herself.

Washing. Tidying. Microwaving. Dodging phone calls from my sister.

Starting to write out Christmas cards before deciding it's nearly Christmas anyway and what's the point.

With the exception of Parnell, of course. My work-dad gets a card depicting a glittery robin perched on an equally glittery branch. He's already moaning that he's covered in the bloody stuff.

"What did Saskia say?" repeats Parnell, blowing hot breath into his glittery hands. "Well, in between saying that Forensics were 'taking fucking liberties' and stressing about having to pack to go to her parents' today, she confirmed, yes, they were having an affair but no, she didn't send anyone to the house."

"Alice could have gone to the Hickses' under her own steam." I suggest. "Maybe she found out about the affair with Saskia and decided to blackmail Nate Hicks. We know she needed money."

"Which gives him motive to kill her," says Flowers, stating the bleeding obvious.

Steele doesn't look too excited. "Yeah, OK, maybe it does, but it's just that—a maybe. We've got no proof whatsoever that Maryanne had any knowledge of Saskia and Nate's affair. And also, why blackmail him? There can't have been a shortage of married men frequenting that flat with guilty consciences and deep pockets. Why pick on the lover of your newfound flatmate? Doesn't make sense."

"Maybe Saskia put her up to it and they were going to share the spoils?" I say.

"Another 'maybe' but that one sits a bit better." Steele chews her lip, twists the holder on her coffee cup. "Devil's advocate, but what do we think about Saskia French as a suspect? She didn't report her missing, that's dodgy, surely?"

Parnell's open to it. "We said we couldn't completely rule out a woman. And she's statuesque enough."

"Alibi?" croaks Renée.

"Another Home Alone," I say. "Damn these early morning murders, eh." I give up trying to claim my patch of heat and plonk myself in the corner instead. "What's her motive, though?"

Steele's not bothered about motive. Means, opportunity and watertight forensics are her Holy Trinity. As long as she's got the who, the when and the how, she's happy to leave it to the psychiatrists to impress everybody with the why.

Parnell's a big fan of motive, though. He likes things tidy. "Wouldn't be the first fight in a brothel to turn nasty. And as they're usually over money or men, that obviously brings us back to Nate Hicks."

I have to say it. "I'm not convinced she was working in that flat, you know. No semen, no condom residue." I look to Parnell. "And do you remember, Saskia said she assumed she saw her clients off the premises, so we haven't even got a confirmed sighting of her with a punter."

Steele sweeps her eyes across us, deadly serious. "While we're on the subject of confirmed sightings, how definite are we that it was Alice on the Hickses' road, because we're basing an awful lot of *hypotheses* around it, m'dears."

"It's not a foolproof ID at the gates," I admit. "But we've definitely got her in the café down the road and it's just too much coincidence to be anyone else, surely?"

"Mmmm," says Steele. It's a long "Mmmm." One that says there's a big gulf between a coincidence and a murder conviction. "Right, let's stop hypothesizing for a minute and look at the latest facts. I've had it off-the-record from Forensics that Saskia French's flat is *unlikely* to be the primary crime scene, nothing obvious flagged up. We're going to have to wait until after Christmas for Maryanne's clothes, bedding, etc., but who knows, maybe we'll get lucky there—I think we're due some luck, don't you?" Steele drapes another cardigan over her shoulders, scowls at the heater. "So what else? Tox screen's come back, nothing exciting there, either. Craig and Ben went over to Silks last night—bless Benny-boy, all those near-naked honeys, Christmas really did come early—anyway, the bar staff recognized Saskia but not Maryanne, and they don't have CCTV for the night Saskia says she met Maryanne as they only keep the tapes for twenty-one days. We've got the rest though so that will keep someone busy after Christmas, Emily or Ben probably. Oh, and there's still nothing on the car."

Parnell turns to Renée. "We've checked the Hickses' and Saskia's names with Thomas Lapaine, right?"

Steele steamrollers on, Renée doesn't get a word in. "Oh, don't talk to me about Thomas frigging Lapaine. He's about as much use as a one-legged man in an arse-kicking contest. Knows nothing about his wife apart from what she wanted him to know." Parnell gives a duty-bound harrumph but it's jovial, mischievous. "We're still keeping tabs on him though. Seth's been stalking his "paramour," Abigail Shawcroft, on Facebook and he reckons Lapaine might have given her the heave-ho. She's been posting all these cryptic quotes about heartbreak and self-reliance: *'Let your tears water the seeds of your future happiness,'* that sort of crap. So if he has dumped her, she's definitely worth a re-interview, see if we can crack that alibi. Renée, sit her down for a woman-to-woman, OK?" Renée nods.

"You know what's bugging me," I say, keen to shift the focus—Thomas Lapaine isn't our guy, I'm almost sure of it. "She went back to using her original name when she came to London. That's certainly how Saskia and the other girl at the flat knew her. Why would she do that?"

"Going back to her roots," says Renée.

Steele points at her. "Aha, which brings me to Mulderrin." A heat sweeps through me, entirely unwelcome. "Who fancies a trip after Christmas?" she says, all smiles. "I'm still not convinced there's anything there but as we're hardly drowning in leads, I think we need to get over there to get a sense of things ourselves. And you never know, maybe Alice, Maryanne, whoever, had been in contact with someone from her past and they'd been keeping it secret? If we get in front of them, there's more chance of dragging it out, right? But if there's nothing to drag out, if we get nothing, then fine. We can officially downgrade it as a line of inquiry."

"I'll go." My voice sounds funny. For a second I wonder if it was even me who said it.

"Bingo. Well done, Kinsella."

Steele claps her hands together like it's the perfect answer she was looking for and in truth, it probably was. For all her *"as long as you report to me"* declarations, I suspect she'd still prefer me on the fringes, chasing flimsy leads in other countries rather than drilling too close to the center of the case.

If only she knew.

Steele stands up. Class dismissed. "OK, I think that's it, folks. Thanks for coming in at hideous o'clock but as you know, I'm tied up with Blake from eight thirty so needs must and all that. See what you can get done today—Nate Hicks' alibi is priority but have a bit of a general dig into him as well—and then for God's sake, have a Merry bloody Christmas. We'll get your flight sorted for Monday, Cat." To her credit she waits until everyone's left the room and walked a few paces out of earshot. "So make sure you call Dolores—Dr. Allen—to see if you can shift your afternoon slot to earlier, OK? Don't think you're getting out of it that easily."

I go back to my desk and spend the morning acting like the thought of Mulderrin hasn't flayed a thick layer of skin from my bones. For four hours straight I flit around the office like a worker bee high on pollen—making tea, chatting theories, powering through paperwork and swearing at spreadsheets. I even think about calling my sister back just to have my mind stuffed full of benign festive fluff, but I haven't quite decided what I'm doing for Christmas Day and I'm not ready to have that fight yet.

As usual I turn to Parnell to neutralize my angst.

"So did you make it back for your concert last night?"

"I did." He leans over, offers me a homemade mince pie. "Raced all the way back to north London, even did a dodgy U-turn on Stroud Green Road, and do you know what their *very important* roles were?" I sense we're not talking top billing here. "Curious sheep," he says, laughing. "That's exactly what it said in the program—Joe and James Parnell: *Curious sheep.*"

And I bet you died of pride anyway. The year I was Mary, Dad had to drive "something" to Manchester at the last minute.

I laugh along. "What were they curious about?"

"God knows? The Angel of the Lord appearing, I think, but bless them, they're not born thespians. Joe was more of a fidgety sheep and James had his back to the audience the whole time."

"A cantankerous sheep?"

"'Bout right," he says, chuckling again.

With my emotions temporarily quietened, I call Aiden Doyle. Just a quick courtesy call to say I'm going to be asking questions around Mulderrin. I can't help feeling a bit disappointed when the answerphone clicks in and I end up leaving a long, garbled explanation about when and who and why and the cost of last-minute flights, along with my hopes that he has a Bearable Christmas, if not a Happy Christmas, in the light of Maryanne and his dad not being well blah blah blah. I'm still rambling on as the answer machine cuts out.

Parnell eyes me strangely. I put the phone down quickly and distract him with a question.

"Any more possible sightings, Boss? Recent or the 'Lost Years'?"

Parnell picks up a stack of papers, jerks them at me. "Plenty of them, nothing that exciting though. Craig and Ben are out all day following up but I'm not holding my breath based on any of the call details. No one's said they saw her with anyone, and there's only a few who are absolutely sure it was her."

I leaf through them anyway, all sixty-seven of them. I'm practically comatose and thinking about lunch when my phone rings. It's the front desk.

"Kinsella."

"Lady downstairs asking for you, pet."

There's a drunk man singing in the background. I think I can just make out that Rudolph the red-nosed reindeer had a very shiny cock.

Oh, the magic of working Christmas Eve.

"Does this lady have a name?" I say—or holler, based on Parnell's reactions.

The front desk clerk raises his voice again. "She does, and she told me, but we've got a D&D down here—quite the Dean Martin, can you hear him?—so I couldn't hear her properly, pet, sorry."

"No worries, I'll be down in a jiffy."

With any luck I'll catch the next verse.

17

For a second I don't recognize her. She's wearing a khaki funnel coat zipped up to her nose and her hair's scraped back tight, not swishing around her shoulders in all its usual caramel and honey-blond loveliness. The frown line gives her away though. That, and the expensive shopping bags arranged neatly around her feet like pets—Liberty, Symthson, Penhaligon, COS. She's staring into space—completely oblivious to the shit-faced chanteur in the snowman onesie, now adding another charge to his sheet by belting out a racist version of "Deck the Halls," peppered with the odd shout of "No Surrender to the IRA." She startles when she sees me, as if she's forgotten where she is and why she's here.

"Mrs. Hicks."

She stands up quickly and the pull-down chair snaps back against the wall, making her jump. She apologizes, gathers up her bags, flustered.

"Gina, please. I'm so sorry to drop in like this, are you busy?"

I swipe my pass and push the door. "Of course not, come through."

I try the squishy room first—I've got a feeling this could be a squishy room conversation—but there's an engaged sign slapped across and a horrible keening noise coming from inside. Some poor soul on the rough end of something. I show her into one of the main interview rooms and resist the urge to thank her for instantly making the room smell nicer.

She takes her coat off. Turns down an offer of tea.

"So what can I do for you, Gina?" My mind's throwing out a hundred hypotheses, the main one being that she's not a complete imbecile and she knows it shouldn't have taken her husband ten minutes to steward us safely out of the main gates last night, and if she can't get answers from him, she wants answers from me. "I assume you weren't just passing?" I say, nudging the Smythson bag with my boot. "Or is there any chance that's for me? I'd die for one of their notebooks."

She glances down. "Oh these." Again, that slight sense of disorientation. "Have it. I'm serious. I've bought them enough already, more than they deserve." She actually lifts up the bag and offers it to me. I shake my head, a little embarrassed. "I just needed an excuse to come into town. To come here."

I say nothing and study her face. It's less remarkable than I'd built it up to be. Attractive but in a commonplace sort of way. The lighting in these rooms is a great leveler.

She lets out a deep breath. "I knew her, you see. Alice." She pauses, rephrases. "Well, I didn't *know* her, not really. Our paths crossed in the past—briefly but intensely, you might say."

Not what I was expecting. There's a pulsing at the top of my head. A frontal lobe reminder that now's the time to use my good judgment and go and get Parnell.

But she asked to speak to me specifically.

I don't want to panic her before we've even got going.

It's also for this reason that I hold back the words, *"lying to a police officer,"* although I do let her know that I need to record everything and then I caution her, in my least cautionary voice possible.

"God, I don't know where to start." She arches her head right back. I hear the tension crunching through her neck. "I just tried to do a good thing and now I'm caught up in all this. I'm so sorry I lied, I truly am. I just . . ."

"Just start at the beginning," I say, my voice as soft as a coo. "It's fine, you're doing the right thing, Gina."

"OK." She lays her palms flat on the table, steadies herself like it's a business pitch. "About four years ago, Nate and I were in a bad place. Really bad. We'd been having IVF and it just wasn't happening and well, it was tearing us apart. I think it's because we'd both had kids with other people." My face says it all. "Oh right, sorry, Leo's mine, Amber's Nate's.

I mean, Amber was only four when we got together and Leo was only seven so we very much consider them our own." She gives a sad little sniff. "Nate's wife died a year after Amber was born, you see. An undetected heart defect." Suddenly, her features harden. "And my ex is a complete waster who's never bothered with Leo so it was perfect, we became an instant little family."

"But it's natural to want children together."

She lowers her gaze, nods at the table. "And we just assumed we would. Took it for granted, as you do. And when it didn't happen . . . well, it's cruel and it's not logical, but when you've made a baby with someone else, but you can't make a baby with your current partner, it kind of does something. It makes you view them differently, view your relationship differently. It did us, anyway, I can't speak for everyone. But we ended up resenting each other, I suppose. It was just an incredibly bad time. Anyway, Nate ended up burying himself in work, which means burying himself in client dinners, and I was on my own night after night with my grief." Her eyes will me to understand. "I know it sounds dramatic, but that's what it felt like, grief."

"I understand," I say, as soothing as I can. "And Alice, where does she come in?"

A deep sigh. "So, as I say, Nate buried himself in work, I buried myself in the internet. IVF forums. Support forums, that sort of thing. It was just a way to pass the time at first but then you start to recognize certain names, the regular posters, and you forge friendships in a weird type of way."

"And you met Alice on one of these forums?"

Another nod. "You end up talking about all sorts, really. It's not all what's on TV, restaurants, tales of woe, you find yourself chatting about husbands, everything. And I'd been chatting to Alice quite a bit and one day I just mentioned how I'd been to Hampton Court and how nice it was to have such a magnificent palace not too far away, and she said, 'Oh, we must live fairly close then' and it turns out we did—she was Thames Ditton, right? Anyway, it went from there, really. We started chatting offline and arranged to meet up. It wasn't a big deal, we just said we'd grab a coffee next time I was down her way or if she was around mine . . ."

"So she gave you the impression she made regular trips into London?"

She gives a small shrug. "I suppose so, yes."

I note this down. "OK, so you met up?"

"Yes, just a few times. Once when I had to pop down her way to buy some hockey stuff for Amber, and then a couple of times at the café near me. The Donatella Caffé, except it wasn't called that then. I forget the name."

"So what did she tell you about herself?"

She leans in, gossipy. "Well, this is it, I ended up doing most of the talking. She seemed quite shy in person and I knew quickly that we weren't going to become best buddies but what I do remember though, is that she and her husband had only been trying for a year or so and she was still young, but she was really, really distressed that it hadn't happened for them." She lets out a shrill laugh. "Here I was in my early forties, and we'd been trying for years, and yet it was *me* who ended up counseling *her*."

"Sounds frustrating."

"It was. It was intense. That's why I phased her out, really. Made excuses not to meet up and so on. She didn't seem that bothered. And then that sort of coincided with Nate and I getting back on track and well, you've seen where that led."

"You got your happy ending."

She smiles. "I suppose I did, didn't I? Doesn't always feel like that when they're doing a poo on the floor in John Lewis or wanting to play picnics at three in the morning."

I laugh. She's good company. I can see why Alice opened up to her.

"Seriously, it's so much harder when you're that bit older." She sizes me up. "What are you, mid-twenties? Well, don't leave it too late would be my advice. You just don't have the energy. I was twenty-eight when I had Leo—whole different ball game."

I smile. "I'll bear it in mind. So you hadn't seen Alice since then, until when?"

She looks rocked by the memory. "About a month ago, maybe a bit less. She just turned up out of the blue. Ambushed me. Not at the house but as I was coming up to the main gates. I had the twins in the buggy. Honestly I'll never forget her face when she saw them."

"Did you feel threatened?"

She's quick to respond. "No, no, nothing like that. She just looked . . . despairing. I know it's stupid but I felt awful. Almost like I'd let her down. I know it sounds ridiculous."

"How did she know where you lived?"

A tiny vexed shake of the head. "She'd *actually* waited in the café on the main road—a few times, she told me—assuming I'd go past at some point and then she followed me."

"And what did she want?"

"I'll tell you what *I* wanted, Detective Kinsella."

"Cat, please."

"I wanted to get her away from my road, Cat. Nate was due back any minute and he didn't know anything about my forum 'adventures' and I wanted to keep it that way." Those pleading eyes again. "The whole IVF thing had nearly broken us. It was such an awful, awful time and I didn't want it all coming back up again."

I nod an understanding that I think is part-genuine.

She goes on. "So I left the twins with Leo—I said I'd left my card in Waitrose and had to go back—and I drove us to King George's Park. She was in a dreadful state, she looked awful."

"Awful, how?"

"Not scruffy exactly, but worn out. Definitely not how I remembered her. Like she'd kind of given up on life, I suppose."

"So what did she want?" I repeat.

She gives me a flat stare. "Money. She said she'd left her husband, that the IVF had finally broken them, and that she needed some time to figure out what she was doing but she couldn't support herself. It was all a bit pathetic to be honest."

Which fits, although there's something I'm struggling to get my head around.

"She needs money so she runs to someone she met for a few coffees, four years ago?"

Her eyes widen in agreement. "I know! It's mad, isn't it? But she said she remembered how kind I'd been to her back then, how supportive, and how I was probably the only person who'd understand because Nate and I had nearly reached a similar point. She said she didn't have any close family or friends she could turn to."

Which fits.

"I just felt so sorry for her. And I felt guilty. It's hard to explain to someone who hasn't been through it but I felt so wretched that she'd seen me with the twins. I know how it feels to see other people have what you want so badly. And with me being ten years older, it must have seemed doubly unfair."

"So did you give her any money?"

"I had sixty pounds in my purse and I gave her that. But I told her, and it was the truth, that I couldn't give her any more. Nate's not particularly stingy or controlling around money, but I couldn't explain away a big chunk of cash, even if I'd wanted to."

"And she was OK with this?"

"Yes, she wasn't being aggressive, if that's what you're thinking. She said she completely understood, and then she said she might have to consider going back to her husband, at least for a while, but that she was certain he was having an affair and it was all so humiliating." Her eyes are on the cusp of watery. "That pressed a nerve, you could say. Leo's *father*, if you can use the term, cheated on me and I stayed with him because I thought I had no other option at the time, and that's exactly the word for it: humiliating."

Nate Hicks and Saskia French. I feel sick for her.

She continues, "So I said—and it was impulsive and stupid, I know—she could stay at one of our properties for a bit, if that would help, and Saskia's place in King's Cross was the only realistic option if I wanted to keep it from Nate. Like we said, she's been so quiet a tenant that we almost forget she's there. Nate especially, seeing as the property's mine."

I frown. "And Saskia was fine to have a roommate all of a sudden?"

"I said she was a family friend, that it'd only be temporary and I'd reduce the rent for that month." Her mouth twists into a scowl. "Saskia knows she's on to a good thing. Do you know, I haven't upped the rent on that place in seven years and how does she repay me—by turning my property into a bloody brothel!"

"So it's true you didn't know about Saskia's . . . profession?"

She looks horrified. "God no, I didn't. I really didn't."

"Saskia must have worried about it getting back to you through Alice?" I write *motive* in my pad. "Did you have much contact with Alice once she'd moved in?"

"No, none."

"Did she have your number, email address?"

"No, I changed my email account a few years ago. We got burgled, you see. I wanted to change everything. And no, I didn't give her my number, I just wanted the least communication possible. I said if she needed to get in contact with me, let Saskia know and I'd call her."

I give her a dubious stare. "And that was it? You were going to let her stay there indefinitely?"

She brings her hands into her lap, clenches them tightly. "Well, no, initially I thought I'd leave her be for a few weeks and then see what her plans were. But then Christmas took over, and what with my dad, I didn't exactly forget about her but it took a back seat. And I wouldn't have asked her to leave just before Christmas. Bit Ebenezer Scrooge, don't you think?"

I sit forward. "Gina, we know that Alice was in the Donatella Caffé on Friday December 12th, just a few days before she died. Do you think she might have been coming to tell you about what was going on in your flat? What Saskia was up to? I mean, it's the least she could do, given the kindness you'd shown her."

"I've no idea. All I can tell you is I didn't see her. She certainly didn't come to the house, thank God." Her hand slams to her chest. "Oh my God, you don't think Saskia has anything to do with this?"

"Not necessarily," I lie, "but Saskia did lie to us. She gave us some cock-and-bull story about meeting Alice in a bar. About Alice also being a prostitute. Why would she say that?"

She thinks about this. "Well, look, I had nothing to do with that particular lie, but I did make it clear that I didn't want Nate finding out about Alice being at the flat, so whatever Saskia said, she was just trying to make sure it didn't lead back to me. As I say, she knows she's on to a good thing. Is she going to get in trouble for this? Christ, am I?"

I ignore this, let her sweat a bit longer.

"Gina, did Alice ever use the name Maryanne, either recently or when you knew her before? Saskia referred to her as Maryanne from the minute we met her whereas you knew her as Alice. Any idea why she'd have used a different name?"

"None whatsoever." She throws her hands up. "Honestly, I've told you everything I know now. And I'm so sorry that I lied, I've never had so much as a library fine in my life, but I panicked. I just wanted to stay out of it. But really, this is just horrendous and I'm devastated by it all. I keep thinking if she'd just gone back to her husband, maybe she'd still be alive." She's edging toward hysterical now, talking faster and faster. "I should have told her to go back to her husband, shouldn't I? But I was honestly just trying to do a kind thing."

"I know, I know," I say, calming her. Then to bring her back to focus, I ask, "Can you remember the names of any of these forums you visited?"

She pulls at her lip, still edgy. "No. No, I'm sorry, I can't. It just seems like a lifetime ago. And I don't have that laptop anymore or you'd have been welcome to check. The bastards took it when we were burgled."

Can't say I'm too disappointed. If Alice had been on the forums recently, Forensics would have found them.

Although she could have been using her phone.

"What happens now?" Gina leans right forward and for a second I think she's going to grab my hands but she stops about an inch short. "What happens about the fact I lied?"

Perverting the course of justice would be a long shot. I doubt it'd be considered in the public interest to waste valuable resources taking down a misguided Good Samaritan. Obstructing a police officer might fly, though. We've certainly prosecuted for less.

And yet when I look at her, all I feel is pity. Pity for a woman who tried to do a kind thing. Pity for a woman who's run ragged looking after toddlers and policing teens while her father dies slowly under her roof.

Pity for a woman whose husband sleeps with prostitutes.

I push away my pity and summon my sternest tone. "We won't do anything on this occasion, Gina. But mark my words, the threat of prosecution will be very real if I discover anything you've told me today to be false, or not the whole story, do you understand?"

Her eyes fill up and she starts searching for tissues in multiple pockets. "Thank you, Detective Kinsella. Thank you. There's nothing else, I promise you. I just want to forget this ever happened and go home to my family."

I stay seated as she gathers up her bags, pulls on her coat.

I say, "You really should speak to your husband though. Once we make an arrest and this goes to court, there's every chance we'll need you to go on record. Alice's last few weeks *will* become public knowledge and he *will* find out."

She shakes her head quickly. "No, no, I can't, he'll be so angry. If I have to in the future then so be it, but I'll cross that bridge then . . ."

I think of Nate Hicks and Saskia French. Of Saskia French performing acts that any *"self-respecting girlfriend would do if she could be both-ered."* I think of Gina's cheating ex-partner. Of the humiliation she endured.

I think about all the STDs that piece-of-shit husband has exposed her to.

"Gina, trust me, you really need to speak to your husband."

And I really need to speak to my boss.

Steele's still out charming the top brass so I download everything onto Parnell, barely coming up for air in the hope he'll be so dazzled by the speed of information that he'll forget to bollock me for not halting the interview and hauling him in.

And he doesn't bollock me. Far from it, in fact. It could be because it seems a little miserly, a little unfestive, to tear a strip off someone hours before waving them off on their hard-earned Christmas break.

It could be because he trusts me. Which makes me feel a myriad of mixed emotions, none of them particularly pleasant.

I made the right call not charging Gina, he says. However, it sounds like Saskia French might not be shown the same clemency. Her story about Maryanne working as a prostitute, especially the supposed "dodgy clients" conversation, could have sent us completely in the wrong direction—hours and hours of time wasted chasing nonexistent punters—and Parnell seems to view this in a much harsher light than Gina Hicks' omission of truth. The CPS could well agree.

But then Saskia *was* lying to protect Gina.

Maybe I should have charged her?

I make tea then Parnell and I pore over the incident board, under-lining Saskia's name in thick red marker twice—one for each secret she had to keep from Gina that Alice Lapaine could have uncovered; her affair with her husband *and* the way she was earning her living. Under instruction from Parnell, I call Saskia to arrange for her to come into the station on Monday—just a chat, nothing to worry about—but all I get is her voicemail. A clipped bored instruction to the caller to leave a message and she'll *try* to call back.

The *try* annoys me. The *"I'm-just-so-busy"* self-importance of it.

Which makes me a hypocrite as I've now had six missed calls from my sister in the past twenty-four hours.

I'm a self-aware hypocrite though. A hypocrite with a conscience.

I dial Jacqui's number and she answers within three rings.

"You called?" I say, with the heavy dose of irony that Jacqui never seems to pick up on.

"Half a dozen times, Cat. No one's that busy, not even you."

There's no nastiness there, just that big-sister righteousness that sets my teeth on edge.

"Look, I'm sorry, Jacqs, it's just . . ."

She cuts in. "Oh, I know how super-important you are so I'll be quick, don't worry. Are you coming for Christmas lunch tomorrow? Well, let me rephrase that, *you are* coming for Christmas lunch tomorrow. I just want to know what time you'll be here. Finn wants help with his Lego Batcave and me, Ash and Dad are 'rubbish' apparently."

Finn's name seals it. I take a punt that his gorgeous little face and boundless effervescence will somehow balance out the crackling animosity that always threatens to surface when my family is gathered in a confined space. Textbook equilibrium, surely.

"I'll be there," I say to Jacqui. "What time's lunch?"

"Around threeish, but that doesn't mean you turn up at two fifty-five. It'd be nice to have a proper family day for once."

My mind boggles at what she means by "proper" but I make a non-committal noise that she takes as a yes.

"Oh, and Finn will probably want to call you in the morning to tell you what Santa brought, so answer your bloody phone, please." I make an affirmative noise this time. "I don't know, Dad's getting as bad. There's definitely something going on with him."

I wish I wasn't so highly attuned to all references to my dad but there's a chink in my armor where the curiosity spews out. "What do you mean? Dad's as bad at what?"

"Answering his bloody phone! He's usually so reliable but lately . . . take last Monday . . ."

The words erupt. "Dad? Reliable?"

"Yes." That scolding voice again. "You should try seeing the good in people now and again. He's amazing to us."

"Oh really, how?" Exasperation, intrigue and a bolt of unexpected jealousy surges through me. That I manage to sound disinterested is a minor miracle.

"In a thousand different ways, Cat, but mainly with Finn. Did you know Dad stays at ours when Ash is on nights, just in case I need someone to come to the hospital with me? Well he usually does . . ."

Everything stops for a moment. "Has Finn had any more seizures? You've got the neurologist any day, right?"

"No, no, just that small one, last Monday night. It's fine. He's fine. But it was Murphy's law, Ash was on nights last Monday and Dad had to cancel staying at ours at the last minute."

"Mr. Reliable," I say without a hint of triumph.

"But that's what I mean," says Jacqui. "It's so unlike him. And I couldn't get hold of him all night either, to let him know what had happened. Voicemail, voicemail, bloody voicemail. To be fair, he was inconsolable the next day."

"And so where was he then?"

I'm starting to feel queasy. I've barely eaten today but it's not lack of food. It's something else.

"Oh, I don't know. Something came up, he said. You know I don't pry." Jacqui's voice is light and I want to shake her. Shake her and shake her and shake her until the happy-mist lifts from her eyes and she sees him for what he is. "I mean, where would anyone be on a Monday night? In bed, I suppose." She laughs awkwardly. "Whose bed is the question. Noel reckons . . ."

What "Noel reckons" fades to nothing, exactly where it belongs, and Jacqui's words fill my head. Deafening, like the peal of a warning bell.

"I mean, where would anyone be on a Monday night?"

I hear drawers opening and closing, cutlery rattling, and the familiar slam of the mammoth fridge door as Jacqui moves around her kitchen busying herself with actions so she doesn't have to stop and think about the fact that Dad put "something" before her and Finn.

I try not to think about it too. I try not to think about the question I've been repeatedly asking people throughout the ten days of this investigation.

"Where were you between eleven p.m. on Monday 15th December and five a.m. on Tuesday 16th December?"

"Something came up," he said.

1998
Monday 1st June

The Guards called at Gran's the next day while I was playing Teddy Detectives—an awesome little game whereby I gathered all my bears in a Poirot-style denouement so that the secret of Maryanne's disappearance could be dramatically revealed.

Mum said the game was "in poor taste" and wouldn't it be nicer if I learned to play draughts?

Dad said draughts was boring-as-shite and asked to join in.

My stuffed penguin metamorphosed into Gabe McShea—a well-known drunk and the last person, according to Jacqui, to see Maryanne, heading up the Long Road toward the town. Dad mimicked him perfectly, slurring his speech as he swore his innocence and lashing out with his flipper when any other teddy so much as looked in his direction.

I laughed so hard that my cheeks started to sting.

Pat Hannon took the form of Brown Bear, an ancient scraggy thing we'd found wedged between a mower and a wheelbarrow in Gran's dilapidated back shed. He smelled a bit of turpentine and his right ear wasn't long for this world, but the frayed stitching around his mouth gave Brown Bear the kind of twisted, malevolent smirk we thought perfect for our prime suspect. He reminded me of some of the men who held meetings in the back room of our pub.

And into this nonsense walked two Guards. A hefty great wardrobe of a man who plonked himself in the best chair while Gran stood crooked against the Aga, and a younger man who said very little, except "I will, yeah" to every offer of biscuits and tea.

The Big Guard picked up Brown Bear by his raggedy left paw and said, "Well, hello there, little fella," before making him dance a stupid jig on his knee. With this one silly gesture, he managed to strip Brown Bear of his ugly, threatening menace and I hated him in that moment for ruining our brilliant game.

"Do you think Teddy might know where Maryanne is?" the Big Guard said, winking at Mum and Dad, utterly charmed with himself.

I told him Teddy didn't talk to the filth and that shut him up good and proper.

Dad let out a roar, a bone-shaking belly-laugh that startled Rosie, Gran's dog.

Mum didn't look quite so amused.

"So Jacqui's name has come up," the Big Guard went on, all stern and business-like now after his failed attempt at being "good with kids." "Could we just have a quick word? Nothing formal, just a chat at this stage."

The "at this stage" seemed to irk Dad, who'd been friendly and chatty up to this point, laughing about various characters in the village with the Big Guard and ribbing the other one about a big match his Gaelic football team had thrown away at the weekend.

"Jacqui's not here," said Dad, landing another pot of tea on the table. This wasn't a lie. Jacqui'd gone AWOL since breakfast when she'd got a pasting from Mum for asking whether it'd be insensitive to go over to Maryanne's to get her Chili Peppers CD back. "But when she does get in, shall I send her up to the station for your 'quick word?' Or is O'Malley's a safer bet?"

The Big Guard glowered at Dad but said nothing.

"What?" said Dad, laughing, his face now the picture of innocence. "Isn't that where you lads drink nowadays? I tell you, they've gone awful strict on the drink-driving back in England but if an officer of the law can't have a pint or two at lunchtime, what's the world coming to, eh?"

The Big Guard laughed too. "You're very good, sir, very good." A nod toward Gran. "Quite the comedian you've got here, Agnes. He'd sell out the Royal Theatre, no bother."

Dad laughed again and I felt confused that people kept laughing at things that weren't even funny, like Noel and his stupid South Park or Dad with that barmaid in the pub.

"Just a bit of craic, Sergeant. No offense meant." Dad offered out his hand and the room held its breath. Eventually the Big Guard grabbed hold. "Rest assured, I'll send Jacqui your way as soon as she's back, although God knows when that'll be. You know how it is, we were all young once, eh."

"Ah sure, no bother, we'll speak to her when we speak to her." The Big Guard looked at his watch then stood up quickly, a bit panicked. "Mother of God, we've been here over an hour, can you believe that? Come on you," he said to the younger one, "let's not take up any more of these good folks' time."

They walked to the door but then the Big Guard stopped, seeming to change his mind about something at the last minute. "Although, while we're here, I might as well ask you, Mr. McBride—have you ever had any dealings with Maryanne Doyle yourself?"

"Dealings? No, none at all. I mean, I saw her around once or twice. In the Diner. Maybe Grogan's? But I don't know the girl, I've never spoken to her. Terrible business though, isn't it? I hope you find her. I hope she's OK."

The Big Guard opened the door a crack and the dog squeezed herself out. At school we'd learned about a panda who'd sensed an earthquake brewing in China.

Dad had said it was a well-known fact that animals had a sixth sense for disaster.

18

Happy Christmas! Get anything nice?
SMS 9:06 a.m.

Parnell
A load of flak for getting home late and a cordless hedge trimmer.
You?
SMS 9:23 a.m.

Yes. A voicemail from Aiden Doyle saying it's a shame he'll miss me in Mulderrin—he could have shown me the sights, ha ha—and would I like to go for a drink when we're both back in London? Oh, and his old fella's still hanging on, although it'd be just like the "fucker" to kick the bucket and ruin Christmas. He signs off saying *Nollaig Shona Duit*—Happy Christmas in Gaelic.

Christmas morning. People all over the country waking up to loved ones, sore heads and a mountain of hastily purchased, naff presents. Chocolate for breakfast. Booze before noon. The Dawsons are away so I have the house to myself, just the sounds of my own breath and the banging and hissing of their archaic central heating system for company. I think about turning on the TV but I quite like the silence. The calm before the inevitable storm. The eerie spell's broken though when sure enough, a little after ten, Finn calls me and in breathless, staccato delivery, lists a load of toys I've never heard of and the exact order in which we're going to play with them. He's already played Pie Face with Grandad but he's saving the rest for me.

Grandad. Such a snuggly, evocative word full of warmth and apple-pie bonhomie. It's never really suited Dad and he hated it for the first few years. Not exactly the kind of moniker that seduces the type of ladies he sets out to seduce.

Michael McBride. Handsome widower. Check.

Successful businessman. Check—if you play fast and loose with the definition of the word "business."

Manager of contemporary London bar. Check.

Grandad. Not so check.

Liar—one hundred percent check.

Dangerous?

At a socially acceptable eleven a.m., I pour myself a glass of wine, then another, and I wait for the edges to blur and for Dad's features to meld so I can't see his face.

Just the strange twist of his mouth as he smiles at Maryanne in the Diner.

The faint smudge of contempt as they row in Duffy's field.

Those groveling eyes as he tells Jacqui, "*something's come up*" and he can't stay over Monday night.

I have to do something.

I'm not sure who jumps higher, her or me.

Steele stares at me across the incident room, surprise and irritation jostling for pole position on her face. She's wearing gray slim jeans, an oversized black cardi and a faded Sonic Youth T-shirt that just about subverts everything I thought I knew about DCI Kate Steele.

"What the hell are you doing here?" she says, parking a buttock on the end of Emily's desk.

"I could ask you the same, Boss."

A wry smile. "You could, but you answer to me, m'dear, not the other way around."

"I was passing."

It's not exactly a lie. As the crow flies, the office is pretty much en route to Dad's and I've always loved walking through London on Christmas Day. The apocalyptic stillness of the place. The frost glittering on untrod paths. I'd managed to walk all the way from home—along Albert Embankment, past the London Eye and over Waterloo Bridge without encountering more than a handful of folk, each one cheerfully bidding me a Merry Christmas where just days ago we'd have ignored each other, probably startled at any form of approach. It wasn't until I'd hit Theobald's Road and a large troop spilled toward me, no doubt fresh from the service at St. George the Martyr, that I'd had to negotiate my path to make way for other people.

Steele narrows her eyes. "OK, so you were passing and you thought you'd just pop in. Why?"

"I forgot something." I stroll over to my desk, willing something to make itself obvious. There's a bottle of vodka I won in a raffle over a year ago. "I'm flat broke," I say, picking it up. "Thought I could regift this. Can't turn up to my dad's empty-handed, can I?"

She clearly doesn't believe me but she rolls with it. "Think I've got the same bottle on my desk actually. Flowers' annual tombola, right?" She stands up, ambles in the direction of her office. "Well, while you're here, we might as well have a Christmas snifter. Be a love and grab a couple of mugs."

I walk into the kitchen, pick up Parnell's Arsenal mug and another with the fewest chips. While I'm there I neck a pint of water over the sink, cursing myself for those two glasses of wine earlier.

I wipe my mouth and walk back to Steele's office.

"Shall I be mother?" she says. Steele pours and we clink mugs, each pulling the same face at the sheer awfulness of the drop. "Christ, unless your dad's your worst enemy, I wouldn't be handing over this cat's piss, Kinsella."

I should laugh. I try to but it sounds false, even to my ears.

She sits back, smirking and swiveling in her chair like a cartoon baddie. "So cut the crap, why are you really here?"

Because I feel calm and competent when I'm in this office and right now, more than ever, I need to feel calm and competent. I need to think straight.

"I told you, I'm broke, I wanted to pick up . . ."

"Rubbish. You only got paid two days ago. And do you think I'm blind? I saw the shopping bags under your desk all week."

She's like a bloody hawk but then I swear it's just with me. She didn't notice for weeks when Ben got a borderline-prohibited haircut over the summer, and Seth's foot was in plaster for two whole days before she finally thought to ask why he was limping.

On a surface level, it drives me nuts—this level of scrutiny she reserves for just me. On a deeper level, it soothes. Reminds me that I don't need to visit clairvoyants to know that someone's watching over me.

"So if you haven't got your dad a present," Steele goes on, "it's because you're disorganized or selfish. Not because you're broke."

"You sound just like my sister. She's always saying I'm disorganized. I'm not though, I just don't do what she wants, when she wants."

Steele screws her nose up. "Typical older sister. I can just about stomach mine a couple of times a year, max." I open my mouth to ask how she knows my sister's older but she shuts the subject down. "So for the third and final time, Kinsella, why are you here?"

I grin a little as if I've been caught out. "Look, I wanted to check out a burglary at the Hickses', OK?" It's not a complete lie. "I forgot to do it yesterday before I left and it was niggling at me."

She raises a toast. "Well, that's very commendable, but sometimes—only very occasionally, mind—you need to ignore those niggles and concentrate on having a life for a few days. Do you have a life?"

I look around. "Do you?"

I instantly regret saying it but she doesn't take offense. "I've got a lot more to lose than you, m'dear. It's been ten days and we still don't have one *truly* viable suspect. We haven't found any skeletons in Nate Hicks' closet yet—well, none that he hasn't told us about anyway, and he's got an alibi for the night of the murder—he was in Cardiff on business. We'll obviously try to pick holes in that, Cardiff's less than a three-hour drive but . . ." *But, it's unlikely.* "There's still Thomas Lapaine, I suppose, but Abigail What's-her-Chops is adamant he was with her all night so we need something more on him before we can even *think* about turning the screw. Unfortunately, there's a very fine line between diligence and harassment as far as the Complaints Commission's concerned, and Lapaine's got a history of complaining."

Of course—the accusation of police brutality twenty years ago. I'd forgotten about it if I'm honest. That first briefing feels like twenty years ago.

"We do have another suspect," I say, sitting up straighter. "Saskia French. *She* had a lot to lose if Alice told Gina she was running a brothel out of the fla—"

"I know, I know, I've read your report, and I agree, we definitely need to reinterview her. But look, that's enough about work, it's Christmas Day."

"So you agree, it's the strongest motive we've . . ."

"Sssh." She pulls a pretend zip across her mouth. "No work, I said."

I wait for her to take the lead because I haven't got the faintest idea what we're going to talk about. I'm hoping "no work" means we don't have to dissect my flip-out in the bedsit again but at least that would be terra firma. The only non-work conversations I've ever had with Steele have been about the stinginess of the sandwich fillings in the staff canteen and once about my shoes—a gorgeous pair of maroon suede ankle boots she couldn't believe only cost thirty pounds.

"Have you got a boyfriend, Kinsella?"

I smile over the rim of the mug. "Nope. Why, do you know someone? I like them over six feet and preferably not still living at home, if that narrows it down."

She takes another sip of vodka, winces as it hits her gullet. "And do you want a family?"

"Have you been talking to Gina Hicks?"

"Eh?"

"Oh nothing, it's just she started going on at me about not leaving things too late. I'm only twenty-six, for crying out loud. That's practically teenage today!"

"I'm not saying you *should* start a family, I'm asking, do you want one? Or a husband, or a life partner, or whatever the correct term is these days if you're not the marrying kind."

"To be honest, Boss, I don't know what shade I want my hair at the moment, so I think I'm going to have to plead the fifth on the bigger questions."

She leans forward, pours the remainder of her vodka into a vase of orchids.

"I'd have liked kids, you know. Never thought I did, but when you get older you see things a bit differently." She pauses for a second—not sad, just reflective. "But it was the right decision, I'm sure of that. I couldn't have got to where I am *and* had kids, it wouldn't have been fair."

I'm enthralled but also slightly embarrassed. This woman-to-woman thing is new territory.

"What I'm trying to tell you, Kinsella, is that it's true you can't have it all but you *can* have *some* of it. You don't have to become the dysfunctional cliché. I've made damn sure I haven't." She holds a hand up, halts my obvious observation. "And yes, I know I'm sitting in this bloody office on Christmas morning, drinking cat's-piss vodka like something out of a Raymond Chandler novel, *but*, I have a lovely man waiting for me at home with a bottle of wine, a four-course lunch and if he knows what's good for him, the Mulberry clutch that I've been dropping hints about since April. So you see, I never did the whole two-point-four kids thing but I do have a wonderful marriage. It is possible."

I nod politely. I can't think of what else to do.

Steele keeps lobbying hard. "This job doesn't have to be your life, Cat. I've got nieces and nephews I see regularly. Fantastic friends. I've got two chickens *and* a greenhouse." She laughs at my shocked face. "Ah see, you thought I was being lazy pouring the vodka into that vase, didn't you? Well, it's good for them, keeps them fresh. And it's all that bloody vodka's good for." I laugh too and it fires her on. "What else? I go to a book club sometimes—bet you didn't know that. Granted, they get a bit narked when they're discussing themes and imagery and I haven't got past chapter two but I try." She folds her arms. "What I'm saying, Kinsella, is you should try to have a life that doesn't involve death."

Maybe I will meet Aiden Doyle for that drink.

I stand up abruptly, banging my knees on the desk. "Look Boss, thanks for the pep talk and all that but I better crack on. My sister will flip out if I don't get there soon and I do want to check out that burglary at the Hickses.'"

"No need," she shoots back. "I've already done it. Fourteenth September 2014. Mainly gadgets, a few bits of jewelry, some silverware." A pause. "Who even has 'silverware'?"

Of course she's already done it. Kate Steele—green-fingered, bookwormish, chicken-owning DCI Extraordinare is always one step ahead.

I reckon she'd have made a great mum.

19

Christmas Day at McAuley's Old Ale House.

Opening for two hours over lunch and badgering old men, who only normally removed their caps for funeral corteges and the Irish national anthem, to don metallic paper hats and play whatever sappy board game I'd got from Santa. Beating Reg at Hungry Hungry Hippos then wiping the floor with Sligo Tom at Buckaroo. Mum and Dad flat-out serving, not watching me close enough. Getting bloated on fizzy pop then leaving half my lunch.

Mum getting angry and Dad getting blamed.

Opening up again in the evening. A younger crowd this time. Dad's friends and their lesser-spotted wives, drenched in new musky perfumes and flaunting new bling.

Being sent to bed but then creeping back down. Sitting on the stairs and watching all the dancing, the laughing, the fighting, the crying.

McAuley's isn't opening today.

All part of Jacqui's "proper family day" treaty, no doubt. A treaty I've already flouted by turning up ten minutes before lunch.

Dad snares me at the kitchen door. The attention's suffocating and feels more like a chokehold than a bear hug. It also seems a little left-field given the last time I saw him I accused him of sleeping with Mary-anne Doyle. I'd expected him to be civil, of course. Maybe to feign a little affection even, if only for Finn's sake. But there's an intensity to the way he's holding me, the way he's breathing me in like I'm a newborn.

I daren't breathe him in. He reeks of something awful—a chemical lemony scent, like bug spray.

Jacqui, flushed from the kitchen, clocks my face. "Yeah, I know, it's disgusting. It's called Silver Man. Finn chose it."

"Because Grandad's got silver hair," says Finn, hugging my thigh as tight as a tourniquet.

Dad looks down, ruffles his hair. "Yeah, thanks for reminding me, champ." A bit quieter. "I'll wash it off in a bit, he probably won't notice."

Which is probably true. He certainly never notices that Auntie Cat and Grandad Mike barely say two words to each other.

"Drink?" asks Dad, loosening his grip and easing me out of my coat. "We have red, white, Prosecco, Aperol . . ."

"That was my choice," shouts Jacqui, her head practically swallowed by the oven. "Apparently it's all the rage in Australia."

"So's skin cancer." Noel's voice lurks behind the kitchen door. I should probably peer around and offer some kind of festive pleasantry but I'm loath to wish him a Happy Anything.

"Wrong actually," says Jacqui. "The Aussies are a lot more sun-savvy than us Brits."

"A white wine, please," I say to Dad, keeping it civil but clipped.

I follow the sounds of Finn whooping at *Super Mario* and find myself standing in the living room. It's less stark in here than the rest of the flat and my face smiles down at me from every surface.

Soaked on the log flume at Alton Towers.

Decked out like a fat fairy for my Holy Communion—a pair of rosary beads in one hand, a packet of Haribo gummy bears in the other.

Me and Jacqui dressed up as witches for Halloween.

That one kills me. We both look so happy and so, so pleased with ourselves in our cute little costumes that it makes me want to weep. It makes me want to go into the kitchen and tell her that I'm truly sorry I didn't get here earlier like she wanted.

But I don't. I've only got the strength for one argument today.

Jacqui's done a stellar job, right down to the gingerbread men garnishes bobbing away at the top of our champagne flutes. Dad sits at the head of the table—perfectly decorated in reds, greens and golds—and I position myself two seats away. Ash stations himself in between, happy to play the human firewall.

And it's OK for a while.

Tolerable, at least.

Ash keeps things interesting with a story about a colleague whose girlfriend jilted him at the altar twice, over two consecutive Christmases, and wonderful Finn acts like a prism, casting rainbows among the rumbling black clouds. The food's complicated enough to warrant long, time-killing explanations from Jacqui about how it came to be on the table. And the crackers are fun, I suppose. I win a giant paperclip.

"So you're working on that case—the Doyle girl, right?"

It's Noel that brings it up. Whatever happens now, I can always point to the fact that it was Noel, *not* me, who tore open the can of worms and dumped them all over the Christmas table.

"There's a lot of people working on it," I say, flatly.

"Have you arrested anyone?" he says, eyes glinting. "It's usually the husband, isn't it? Bet it's the husband."

"Can we talk about something else?" I tap Jacqui with my foot under the table. "Hey, have you still got that Saturday girl in the shop, Jacqs, the one with the crazy eyebrows?"

She taps me back, a little harder. "Ah, come on, Cat, give us the scoop. We knew her, for God's sake!'

Dad stares blankly but there's a microscopic flutter in his eye—the kind of thing you only notice when you know someone inside out. When you're alert to every slight mood shift.

"Well, I suppose we didn't *know* her." Jacqui loads more carrots onto Finn's plate—a futile endeavor. "I remember her though, I hung about with her a few times. You probably don't remember Cat, you were only a kid."

"I do, actually." I look straight at Dad. "She was gorgeous. You'd hardly forget her in a hurry."

Jacqui laughs, elbows Noel. "Do you remember, Geri had just left the Spice Girls and Cat reckoned Maryanne was going to replace her, that's why she'd disappeared."

I don't remember this at all, not one misty memory of ever saying that. And I'd have staked my life on being able to recount every single thing that happened that day.

What other details could I be missing?

Noel grunts. "Didn't think she was that fit actually. Average, I'd say."

Ash laughs. "Oh, you've turned down better, have you?"

"Too right I have, mate. You want to see some of the Spanish women, some of the dancers at the club." He kisses the tips of his fat gnarly fingers. "*Precioso*."

"Very good, Noel," I say, giving him a slow handclap. "That the sum of your Spanish? Not a lot of need for prolonged conversation where you work, I suppose."

"Oh, I get by," he says, smiling savagely. "How about *Que te jodan*? That means 'Fuck you.'"

"Noel!" yelps Jacqui, looking at Finn.

"That's ENOUGH."

It's not Dad's tone that shocks, it's the fact he's spoken at all. He hasn't made a sound since we sat down other than to laugh halfheartedly at Finn's cracker joke.

Noel plays the innocent. "Enough what? She said she didn't want to talk about her job so I'm just telling her about mine."

Finn asks to get down from the table. I wait until he's out of earshot and safely goggle-eyed in front of *Super Mario* before I speak.

"I'll tell you something about my job, Noel. I'm going to Mulderrin on Monday. How's about that?" Dad puts his fork down, pushes his chair away from the table. For a second I think he's going to walk out but he's just lost his appetite. "I'm looking forward to it actually," I say, hitting my stride. "It'll be nice to go back after all this time. Why did we never go back there, Dad?"

Dad tops up his wineglass, avoiding my eyes. "On holiday, you mean? Wasn't Florida good enough for you, sweetheart? Couldn't the Maldives hold a candle to Mulderrin, no?"

Jacqui laughs, that shrill *keep-the-peace* laugh that's become second nature.

I shrug. "Just always seemed a bit unfair to me. We saw Nan and Grandpa all the time. Why did you never take us back to see Gran again?"

He knows the subtext. He knows where this is heading but he's not ready to draw weapons.

And so he tries humor.

"Listen to her," he says, flicking his head toward me and smirking at Jacqui and Noel. "Always with the why, why, why. Same as when she was a kid, used to drive us all mad. '*Why are flats called flats when they're not flat, they're high?*'"

Jacqui laughs. "'*Why do we have chins? Why's water wet?*'"

I nudge the conversation back. It's a sharp vicious nudge. "Auntie Carmel told me Mum wanted to be buried in Mulderrin but you wouldn't have it. I doubt Hatfield Road Cemetery held a candle to Mum's birthplace."

"Since when have you and Carmel been so pally?" Dad sneers.

"For years," I lie. "We've got similar interests. Similar likes and dislikes."

We both like the act of disliking Dad.

He stiffens. "It's none of Carmel's business, anyway. I wanted your mum near me, Cat, not in another bloody country."

Jacqui gives a small wistful mew, reaches across for Dad's hand.

"Shouldn't it have been about Mum's wishes though," I say, "not doing what suits you? I mean, when did you even last visit her grave?"

He meets my eyes for the first time. "Yesterday, actually. Tidying up the flowers I'd left earlier in the week. You?"

"On her birthday."

A tiny smile but there's no satisfaction in it. "Right. So five months ago then."

Jacqui cuts in, light and airy, willfully ignoring the storm that's brewing. "Lots of people don't like the ritual, Dad. It's a personal thing." She squeezes his hand tighter. "Although I'm with you, I like to visit Mum regularly. I think it's a mark of respect. A mark of honor."

Her cloying tone needles me. "I honored Mum in life, Jacqs, I think that's more important, don't you?" I tilt my head, mock inquisitive. "Dad, is that why you go to Mum's grave so much? To make up for all the shit . . ."

His fist on the table is loud and final. A glass of wine topples and the dark ruby stain spreads ominously across the tablecloth. Jacqui jumps to attention, relieved to have something practical to focus on. Noel sits back and returns my slow handclap, barely concealed amusement dancing across his face.

Dad stands up, chin high, shoulders squared, and walks out of the kitchen.

Out of the flat.

Clearly I'm not proud of myself but I'd be lying if I said I felt shame. Finn didn't notice and that's the only thing that matters to me, really. While I'd never intentionally set out to hurt Jacqui, her mealy mouthed insistence on sticking to this Dad-of-the-Year fantasy makes her collateral damage as far as I'm concerned and maybe it'd be for the best if I did push her away for good. She and Finn are the only ties that bind me to Dad, the physical ties anyway.

The emotional ties have the elasticity of spider silk. A tensile strength comparable with steel.

Much later, I see Dad in the kitchen, standing over the sink and staring out of the window into the semidarkness. He's smoking, taking long luxurious draws, every inhale as sacred and fulfilling as a silent prayer. He turns his head slightly when he hears me and there's a sly twitch at the corner of his mouth that says he's been expecting me. There's no corrosive energy, just an air of sad inevitability. A sense that it was always heading here.

Just me, him and the sliver of the moon lighting the rooftops of north London.

I sit at the table.

"Where'd you go?"

"Out." It's an inane icebreaker and he knows it. "Just say what you have to say, Catrina."

On the outside I think I'm doing an OK impression of calm but inside my body's gone rogue. Heart racing, head pounding, fingers tingling. Panic attack 101. Something stops me from being completely consumed by it, though.

A purpose.

I take a small shaky breath. "You told the Guards you didn't know Maryanne Doyle. Why did you lie?"

If I'm expecting catharsis, it doesn't come. If anything I feel worse.

"I didn't know her." He sounds calm, almost relieved. As if he was expecting much, much worse.

"You did, Dad. We picked her up in the car. She was hitchhiking."

"Did we? I must have picked up twenty hitchers that holiday, the place was rife with them back then. It was the only way some people got to work." Over his shoulder, "Maybe we did, I honestly don't remember."

I sit up straight, anchor myself. "It was only a few days before she went missing. You'd have remembered then, when the Guards asked you, even if you don't remember now."

He gives me that look. The one that says I'm the apple of his eye and the bane of his life and his world would be a whole lot easier if he didn't love me so much. I've been staring down that look for so long now, I recognize it even in his blurred reflection.

"I'll tell you what I do remember, sweetheart. I had forty stolen mobile phones stashed under Gran's dresser, two feet away from where that fat fucking Guard had planted himself, and all I cared about was keeping him talking, keeping his eyes pointing forward, you know?" He turns around, offers his wrists across the kitchen floor. "So go on then, arrest me if you want. Historical handling of stolen goods, is that a thing? Because if it isn't, we don't have anything else to talk about."

For one soaring, luminous second I let myself believe him. He's just Michael McBride, your average dodgy London geezer with his stash of knocked-off phones and his cockney heart of gold who can't resist helping out the odd honest, hardworking hitcher. And if they're pretty, hard-working hitchers, well what's a man to do?

And it'd all sound so feasible if I hadn't seen what I'd seen.

"You were with her in Duffy's field, Dad, a day or two after we'd picked her up. I heard you arguing. You implied she was blackmailing you."

He sways a little, like a boxer seeing stars, riding out a blow to the head. All his questions collide at once. "But how did you . . . why didn't you . . . I mean, what the hell were you doing there?"

I give it to him straight. "I followed you. You were hardly ever around and I missed you. And I was bored," I add cheaply, to sour the sentiment. "Jacqui and Noel were off doing whatever. Mum was always busy with Gran. I had nothing to do, so I followed you. I thought it was a great game."

If I was prone to arrogance I'd say he looks impressed, although by what, I'm not sure. The eight-year-old me with the keen ear and the sharp eye? Or the grown-up me who's kept his secret hidden for so long?

He stubs out his cigarette, lights up another. Takes a seat straight across from me, settling in for the duel.

"So?" I say, chin high. "Why were you with her in that field?"

His answer is a long plume of smoke but I see his eyes wavering through the trails, weighing things up, charting the path of least resis-tance. He doesn't speak for a long time. The fridge hums in the back-ground and there's raucous canned laughter from a distant TV. He takes another deep draw of his cigarette and during the long inhalation, he seems to make a decision about something.

My stomach churns as I wait for the exhale.

"It was your mum's fault."

I recoil like I've been slapped. Actually, scrap that—like I've been headbutted.

He backtracks. "Well, OK, maybe that's unfair. It was your mum's idea though."

Fault. Idea. The interchange of words means nothing.

Mum?

"Maryanne was a wild one. A bad influence on Jacqui. She'd given her some weed, you see, and your mum found it in her pocket, completely lost the plot." He shrugs. "She told me to put the hard word on Maryanne, threaten her with the Guards if she didn't steer well clear of Jacqui."

I think of fourteen-year-old Jacqui, of that sweet leafy scent that had hung off her for months, long before she encountered Maryanne Doyle. And then I think of Mum, her warrior-like approach to protecting her kids. She'd have had no qualms about tackling Maryanne Doyle herself. She'd have relished it, in fact. It doesn't make sense.

And nor does another thing.

"So why didn't Mum say all this when the Guards came around? I mean, it could have been relevant, a drugs slant. There's no way Mum would have held that back, not when a girl was missing."

He rolls his eyes. "Yeah, because your mum was faultless, Catrina. A real modern-day saint." He knows it's a low blow, I don't bother pointing it out. "She was protecting Jacqui, I suppose. Weed was still a big deal back then and there was no way your mum was going to drop Jacqui in the shit, didn't matter who'd gone missing." His face softens. "That's what you do when you're a parent, sweetheart. You protect your own kids first and sod all the rest. It's just the way it is and your mum was no different."

Protecting Jacqui, or protecting Dad?

The latter's too dire to contemplate so I quickly file it under "no go" in the locked box in my brain—the place where I stash the taboo stuff, emotions I can't bring myself to cope with.

"So why the secret meeting in Duffy's field? Why didn't you go to her house? Have a quiet word in the Diner?"

Eyes wide. "Are you joking? If I'd gone to the house, Jonjo Doyle would have put her in hospital, and I'd have been in the next bed. And I didn't go to the Diner because"—he blows out his cheeks, thinks for a minute—"well, I don't know why, to be honest, it was eighteen fucking years ago, I can't remember every last detail. I saw her having a cheeky smoke in the field one day as I was passing and I took my chance, that's all."

I know that's not true. He was meeting her there. I know it on a bone-deep, intuitive level but if being a detective's taught me anything, it's that it's not worth fighting over points you can't prove.

I nod slowly. "OK, so that's why you were threatening her. But you accused her of threatening you. You said the word 'blackmail.'"

He lets out a laugh, a quick scornful breath. "Christ, did I really say that? It was hardly blackmail. It was just a seventeen-year-old girl thinking she was the Mata Hari of Mulderrin and wanting me to know about it."

Which explains nothing. My face tells him as much.

He pulls in a bit closer, every bit the cozy raconteur with the juicy anecdote, not the man teetering on the edge of "suspect." "So I said exactly what your mum told me to say, right. 'Stay away from Jacqui or we'll tell the Guards about your dirty little habit.'" He pauses, gives me a look that I can't quite read. "And then she—Maryanne—says, 'Well maybe *you* should stay away from Tina McGinn, or I'll tell your wife about *your* dirty little habit.'"

I'll process that anger later. "Right, so she was blackmailing you?"

He flicks a hand, dismissive. "Well, she was trying, bless her, but there was absolutely nothing going on between me and Tina McGinn and she knew it. She was just a barmaid in Grogan's who'd flirt with her own shadow and she must have seen us having the craic a few times. Tina knew your mum, for God's sake, it was all bullshit." My face says "*yeah yeah*" but I keep it buttoned. "So anyway, I said to Maryanne, 'You can put an announcement in the parish newsletter for all I care, darling, just stay away from my daughter, OK.' Best thing you can do with people like her, just call their bluff." Another pause. "And that was that, really. She piped down after that."

He grinds out his cigarette. Story concluded.

And they all lived miserably ever after.

I feel like I'm floundering, losing leverage. I need to pull myself up, draw myself back level but I can't find anything to hook onto. Plausible lie after plausible lie, Dad's dismantling everything I've ever believed, and even if I don't believe half of what he's telling me, there isn't a lot I can say. The only two people who can contradict him are dead.

And so I ask the unthinkable.

"Where were you last Monday night, Dad?"

His head jerks back, utter confusion. "What?"

"The night Maryanne was killed. Jacqui said you were supposed to be staying at hers but that you canceled and that's really unlike you. She reckons she couldn't get hold of you all evening as well, your phone was off." I swallow quickly, keep going. "So what came up, Dad? What was so life-or-death that you couldn't put your 'precious' kids first?"

Confusion contorts into anger. Panic and anger. "Where are you going with this?"

I lean back, lengthening the distance between us. "I'll tell you exactly where I'm going. A girl blackmails you, threatens you, whatever you want to call it. She goes missing, you *lie* about knowing her to the Guards, and then eighteen years later she turns up dead, less than five minutes from your door and around the same time that you go inexplicably off the radar."

I'm going with conspiracy over coincidence. Sod Parnell and his "rare breed."

"Did you hurt her, Dad?"

The words burst out of me, flailing and unfettered, and in that moment I know it's over. Any hopes for the future, all nostalgia for the past, obliterated with one unutterable accusation.

"What the fuck is this?" His face slowly twists in pure undiluted disgust. "I mean, who the fuck are you?" He bangs the side of his head. "You're not right up here, sweetheart. Your mind's diseased. *You're* a disease."

It takes a second to realize I'm crying.

When I was little, Dad used to say he'd rather go blind than see his baby girl cry. No sooner would my knee hit the concrete or my pacifier hit the floor than he was scooping me up, making it all better, stemming the flow with kisses and wild promises.

I want him to stem the flow now. To make it all better with just one rock-solid alibi.

"Just tell me where you were." I press my fingers into my eyes. "Tell me where you were last Monday night and I'll stop all this, I promise. We can start again. Have a proper relationship. No more fighting . . ."

Something flickers in his eyes, something like longing. But it's just that; a mere flicker.

"I'll tell you nothing. I don't answer to you, Catrina, remember that."

I blink hard. "As a daughter, maybe not. But as a police officer, you should really think about it."

His eyes flash dark, almost black. "And unless you're arresting me, you should really think about getting out of my fucking house."

20

"Did you have a nice Christmas?" she asks.

I wonder what a nice Christmas means to Dr. Allen. A houseful of emotionally balanced relatives, effortlessly adapting to the radical shifts in daily routine with humor and good grace? Friends happily discussing their feelings between courses, sipping moderate and responsible amounts of alcohol and only eating until they're satisfactorily full?

I attempt a smile. "Not bad, thanks. You?"

Her nose wrinkles. "Oh, quiet," she says, softly. "Peaceful."

Which sounds just peachy but could be her way of saying it was bitterly lonely and crushingly dull. We all have our own stories to frame.

I'd had an OK Boxing Day, all things considered. An empty house. Curtains closed. Heating cranked up to Caribbean setting. Just me, chocolate and enough weed to guarantee a twenty-four-hour moratorium on dark feelings. I'd switched my phone off after Jacqui's third call. Ignored the front door when it buzzed sometime in the late afternoon. Didn't even peer out to see who it was. The only contact I'd attempted with the outside world all day was to try Saskia French's phone again but got no joy there. A fairly joyless day all round, I suppose, but as Dr. Allen said it was "quiet." "Peaceful."

"You're off somewhere?" says Dr. Allen, looking at my wheelie case. "A short break before the New Year?"

"No, no, it's work." I spot an escape hatch. "Actually, is it OK if we finish a bit early today? I'm cutting it fine for my flight as it is."

"Of course. What time's a bit early?"

I push my luck. "In about ten minutes?"

She arches an eyebrow, writes something down quickly. It can't be more than one word.

Liar?

Futile?

Stoned?

She puts the pad to one side, it wobbles precariously on the arm of the chair and I will it to fall off. A burst of activity to liven up the routine.

"So"—she looks at me hopefully—"things must be going well if you're being sent off on international assignments."

"Yeah, or you could look at it another way. Steele's sending me off on pointless day trips to keep me out of the way."

A tilt of the head. "Is it pointless?"

I shrug. "It's background stuff. And when we've got a possible suspect coming into view—someone *I* identified—it just feels a bit lower-league, that's all."

She lifts her hands, palms forward. "Well, clearly I don't know the ins and outs of the case but I think it means she trusts you to operate alone, and that's a good thing."

"It means she trusts me to keep my passport up to date, that's about all."

"Come on, is that really what you think?"

My head's still a bit woolly from the weed and I haven't got the sharpness to fight. "No, probably not," I concede with a sigh. "Anyway, I'm only going to Ireland, is that classed as international?"

She smiles. "Your family's Irish, aren't they?"

"Yep. My dad's second generation but my mum was born there, she was from the west coast."

"A beautiful place, I hear." Eyes slanted. "You said she 'was.'"

"Yeah, she died a few years ago. Actually, it was five years ago. Is that still considered 'a few years?' Feels like yesterday to me."

"I'm sorry to hear that, Cat. There's never a good time to lose a parent, of course, but you were, what?"

"Twenty-one. The year before I joined the Met."

She shuffles in her chair, instantly piqued. "Are those two things connected?"

Oh, on so many levels that I can't even go there. Craving a new family, a new sense of belonging when the only person I felt I ever belonged to had gone. Finally having the freedom to *totally* fuck with Dad's head, now that I didn't have to worry about Mum's censure.

I opt for telling a part-truth. "There's probably some connection, yeah. The world seems a scarier place when your mum's not in it. I suppose by joining the police, I thought I could make it less scary."

"For you or for other people?"

Good question.

"For both, I think."

She nods, steeples her fingers. "What else do you get out of your job?"

Another decent question and far more preferable to our first half hour when every question centered around how I was feeling, how I was sleeping, how I did nothing wrong in that bedsit and so on and so on.

This time I go with a whole truth. "I get firsthand reassurance that the rules work."

Dr. Allen loves an abstract statement, delights in them like a kitten with a ball of wool. "Well that's a very interesting way of putting it, Cat. What do you mean? What rules?"

"I've just always had a bit of an obsession with fairness, I suppose. Take school, for example, if the wrong kid ended up getting blamed for something, it'd really upset me. Like, *really*. And God, if someone got a bigger slice of cake than me, there'd be blue murder—but then I always had to make sure that I didn't have a bigger slice than anyone else either."

"Fairness." Dr. Allen chews the word over. "So you're talking about justice?"

I laugh. "Justice? That's a bit of a lofty goal. I'll settle for the basic rule that says bad people get punished."

A glance of recognition, things clicking into place. "But the rules didn't work for Alana-Jane and her mother though, did they? Her father's still walking free. No one's been punished for that. Is that why you find it so tough to deal with?"

"He will be punished. One way or another." And I really do believe that. One look at my dad's face as he realized his "baby" believed he could actually be a killer has given me new perspective on the word "punishment."

The most devastating punishments aren't always the legal ones.

Dr. Allen leans forward. "What's the difference between punishment and justice, Cat?"

This doesn't take me long. "Punishment's tangible. It's something that's actually meted out. Justice isn't tangible, it's just a feeling that things are as they should be."

"And is that important to you?"

"Of course it is," I reply. "That's like asking a cleaner if bleach is important to him."

A tiny thin-lipped smile. "Well yes, it's just that some of the officers I see struggle with the idea of true justice. I'd go as far as to say they don't think it exists."

"Well, I bloody hope it does, because if it doesn't, we might as well all become cleaners. At least what they do *is* tangible, it's something people actually need—the crap removed out of their lives." I ponder that for a second. "Although maybe that is part of what I do. And you," I add.

She seems to like this answer. "So do you think we have removed some crap together, Cat? How are you feeling?"

I check the clock. Time to go.

21

There's nothing quite like a turbulent flight sat next to a hysterical first-time flyer to temporarily distract you from your own mental chaos and I'm grateful for both as we judder to the ground at Knock airport, battling a stubborn crosswind.

"Hurricane Something-or-other," says retired ex-sergeant Bill Swords, tossing my case into the boot of his seen-better-days Volvo. "We always cop the tail-end here. Rap music and fierce winds, that's America's gift to the west coast of Ireland."

When Swords said he'd pick me up, I assumed it was some sort of professional courtesy, however it turns out that retired ex-sergeant Bill Swords is now a taxi driver and it'll cost seventy euro to take me, thanks very much. He's an interesting sight, that's for sure. Tracksuit trousers paired with shiny black work brogues. A green Aran sweater with the sleeves rolled up.

No coat. They build them hardy in this part of the world.

He informs me this is my interview slot. He has to bring a stag do to Westport as soon as he drops me off and then he's flying to Lanzarote tomorrow for a blast of winter sunshine and "a few rounds of the ol' golf." I bite back telling him that it might have been nice to have known that before and instead I silently riffle through my bag for my interview apparatus—my pad, a pen, the file, etc. Swords entertains himself by passing comment on just about every other person's driving ability and singing along to *Sounds of the Sixties*. I wait for the last chorus of "You Don't Have to Say You Love Me" before I start.

An unprofessional courtesy, you might say.

"So did you ever wonder about what happened to Maryanne, Bill?"

In a flash, his face changes—deadly serious—and his answer is instant. "Wondered, yes. Worried, no. People go missing all the time, Cat. Honestly, you wouldn't believe the number of folk who say they're popping out for the paper and then, poof"—he takes both hands off the steering wheel—"never seen again. It's unusual, right enough, but it's not uncommon and unless we have evidence of foul play, or unless it's *completely* out of character, which it wasn't in the Doyle girl's case, there's not a lot we can do." He stops for a second, gives the finger to a speed freak flying out of a side road. "Anyways, I spoke to the people who knew her best, put the wind up them a bit, but they all kept saying the same thing—well, apart from the father and the brother but then it's the family who normally know *the least* about someone—everyone else kept saying it didn't surprise them one bit that she'd took off."

I nod. Fickle as I am, I decide I quite like Bill Swords—even if seventy euro does seem a bit steep for a forty-minute journey in a rust bucket of a car that smells faintly of feet—and I'm given to thinking I might have been a bit hasty in my assessment of him. While nothing he's said particularly differs from the words he committed to paper eighteen years ago, face-to-face it seems less half-arsed and dispassionate, leaving me wondering if I'd really have done anything different.

"So are you stopping long?" he asks.

"Afraid not. I'm on the fifteen-forty back to Gatwick tomorrow." I glance at the clock on the dashboard. "I've got twenty-four hours."

Swords hits the steering wheel, delighted. "That's what they say in the movies, isn't it? You know, the angry lieutenant giving out to the detective: 'You've got twenty-four hours or you're off the case, goddammit.'" He laughs to himself, bouncing in his seat. "'You've got twenty-four hours or I'm having your badge!'"

He's kind of infectious, I can't help but smile. "Yeah, well, it might come to that yet, Bill."

He screws his face up. "And sure, what are you doing here then, loveen? 'Tis London that finished that girl off, nothing to do with Mulderrin."

I trot out the party line. "Maybe, maybe not. Maybe she was in contact with someone and they can tell us something? Maybe she asked them not to say anything but now she's dead, they might? I don't know, Bill, clutching at straws is better than sitting around scratching our heads."

He's not convinced. "Something like that'd get out around Mulderrin, I don't care how much someone said they'd keep it a secret. This isn't London, Cat. You might be able to run across Piccadilly Circus, naked as the day you were born and no one'd pay a blind bit of notice, but around here, if your washing's out too long, folk start to speculate. Secrets are just gossip you haven't been drunk enough to spill yet, you know?" I must look despairing because he suddenly changes his tune. "Ah sure, you never know, I suppose. What harm will it do talking to folk . . ."

I open the file, take out the list of names. "So given I don't have a lot of time, who's still knocking around? Who should I prioritize?"

Swords laughs. "You'll have plenty of time, loveen. Half of them have gone to meet their maker, the Lord have mercy on them. Another good few emigrated. We've got Mulderrians in the US of A, a few Down Under. One in Papua New Guinea, of all places!" He seems to find this riotously funny and for that same infectious reason, so do I. "Colette Durkin's still around but, God love her, the lift wouldn't be going to the top floor, if you know what I mean. A few fries short of a Happy Meal."

I strike a line through "CD." "What's wrong with her?"

He tuts. "Ah sure, what's wrong with anyone? Depression, I suppose. Anxiety—isn't that what they call it nowadays?"

"Lot of it about, Bill."

"Well, not near me, thank Christ. I finished me thirty years in 2012, got me pension, bought this car, and now I have a grand old time driving about the place, listening to the radio, having the craic with folk. And a few pints at the weekend o' course."

Sold. I wonder if he wants an apprentice.

"Anyways," he goes on, "the only two you need bother your head talking to are Manda Moran and Hazel Joyce. Now the three of them were *very* cozy. Manda Moran's still Manda Moran. Never did marry, God love her, but she has a B&B behind St. Benedict's. Does well, I think. A great girl, altogether. Hazel Joyce's now Hazel O'Keefe, I think. She lives in the next village up."

For no other reason, other than my kamikaze tendencies, I look down at the file and say, "Oh look, how funny, there's a Kinsella! No relation of mine, ha ha."

His face pinches. "Now why in God's name would I have questioned Agnes Kinsella?" He thinks for a minute. "Ah, I know, she'd relatives over from England. One of the kids was sorta pally with the Doyle one."

"The McBrides?" I say, casually, just shooting the breeze.

"If you say so, I forget their names. Ah now, Agnes Kinsella, she was a nice woman. Decent sort. She died, oh, it must be ten years ago now."

Eleven years. I had my GCSE Double Science exam so I couldn't go to her funeral and only Mum ended up going in the end. Dad had to work for "Uncle" Frank at the last minute. Work that involved flying to Rotterdam and back in a day.

Mum seemed to placidly accept it. I raged for months.

"Here we are," Swords says, nodding toward the road ahead. "Didn't take long now, did it?"

We drive into Mulderrin up the Long Road, a narrow winding track flanked by tall blackthorn hedges and gray drystone walls. Red and gold balloons, starting to wither and deflate, are tied in clusters to the ash trees that still border Duffy's field.

"Big wedding last weekend," explains Swords in a crabby tone. "Children starving in Syria and they spent €2,500 on flowers, can you believe that? Plain scandalous."

As we get closer to the town, the sign comes into view— "**MULDERRIN**" written in austere black lettering. I'd have sworn there was a "Welcome to . . ." back in the day but that could be me over-sentimentalizing. Embellishing the facts, the way memories often do. There's an instruction to drive carefully that I don't think was there before. And a twinning with a town in Brittany—some lucky local dignitary quaffing Chablis at the taxpayers' expense, no doubt. The houses look newer and it feels like there's twice as many. Huge great piles with twin garages and pillared porches, monuments to the time when the Celtic Tiger was still having its tummy tickled and ostentation was de rigueur.

The town square's empty. Just a few stationary cars and a lone old man creeping along the footpath with a stoop and a tin of dog food. The Diner's called something else—we pass it quickly and I don't catch the name—and Mrs. Riley's is now a Londis.

There's also a bookie's, three pubs and a funeral parlor.

Somewhere to eat, somewhere to shop, somewhere to bet, drink and die.

A blueprint for a life simply lived.

My B&B's about a kilometer outside the town. Swords insists on helping me with my tiny case and introducing me to the owner, a tall woman with a bad bleach-job that's left her hair the color of turned milk. Before he sets off, he gives me the lay of the land.

"Now, if you're wanting a drink, you'll have to wait awhile. They don't open till late, although if you've a real thirst on, you could probably give Grogan's a bang. Matty Grogan'd be likely to open up for the likes of you." He gives me a wink, and a gentle tap on the forearm. "Well, ta-ta then, Cat Kinsella. Take care of yourself, loveen . . ."

It's unexpected—unexpected and self-indulgent—but for one clear second, as I watch Swords pull away, I feel a calm sense of restoration being back in Mulderrin. A return to who I once was. A quirky, trusting eight-year-old with a head full of greasy curls and a mouth full of wobbly teeth, and almost certainly wearing a Pokemon T-shirt.

Mum's still alive and fussing around Gran.

Jacqui's still someone I aspire to be like.

Noel's still Noel. Just slimmer and with bad acne.

Dad's still my hero and all's right with the world.

Ignoring Swords' advice to take care of myself, much later, after the wind's died down and I've eaten a home-cooked stew, I take a dark and perilous amble up to Gran's old house, using just the light of my phone to chart my half-remembered course. Heading back down the Long Road, I turn right at Duffy's gate, doubling back on myself when it becomes apparent I should have gone the other way, and then past the field where Pat Hannon kept his cows. This brings me out at the foot of the Pot-Holey Road, otherwise known as the Road Where Gran Lives.

Or now to my mind, the Road Where I Was Last Truly Happy.

Gran's house hasn't changed, not in an obvious way. It's still small, pebble-dashed white and with that stone slate roof that Kinsella clans carefully maintained for well over a century. But now there's a satellite dish fixed to the front. A child's trampoline where there should be a chicken coop. The paint's definitely fresher. The windows look brand-new.

Through thin gauzy curtains, though, I see the familiar glow of a turf fire and I instinctively breathe it in, convinced that I can smell it, taste it, see us all sat around it, snacking and bickering and watching game shows before bed.

Getting our last fill of Dad before he kissed us all and went out.

In the window of the largest bedroom—the one where Gran used to sleep—there's a little girl bathed in light, no more than ten years old. She's smiling broadly, clapping her hands and making faces so I smile back and take a photo.

She startles at the flash and retreats from the glass.

Or maybe I'm just dog-tired?

"Overtired," Mum used to say when I claimed monsters were in the wardrobe or ghosts were rattling chains in my face.

Later when I check, there's no child in the photo. Just the shadow of a coat stand where Gran's grandfather clock used to be.

22

I find Manda Moran the next morning, explaining the difference between black and white pudding to a group of California tourists. Reactions range from skeptical to repulsed.

"Coffee and toast it is then," she says cheerfully, probably relieved to put the frying pan away for another day. The state of the wood-paneled breakfast room suggests it's been a busy few hours and I'm tempted to start helping her clear things away.

I can't say with any certainty that time hasn't been kind to Manda Moran because I honestly can't place her, however I'm fairly sure she couldn't have looked like this as a teenager as I'd have surely remembered this strange triangular-shaped person. Normal(ish) on the top half, the width of a two-lane highway from the hips down. Like a tepee on legs.

"He said you'd be calling, all right." She points toward a set of frosted double doors. "Go on through, I'll be there in a minute."

"Who said, Aiden Doyle?" I feel a tiny prick of irritation. I'd wanted to catch them on the hop.

"No, that old gobshite, Swords."

Poor Bill. "He was a bit more complimentary about you," I say, smiling.

This surprises her. "Was he? I wonder what he's after? Is it me body, y'think?" She whoops with laughter, happy to be the butt of her own joke. "Aiden Doyle though," she adds, salivating comically like the Big Bad Wolf. "Now didn't he grow up to be a pure ride."

I grin a "no comment."

Walking into Manda's living quarters is like stepping through the wardrobe to Narnia—a whole different world awaits you. While the B&B's all chintzy sofas and embroidered curtain drapes, Manda's private space has been well and truly pimped. Less "nursing home," more "footballer's crib." An open-plan space with white leather sofas, black marble flooring and a television the size of a pool table.

The most telling thing though is the two-hundred or more Christmas cards that cover every shiny surface and every available wall. That's a few hundred people who didn't include Manda Moran in a communal Facebook share. They didn't send her a round-robin email. They got a pen, wrote her name, licked an envelope, found her address, bought a stamp and walked to a post office and that tells me what Swords said was probably true—*"a great girl, altogether."*

"Sorry about the state about the place," she says, walking in and attacking a nonexistent mess, fluffing cushions and moving magazines. "I don't get a frigging second to meself around here. I don't think half these eejits get the concept of B&B. You know, 'Bed' and 'Breakfast'— and maybe a light evening meal if you ask me nicely. Do you know what one of them asked me for last night?" She doesn't wait for my guess. "The wine list and a fecking ice bucket!"

"They'll be asking for spa treatments next."

She likes this. "It wouldn't fecking surprise me! You'll have tea o' course."

It's an instruction not a question but I give her the thumbs up anyway.

She shouts over from the kitchen space. "So what in the name of God can I tell you about Maryanne Doyle? Terrible business, though, isn't it? Swords told me she was strangled, is that right? And that she was living in England all this fecking time! A fifty-minute flight away." Hands on those considerable hips. "So strange that she never came home, hey?"

Very.

I shout back. "She hadn't just lived in England. She'd seen the world, Manda. Sydney, Hong Kong, Cape Town."

She makes a catty "lucky for some" noise, then catches herself. "Ah well, I suppose that's something." There's a note of regret in her voice. "She'd done something with her life, at least."

I walk over to the kitchen island and watch her for a minute—kettle on, mugs out, milk poured, sugar spooned, without ever looking at her hands once. A sad little choreography.

"So am I right in thinking you never heard from Maryanne again?"

She goes misty-eyed, the way Gran used to go when she relived the moment she heard Elvis Presley had died.

"I last saw Maryanne Doyle on Friday May twenty-ninth 1998, sometime in the afternoon," she says, peeling the cellophane off a tin of biscuits. "And not one fecking peep since. I can still see her now, she was sitting on the wall of St. Benny's, smoking a fag and flashing her bra strap at some young lad. Pure Maryanne, like. She reckoned she'd gone up to a D-cup since Easter. She never stopped going on about it."

"And do you remember anything odd about the days or weeks leading up to Maryanne's disappearance?"

She hands me a mug. "Not really. Hazel has a better memory for that sort of thing. Are you seeing her?"

I nod. "Anything at all, Manda? Anything she said, anyone she'd met, plans she had for the future, that sort of thing."

A funny little snort. "Oh, she'd plenty of plans, all right. Usually America though, never England. I mean, what she thought she was going to do in America, I haven't a clue, but you're full of big dreams when you're that age, aren't you?"

I gulp my tea, ignore the fact it's far too milky. "So, what was Maryanne's big pipe dream?"

She shrugs me off. "Ah sure, I can't remember, and even if I could, how in God's name would that help you?"

I put my cards on the table. "We're not sure what Maryanne was doing in England until around 2001, when she turned up in Brighton, and if we understood a bit more about her motivations, her interests, it might give us more of a clue where to start, Manda. It's a long shot, I know, but we don't have too many short ones."

She puts her mug down, gives me a conspiratorial smile. "Christ, Cat, you must have really pissed someone off to get this gig. Talk about the short straw! What'd you do? Punch your boss?"

I smile and feel a surge of affinity for canny Manda Moran. She may have the jolly spinster act down pat, but she's as shrewd as they come.

And she's not finished either.

"Well, look," she says, examining her short, neat fingernails, "and I'm pure speculating here, but I'd say there's one very obvious reason why an Irish girl would slip off to England on the hush-hush, and it's not to chase any big pipe dream, you understand what I'm saying?"

Perfectly.

"You think Maryanne was pregnant and wanted an abortion?" I hold back the fact that we know she had a child; Manda doesn't need to know this and it might derail her. "What makes you think that?"

She won't be drawn, gives a little twitch of the shoulder. "Pure speculation, like I said. Hazel's sure of it, though. When are you seeing her, by the way?"

I look at the clock. "In about half an hour. Do you still see a lot of each other then?"

She pours more tea. I don't bother arguing. "Ah sure, what's a lot? I'm run off me feet with this place. She has three nippers under seven and a useless lump of a husband—although a handsome lump, I'll give him that." Melancholy cracks her voice again. "Sad though, isn't it? We used to be the best of pals and here she is, only in the next village, and we're lucky if we see each other once every three or four months."

Something suddenly occurs to her and her face lights up. I find myself beaming back even though I don't know why.

"Do you know what, feck this," she says, switching off the kettle and picking up her car keys. "If I drink one more cup of my own fecking tea, I'm going to go loopy. We'll go down to Ganley's. I'll call Hazel and tell her to meet us there. It'll be a gas! They've got *gorgeous* pastries too." She picks up the phone, eyes blazing with excitement at the thought of a break in the routine. "And Hazel'll be a lot more help than me, I promise. Nothing got past that one. She's exactly the same now."

Nothing gets past Hazel O'Keefe apart from her useless lump of a husband's super-sperm, it seems, and Manda's face is a picture as Hazel strides into Ganley's with an obvious round stomach and a *"don't-fucking-ask"* expression.

"He got his mojo back, I see," howls Manda, barely able to breathe from laughing.

The Diner's now Ganley's, a chi-chi little "bistro" with red-and-white-checked tablecloths and paintings of mournful Pierrot dolls gazing down from every wall at our raspberry *mille-feuille*.

Hazel plonks herself down, shaking her head at Manda. "Shut up, you. It's a fucking disaster. Seriously, he only has to sneeze near me and I'm up the pole again." She picks up the menu, looks around. "Right, I've only got twenty minutes, I'm afraid, *as per fucking usual*."

Hazel O'Keefe, *nee* Joyce, doesn't have long red hair clamped in a ponytail anymore. She's got a low-maintenance mum-cut and high-maintenance eyebrows, like she had to make the choice between one or the other and drawing caterpillars on her face seemed like the better option.

She also has a slight edge to her. A spikiness that suggests she's not mad about being summoned to eat French pastries with law enforcement officers in the middle of the day.

"We were just talking about Aiden Doyle," Manda says to Hazel, which is an outright lie. We'd actually been talking about Manda's hair, a lovely rich auburn.

"Oh yeah? I heard he was back visiting the father over Christmas, all right. I bet he had nice things to say about us, hey?" She catches my face. "Ah go on, what did he say? We'll have probably deserved it, honestly, it's fine."

I give them the short version. "Just that you could be a bit harsh sometimes."

"Yeah, and the rest," says Hazel, hailing the waitress. "He was such an oik back then though. Hear he's a big hotshot in London now. Hey, d'ya think he'd be in the market for a ready-made family? I could just see me and the kids tearing it up and down Bond Street."

"Speaking of London," I say, once she's ordered her hot chocolate. "Hazel, do you know if Maryanne knew anyone in London, or even England would be a start?"

"No. Not that she ever mentioned, anyways, and believe me, she'd have mentioned it. She had these couple of cousins in Chicago and seriously, you'd think she had the key to the city, the way she went on about it." She sits back a little, rubs a rhythmic hand over her bump. "There was this English family in the village around the time she went missing, they were over from London, I think."

My heart stops.

"Oh God, yeah, I'd forgotten about them," says Manda. "See I told you, Cat, she remembers everything. I'm fecking useless. Memory like a goldfish."

"What, and you think . . . ?" I don't know how to finish this sentence and I'm grateful when the arrival of Hazel's "chocolat chaud" forces a brief pause.

Hazel takes a sip, mutters, *"Luke-fucking-warm as usual.* Ah no, I didn't mean anything by it. You mentioning London made me think of them, that's all. We didn't really have much to do with them. The girl knocked around with us a coupla' times, I think, that was about it."

Manda nudges Hazel. "That'd have been pure Maryanne, though. Decides she likes the accent and then takes off to England without so much as a backward glance."

"Ah, you're such a gom, Mands. Look, Cat—it is Cat, isn't it?— between you, me and the gatepost, Maryanne was pregnant, and there's only one reason you go to England if you're pregnant. I've half a mind to pay a visit meself!"

"You never told this to Bill Swords?" I say.

It's not meant to sound like an accusation but Hazel takes it as one.

"Course I fucking didn't. You don't grass on your mates, and anyways, I thought she'd probably be back, so why would I make trouble for her by going round telling people her business?"

"How are you so sure she was pregnant?" I keep my voice light, careful not to wind her up again, although I get the feeling Hazel O'Keefe could get wound up by a Buddhist monk. "Did she tell you?"

A lightning shake of the head. "No. But come on, she'd gone up a cup size in less than six weeks. And I'd caught her throwing up in the Diner a few times"—she prods the table—"in here, I mean, that's what this place used to be called. She blamed the drink but she wasn't drinking much either, that's another thing. I mean, she hadn't *stopped* drinking or anything, but she wasn't getting plastered like usual. I'm telling you, as sure as I've a hole in me arse, she was pregnant—fact."

I don't disagree. "It'd have cost a lot of money though, if she was planning a termination—flights, travel, staying over? Where would Maryanne have got that kind of cash?"

"She did well on the tips in here," offers Manda.

Hazel's more cynical. "Ah, she was fierce resourceful, was Maryanne. Sweet-talked it out of some lovesick eejit, I'd say."

Blackmailed it?

"Any ideas on the father?"

"The father," repeats Hazel, laughing. There's a line of chocolate milk running the length of her top lip—Manda doesn't point it out so I don't either. "My money'd be on Ryan Roland or Shane Dillon but it could have been anyone, really. She had a thing for older fellas too, so God knows. She wasn't exactly . . ."

Manda scowls. "Ah now, stall the ball, Hazel. You're making her sound like a proper skank and she wasn't." She turns to me. "She was just gorgeous, that's all. Never short of a few offers, you know."

My phone vibrates. I glance down, praying for it to be anyone other than Jacqui. I know I'll have to face that fight eventually but it can definitely wait another day. Or another week. Another lifetime.

Parnell
Saskia French still not answering. Hicks don't have next of kin. Have a lovely old Doris from flat 12a keeping a watch out for her. When u back?
SMS 12:03 p.m.

I tap out a reply while Hazel gestures for the bill.

Covert surveillance, love it ☺ ☺ Should be back at HQ 5:30ish. Looking like Maryanne was preggers when she left Ireland.
SMS 12:05 p.m.

Once it's sent, I turn my attention back to Hazel O'Keefe, conscious she's going to stride out of Ganley's in the next few minutes just as quickly as she strode in, and Manda Moran was right, she has been a lot more use.

"So what did you think when Maryanne didn't come back?" I ask. "I mean, fine, maybe she *was* going to have a termination, but didn't you find it odd that she never came back? Never even made contact again?"

"Sure, why would she come back?" Hazel says, wiping her chocolate moustache. "What was here for her in Mulderrin? A bollix of a father and a cranky little brother?" She shrugs. "Good luck to her, I thought."

"And you, Manda?"

"I was a bit hurt," she admits, "and maybe a bit worried, yeah. But I had me own shit to deal with, you know. I thought she'd probably just hitched up with some rich, hot fella and like Hazel said, good luck to her." She looks at me earnestly, like it's important I understand something. "But I did think about her a lot though. I've looked for her on Facebook, but sure, I didn't know if she was married, if her surname had changed."

"She'd changed her first name too. She was calling herself Alice."

A dewy-eyed look passes between them. "Alice," says Hazel, smiling, and it's a proper smile too. A genuine smile that says Maryanne had meant *something*. "Alice in Wonderland. That's what we used to call her 'cos she always had her head in the clouds, you know? Living in this dreamworld about all the places she was going to go, places she wanted to live. We were only teasing though and she loved it. She always said she loved the name."

Manda's dewy eyes give way to tears—tears which surprise her and appall Hazel.

"Jeez, cop yourself on, Mands," she says, looking around to make sure no one's noticed. "We'll be the talk of the town, you big gom."

I fish a tissue out of my bag and Manda sniffs gratefully. "So who else are you talking to, Cat?" she says eventually.

"No one else. It's been a flying visit." Something stirs in me—the chance to plunge my hand into another wasp's nest. "Actually, Swords mentioned someone called Tina McGinn," I lie. "Said she was a bit of a character, would flirt with her own shadow, that sort. They're often the best kind of witnesses. Maybe I'll call in on her."

It sounds weak to my ears and I'm not even sure what I'm hoping to achieve. Do I actually want to speak to Tina McGinn, or do I just want to gauge if she'd have been Dad's type?

Hazel O'Keefe's eyebrows hit her hairline. "Flirt with her own shadow? Is that what Swords said?" A fast glance toward Manda. "Fucked her own shadow, more like. More cocks than a henhouse, that one."

Manda doesn't protest. Her pious face says it all. "She doesn't live around here anymore, not for years. Last I heard, she'd broken up another marriage down Spiddal way."

I sense there might be a story here—maybe a Moran man who fell for the wanton charms of Tina McGinn? I get an even stronger sense that contrary to Dad's assertion that *"there was absolutely nothing going on"* between him and Tina McGinn, I'd bet everything I hold sacred on the fact there absolutely was.

Which gave Maryanne stronger leverage to blackmail him to do what?

"Right." Hazel O'Keefe stands up abruptly. "I better get home, I suppose, if I want the house still standing." She kisses Manda on both cheeks and they make promises to meet up properly in the New Year, promises they both know they won't keep. "I hope you catch whoever did it," she says to me. "She could be a right cow sometimes, but sure, couldn't we all at that age."

"Ah now, she wasn't that bad, Hazel." Manda dabs at her eyes again, more for effect than necessity. "Don't be speaking ill of the dead."

Hazel picks up her phone. "It was just that she was snide, you know, that's what I could never stomach. Me and Mands, and even Durkin Donut—that's Colette Durkin—we fought and fell out and we slagged each other and all that, but Maryanne could be proper, proper snide. Putting you down in front of folk. Taking the piss without you realizing."

"And always taking your stuff," chimes in Manda, clearly thinking "*if you can't beat 'em, join 'em.*" "Not stealing it, she was more wily than that. She'd just suddenly be your best pal, you know? All over you like a rash, flattering you, saying whatever she had her eye on was *soooooo* gorgeous and she was so jealous, that sort of thing. Before you knew it, you'd given it to her—'*here, it'd look better on you,*' I'd end up saying. Sad thing is, it always did."

"Hey, I like your Tinkerbell," she said, touching the tiny pink pendant that hung around my neck—a Holy Communion gift from an aunt who wasn't big into Jesus. "Where'd you get it? It's gorgeous! Look, it matches my belly-button ring, dead-on!"

1998
Saturday 6th June

"Can I have a car hoover for Christmas?"

Mum looked at me with the annoyed face, thin-lipped and beady-eyed. She'd been looking at me with the annoyed face all morning. And all of yesterday. All week, really. She was cross that I'd lost my Tinkerbell pendant, a gift from Auntie Someone in America who doesn't have the money to be wasting on spoiled little girls who don't look after things properly.

She'd be even more cross if she knew I'd given it away.

"Course you can, sweetheart," said Dad, fishing crisp and fag packets out of the side pockets of the car. "Or you could have it for your birthday, that comes first?"

Problem was, I wanted a leaf blower for my birthday. A great big red one with a cruise control throttle like the one "Uncle" Frank used for clearing his posh drive. And I couldn't have a leaf blower AND a car hoover for my birthday because Jesus said we shouldn't be greedy. I'd learned that in Holy Communion class too.

Mum stuck her head into the back seat, pulled out a banana skin. "This is disgusting. It's only been two weeks and look at the state of the car."

I jumped in beside her. "It hasn't been two weeks, actually, it's been twelve days." I counted them out on my fingers. "Tuesday, Wednesday, Thursday, Friday, Saturday, Sunday, Monday, Tuesday, Wednesday, Thursday, Friday, Saturday."

"All right, smart-arse, less cheek to your mum," said Dad, pulling a map of Ireland out of the glove compartment. "Here, Ellen, do you think your mam will use this?"

Mum gave Dad the annoyed face. "What would Mammy want with a map of Ireland, Mike? She hasn't left the county since I-don't-know-when. She hasn't left Mulderrin for over a year."

We hadn't left Mulderrin in twelve days. I didn't know why Dad needed a map of Ireland either.

And I didn't know why Mum insisted on calling Gran "Mammy." It made her sound like a baby.

"Mum," I said, stressing the word. "Can Gran come back with us? I think she might like London."

Dad laughed, shouted over the top of the car hoover, "She might, she loves EastEnders!"

I thought it was a good point but Mum put her hands on her hips. "Don't be ridiculous, Catrina, where would she sleep?"

But I was ready for this. I'd thought it all through. Gran could have my bed, I said, which meant they'd have to get me a new one and if they weren't sure which one to get me, I'd seen one shaped like Buzz Lightyear in the Argos catalog. Or, I suggested, Gran could have their bed because Mum often stayed at Auntie Carmel's anyway and Dad was well used to kipping on the couch. Then, and this was my favorite idea, I said maybe Noel could move out and Gran could have his room (only after we'd opened the windows for a week though!). My last (and to be honest, least favorite) suggestion was that I give up my room and share with Jacqui again, like I ALWAYS had to do when one of our barmaids lived in.

Not that anyone had lived in since Alina—our Latvian barmaid—had moved out.

That last suggestion was definitely Mum and Dad's least favorite too because they looked at each other funny and Mum popped the car boot open, saying something grumpy under her breath.

Dad turned off the car hoover, walked over to me and gave one of my curls a ping. "It's a lovely idea, sweetheart, but the World Cup's starting in a few days and it'd be much too noisy for Gran. And she'd never make it up the stairs. We've got a lot more stairs at the pub than Gran has here, haven't we?"

We had. Fourteen up the fire escape to get to the front door. Another fourteen to get to the kitchen and the living room. And then ANOTHER fourteen to climb when it was time to go to bed.

Dad was right. Gran would never make it.

I was disappointed but at least Dad thought about things and made good points. He didn't just stand there with a grumpy face or whisper grumpy things under his breath like Mum did.

But suddenly Mum didn't have a grumpy face anymore.

"Look, Cat," she said, pointing in the boot. I ran over to see what was making her less grumpy. "It's amazing what you find when you actually look for things properly, isn't it?"

I peered closer. Saw it glittering in between a wellie and one of those sealed brown boxes that Dad warned me I was never to touch.

My Tinkerbell.

But I'd given my Tinkerbell to Maryanne Doyle?

Maybe she'd heard that Mum was cross with me for losing it so she'd done a kind thing and snuck it back? Ever since she'd disappeared people had said mean things about her but if she'd done that, she definitely wasn't all bad.

Stupid place to leave it, though. In the boot of Dad's car.

23

"So you've got a better sense of what she was like, you think she was pregnant when she left Ireland, and you remembered how to say 'hot chocolate' in French, but that's about it?"

It's a fair summation. Steele's not being snarky either, she just never has the patience for the nuances of the long version.

"Yup. Report on the back of a fag packet OK for you?"

She raises her hand. "Er, quit with the negativity Kinsella. How sure are we she was pregnant?"

"She had all the early symptoms, and it works as a theory—Irish girl comes to England for an abortion on the QT."

Steele nods. "But obviously something changed her mind as we know she gave birth."

"Again, on the QT," says Renée, packing up for the day. "It's not registered anywhere, it's not in her medical records."

"Illegal adoption?" I chip in. They both nod like they've been discussing it. "It'd explain the IVF desperation, anyway. Gina Hicks said that even when she first met 'Alice' a few years ago, she was already strung out about the IVF not working, which seemed a bit odd as they hadn't been trying *that* long."

Renée sees where I'm going. "Yep, that's definitely going to sting. Struggling to conceive a child when you already gave a perfectly good one away."

"It doesn't explain why she'd put the brakes on the IVF though," says Steele.

It does to me—*"Maryanne was fierce resourceful."*

"They'd been through so many rounds already, I think she was giving Thomas Lapaine up as a lost cause, looking elsewhere."

"So she came to London to seek a new sperm donor?" Steele weighs it up. "It's a bit of a stretch but I'll go with it."

"Well, it wasn't just that, remember. She told Gina Hicks that she was sure Thomas Lapaine was having an affair, so I think it was more a case of 'you're cheating on me, and you can't give me what I want most in the world anyway—a child—so why am I putting up with it? I'm off.'"

"Makes sense," says Steele. "Of course it contradicts his version—the loving note she supposedly left which we only have his word for, but to be honest I think I'd struggle to believe the sky was blue if it came out of Thomas Lapaine's mouth."

"But we've definitely ruled him out, right?"

Steele hands me a marker pen. "Well and truly as of a few hours ago. Emily took a statement from Abigail Shawcroft's nosy neighbor and she confirmed seeing him at the house that night *and* leaving again the next morning."

I walk over to the incident board, draw a thick black cross through Thomas Lapaine's name, then change markers and write "Illegal adoption??" across the top in red.

It feels like a red kind of theory.

Nate Hicks' name has already been crossed out. "Definitely schmoozing in Cardiff then?" I ask.

"Looks that way," replies Steele. "Hotel confirms him checking in and out. CCTV has him going up to his room at twelve ten a.m. and he doesn't appear to leave again until breakfast. His car didn't move from the car park all night."

"Bollocks. I'd have liked it to be him."

The door opens and Parnell walks in, instantly making a beeline for me.

"Well, look who it is, the international jet-setter. Glad to be back, are we?"

The answer's a definite no. Right now, I'd give anything to be back in Mulderrin, strolling up the Long Road, burning off the last of my raspberry *mille-feuille*. In fact, I want to be Bill Swords. I want to cruise around the county in my rust-bucket of a car, singing along to Dusty Springfield songs and making "tosser" signs at other drivers. Or I'd settle for running a B&B like Manda Moran. Hell, I'd settle for running a B&B *with* Manda Moran—she looked like she could do with the help.

Basically, I want to be anything other than back here, in this room, soul-deep in this wretched case.

Steele's feeling the same. "How bad is this, folks? There was a woman murdered in Wimbledon on Sunday night, a strangulation, and I was almost *relieved* thinking it could be linked to our case. I was actually hoping for a serial killer, can you believe that?" I can, wholeheartedly. "Turns out it was some scumbag she'd given the brush-off after a few dates. He walked into Mitcham nick last night, confessed the whole thing." She pulls her hair back off her face. "We can dream, eh?"

I look at Parnell. "Still no Saskia, I take it?"

There's a rising worry in his eyes. "No. Phone's still off and there's no sign of life at the flat. I've got a Mrs. Stevens across the hall doing covert surveillance"—a quick smirk at me—"so as soon as Saskia or anyone else turns up, we'll be on it."

"Facebook?" I say. The solution to everything.

"Can't find her," says Renée. "She's obviously got tight privacy settings."

I sigh, throw my pen down, agitated. "It just feels like we should be doing more. Saskia's got motive, she lied to us, she's gone AWOL for God's sake and . . ."

Steele halts my tailspin with one point of a finger. "OK, OK, OK, she *possibly* has motive—if she thought Maryanne was planning to grass her up to Gina Hicks for either shagging her husband, or shagging other people's husbands for money, then absolutely, that's reason to shut her up. But we don't know Maryanne was planning to do that."

I take a breath. "Gina Hicks specifically told her to make any contact through Saskia, but we know she was in the café down the road on the Friday before she died, so she obviously wanted to speak to Gina without Saskia knowing. What other conclusions can we draw?"

Steele throws her hands up. "That she thought the Donatella Caffé did the meanest espresso ristretto this side of the equator? That she was dropping off a Christmas card? That she was lunching with Lord Lucan? We don't know!"

I bite my cheeks but Steele's wise to my little angry tics.

"Look, we're all on the same side here, Kinsella, and I agree there's motive to be explored, but Saskia French hasn't lied to us any more than anyone else, including Gina Hicks, and at this point we don't have any reason to believe she's even gone AWOL. She's gone to her parents, that's what she said, isn't it, Lu?" Parnell nods. "Which is entirely normal at this time of year and given the fact she wasn't under arrest or even a formal suspect, we had absolutely no right to stop her. No right to even ask for the address."

Renée asks Parnell, "Where do her folks live?"

"Somerset, apparently."

"If it's rural Somerset, mobile reception's not great," says Renée.

"Or she's switched her phone off because she doesn't want clients calling her at her parents'?" adds Steele.

I've got no choice but to nod along. Steele calls the shots and she invariably calls them with a combination of searing logic and calm reason. She's virtually impossible to argue with.

"And another thing," she continues, "I've been looking at the CCTV again and yes, I'm going to keep an open mind, of course, but honestly . . . I don't think it's a woman. I don't think a woman could have lifted the body that leisurely. Maryanne, Alice, whatever we're calling her, she wasn't exactly tiny, was she?"

"Five feet six, just under ten stone," I say, keen to show I have concrete facts as well as unsubstantiated theories.

"Saskia French's a unit, Boss, I wouldn't rule it out," says Parnell.

Steele puts her palms flat on the table. "I'm not, Lu. I'm just not prepared to start panicking and canvasing the Somerset countryside just yet." She nods toward Renée, who's packed up, wrapped up, and ready for the off. "Now if you don't mind, I'm going to follow my learned friend's lead and bugger off home. Tomorrow, we go again."

But I'm not ready to go home yet. I'm not ready to be alone.

Parnell reads my mind with a resounding, "No, Kinsella! No pub today. I'm in the doghouse enough already. Turns out that buying your wife and your mother the same perfume for Christmas is a bit of a no-no." He looks to us for sympathy, finds none. "I don't know . . . women . . . it's a bloody minefield . . ."

Aiden Doyle doesn't knock me back, though. He says he has an appointment with Sky but if I give him ten minutes, he'll try to change it. Then he asks me if I enjoyed Mulderrin. Did I get a chance to do the open-top bus tour? Have a ride on the Mulderrin Eye?

The joker.

As promised—well, fourteen minutes later, but who's counting?—he calls me back to say we're on. An hour later, we're sitting in the upstairs window of the Chandos, sipping cheap ale while overlooking the relative calm of Trafalgar Square as it braces itself for tomorrow's New Year's Eve onslaught. He's looking even more handsome than I remember. The same distressed jeans but with a white long-sleeved top that shows off a chest that manages to stay on both the right side of toned and the right side of vanity.

"So you canceled your Sky Engineer, I'm honored," I say.

It's tragic but I actually mean it.

"Ah sure, I hardly watch the bloody thing anyway. What is there to watch? Baking shows and bad news, that's about it." His accent seems stronger, richer, from his flying visit back to Mulderrin—more of a pulse than a lilt. "I reckon you've saved me forty pounds a month *and* you've introduced me to London's cheapest pint. You're like my financial guardian angel."

I catch myself in the window, wish I'd put my hair up. "God, don't let my boss hear you say that. She's threatening to second me onto Financial Intelligence as it is."

"Don't fancy it?" he asks, trying and failing to open a bag of peanuts.

I take over, tear the corner with my teeth and hand them back. "Would you? Spending eight hours a day analyzing SARs."

"SARs?"

"Sorry, Suspicious Activity Reports."

"Sounds like heaven to me, but then I am a bit of a numbers freak."

I pick up my bag, pretend to leave. "Look, if I'd known you were such a nerd, I'd have never called . . ."

"I am," he says, laughing. "A proper nerd. I've even got a T-shirt that says 'I Heart Sums.'"

"You sure know how to impress a lady." I sit back down. "So what is it you do then? You don't look like a banker, or an accountant."

"You don't look like a detective."

"What's a detective look like?"

He struggles to answer. "Oh, I don't know. Long brown mac, disheveled hair, a big fat cigar."

A deadpan stare. "Columbo, basically."

"That's yer man. You don't look anything like him."

"They're not wrong about that slick Celtic charm, are they?" He smiles. We smile. "Seriously though, what is it you do?"

"I work for an online betting company. I'm a risk analyst, well"—he doffs an imaginary cap—"a senior risk analyst, if you please."

I look impressed even though I have no idea what this means. "My dad always used to back a horse for me on the Grand National, that's about my experience of betting, I'm afraid."

"Any luck?"

"I won thirty pounds once. I was only six, it seemed like a windfall."

"I hope you invested it wisely, you being so financially intelligent 'n all."

"Very. I bought my dad a West Ham key ring, myself a Barbie Porsche and I gave ten pounds to the PDSA." He doesn't recognize the acronym. "Poorly animals," I add.

"Sweet kid. I send my nephews in Canada fifty dollars every Christmas. All they buy are computer games where you slaughter people."

"Well, I don't know about 'sweet.'" I put my hand out for peanuts and he holds it steady as he pours. It's nice. "As my brother never stopped pointing out, I won the money on a sport that's cruel to animals and then made myself look good by giving some of it back to animals. Bit Machiavellian, don't you think?"

He sips his pint. "I think that's a shitty thing to say to a six-year-old, to be honest, but hey, I'm trying to impress you—you know, after getting off to a great start with the whole 'I Heart Sums' thing—so I won't start slagging your brother off as well."

"Oh please do, slagging him off will impress me big-time."

His eyes narrow. "Mmmm, I'm not sure, I feel like I'm being walked into something I'll regret later. Can I not just send a massive bouquet of flowers to your work with a balloon and a 'I Wuv You' teddy?" Eyes twinkling now. "That always impresses, right?"

I twinkle back. "Oh every time—flowers, cuddly toys and equal pay, that's all us women want in life."

He laughs. "For that dig, I might just do it, you know. Send you the biggest, tackiest bunch I can find." He starts Googling florists on his phone. "Are you based at Holborn all the time?"

"No I'm not and don't you fucking dare." I snatch his phone. "My boss would have a fit if I got flowers from you. She'd have a fit if she knew I was here."

"Why?" He looks momentarily confused before remembering that we aren't just two ordinary people enjoying an ordinary pint. "Christ, I'm not still a suspect, am I?" Panic with a tiny hint of boyish excitement. "Seriously, was I ever *really* a suspect? Or do you have to go through all that, 'On the night in question' stuff with everyone?"

I'm not prepared to answer that. I may be two pints down, and more than a little smitten, but I haven't completely lost the run of myself.

I do have a question for him though. A serious one.

"Can I say something?" He looks ominous, which is the only way you can look when someone utters that statement. "You don't seem that cut up about Maryanne."

He turns his head and looks out of the window, despondent. I instantly wish I could claw my words out of the ether and ram them straight back down my stupid fucking throat where they should have fucking stayed.

I try to make amends. "That's not a judgment, Aiden, honest, it's just an observation."

God, that's worse. Condescending.

He stays gazing toward Nelson's Column. "I don't know how I feel is the honest truth, Cat. I don't know how I'm supposed to feel. You know, I met her husband in the end." He smiles apologetically, warding off a lecture. "He's a strange guy, isn't he? An awful dry shite, as we say back home." *Agreed.* "Anyways, I was pleased, you know, when he said he'd meet me. I thought maybe it'd make me feel closer to her."

"I can understand that. I'm sensing it didn't, though?"

He swills the foam around at the bottom of his pint. "It was just plain weird, hearing him talk about 'Alice.' And the way he described her too—quiet, passive. I nearly said, 'Who? Motormouth Maryanne?' a few times." He takes a sad little breath. "I dunno, I just came away feeling further away from her—Maryanne, that is. I mean, this Alice woman, I don't know her at all, and I can't grieve for someone I didn't even know." He rubs at his face. "God, I'm talking some existential shite this evening, aren't I?"

He's talking sweet, perfect sense to me. I hope my face shows it.

"He's going back to Sydney," he adds.

My investigative ears prick up. "He is? When? Soon?"

"Soon-ish. Well, that's what he reckons, anyway. Said he wishes they'd never left, they were happy there apparently. I said he shouldn't rush into anything. I said it's easy to make the wrong decision when you're raw, but he just looked at me as if to say, 'Who are you to tell me what I should do?' And he's right. Who am I? I don't know him. I didn't know 'Alice.' We're all just strangers to each other."

"I'm so sorry."

"Don't be. There is one reason I'm glad I met him, you know. He told me about all the places they lived overseas, and how he'd met her in Brighton." I smile encouragingly although I don't know where he's headed. "And it made me think—she always wanted to be by the coast, didn't she? And he said that himself—that this Thames Ditton place was a massive compromise for her, but at least she was by the river. So I'm thinking that must mean she'd been happy growing up in Mulderrin, right? I mean, we were only a mile's walk from the Atlantic fucking ocean. Just made me feel better to think she hadn't completely forgotten where she came from, even if life at home was shite a lot of the time."

Speaking of. "How is your dad?"

"Ah sure, not good, Cat, not good." He looks out the window again. I follow his gaze but I'm not looking at Nelson's Column or the skeletal, riderless horse standing on top of the Fourth plinth. I'm looking at his reflection. His faraway, sad expression.

"If there's anything I can do . . ." It's woefully inadequate but it's all I can think to say.

He brightens quickly. "You could let me take you out for dinner sometime. Sometime soon," he adds, quickly. "Or I could cook you dinner? If you've got a particular fondness for cheese and ham toasties or microwaved pizza, I'm your man."

"How about cheese and bean toasties?"

He rolls his eyes. "Fuck's sake. There's always one who goes off-menu, isn't there?"

I like him. I really like him.

My moonstruck spell is broken by the hypothermic heap waiting on my doorstep when I get home. I didn't even know she knew my address. I've always kept things deliberately vague.

Lesson sorely learned. *This* is what happens when you don't answer your phone.

"Jacqs, what are you doing here, it's freezing? How long have you been there?"

She doesn't answer but the color of her nose tells me it's been a while. I open the front door, half-hoping to hear noise, but realistically, it's good that the Dawsons still aren't back.

They really don't need to see this.

I walk inside, slip off my coat and hang it at the bottom of the banister. Jacqui doesn't follow. "Are you coming in then?" Her eyes bore into me. "Look, I'm shutting the door, Jacqs, so make up your mind."

She steps into the hall and looks around, baffled by the framed artwork and expensive Turkish rugs. I'm about to ask what her problem is but then it dawns on me. She thinks this is all mine. That I'm renting this whole place. It doesn't occur to her that some people live in ten by eight attic rooms and have two shelves assigned for their food.

"Tea?" I say, heading toward the kitchen. "You look like you could do with a hot drink."

"Fucking tea?"

They're only two words, not even a coherent statement, let alone a sentence, but these two words sound truer than anything Jacqui's said in a long time. She's hardly sworn in years.

"OK, do you want some fucking tea?" I know it's a mistake as soon as I say it.

She steps toward me. "Why do you do it, Cat?" Under the hall light I see it's not just her nose that's red, she's been crying. "Why do you have to make everything so unbearable? Can't you accept people for what they are?"

I drop heavily onto the bottom stair. This isn't going to be a cozy kitchen type of chat. "By people, I take it you mean Dad. What's he been saying?"

Her face twists in indignation. "Nothing! That's the whole point. He won't answer my calls. He won't answer the door. I even asked for him in the pub on Sunday night but they said he wasn't around, even though I could clearly see the lights on upstairs."

"Maybe he . . ."

"Maybe he *what*, Cat? Maybe he's decided daughters are too much hassle and he's cut me off too. What exactly did you say to him on Christmas night?"

I'm too tired for this, too unprepared. I've dreamed of having this conversation with Jacqui—for her to spar with me, face things head-on—but just this once I wish she'd stick her head right back in the sand.

"We had a disagreement, that's all, nothing for you to . . ."

"Fuck off, Cat. You and Dad don't 'disagree,' you destroy each other." *So she does notice.* "I knew you were both in the kitchen on Christmas night. I said to Ash, 'Oh here we go,' but when I didn't hear any shouting, I thought maybe you were talking—you know, talking like normal people. Next thing I know, the door slams and Dad's walking into the living room and ordering us to leave." She pounds her chest with a gloved fist. "Us! Me, Ash and Finn. So Ash says he's drunk too much to drive and that a taxi back to Edgware will cost a fortune on Christmas night and Dad just whips out two twenties and says, 'Now get out of my house please, I've already asked you nicely.'"

I can hardly believe it. "He kicked out Finn?"

"Well, not exactly," she admits. "He did say we could leave Finn where he was, but I was livid, Cat. I said, if we're not welcome nor's Finn, so then I had to wake Finn up, put him in the taxi in his PJs."

There isn't an affirmation self-congratulatory enough, or a vat of wine big enough, to stop me feeling awful about this until the day I die. I push my fingers deep into my sockets to try to blur the image of a confused and sleepy Finn, shivering in his dinosaur PJs.

"I'm so sorry. Really, I am." I want to take her hand but I know she'll swipe it away. "He shouldn't have taken it out on you. I don't understand why he did. Can you see now that he's an arsehole?"

Her voice is firm. "I can see that he must have been massively upset about something."

"Oh for God's sake, stop sugarcoating him."

She kneels down, eye-to-eye. "What, like how you sugar-coat Mum? Canonize her, even? I loved her too, Cat, but she wasn't perfect."

"So? Who is?" I snap back.

Jacqui cranes her neck closer. "Have you ever wondered why an angel like Mum would stay with such a supposed 'arsehole' as Dad?"

Yes, many times. I've come up with, in no particular order—love, money, stability, religion, habit, fear of the unknown and low self-esteem. But I'm not about to share these.

Instead I say, "Your point is?"

"Well, just that Dad can't be all bad. Not if the holier-than-thou Ellen McBride loved him."

I catch fire. "Show some fucking respect, Jacqs, that's Mum you're talking about."

"And she had her faults, Cat. She could be *so* moody sometimes, re-member? Nothing was ever good enough. Even the way she drew the curtains could make you feel like you'd somehow disappointed her when she was in one of her sulks."

"At least she made us feel safe."

She jerks her head back, bewildered. "I *literally* don't know what you mean by that. Dad's always made me feel safe. God, I don't know where we'd be if . . ."

"You're talking about money, Jacqs."

A nasty expression. "Oh, and you're not?"

This sideswipes me. Money?

Jacqui takes my silence as confirmation of something, she almost looks pleased. "I had a feeling it was about that," she says, nodding to herself, "but I wanted to hear it from you. I told Dad not to men-tion it, I said you'd kick off, *I told him*, but obviously he wanted to be straight with you." She looks around again, gives a haughty little sniff. "I mean, you're obviously doing OK, and we're going to need that renovation if we have another baby. And we said it should be a loan but Dad insisted . . ."

A loan.

A fucking renovation.

That's what she thinks this is about?

Rage rips through me like a forest fire. I try counting to ten, focusing on my breathing, thinking about Aiden Doyle and the shards of possibility there.

But, of course, there are no possibilities. There never can be. Because he is Maryanne Doyle's brother and my father is . . .

What?

"Do you really want to know, Jacqs?" I stand up. "Do you really want to know what this is about, and what I think Dad's capable of?" The flat look on her face says "we've been here before" and it only serves to pour petrol on the ravaging blaze. "Wait there."

I fly up the stairs before reason sets in and pull the shoe box out from under my bed.

Underneath the family photos that Mum took in Mulderrin and the red fluffy notepad where I write the unspeakable things, something glitters, as good as new.

I haven't taken it out for years. A stupid, supernatural fear of what it could unleash, maybe? But then hell was unleashed the minute that desk clerk walked into our squad room and said, *"A body. A woman. Leamington Square."*

I fly back down the stairs, resolute.

"This." I hold the Tinkerbell pendant between my thumb and my forefinger. Jacqui doesn't blink. "Do you remember this?"

Her head moves up and down, then side to side, as if to say, *"Yes, I remember. No, I don't have the faintest idea why you're showing it to me."*

"I found this in the boot of Dad's car in Mulderrin. It was the day we were leaving and I was helping him clear all the crap out." Jacqui's chin retreats into her neck—she knows this is bad but she doesn't know why. "I gave *this* to Maryanne Doyle the day before she went missing. She said it was gorgeous and that it matched her belly-button ring, and because she was so bloody pretty and I was so bloody gormless, I said she could have it."

She starts backing down the hall, more wary of me than of what this could mean about Dad. I can hear her later:

"Seriously, Ash, she's not well. She's finally flipped. I was frightened."

Her hand is on the door-catch and I realize she's going to leave without saying a single solitary word, leaving me with no choice but to spell it out to her. No sugarcoating. No filtering.

No-holds-barred.

"Do you understand what I'm saying? I gave it to Maryanne Doyle, Jacqs. She put it in her pocket and I didn't see it again. So how did it end up in the boot of Dad's car? What was Maryanne Doyle doing in the boot of Dad's car?"

24

I've never subscribed to the cult of New Year's Eve. Never grasped the fascination. All that reflecting on the past and hoping for the future always strikes me as a profoundly bad idea when you've been poisoning your body for seven days straight, and your nervous system's shot to pieces by marathon-style boozing and energy-sapping grub.

It's especially a bad idea at five a.m., when you're alone and lying in the pitch-black silence, waiting for the orange glow of the streetlamps to bring another dark night of the soul to a close.

Good old five a.m., though.

There's comfort to be found in consistency.

Unsurprisingly, sleep was fractured last night. Just the odd twenty-minute snatch dreaming of shadowed, wailing women emerging from dark corners to plead with me about *something*.

Mary Shelley had Frankenstein haunting her "midnight pillow." Basically, I'd had Jacqui.

Around three a.m., I'd switched the light on and pounded out a text to my sister. An incoherent essay full of pseudo-apologies and rambling justifications. The worst kind of grovel—"I'm really sorry, *but . . .*"

Thankfully I hadn't sent it.

I hadn't sent the one I'd written to Aiden Doyle either.

Thanks for the drink. Don't think we should meet up again. Sorry.
Cat x.
SMS 3:32 a.m.

I stir myself and drift zombie-like into the shower. The water's warm but sparse, another thing in this house that needs fixing. Still in my towel, I mainline carbs and caffeine for half an hour, sitting on the stair where my relationship with Jacqui ended last night until I realize I'm shivering. Proper cartoon shivering. I crank the heating up and go back upstairs. Fill my room with the tinny, mindless sounds of breakfast TV.

A shower. Carbs. Caffeine. Vacuous noise. Usually a winning combination for shaking off the worst of the bad-night blues but I can't seem to find solace today. My heart's too heavy and my chest's too tight and for the first time ever I think about phoning in sick.

That is, until Parnell calls.

"Boss," I croak, giving myself the option depending on what he has to say. "You're up early, you all right?"

His voice sounds odd, softer. "Better to be a lark than an owl, Kinsella, and in answer to your question, no, I'm not all right."

I mute the TV, silencing a far-too-chipper brunette preaching about how to get a flat stomach in twelve hours. For the "big night" as she calls it.

"Why? What's happened? You sound weird."

What's happened to Parnell is a tooth abscess, "more painful than labor" he insists as Maggie shouts obscenities in the background. What's happened to our case is a call from Parnell's "snout," Mrs. Stevens, to say that "a dark woman with a suitcase" turned up at Saskia French's flat last night and was heard saying to someone on her phone that she'd come back the next morning when she'd found her spare key.

Which leaves me sitting outside Ophelia Mansions for nearly four hours, cursing this woman and her loose definition of the word "morning," and Parnell sitting in the emergency dentist's chair, cursing himself for not taking better care of his teeth.

Just after noon she turns up. As we climb the six flights of stairs, I give the woman with the mellow-brown skin and the cut-glass accent a two-minute version of our two-week-old case.

She doesn't seem too moved by it.

"Maryanne's dead?" She pats the pockets of her Afghan coat, shoving her handbag into my arms so she can rummage for the key. "Sorry,

I had no idea. I've been in the Seychelles for the past three weeks with a client."

Her name is Naomi Berry. She's been working *"with, not for"* Saskia French for several years and she has a key because when Saskia's away, she likes Naomi to keep half an eye on things. She explains that she called by the flat last night as Saskia lets her keep her work "things" here—it saves her carting them backward and forward between here and her respectable life as a trainee acupuncturist in Crouch End—and she was very surprised to find Saskia gone as the week between Christmas and New Year is usually highly lucrative. Clients who've been cooped up with their families are desperate to "relax," apparently, and a wintry woodland walk or a quiet pint in the local doesn't quite cut it.

All this before we've got through the bloody front door.

"So you met Maryanne?" I finally get a word in.

"Briefly." She jangles the key triumphantly then twists it in the lock. "She was here for about a week before I left."

There's a mound of literature on the doormat, mainly junk—pizza flyers, taxi cards, letters addressed *"to the occupier,"* and there's a sweet rank smell stifling the air. Naomi eyes me warily in the dim light—she's clearly watched her fair share of cop shows—however it's definitely not the sweet stench of death. Decaying fruit, I reckon. Or an unemptied trash bin. Naomi puts her case down and goes into the kitchen to investigate. I walk into the living room and start opening windows.

"So what can you can tell me about Maryanne?" I say, keeping my question nice and open.

She stands in the doorway holding the offending trash out in front of her like a dead rat. Sundown in the Seychelles must seem like a very distant dream right now.

"Nothing. Like I said, our paths didn't cross for long. We barely spoke other than to say hello."

I nod, leave it at that. "Naomi, we really need to speak with Saskia and we haven't been able to contact her for nearly a week. Have you heard from her at all?"

"No, but then she knows not to call when I'm holidaying with a client. They tend to want the full 'girlfriend experience' and they don't appreciate your phone going off every two seconds. It rather reminds them of what you are." She pauses, pouting. "Saskia could be away with a client I suppose?"

I shake my head. "She said she was going to her parents. I don't suppose you know their address, or have a contact number?"

Her lip curls slightly. I'm not sure if it's the trash or the question. "Her parents? As far as I'm aware she never knew her father and her mother died well over a year ago. She was very distressed about it even though they hadn't spoken in years."

OK.

I relieve her of the trash, offer to ferry the bag down the six flights. There's no thank-you, just a tight smile that suggests I'm probably better suited to the chore anyway. On my way down, I put a call in to HQ and get a message to Steele, through Renée, that it looks like there's no parents in Somerset, or any other rural cider-drinking county for that matter, and therefore we have the very real possibility that Saskia French has done a bunk. Then I call Parnell who I tell the exact same thing.

Parnell tells me, as best he can in his semi-anesthetized state, that he's just jumping in the car and he'll be as quick as he can.

When I walk back into the flat, the hall light's now on and Naomi's bent over a small puddle of water, holding a dustpan and brush awkwardly, like she's not quite sure how to use it. A cylindrical vase lies on its side and small shards of broken glass are scattered around a few limp gerberas—once a cheerful yellow, now heading toward a murky light brown.

I address the top of her head. "Accident?"

"No, I only just noticed it when I switched the light on. That table's a bit crooked as well." She looks up. "This is odd. Saskia's usually quite tidy. I'm surprised she'd leave behind a mess like this."

So she left in a hurry, of her own accord or someone else's.

"Look, leave that, Naomi. Don't touch anything." I gesture toward the living room. "Can we sit down? I need to ask you a few more questions."

She thinks about this for a minute and I play along, allowing the pretense that she actually has a choice. Eventually she shrugs, pushes past me. "OK, I can't imagine how I'll help but if you must."

I take the sofa—chic, angular, uncomfortable, like the sofa in Dr. Allen's waiting room. Naomi stays standing, leaning lightly against the windowsill. The low midday sun frames her beautifully and if it wasn't for her completely flat expression, I'd say she almost looks celestial.

"Did you ever hear Maryanne or Saskia say they were scared of anyone?"

"No. But as I explained, I didn't hear Maryanne say very much at all."

I get specific, eyes primed for the slightest reaction. "Do you know Nate Hicks?"

The name doesn't faze her. "I know who he is. I don't know him personally."

"Did you ever see him with Maryanne?"

A languid shake of the head. "No."

"Have you ever seen him here?"

"Not in a long time, but then I'm only here a few times a week."

"What about his wife, Gina Hicks?"

Her face stays blank, unreadable. "No."

"Did you know Saskia was having a relationship with Nate Hicks?"

Her head tilts. "You mean he's a client?"

"Well, it was a bit more than that. They were having an affair, a relationship. In Saskia's mind anyway."

She seems to find this amusing and lets out a deep gravelly laugh that doesn't quite match the la-di-da accent she obviously works hard to maintain. "That's an absurd idea," she says, recovering quickly. "A client maybe, but a lover?" Her brown eyes sparkle as she says the word.

"Saskia likes them young, skinny and arty. I don't think I've ever known her to date anyone over the age of twenty-five and the Hicks chap must be in his mid-forties at least?"

"Saskia confirmed it," I say.

"Well, that surprises me." She concedes quickly, too disinterested to argue the toss. "Why are you asking about him anyway? Has he got something to do with what happened to Maryanne?"

There's a boredom to her voice that I find refreshing. A complete lack of emotional investment which means she's less likely to lie, unlike every other person involved in this case.

On this basis, I decide to make her my trusty assistant.

"I need to make a quick call," I say. "Can you see if there's anything obvious missing from Saskia's room? Do you know where she keeps her passport, for example?"

She looks unsure. "Well . . . I . . . I'm not really sure Saskia would be comfortable with me going through her things. I . . ."

"Naomi, she's been out of contact for nearly a week and she's been sharing a flat with a woman who was murdered. We're extremely worried about her, as I'm sure you are."

I'm sure she's nothing of the sort but she has the good grace to pretend at least, nodding solemnly and heading toward Saskia's bedroom, if not exactly at a worried pace.

Parnell answers instantly on his crackly hands-free. "Calm down, kiddo, I'm about fifteen minutes away."

"Listen, Boss, I'm not sure Saskia has done a bunk. It looks like there's been some sort of scuffle here. Nothing major, no blood that I can see, but a table's been knocked into and there's a mess on the floor, a broken vase. I've got a bad feeling about this."

Nothing for a second except static and the sound of car horns. "All right, I'll let Steele know and I'll get the team down to start knocking on doors. See if anyone heard anything, saw anything."

"OK, I'm going to have a root around Saskia's room."

The crackling intensifies. "The previous warrant covered the whole flat," he shouts as best he can. "Forensics have already gone through Saskia's room."

"Yeah, but they were looking for Maryanne's bag and phone, things related to her. I'm looking for something that might tell us where Saskia is."

A pause. "OK, fine, there might be something they wouldn't have considered relevant the first time. I'll get someone from Forensics over to check out this scuffle, OK."

He hangs up without a goodbye. I open the door to Saskia's room.

"Any luck?" I say, taken aback by the messy, windowless box. It looks like a modern art installation called "Pandemonium."

"I'm surprised she'd leave her room like this." Naomi's sitting on the bed, a king-size divan with a brass metal headboard. Clothes, make-up and an arsenal of electrical beauty gadgets that I'd struggle to even identify are strewn across the wooden floor. I have to tiptoe across just to reach a clear patch. "Her passport's still here," she says, pointing to a nightstand. "But it's strange she didn't take this." She leans toward the headboard and unscrews a brass knob from the railing, pulling out two bulging rolls of twenty-pound notes. There must be easily £2,000.

"And she's definitely not with a client." She slides open the fitted wardrobe and presents various swatches to me—red velvets, black silks, a sky-blue lace number similar to the bridesmaid dress I wore at Jacqui's wedding—the memory slices through me. "Because she hasn't taken any of her good stuff."

Much as she's being helpful, I want her out of here now so I can have a proper scout around.

"Thanks, Naomi. Any danger of a cup of tea?" I'm used to this being a reasonable request to make of anyone. Naomi Berry looks affronted. "Weak, no sugar," I add, smiling. "Not too much milk."

She realizes I'm being serious and walks out of the room, her posture straight out of finishing school. Spine straight, head high.

I take the wardrobe first, fishing among the clothes and shaking out every shoe, completely clueless as to what I'm looking for. There's a few handbags flung at the back—designer labels, although I think they're fake—each one containing nothing more than a few screwed-up receipts and half-used lipsticks. The shelves are full of cozy winter sweaters and throwaway tops, apart from the top shelf where a small suitcase sits with the baggage tag still on—London Heathrow to Prague. There's nothing in the case. I turn my attention to the bed, checking under the mattress and then pulling out the drawers where a suite of sex toys rests on top of neatly folded towels and bed linen. I check the nightstands on both sides and discover nothing more revelatory than the fact Saskia French takes Microgynon for heavy periods and hydrocortisone cream for dry skin.

There's little else to search as the bed swamps most of the room and I'm just about to start thumbing through a handful of paperbacks on a slightly wonky shelf when my phone rings. It takes me a minute to locate it and when I do, the caller's voice is impatient and crabby.

"Are you still there?" It's Steele.

"I am. So you heard? About the parents? Well, the potential lack of parents . . ."

"Zip it, Kinsella." The line's echoey—speakerphone? "Listen, I've got Sonny Shah from SERIS with me. He's been going over the videos from the search of Saskia's flat before Christmas."

SERIS. Specialist Evidence Recovery Imaging Services. Responsible for a smorgasbord of tasks including crime-scene video recording. Essential to all murder investigations as you just never know what innocuous item might become relevant further down the line.

"Hey there." A meek, nervy voice. Birmingham, I think.

"Sonny, you explain," says Steele.

He clears his throat. "Um, well, as you know, we take panoramic recordings of every room and um, what with Christmas and that, there's been a bit of a delay in getting through everything but I, um . . ."

Steele cuts in. "Basically, Sonny thinks he's spotted something on the video and I need you to check." My heart quickens, she'd have left this to Parnell to sort if it wasn't critical. "There's a room at the bottom of the hall, across from the kitchen. There's a single bed in it but it looks like more of a spare room, a dumping ground."

I'm standing in the doorway before Steele's finished the sentence.

Sonny Shah comes back on the line. "Um, there's a photo on the wall. Er, well, it's more of a collage really."

It's to my left as I walk in, twenty-plus versions of Saskia French looking back at me. Saskia French and various people—smiling, pouting, smoldering, posing and probably a whole load of other "ings" that I'd be able to identify if I put my glasses on. I fish them out of my pocket, give them a cursory wipe with the sleeve of my coat. "OK. Got it."

Steele again. "Toward the top left-hand corner. It's a bit faded, it's an old photo."

I step closer.

"Um, I'm not a hundred percent sure, she looks very different," says Shah, getting his excuses in early. "I've blown it up as much as possible. I *think* it's her."

I'm a hundred percent sure though.

A hundred and ten percent sure, as annoying people often say.

It most definitely is Maryanne Doyle.

I say the words out loud but I'm not sure if they hear over the sound of my phone crashing to the floor. Almost instantly it rings again but I stay rooted to the spot, fearful that if I crouch down, I might never find the strength to get up again. Eventually it rings off.

Maryanne Doyle and Saskia French. Together. Standing, maybe dancing, on a coffee table. Maryanne with her licorice-black curls and Saskia with a shaggier bob, a couple of shades lighter than the coal-black hue she currently sports. They can't be more than eighteen, nineteen, tops, with their bottles of lemon hooch and their matching denim miniskirts. Smiles broad and cheeky. Clearly loving life.

But it's not the girls who chill my blood, it's the men in the background. The men leering and laughing with their lager cans brandished high like trophies.

The men I remember from Dad's pub.

The men who'd count money in the back room when Mum was away.

And "Uncle" Frank, sitting on the arm of a sofa wearing a West Ham shirt identical to Dad's, except Dad's had *"Di Canio 10"* printed on the back whereas Frank's had *"Frankie 666,"* the crass, egotistical prick.

No sign of Dad though, and it definitely wasn't taken in the pub which is something. One molecule of mercy in this mountain of dirt.

Although someone had to be taking the photo. The thought that it might have been Dad is so riddled with dirt that I've got no choice but to temporarily block it out.

I hear voices in the distance as I try to steady my breathing. Familiar, comforting voices. Parnell pacifying Steele over the phone. Emily whining about the stairs. Seth out-poshing Naomi Berry with his upper-class pronunciation and use of the word "splendid."

Suddenly, a voice gets closer. I hadn't even registered him walking in.

"Well?" says Parnell, breathless from the climb. "Is it her?"

I don't answer, I just point toward the top left-hand corner. There's a tremor in my hand that I pray is only visible to me. Parnell's mouth makes a puckered "O" as he clocks the mini-skirted buddies. He confirms to Steele that it's definitely her and hangs up.

Somewhere outside the room, Naomi Berry shouts, "Tea."

Parnell pokes his head out. "No time for tea, I'm afraid. Can you go and see Detective Swaines, please? He'll take a full statement from you. He's out on the landing now—tall lad, fair hair, makes Brad Pitt look like a warthog, you can't miss him."

Her protest about "not knowing anything" gets fainter as she sashays back up the hall.

Parnell picks up my phone, hands it to me with a funny look. "So what does this mean then?"

Usually when Parnell asks me questions like this, it's some sort of test. It's Parnell doing his sage, avuncular thing. Today I think he's genuinely stumped.

"I don't know exactly." My feet prickle with the urge to run away but my legs feel too heavy. I clear some junk off the bed and sit down. The mattress feels saggy and lumpy, decades old. "It means Saskia's been lying through her teeth which has to mean Gina Hicks is lying too, unless we're supposed to believe that Maryanne was friends with Saskia from way back but then *just happened* to turn up on the same IVF forum as Saskia's landlady four years ago. I mean, I know you believe in coincidences, Boss, but I'd like to see the odds on this one."

Parnell takes a photo of the photo on his phone then sits down beside me, staring blankly ahead. "But who's covering for who? And why? What are we missing?" He puts his hand to his jaw. "Damn it, my tooth hurts."

"My head hurts. We've got a victim with two identities, a missing/dead baby, a load of people who couldn't lie straight in bed but no stand-up-in-court motive for any of them. Saskia French's missing. Gina Hicks is clearly hiding *something*. And even though it's the women who are wrecking our heads the most, we're fairly sure our killer, or at least the person who dumped the body, is a man!"

Parnell scratches his head. Half-laughs, because you might as well.

"Aiden Doyle is some big-shot algorithim-analyst-nerd," I add. "He'd have a better shot at solving this headfuck than us, I reckon."

Parnell nudges me. "Hey, we're not quite the Keystone Cops, kiddo, we're getting there. I think we can safely say Saskia French's now a person of interest so we'll get an appeal out for information—Her Majesty can get on to the Press Office. We"—a wiggle of the fingers to confirm he means me and him—"need to find out what the Hickses make of all this. I'll run it by Steele but I don't want to arrest them or bring them in at this point, they'll only lawyer-up if we do. I say we surprise them at home, and then cross our fingers they decide that a cozy little chat on the sofa, under caution of course, doesn't warrant getting their brief over. I just want to see how they explain this away before we get heavy. We won't be able to record it," he adds, "so make sure you note everything down, OK?"

Emily sticks her head around the door, a giddy look on her face. "Sir, I think I might have something. A woman at 12b says she saw Saskia let a guy into the flat on Christmas Eve morning and heard raised voices. She doesn't usually pay much attention to men coming and going—she seems to know the score—but she remembers this one because he looked pretty young."

Young. Not in his mid-fifties with salt-and-pepper hair and a smile that could melt granite. I nearly combust with relief.

"Saskia likes them young," I say. "According to Naomi, anyway. So maybe she's got a boyfriend? Maybe she's *with* a boyfriend?"

Emily hasn't finished. "You know who the description sounds like, Cat? The eldest Hicks lad. The one who came into the kitchen when we were there. You know, the one with the faux-hawk."

"Spiky hair," I confirm to a frowning Parnell. "She means the sweary one with the violin."

Emily continues. "I found him on Instagram. His profile pic's not great, he's used this stupid psychedelic filter which obviously distorts things a bit, but she's still about eighty percent sure it was him."

Parnell stands up abruptly leaving the knackered mattress rippling. "Right, come on," he says to me. "We need to get over there now." To Emily, "Get this collage bagged up, please. Let what's-her-name know we're seizing it on the grounds it could be evidence in relation to an offense."

I snatch one last look at the photo, wishing with every fiber of my being that we could leave it here, displayed in this safe, unthreatening place, far from the world of evidence bags and incident boards. Because, make no mistake, once it's up on our board and "Uncle" Frank's familiar face becomes permanent MIT4 wallpaper, my failure to identify him definitely puts me in losing-my-job-territory.

As if I wasn't there already.

It possibly puts me in losing-my-freedom territory too—attempting to pervert the course of justice wouldn't be too much of a stretch for a particularly pumped-up prosecutor and misconduct in a public office would be mere child's play. A prosecutorial walk in the park.

I trail Parnell back down the hall. His step's surprisingly sprightly given he's got nearly thirty years on me and over thirty kilos, but then he's full of purpose while I'm full of guilt and the guilt is weighing heavy on me. My legs feel like lead. As I pass by the living room, I remember I opened a window earlier. I call out to Parnell to wait a second while I close it.

And that's when I see it.

"Boss," I shout.

Parnell's talking to a recently-arrived SOCO and doesn't come straight-away. I walk out into the hall and tug on his arm like an overwrought child wanting attention. "Boss." He shakes me off, tries to finish his con-versation. "Parnell, now! Please! You need to come and look at this."

The SOCO mutters something sour but I couldn't care less. All I care about is another pair of eyes confirming what I think I can see.

I literally push Parnell into the living room. "Wait there," I say, run-ning back to the spare room where I take the collage out of Emily's hands without explanation. Back in the living room, Parnell's looking grumpy, jiggling his e-cig in his pocket, and so I bypass all the usual preambles of *"I can't be sure"* and *"Now, I might be wrong"* and cut firmly to the chase.

"Look." I point to the wall then back to the image of Maryanne and Saskia. "The paint's a different color but the flouncy plasterwork hasn't changed one bit."

Words I never thought I'd hear myself say.

Parnell swipes my glasses off my nose and onto his, holding the photo close to his face, looking back and forth, his smile growing wider with each gawp. "You know, I think you might be right, kiddo."

"Too right, I'm right. It's unmistakable. It's unmistakably hideous." It's harsh, but roses and ribbons really aren't my thing. "I'm telling you, Boss, that photo was taken in this flat."

25

Amber, the teenage daughter, answers the door, sullen-faced and red-eyed. She jerks a thumb toward the family room then tiptoes quickly up the stairs, hunched and uninterested, eager to get back to the sanctuary of her bedroom.

There's a definite frost in the air. A bleakness that can't be masked by lavish decorations and cozy festive scents. It's there in the quietness of the house, the unnatural stillness. The sheer distance between them as they occupy the same space—Gina Hicks sitting stiffly on the window seat, scrolling through her iPad, Nate by the opposite wall, idly browsing the *Times*. Instantly, I'm thrust back to the countless days when Mum and Dad would skulk around each other, brooding and wallowing in whatever argument had caught light the night before. Just the occasional slammed door slicing through the pained, loaded silence. Me, Jacqui and Noel quietly going about whatever business we'd have usually executed at ear-shattering volume.

The atmosphere is obvious.

Gina knows about Nate's affair.

However, it's amazing what a police caution can do to reconcile a couple. The words seem to bond them as they move in sync from the far corners of the room to the sofa, side by side, hand in hand, looking for all the world like a staged royal photo.

While I get my notepad out, Parnell explains why we're here. Explains why he had to caution them in as reassuring tones as possible. *"We have to cover ourselves, you see? Just in case you have information that can help us."* Gina barely reacts, her thousand-yard-stare suggests this is just one more punch in the gut and she's getting used to it. She also must be the only person in the world who appears to have lost weight over Christmas. A gray silk vest sags lightly over her birdlike frame.

"I appreciate this isn't an ideal time," says Parnell, playing nice, hoping to keep all thoughts of legal representation out of their heads for as long as possible.

"We haven't made plans," replies Gina. "We rarely go out on New Year's Eve. It's all a big con, isn't it? Venues charging through the nose for sub-standard food and entertainment. Taxis are a nightmare . . ."

Hear hear.

"We're worried for Saskia French's safety," says Parnell, all earnest eyes and open hands. "She's been out of contact for some time now and we believe she may have left her flat in a hurry. Can I ask if either of you have heard from her?"

Gina drops her husband's hand.

Parnell directs the question. "Mr. Hicks? Has Saskia been in touch lately?"

Everything about Nate's body language screams tough guy—the balled fists, the clenched jaw, the taut, raised shoulders.

"No, she hasn't," he hisses.

Parnell keeps needling. "Any ideas where she might have gone then? Places that are special to her? Close friends? Did you ever discuss this type of thing?"

He doesn't answer, just emits small angry breaths from his nose.

"I'll take that as a no," says Parnell. "And you Mrs. Hicks?"

She stiffens, regally poised. "No, I haven't heard from her."

Looking up from my notepad, I wince slightly, as though the piece of information I'm about to share pains me as much as them. "Your son, Leo, has been identified as a man who was heard arguing with Saskia on Christmas Eve morning. We naturally need to speak to you—and him—about this."

I'm surprised by the calmness in my voice, the professionalism. I feel anything but.

A blast of confused laughter from Nate. "Leo? Arguing with Saskia?"

I nod. "I think 'raised voices' was the actual term."

"I wasn't debating the nature of the altercation, Detective Kinsella." The smug fuck is back. "I was suggesting there was no altercation at all. Your witness must be mistaken." He laughs again to himself. "Bloody ludicrous."

Gina grips Nate's thigh, quietens him. "I'm afraid you won't be able to speak with Leo. He's away for a few days, playing at a concert in Vienna. He's a very talented violinist—and pianist, of course."

Of course.

She raises her chin. "However, I can tell you *I* sent Leo to Saskia's flat to deliver an eviction notice." Nate shifts, struggling to keep his surprise in check. "He mentioned they'd had words, Saskia can be a little fiery, shall we say, but that's all it was—words. The walls in those flats are so bloody thin, every conversation sounds like raised voices."

"You sent a teenager to deliver a legal letter?" Parnell doesn't hold back on the parental judgment.

Nate cuts in. "Leo's at that age where he wants to feel part of the family business. We've been giving him more responsibility."

"And what exactly is the family business?" asks Parnell, starting to enjoy himself. "I'm aware you have a number of non-executive directorships, Mr. Hicks, and you own a chain of beauty salons . . ."

"Nail bars, actually." He tries to sound blasé but I can tell his feathers are ruffled. No one likes having their background checked.

"My apologies, *nail bars*," says Parnell. "But assuming you don't do the filing and polishing yourself, what is it that you do on a daily basis?"

"Property development and management," he says, vaguely. "Here and overseas."

"Property development *and* management." Parnell pretends to look impressed.

I'm not actually sure where Parnell's going with this. In fact, I'm not altogether sure it's not just a spontaneous pissing contest.

I pull the conversation back to Gina and Leo.

"I'm sorry, Gina, you say you got Leo to deliver the eviction notice?" She nods. "But you were in town yourself on Christmas Eve morning. You came into the station, remember?" Another surprised shift from Nate Hicks. "Why didn't you deliver it yourself? Our station is less than a mile from Saskia's flat."

She bristles. "Because I had no desire to come face to face with Saskia French, that's why. Leo was going into town anyway, skating with friends, so I asked him to drop it in." She looks at me, disappointed. Like I've somehow betrayed her confidence. Betrayed the sisterhood. "And *as you've pointed out*, I came into the station, I had last-minute shopping to do. I wouldn't have had time to go to King's Cross too."

Nate frowns. "Darling, why did you visit the sta—"

She silences him again with another thigh-grip. "I'm sorry Leo's visit seems to have caused an issue, Detectives. If I'd known Saskia would be there, I wouldn't have asked him to do it. She often goes away at Christmas so I thought what harm would it do, Leo shoving a note through the letterbox?"

I tap my notepad with my pen. "Hold on, you said you feared coming face-to-face with Saskia. Now you say you didn't expect her to be there anyway?"

A pinched smile. "I just didn't want to risk it."

"Why?" asks Parnell. "Why didn't you want to risk coming face-to-face with Saskia French?"

Nate shrinks into himself, his pallor whiter than the marble fireplace.

Gina lowers her eyes. "I believe you already know the answer to that question, Detective. I don't know why you feel the need to humiliate me in my own home."

"Can we see the eviction letter, Gina. Take a copy?" I say it softly, in a way that suggests I'm trying to help, trying to divert things away from her husband's indiscretion but if anything she looks more uncomfortable.

"I didn't make a copy. I just filled it out quickly and pressed print. Sorry."

I shrug, note this down. "Not to worry, we'll assume it's in Saskia's flat somewhere. Our Forensics team should turn it up."

Stony-faced, she says, "I'm actually very sorry to hear Saskia might be in danger. I wouldn't wish that on anyone, despite *everything*, but I don't see what more we can do."

Parnell doesn't bow to the pious act. "What you can do, Mrs. Hicks, is have your son return on the next flight for questioning."

A hand to her chest. "That sounds rather extreme!"

"Not at all. As far as we're aware, Leo was the last person seen with Saskia French. You must understand that we need to speak with him."

Nate appeals to Parnell. "Look, mate, do you have sons?" The *"mate"* sounds ridiculous. Plummy and contrived.

"Four," says Parnell.

"Gosh." *"Gosh"* suits him better than *"mate."* "Well then, you'll know that young lads love playing the big man. That's all Leo was doing, I'm sure of it." He gives Gina a fond—some might say condescending—smile. "You really should have judged that better, darling, but honestly, Detectives, there's really nothing we—or Leo—can tell you."

He's either brave or stupid—lecturing his wife on her judgment when he's been sweating up the sheets with their prostitute tenant.

"We'd rather hear that from Leo, all the same," says Parnell.

Nate's eyes dart. He's looking for an escape route. "Well, actually, there's a problem with the flights apparently. Storms and strong winds of up to a hundred kilometers an hour across northern Austria, we're led to believe. The forecast isn't looking great either so God knows when Leo will get back. How about a Skype chat?" He looks pleased with this suggestion. "Although I suspect reception won't be great. We haven't heard from him since Monday, not that that's unusual with teenage boys. We'll try to arrange something in the next day or two, does that work?"

Parnell bites back a smile—I mean, Nate Hicks' arrogance *is* pretty amusing.

Deciding it's time to hit them with something tangible, Parnell takes out his phone and starts tapping the screen, doing his bumbly Luddite act, muttering *"bloody technology"* under his breath.

Nate looks bemused but Gina senses something serious is in the offing. I sit back and watch the rapid rise and fall of her bony chest.

Eventually, Parnell leans forward, offering his phone.

"This is a photo of Saskia French pictured with Maryanne Doyle, or we can call her Alice Lapaine for argument's sake. Would you both take a look and tell me if you agree."

Nate studies the photo, making it bigger, then smaller, with the ease of a man who spends his life on his smartphone. "Well, it's certainly Saskia, a much younger Saskia. I don't know the other woman, other than the photos I've seen in the media and the one you showed me, so I wouldn't be able to say with absolute certainty that it is her."

Gina takes the phone, holds it with both hands, frowning. "They both look a lot different but yes, I'd say that's Saskia and Alice."

I put my pad down, stare at her intently. "So bearing in mind you've agreed that this is Saskia and 'Alice' pictured many, many years ago, we have to ask, Gina, is it true that you only met 'Alice' four years ago?" She says nothing. I soften my tone, see if that works. "Come on, you have to admit, it just seems too coincidental that the woman you claim you met on a random IVF forum four years ago turns out to be a longtime friend of one of your long-term tenants?"

I shouldn't have used the word "coincidental." It gives her an out, no matter how poor an out it is. She hands the phone back to Parnell, bolder now. "It must be, as you say, a coincidence. There's no other explanation."

"Oh, I think there is, Mrs. Hicks." Parnell's voice is thick with warning. "What would you say if we told you that this photo, which we're putting at around 1999, maybe 2000, was taken in *your* King's Cross flat. Do you see why this makes it very hard for us to believe what you're saying?"

Nate sighs irritably. "Gina didn't own the flat then so this really is pointless. Tiresome, even."

"Honestly, I don't know what to tell you," she says, sounding desperate. It could be an act but the frown line, once deep, is now cavernous. "This just isn't making any sense. We got the flat in 2005, Saskia French was a sitting tenant who came with excellent references . . ."

Nate takes her hand. "I've explained this to them, darling, they just don't want to listen. Perhaps we should call Felix?"

No need to guess who Felix is.

Parnell powers on and I don't blame him. *"Perhaps we should . . ."* isn't the same as *"I demand to see . . ."* but we've probably got a matter of minutes at most.

"Mr. and Mrs. Hicks, a murdered woman, who you"—a point to Gina—"have at least admitted knowing, is pictured many years ago in a flat that you now *just happen* to own. Now I'll be honest with you, I don't know what you're lying about but I know you're lying. A woman is dead and she's continually being linked to your King's Cross flat."

"Did you hear what my wife said? We didn't buy the property until . . ."

I'm sick of the sound of his voice. I don't know how Gina sticks it. "From who?" I say, sharply. "Who did you buy the flat from? And it will only take us ten minutes to find out so do yourselves a favor . . ."

"From me."

A voice from the doorway. Frail but commanding.

The grandad.

He of the Santa beard and stage-four cancer.

"Well, Gina didn't buy it from me, of course. I transferred it over to her." A quick chuckle. "I got it off Lenny Spoons in the seventies, if you're interested. Didn't buy it, I won it in a poker bet. They were good times, back then. Lawless."

Gina jumps up, moves toward him, arms outstretched. "Dad . . . please . . . don't . . . we've got this . . . don't say anything else."

Parnell stands up, astounded, mouth gaping like a fish. I glance from one to the other, waiting to be put in the picture, but they just eyeball each other, locked in their own private reunion. There's a hint of a grin on Parnell's face. "Mr. Mackie, it's been a very long time," he says eventually. "Did the craving for a decent cup of tea finally get to you? Or is it the weather that tempted you back?"

The old man laughs. "Tell you the truth, it's that copper sense of humor I missed the most. The *Cuerpo Nacional de Policía* take themselves far too seriously. Bit of a mouthful, ain't it? *La Pasma* tends to do. Means 'the cops,' 'the pigs,' y'know?"

Parnell turns to Gina Hicks whose face is the color of glue. "OK, I think it's time we swapped places, people. You all need to come to our place and our guys need to move into yours. Oh, and Mr. Hicks." Nate Hicks has his head in his hands but at the sound of his name, he looks up. "I'm arresting you both for assisting an offender, and quite possibly for perverting the course of justice, so I think you might be right—perhaps it is time you called Felix."

It turns out Felix Whiteley is a bit more partial to a New Year knees-up than Nate and Gina Hicks and when they do finally get hold of him, two hours later, he's already halfway to the New Forest, where he and his good lady wife are attending a seven-course dinner and a "Masquerade Ball."

Whatever that may be.

Of course, he agrees to turn around and come charging back up the M3, however with warnings of a jack-knifed lorry just before Basingstoke, he really can't say what time he'll be able to join our little NYE soiree, which leaves the Hickses contemplating life in a holding cell and Patrick Mackie with the police surgeon. Word is, he'll be deemed fit to be detained as long as he's kept under regular observation.

Steele's appeal for information on Saskia's whereabouts went out a short while ago. I'm not sure how many people actually watch the six o'clock news on New Year's Eve—most people have started the final blowout by then, I suspect—but we've all agreed to stay in the office on standby, manning the phones and ready to leap into action if required.

Someone's ordered in pizza but for once I don't feel hungry.

Parnell's in his element though, regaling the team over slices of deep-pan Hawaiian.

"Patrick Mackie. Quite the face when I was a wet-behind-the-ears bobby."

Ben can't help himself, grabbing a clutch of fake snow from the base of the Christmas tree and sticking it in front of his chin. "Here, Boss, do you recognize me in this cunning disguise?"

To be fair, Parnell takes it in good humor. It's not every day you over-look one of the UK's Most Wanted because they were dressed like Father Christmas.

"In my defense," he says, "Mackie answered the door once and I saw him for all of two seconds and as you've pointed out, I could hardly see his face. Them pair"—a point toward me and Emily—"had a whole bloody conversation with him."

"We've never heard of him though," Emily protests. "We can't be ex-pected to recognize every criminal who's ever existed since the Second World War!"

I smile but I'm too drained to enter the fray. And I know Parnell's only messing.

"Second World War! Cheeky mare," he says, smiling. "Anyway, as I was saying before I was *so* rudely interrupted, Patrick Mackie was defi-nitely something of a big shot back in the day. Made his name in the seventies but really came into his own in the eighties and kept going until around 2007. Drug trafficking, protection rackets, prostitution, se-curity fraud, you name it. There were rumors he was involved in people trafficking too—maybe not actually running the show, but putting the money up. Same with a number of big-league armed robberies."

"Mainly London?" I ask, just to say something. Asking questions makes me feel a little less isolated.

"Mainly, but the big networks always spread it out a bit. That way, they exploit the fragmented nature of our so-called 'great' British polic-ing structure. It was definitely fragmented in those days, anyway."

"So what happened to knock him off his perch?" asks Flowers.

"SOCA, that's what happened." Serious Organized Crime Agency. "Tony Blair's vow to make life hell for the 'Mr. Bigs.' Mackie got a tip-off we were closing in on him, did a flit. Amsterdam for a while, apparently, then Spain. Not a peep out of him since."

"I suppose it was one of us that tipped him off?" says a world-weary Flowers.

Parnell rubs his hands. "A high-ranking politician, if you believe the rumors."

"Bit of a risk coming back to the UK?" suggests Craig.

"He's old, terminally ill. Not got a lot to lose, I suppose."

Maryanne. This is about Maryanne, not some washed-up gangster in a Santa suit.

I look at Parnell. "Boss, this is all very interesting but what are we saying? Maryanne was mixed up in some sort of organized crime thing? And anyway, Patrick Mackie had retired, right?"

"His sort never retire, they just retreat into the background. I mean, those nail bars that Nate Hicks supposedly owns. They've got Patrick Mackie written all over them. Nail bars, tanning salons, what have you—classic fronts for money laundering."

Renée shouts over. "The Hickses both came up clean as a whistle though, nothing on the PNC. Nothing for a Gina Mackie either."

"They're involved," says Parnell without a shadow of doubt. "Somehow. They have to be. We just need to pray Forensics turns something up at the house and we can worry about the why later. For now, we just need *something* to hang our hat on. How are we going on Leo Hicks, Cat?"

Honest answer—we aren't.

"I've been on to Passport Control in Vienna. He definitely entered the country on Sunday 28th so maybe they are telling the truth about that and it's nothing? Maybe he was sent to Saskia's with some sort of message, he did his Billy-big-balls thing, and then he left? I managed to get hold of his head teacher—you know, in case the concert was a school thing and he could give me a location, but apparently it's not. First he'd heard of it, actually. Kept going on and on about what a talent Leo is and how they're hoping he'll get into the Royal College of Music."

"We'll find him," says Parnell, "it's a matter of time. Even if Nate and Gina have stopped talking, we've got their phones now and they must have been in contact with him, surely? They both seem pretty hot on deleting texts but once Digital gets digging, we should get something."

"I've got something!" Across the other side of the room, Seth slams the phone down then struts a victory walk across the floor. "Saskia French." Parnell reaches for his car keys. "No, no, don't get too excited, Boss, it's not a sighting—it's someone who thinks she worked with her in the late nineties/early noughties at an abortion clinic in Camden. She knew her as Sarah Finch though—very inventive—and she was a receptionist/admin type. They fired her early 2001 when she was caught taking sensitive information home, basically clients' personal details. They thought she was maybe planning to blackmail some of them. Apparently, they didn't call the police at the time because they didn't want the drama—it's hard enough for some women to visit them without hearing about that type of thing—but anyway, she just thought it was worth us knowing that if Saskia is this Sarah Finch, she's always been a bit of a shady character."

"So she's not certain it's her?" I say, raining on Seth's parade which absolutely isn't my intention.

"Fairly sure but she wouldn't 'put the house on it,' were her exact words. I think it's the same person though. She was able to give me a lot of physical detail—well, as much as you can fifteen years later—and I've just cross-checked with the extra description Naomi Berry gave to Steele for the TV appeal."

"What extra description?" I ask.

I didn't actually watch it. Couldn't bring myself to.

"Distinguishing features, that sort of thing."

"She's not far off six feet, that's fairly distinguishing," says Craig.

Seth nods. "Indeed, but she's also a bit of a tattoo and piercing junkie apparently. My caller said this Sarah Finch used to have several piercings *and* tattoos. She'd get a little contrary when they'd ask her to cover them up on reception. That fits with what Naomi Berry told Steele about how when Saskia's 'off-duty', she usually wears a ring in her nose, one in her eyebrow." He points to the deep groove under his bottom lip. "And a stud just here."

An ice-cold sensation sweeps the surface of my skin. Seth's voice fades to nothing and a sharper voice comes into unwelcome focus: Noel.

"At a rough guess, I'd say he's shagging that sweet-ass with the lip-stud, the one who comes in here."

The one who stood with her back to me in McAuley's. Tribal tattoos snaking all the way down her spine.

What had Dad said about her?

"She's in her thirties, actually, and anyway she's just a friend."

Dad knows Saskia.

I wait until Seth's finished then pull Parnell to one side. Tell him I need to pop out for a while. Say I know it's not ideal but I'm not feeling great. Nothing major, no dramas, but I need some fresh air and maybe a trip to the chemist. Just an hour, I say, tops.

Of course, he says, no problem. Take as long as I need. Come to think of it, he thought I was looking a bit ropey.

I thank him, say he's the best boss ever, say I'll just finish my notes on the call with Leo's head teacher and then I'll head off.

I don't say there's a chance I might never be back.

26

I sign out a pool car and head straight for McAuley's, fairly sure that Dad won't be there but still inclined to check. Parnell's definitely rubbed off on me over the past six months.

"Time and patience got the snail to America, kiddo."

"Every dead end is another box ticked."

I picture his face in a few hours' time. Those kind, smiley eyes clouded by betrayal and disappointment. The thought turns my heart to wet sand.

I park across the street. There's no light upstairs, no sign he's here at all, but I head over anyway. Argue with some bureaucrat on steroids who says I need a ticket to come in. My warrant card twitches in my pocket but I try out my daughter credentials first. He doesn't believe me though so I tell him to get Xavier. Cross my fingers that a sexy Spanish barman remembers a plain girl in a parka from nearly a fortnight ago.

He does, and I'm in.

"He's not here though," he says, frowning. "I thought he was with you."

"Me?" The absurdity of it actually makes me laugh, despite everything.

Xavier calls to another barman, checks he hasn't picked it up wrong.

Other Barman confirms it. "Nah, he's not been here for days. He's away with family. Skiing in Val d'Isere, I think?"

Dad took us to Val d'Isere once. Mum said it was important to learn how to ski now I was at a posh school. I wasn't exactly a natural though and I felt self-conscious the whole time. My single happy memory is of the caramel apple crepes I used to scoff after each and every meal.

But Dad's not in Val d'Isere now.

The New Year's Eve roads are quiet as I shoot north into Hertford-shire, and I rocket up to Radlett in less than an hour, only nudging the speed limit twice. All the way, I get green light after green light and gracious drivers wave me out of side roads. I should be pleased—I'm not exactly a patient driver at the best of times—but instead I have this burning, twisting feeling that the world's conspiring to get me there as fast as possible and I'm terrified of finding out the reason why.

The house is in darkness. The cul-de-sac's one and only party-pooper. Even Kevin Farrow, Kevin "Killjoy" Farrow as Dad used to call him, ap-pears to be having some sort of get-together and a glut of cars are parked bumper-to-bumper around the horseshoe of the street.

I can't see Dad's car though.

Could I have got this wrong?

I go through the gate and walk down the side of the house, the nar-row space between the kitchen extension and the garage where I used to smoke crafty fags and text even craftier boys. I peer through the garage window but again, no car.

My phone vibrates: Parnell.

Hicks' lawyer still having a 'mare on M3. Interview in morning.
Don't come back if you feel poorly, think we've got enough cover.
SMS 19:36 p.m.

I tap out a "fanks!" and a thumbs-up emoji. This buys me a bit of time at least.

It's drizzling now. Freezing rain, not quite sleet. All the doors at the back are double-locked and the kitchen blinds are closed. I look for evi-dence in the trash that someone's been here recently but there's noth-ing. Nothing in any of them. Just a frantic spider in the recycling bin, dizzying itself in circles.

I know the feeling, mate.

I take the spider in my hand and flick it gently onto the path, wondering if I've just rescued it or made its predicament worse. Suffocation versus hypothermia? Two brutal ends of a particularly shitty stick.

The analogy isn't lost on me as I watch it scuttle away.

I look at my phone and scroll for Dad's number. I'd wanted the element of surprise but this is getting me nowhere so there's nothing else for it, I'm going to have to do things the long-winded way. I'm going to have to call him, hope he answers, ask him very nicely where he is and then ask even more nicely if he'll talk to me. I fully expect to get his voicemail—that deep, cheerful voice saying, *"Bollocks, I've missed you. Leave a message"*—but to my surprise it rings.

And it's ringing inside the house.

I vault toward the patio doors, hammering my palms against the glass. "Dad, it's me. I know you're in there."

Nothing. Somewhere up the street a bass thumps out a generic dance hook.

"Let me in," I shout into the dark. "I know you know Saskia. And that she knew Maryanne." More nothing. I keep the volume but change my tone. "Listen, it's either me or my colleagues, Dad. And they'll be baying for blood, I just want to understand."

I've no idea whether I mean this or not.

I dial his phone again. And again. When it goes to voicemail the third time, I walk over to the rock garden, now neglected, and pick up the largest stone I can find. Standing by the back door, I take three breaths to consider the consequences of what I'm about to do. An alarm could go off? *Would Dad actually hurt me?*

I'm about to lose my nerve when the door clicks open.

His silhouette's enough to shock me. The heavy droop of his shoulders and the hang of his head. He looks smaller, somehow. Diminished. To think I've spent most of my life kicking against all his swagger and the gangster-lite bravado. Now I can hardly look at this sunken version.

Just a scared middle-aged man, hiding out in the dark.

"You can't stay long," he says, retreating into the house. "It might not be safe."

I step into the kitchen, instinctively reaching left for the light. He grabs my arm and pulls me with him. "What do you mean, 'not safe?'" I try to shake him off. "What's going on, Dad? What's with the blackout?"

"In the study," he says, shoving me forward.

I walk into the so-called "study." The small enclave at the center of the house, accessible through the dining room on one side, the "good" living room on the other.

No windows to the outside world. So no announcements to the outside world that anyone's here either.

And no ventilation. The air's sour and smoky.

"It's all right during the day," he says, sitting down behind an oak desk that was bought purely for show. "I just stay away from the main windows. But at night, it's the only room where I feel safe turning the lights on."

I stay standing, sizing him up, waiting for an explanation. When it doesn't come I sit down, taking the chair opposite. Committing myself physically to however long this is going to take.

"Just tell me, Dad. Tell me what you did, or what you've done, and I promise things will feel a whole lot better."

It's the oldest trick in the book, of course. "*Interrogation for Dummies*." My soft voice, the bedtime-story tone, I've done it countless times—"*Come on now . . . I know you're a good guy . . . you'll feel a whole lot better when you get it off your chest . . .*"

He doesn't fall for it though so I revert to basics. The "Specific-Closed" I think they called it at Hendon.

"Do you know where Saskia is?"

"No."

"Do you know if she's in danger?"

Silence.

"Did you hurt Maryanne?" My mouth won't form the word "kill."

He gives me a look so heartsick that I swear I feel the heavy sadness that's crushing him. For a second I can actually taste his shame.

"No," he says, a mere whisper.

"Then who did?"

His eyes fix on a photo, just to the right of my head. One of those expensive family portraits that make it look like you all like each other.

"It was supposed to be a one-off," he says eventually, sighing deeply. "Just Maryanne. But it spiraled out of control. I didn't want what happened . . . I'm not a bad person, Catrina . . . I know you think I am, but I'm not . . . nor was Maryanne, really . . ."

I say nothing. He's trying to convince himself, not me.

"I was in deep shit, you see. I owed money to this . . . well, this guy you don't want to owe money to, let's just put it that way. I was playing a lot of poker back then. Underground poker, backroom stuff. Winning big sometimes, losing big more often. Anyway, this guy wanted his money back. One of his men approached Jacqui, you know. Stopped her in the street, told her how pretty she was, gave it all that 'you could be a model' bullshit." He laughs, sadly. "Christ, she was hyper that night, do you remember?" I do. Hyper's not the word I'd use. Try insufferable. "I knew it was him playing games though. I knew what the threat meant."

"Patrick Mackie?"

A quick nod. If he's surprised I know the name, he doesn't show it. "So I needed to get away for a while. Get us all away. Lie low. And your mum felt guilty that she hadn't been home for years—I mean, we hadn't been back since you were born—so I thought two birds, one stone, why not? Just for a few weeks while I worked out what to do."

"So you were always a fuck-up, Dad. That really isn't big news. What's it got to do with Maryanne?"

He picks up a bottle of something clear; gin, maybe vodka, I can't see the label. "We need to get one thing straight, sweetheart. I never laid a hand on Maryanne, then or now. That isn't what this is about."

I stay stock-still. "OK, I'm listening."

Something unlocks and the words spew out. Maybe if I'd offered to hear him out years ago, instead of all the teenage histrionics and grown-up passive-aggression, we might have got to this point sooner.

"It started with that bloody barmaid in Grogan's." He shakes his head bitterly. "We had a drunken kiss one night—and that's all it was, Catrina, a stupid drunken kiss, I could hardly remember it the next day. But Maryanne saw us. She was a sharp one, I'll give her that—had a bit of scandal on everyone and wasn't afraid to use it if it benefited her. Anyway, she threatened to tell your mum what she'd seen and well . . . me and your mum were on a sticky wicket already, and on top of all the shit with Mackie, I just didn't need it."

"So how did blackmailing you benefit her? What did she want?"

He closes his eyes, sighs again. "She was pregnant."

I knew this, of course. We've suspected it ever since the post-mortem and Hazel O'Keefe more or less confirmed it yesterday. *How can that only be yesterday?* But hearing it from Dad adds an ominous weight to it. He says the word "pregnant" like it means everything. Like it's the reason we're here. The reason we've spent a lifetime splintering each other's hearts.

"She said she'd keep quiet if I gave her a few hundred quid and a lift to Dublin that Saturday, to the ferry. She wanted an abortion, you see, she had to get to Liverpool."

I remember that Saturday. Dad gone since lunchtime, Mum perming Gran's hair. Jacqui and Noel off somewhere. "Gallivanting," Gran called it.

I was so bored that day I actually did my maths homework.

"So I said yes . . . eventually. What else could I do?"

"You could have told Mum? I mean, what was one more . . . especially if it was just a drunken kiss."

He cuts me off quickly. "But you see, I felt sorry for Maryanne too, even though she was a crafty one. Jonjo Doyle was a nasty little shit, especially after a few pints, and I knew the beating she'd get when he found out she was up the spout." He looks at me for a long second, trying to communicate something. I think he's begging me not to judge him too harshly. "So I hit on an idea, see? The worst fucking idea of my life, sweetheart, but you've no idea how stressed out I was about Patrick Mackie and for the first time in weeks, I could actually see a way out."

He pushes the bottle toward me, doesn't offer me a glass. I want to say no but it might steady my heartbeat.

I drink straight from the bottle. Neat white rum.

"Patrick Mackie was a nasty, greedy bastard." He points a finger. "Now I wasn't involved in *this* at all, you understand, but I knew he had this racket going—paying prostitutes a few thousand quid to get pregnant and then selling the babies on the black market."

There were rumors he was involved in people trafficking . . .

"He made good money off it too. There's plenty of desperate people with deep pockets who can't have kids. Problem was, half the time the girls were addicts. They'd promise to stop using but they never did, and then the babies were born addicted, or with low birth weights, what have you, and I think it was getting to the point where he was wondering if it was worth the hassle. I had *nothing* to do with this, you understand," he repeats. "I just heard a lot of things, knew a lot of people . . ."

It's obvious where this is heading but I need to hear him say it.

"So Maryanne got me thinking—'cos she was upset, you know—she wasn't blasé about the abortion, she just thought she didn't have a choice. And so I looked at her—fit, healthy, good-looking, smart, that perfect Irish colleen thing going on, and I thought, 'Well maybe you *do* have a choice, missus?' Patrick Mackie had all the contacts and I mean, it was obvious any rich couple would take one look at Maryanne and fall in love with her, which meant falling in love with her baby ten times over, so I knew it meant big money. Enough for her to make a clean break away from that shit of a father. So I made that clear to Mackie, when I finally got up the guts to make contact. I made sure he understood this wasn't some skank-whore he could palm off with a couple of grand, he'd have to pay big but then he'd get paid big as well—at least five times what he was paying Maryanne—so it was a good deal for him . . ."

"And a good deal for you. You'd be back in the good books. Everyone's a winner, eh?"

Defensive. "Everyone *was* a winner, sweetheart. Maryanne didn't take much persuading, I can promise you that."

"Everyone apart from the baby, sold off to the highest bidder like a meat raffle."

I should want to spit at him. Bounce his head off the wall. Tear at his face. But I don't feel angry, I feel nothing. Hollow and weightless. I dig my nails into the palms of my hands just to feel the sensation.

"I thought the highest bidders were good people. Criminals maybe, but having a few brushes with the law doesn't mean you can't give a child a good life. It doesn't mean you don't know how to love. Do you know how hard it is to adopt legally if you've got more than a speeding fine? Might have changed now, of course, but back then . . ." His voice trails off.

"So what happened next?"

"What she'd asked to happen. I picked her up, she hid in the boot until we were well out of Mulderrin . . ."

The Tinkerbell mystery solved, eighteen years and a hundred battles too late.

He frowns, confused as to why I'm so shaken by such a small detail. "Well, it's just you never knew who you'd pass on the road," he says, explaining, "or who'd flag you over for a quick chat. We just didn't want to take the risk, that's all. But as soon as we were a good few miles away, she jumped into the back, went to sleep I think, and I drove her to Dublin as planned and she got on the ferry. Only difference was that someone from Mackie's crew was waiting at the other end to take her to London. And she didn't go through with the abortion and she got paid ten thousand quid."

Ten thousand pounds. Around twelve thousand pounds in today's money. The watch on Dad's wrist couldn't have cost much less.

"So if it was such a happy-ever-after, why is Maryanne dead? Why are you hiding in the dark in your own bloody house?"

"Maryanne was supposed to be a one-off," he says, pressing his fingers into his forehead, squashing the memories. "I mean, I can't believe *now* that I was so fucking naïve, but it never occurred to me that Mackie would want to run with it, turn it into a separate operation. And Maryanne, you know, she'd got a taste of the high life, she wanted more. It was her idea to target someone working at an abortion clinic."

"Saskia."

He nods. "A lot of the Irish girls headed for Manchester or Liverpool, nearer to the ferry I suppose, but some of them would get the train down to London and Camden was the nearest clinic to Euston. That's where Saskia worked. Basically, she'd tip off Maryanne about any girl who sounded like she was wobbling, pass on their contact details. Maryanne would make the approach and the odd one would go for it. There you have it, big business," he adds with a sneer.

I almost laugh. "And what, *you* didn't approve? Don't tell me you weren't getting a decent kickback. Commission, was it? Payment on delivery? Literally." I look around the room at all the handmade furniture, all the gadgets, the *stuff.* "Oh my God, that's what paid for everything, isn't it? For all this shit. For my fucking education."

He picks up a coaster, turns it over, turns it back again—something to do to avoid meeting my eyes. Eventually he says, "You won't believe me but I wasn't comfortable with it all. Not one bit. I hadn't meant it to spiral like it did—but Maryanne and Saskia, *especially* Maryanne—it was like she thought they were performing some kind of public service, helping girls make the best out of a bad situation, that was her argument—no abortion required, girl gets paid, *we* all get paid, doting parents get bouncing baby, where's the problem? She had me convinced for a while that it was a kind of victimless crime. And yeah, I liked the money so I just blanked out the bad feeling."

"Which was what?"

A bold stare. "That it was wrong."

Does that change anything? Mean anything? Does it make him a better man than I thought, or worse?

"Did Mum know about this. About any of it?" I choke on the words, fearing the answer.

Mercifully, he shakes his head, appalled. "No, never, absolutely nothing. She turned a blind eye to a lot of stuff, your mum—she wasn't Mother Teresa, you know, she liked the high life too, the nice things—but she wouldn't have turned a blind eye to this, no way. The less she knew the better."

So there we have it. I might have to do a surface edit of the past, lightly reconfigure my image of Mum so that she's less righteous and more mercenary, but essentially it's quite simple.

She was human. She was flawed. She liked fancy things. She loved Dad.

But she had her limits.

I can live with this.

I turn my focus back to Dad. "You said Maryanne had you convinced 'for a while.' What changed?"

"I learned things." His mouth twists and quivers, fury and disgust. "Most of those babies weren't being sold to doting parents, they were being sold on to other trafficking networks, global networks. God knows where they ended up, who they ended up with." He rocks slightly, his knuckles white around his glass. "I actually can't bring myself to think about it, Catrina. If I think about it too much I . . . it haunts me every day of my life what I started." He looks at me, desperate for understanding. "As soon as I knew, I told Mackie I didn't want anything more to do with it, not that I had much to do with it by that time anyway, I was just helping out on the sidelines really, driving the girls around, maintenance of the flat, that sort of thing."

"Girls?"

He nods, the effort seems to pain him. "Yeah, there'd be three or four pregnant girls in that flat at any one time. Maryanne and Saskia lived there too, minding them. 'Guiding them' Maryanne used to call it."

A baby factory right in the middle of central London. Right now, I wish there was a window to look out of. Something to remind me there's life—stars, sky, people, laughter—outside this snake pit of a room.

"What about medical care? I mean, how did they . . . ?" My voice is cracked, hoarse.

"Mackie's daughter, Gina. She was a trainee doctor back then. Daddy insisted she had a respectable job and a doctor's a handy person to have in the family for people like Mackie. Gina's the one who actually oversaw things on a daily basis. She was Maryanne and Saskia's boss, I suppose."

I lean forward. "What happened, Dad? This was years ago. What brought everything back up?"

"*Maryanne* brought it all back up. She tracked me down a few months ago. I literally hadn't laid eyes on her in fifteen years and there she was, standing on my doorstep one night, saying she wanted to contact Gina. Wouldn't say what for. Just that she'd been thinking about the past and . . ." He puts his hands up in a *"who knows?"* gesture. "Anyway, she said she'd seen Saskia but Saskia wouldn't tell her where Gina was. I said that was probably for a bloody good reason—I knew Gina'd gone all respectable in her old age and she wouldn't thank Maryanne for turning up. But Maryanne wouldn't let it go. She seemed a bit desperate, pitiful really. And I felt guilty for what I'd got her involved in all those years ago, so eventually I cracked and I told her. Not that I knew Gina's exact address but I know people, I can find out things." He stares into his drink, broken. "Week later, Maryanne was dead."

I wait awhile, although it's probably only seconds. "So Gina killed Maryanne, is that what you're saying?"

A small twitch of his shoulders. "*You're the detective, you do the maths.*"

Fear and love combined equals panic. "So does she blame you for sending Maryanne her way? Have you been threatened? Is that why you're hiding? Jesus, Dad, couldn't you think of somewhere better than hiding out in your own house?"

He shrugs, a hint of the old bravado. "I doubt Maryanne told her it was me, and I don't know if Gina'd remember me that well, anyway. I worked for Mackie, not her. Gina just saw me as this well-paid handyman. And Mackie, well he hasn't been seen for years. Went on the run. Could be dead for all I know."

"So why all this?" I say, circling two fingers.

"A precaution."

"Against what? You said you don't think they'll come after you."

The door opens. I age twenty years but Dad looks more annoyed than afraid.

"He's protecting me, not himself."

Saskia.

"I came to him," she says, edging into the room—"*so lay off him*" being the obvious subtext. "That thug turned up . . . threatening me— 'delivering a message,' he said . . . I couldn't stay there . . . I didn't know where else to go."

The "thug" throws me. "Patrick Mackie?"

She looks to Dad, her face blanched with dread. "Why's she bringing him up, Mike? You said he was long gone? Dead, with any luck." She turns to me. "I'm on about Gina's son. Mummy's little henchman. You know, he actually thought I was scared of *him*—as if I'd be scared of that little twerp—but I'm scared of that family. Fucking terrified."

I break it to them. "Patrick Mackie's not dead and he's back in England." Dad jumps up, shifting the desk a few inches. "Relax. He's dying, if that's any comfort. And he's in police custody, as is Gina Hicks. You're safe so turn the rest of the fucking lights on!"

"Custody," snarls Saskia. "You think the Mackies don't still have a long reach? If they want to shut me up, they'll find someone to do it, doesn't matter if they're in *custody*."

"Why do they want to shut you up? Because you know about the past? Or because you know what happened to Maryanne?"

Dad gives her a nod, a resigned go-ahead. "Two sides of the same coin, really. I know everything." She slides down the wall, slumping hard to the floor, exhausted. "So how did you nail them? Who talked?" Her head snaps up, eyes wide. "There's no way they'll get bail, is there? Not for this?"

I can't lie. I mean, literally, I can't. I don't have one ounce of guile left in me.

"We don't have them for this. We've arrested them on other grounds for now but they aren't exactly top-drawer. They're locked up for tonight, that's all I can promise you." *So make a decision, quick.* "We're going to need more to hold them for longer. Can you give us more? We can protect you, Saskia, if you tell us everything you know. It's the only way you'll be safe in the long run."

I say "we" but my career's surely over. It was over after the first lie. I don't need to read the College of Policing's *Standards of Professional Behavior* to know mine have been utterly abysmal.

Saskia looks to Dad again and something weighty passes between them. I'm not sensing a romance but something deeper. True friendship might be Disney-coating it, more a mutual kind of dependency.

She takes a deep, trembly breath, a life-changing one. "OK, I'll tell you *everything* on one condition. You keep Mike—*your dad*—out of it."

Has she always known who I am? Did she know the day I was at the King's Cross flat?

"He doesn't need to be involved. He wasn't really involved anyway, not in a big way, or in the worst way. And he took care of me that night, the night Maryanne died, when I had nowhere else to go, and I won't see him punished for this. I won't. He's the only person who ever gave a shit about me and Maryanne, then and now. He looked out for us, had a laugh with us, treated us like human beings, not like prison guards and the girls like cattle. So that's the deal. You don't need Mike to take them down, you only need me."

It's a lovely spin to put on things and I nearly ask her to keep talking. To pull up a pew and tell me all about the great man I've missed out on, all the wonderful traits I could never see. And it's a lifeline too. A chance to cling on to the job I love for that little bit longer—because I'm not stupid enough to think that it wouldn't come back to bite me in the end, of course. But just a little bit longer would be nice. Long enough for me to be remembered for more than just this.

It'll never happen though. How can it?

"You might want to keep my dad out of it, Saskia, but when we charge Gina Hicks, she might have other ideas. And Patrick Mackie."

She slaps me down quickly—she's clearly thought this through. "That's not the way they work. Their type don't drag people down with them, certainly not—no offense, Mike—the small fry. What would be the point? You're only giving someone ammunition to spill more shit on you and Mike has plenty of shit on them, stuff that goes beyond this. They wouldn't run the risk, I know it. There's no benefit in dragging him into this for anyone." A pointed look toward me. "Including you, I'd have thought?"

So Saskia tells all. The Hickses go down. One of the UK's most wanted villains is back under our jurisdiction and Maryanne gets justice.

And I get to keep my job, or at least have a wild, gutsy, come-what-may stab at keeping it.

Everyone's a winner, right?

I slowly nod my head but I feel laden with loss.

27

I picture us in the pub when this is all over. Flowers is getting the round in. Ben and Seth are monopolizing the jukebox as usual. Me and Parnell have bagged our regular table—the oak-paneled booth, big and round enough to house a midsize Murder team—and Renée's swearing she's only staying for one, later claiming she meant one bottle, not one glass. Emily's being chatted up by *someone*—could be one of the old boys who drink in here because the beer's fairly cheap and they show the Channel 4 racing, or maybe one of the young suits, who pour out of local offices, professing their love for a "proper old boozer" before loading up on low-strength bottled lager and bags of vegetable crisps.

As ever, the busiest woman in Christendom—DCI Kate Steele—"will be there in a minute."

Then once the booze has been bought and the tunes have been chosen, conversation will inevitably turn to the moment this case cracked open. Our breakthrough. Everyone will stake a claim in it, of course. Exaggerate their part in its unraveling. But the fact of the matter is nobody swung this case one way or the other. No one gets the bragging rights. Because as far as anyone except me is concerned, at nine fifty-two p.m. on December 31st 2016, Saskia French walked into the reception of Holborn police station and voluntarily, and of her own volition, asked to speak with whoever was in charge of the Maryanne Doyle investigation.

Parnell was out at the time, having a quick walk around the block—his "evening constitutional" to quote the great man himself, so Seth got the gist down while Parnell hotfooted it back to HQ, read Saskia her rights.

She refused a solicitor.

This is how it happened, no matter how it's romanticized and re-configured in the annals of MIT4 history.

This is how it's happening right now, in fact.

Present in the interview are Acting Detective Inspector Luigi Parnell and DC Renée Akwa. Parnell and Renée are a good combination. More nuanced than good cop/bad cop, they aim for friendly cop/formal cop with Parnell doing the empathy, Renée the direct questions.

Slumped in the observation room watching everything on TV is me.

I haven't worked out what I'll say to Parnell about why I'm back here. Why I'm not tucked up in bed nursing my sudden mystery illness. All I know right now is that I need to be here. There's no way I can let Saskia out of my sight, not now that she is a significant witness.

A significant witness with an incendiary energy you can never quite trust.

A significant witness who's wearing a sweater of mine, nicked from the wardrobe of my old teenage bedroom.

"OK, Saskia, let's start at the beginning." Parnell leans back, getting comfy—a signal for her to do the same. "It is Saskia? Not Sarah?"

A slow smirk as she trails a finger along the edge of the table. "Saskia."

"Why did you change it?" asks Parnell, as though just curious.

"There's no big story. I just wanted something more exotic for work. Sarah seemed a bit conventional, a bit wifey. That's not what clients want."

"Fair enough."

Renée takes over, masking her innate warmth with a cool, factual tone. "When did you first meet Maryanne Doyle, Saskia?"

She stretches out her hands, examines her chipped nails.

Arrogance personified but I know it's all front.

"In 1999. I was having a fag at the back of the clinic and it was fucking freezing so it can't have been any later than say, February. She bummed a light off me, said she worked in an office across the road, and then every fag break for a few days after, there she was. Anyway, we got talk-ing, just about bands and that, and then one day she produces these tickets—Faithless, Brixton Academy. I thought it was sold out but she just laughs, says she knows people, and then she says none of her mates are that into them, so do I fancy it? I mean, I thought it was a bit weird but I really wanted to see them so I thought 'fuck it.' And then we sort of became mates. She always had loads of money, she was always paying for things—more gigs, swanky bars, the best clubs . . ." She draws her hands back, sits on them. "Anyway, this went on for a couple of months and then she asked me. I knew she'd been building up to it then, this 'new best friend' act had just been a load of bollocks."

"Asked you what?" asks Renée.

She looks downward. "If I'd be up for passing on the details of any girls booked in for abortions, or consultations, who I thought might be wobbling, especially Irish girls. She said she knew some guy who'd pay big for that kind of information. I worked on reception, you see—booked the girls in, watched them. You get to know the signs."

"And you agreed to do this?"

She rolls her eyes. "Well, I didn't exactly say 'yeah, no problem' the first time she asked, but I was skint, OK? Minimum wage had just come in, literally that week, and I was getting a pay rise to three pounds sixty an hour—when I told Maryanne, she burst out laughing. That kinda sealed it."

Parnell nods, all compassion and understanding. "And that was it? You'd pass on the details, they'd bump up your bank balance?"

"In the beginning. But then I started to learn more about how it all worked, more about Maryanne, how she'd sold her baby, started up a 'business' with this guy. It just seemed like she had the life of Riley, living in this flat in the center of town, earning a few thousand a month just for babysitting a couple of pregnant girls. I mean, I soon learned it wasn't 'babysitting,' it was guarding, but at the time it sounded amazing and I wanted in. So I said to her, surely if there were two 'babysitters' they could have more girls, right? She said she'd speak to her 'guy.'"

"This guy's name?" asks Renée, flat, expressionless.

She hesitates, knows she's about to go over the top. "His name's Patrick Mackie, but I think she spoke to his daughter, Gina. Gina was more involved on a daily basis. She delivered the babies too."

Renée's voice is stern. "For the benefit of the tape, you're referring to Gina Hicks, your landlady."

Saskia leans over, mimics Renée. "*For the benefit of the tape*, that's right." She smiles to herself, cracking the center of her bottom lip, drawing blood.

"Carry on," says Renée, not rising to it.

"Yeah, so Maryanne speaks to Gina. Few weeks later I've got the life of Riley too. Although I had to keep my job at the clinic, of course."

Parnell leans in. "So let me get this straight. You'd give the details to Maryanne. She'd approach a girl, someone who didn't seem that sold on having an abortion, and she'd make them an offer they couldn't refuse? Is that how it worked?"

"Well, it wasn't exactly *that* straightforward but in a nutshell, yeah. It was a good sell—a nice long stay in a luxury London flat—it was luxury back then—you got all your needs catered for and then eight grand at the end of it. I mean, the sell *had* to be good. The girls had to lie to their families about where they were for months on end, it wasn't easy. But then eight grand's a lot of money. Maryanne used to brag she'd been paid ten grand but Mackie wouldn't pay that again, not when he had 'overheads' to factor in. That's what he used to call me and Maryanne—fucking 'overheads.'"

Parnell puffs his cheeks out. "Risky business. Didn't Maryanne worry about someone telling her to bugger off and going to the police?"

"Some did tell her to piss off, but they were hardly likely to blab. If they weren't interested they just wanted to get it over and done with as quietly as possible, they weren't going to start making big noises about the fact they were in England for an abortion. And I mean, she didn't approach *that* many. I got good at knowing who looked good for it so our hit rate was high." Hands open, explanatory mode. "Like, it didn't matter how wobbly they were, if they were too young I knew they'd have a hard time getting away with the seven-to-eight-month disappearing act so we didn't bother. Too old and they could be a bit too feisty, knew their own minds more, not as easy to control." She catches herself. "God that sounds fucking awful, doesn't it? But I was nineteen, I'd had a shit life up until then and I liked the money."

Parnell's voice is soft and steady. "Look, we're not here to judge you, Saskia. Don't flog yourself on our account, just keep going. You're doing great." She gives a grateful nod. "OK, so when a girl agreed, what happened?"

"We'd send them to 'host families' for a few days while we got things sorted. Some clinics do that, you know—for women who can't afford the few nights in a B&B—so Maryanne thought it made it sound a bit more legitimate if we did it too. 'Course, the 'families' were just people on Mackie's payroll, it was a big farce. Soon as we could though, we'd move them into the flat."

Renée picks up a sheet of paper. "12c Ophelia Mansions, Frederick Street, King's Cross. Where you currently still reside?"

She nods, flashes a sarky smile. "Yes. Where I still *reside*."

"And what, you'd literally hothouse these girls until they gave birth?"

She mouths the word "*hothouse*," ponders it. "I suppose you could call it that. But it wasn't exactly the workhouse. Only the best food, you know—Gina, she was a GP, she was obsessed with nutrition—and then there was Sky TV, every channel going, and basically whatever they wanted, books, magazines, fancy toiletries—and some of them really took the piss with the brands they'd ask for—me or Maryanne would get it for them. Usually me as I was out more because of my job."

Parnell rubs his chin. "So you're saying they never left the flat? Forget nutrition, that can't be healthy?"

"Maryanne took them for walks sometimes, once she trusted them."

Renée's look is pure ice. "Like dogs?"

Saskia bolts upright in her chair, jabs a finger toward Renée. "She didn't have to do that, you know? Gina never insisted. It was an act of kindness." Parnell smiles, smooths things over. "'Course she wanted to get out too. She'd take the girls for picnics on warmer days—just to Leamington Square Gardens, it wasn't far. She bloody loved it there, said it was exactly how she'd imagined London to be, all posh Georgian houses and old-fashioned streetlamps." She pauses, catches a tight little breath. "That's where she was found, wasn't it?"

Parnell nods reverently.

Her jaw tightens. "Bastards. I bet that was a warning to everyone to keep their mouths shut. Any girl who passed through the flat would have got the message loud and clear—they all loved the gardens, see, it was the only place they ever got out to. We were *all* pretty much prisoners, we just didn't see it that way." She smiles and it's a genuine smile, no side helping of sarcasm. "Me and Maryanne did sneak out sometimes though, at night, left the girls on their own. Turnmills was a favorite, it was less than a mile, you see. We went as far as Heaven once though, over by Charing Cross. It was risky but it was worth it, you know. Just to be able to do normal things for a few hours—dancing, flirting . . . not sitting in night after night, watching repeats of *Friends* with a load of hormonal women."

"What about men?" asks Parnell, leaning back again. "Any male visitors?"

"What's that supposed to mean?"

I put my hand to the back of my neck—not clammy, red-hot.

Don't be defensive, I will her. Don't flat-out deny it.

But Saskia's a smart cookie, she knows they're asking for a reason. "There were a few around occasionally, just Mackie's associates. The odd party, or drop-off."

"Drop-off?" asks Renée. "Stuff for the girls?"

A hollow laugh. "Not exactly. They'd store drugs in the flat sometimes. Money. Weapons occasionally, although Maryanne kicked off about that. I can't remember names, though. I can barely remember faces."

"Well, this was hanging on your wall." Parnell slides the photo over, points at the men. "Jog any memories?"

She stares for a long time, poker-faced. "Nope," she says, pushing it back. "It was a long time ago. I forgot that photo was even there, to be honest. I hardly ever go in that room. God, I was gorgeous back then," she says, changing the subject, looking to Renée. "You don't realize it at the time, do you? You don't appreciate it."

Renée stays stony-faced while Parnell taps his palms on the table—a chirpy move, almost like a drumroll. "So all good things come to an end, as they say. How long were you and Maryanne involved?"

She answers instantly, like it's just yesterday. "Maryanne took off for Brighton early 2001—she was always going on about wanting to live by the sea. I kept going for a bit but it was too much for just one person. I started making mistakes at the clinic, being too obvious, I suppose. Anyway, I got fired when they caught me with clients' details on my phone."

"The Mackies must have been angry at Maryanne for leaving?"

"Yeah, but not as much as I thought. I think Mackie was wanting to wind things down anyway. Bigger fish to fry, easier scams to run. And I reckon Gina'd lost interest—don't know if she ever had any interest, to be fair—she was just following Daddy's orders. She was like a robot."

"So is that what happened with Maryanne?" There's a taunt in Renée's tone, I wonder how Saskia will take it. "She lost interest in earning lots of money for having picnics and watching Sky TV?"

Saskia blinks slowly, doesn't react. "She lost faith in what she was doing."

"Faith?" echoes Parnell.

"Yes, *faith*. Look, I'll hold my hands up, I did it for the money, pure and simple, but Maryanne—now I'm not saying she wasn't a greedy cow, 'cos she was—but she did genuinely think we were doing a good thing. Giving someone a good option. I used to take the piss out of her, laugh at her fairy godmother act, but to be fair she'd been through it, not me. She knew what a lifeline it had been."

"Sure, sure," says Parnell, nodding quickly. "So what changed? Why'd she lose faith?"

She stares at the table, bites her lip. Blood pools at the center again but she doesn't seem to notice. "Something happened, late 2000, coming up to Christmas. There was this girl, her name was Kristen. Nice girl, but she kept chopping and changing her mind throughout the pregnancy, she was high-maintenance, a pain in the arse, really. Maryanne was always having to talk her around—I left that side to Maryanne—like I say, she'd been through it, not me. Anyway, after Kristen gave birth, that was it, she was keeping her baby and that was the end of it. It was the first time it'd actually happened. Maryanne was shitting herself, expecting Gina to go mental . . ."

"And she didn't?" asks Parnell.

Her face sours. "No, because she just walked into the flat and took it anyway. Literally just lifted the baby out of the Moses basket with Kristen sitting there screaming."

Every hard edge I've tried to cling on to begins to dissipate, liquefy.

Renée adjusts her ponytail—beats punching the table, I guess. "Surely this Kristen went to the police then?"

Saskia looks from the table to the floor and her voice becomes a mumble. "No way, she wouldn't dare. We had their contact details from the clinic, remember? She told Kristen in no uncertain terms, '*We know where you live, where your family lives.*' I mean, that was always sort of implied once a girl had given birth and she was getting ready to leave the flat, just to keep her in line, you know, but it was the first time I'd heard it said so blatantly."

"What did you take it to mean?" says Renée.

Saskia throws Renée a "*you-work-it-out*" stare.

"That they'd harm her family if she said anything?" offers Parnell.

Saskia shrugs. "I don't know that for sure. Harm her family, make trouble for her family, I dunno. I just know you wouldn't want to risk finding out."

"And this got to Maryanne?" asks Parnell. "Didn't fit with her fairy godmother image?"

She nods, keeps her gaze on the floor. "It gets worse. Gina, after she'd effectively threatened Kristen, says it's *our* job to bring her back into line, make her realize it's all for the best. So she gives us five hundred pounds to go up to Oxford Street and buy her some treats. *Fucking treats.* Few hours later, we walk back into the flat, Kristen's slit her wrists in the bath and we're standing there with fucking Topshop bags." The memory pales her. "I was gutted but seriously, Maryanne was inconsolable. I watched her for weeks afterward. I was worried she'd slit her wrists too, the way she was moping around. But she didn't, she just took off. Didn't even say bye, just left a two-line note. '*Gone to Brighton, have a nice life,*' pretty much. It hurt, you know? We'd been through a lot."

"Was Kristen dead?" says Parnell—his tone light, his body language relaxed.

Minimize the crime, keep them talking—"*Interrogation for Dummies: Intermediate level.*"

"No. She was in a really bad way but she had a pulse."

"Did you call an ambulance?" asks Renée.

"We called Gina." Saskia goes from pale to a deep blush—an appreciation of how piss-poor that sounds, at least. "Some guy was there within minutes. Gavin something. Like I say, I don't remember names. He told me and Maryanne to get out."

"Do you know what happened to Kristen? Did she live?"

"I don't know. Neither of us could face asking." She looks away, loses herself in the oppressive gray walls. "Jesus, she was so young."

"So were you." Renée's tone stays cool but there's compassion in the statement. Saskia's eyes well up. "You must have thought of taking off too?" adds Renée, back to business. "What kept you there? What's kept you there this whole time?"

"I did, at first, but then I was flavor of the month, you see. The one who stuck around. So once the baby thing wound down, Gina said I could stay on for a bit while I found my feet. All I had to do was 'entertain' Patrick Mackie's friends now and again, turn a blind eye to whatever business they were doing. It was all right for a while, but then one of Mackie's crew got me into drugs big-style and soon I wasn't just entertaining the odd villain, I was turning tricks full-time. Earning my keep, they told me. And then they moved other girls into the flat. I recognized one of them—she'd been with us about a year before, one of the girls who'd sold her baby. She'd been this real A-grade student, I remember her telling us she had a place lined up at uni for the following year, she wanted to be an architect. God, by the time she turned up back at the flat, she had a coke habit and two black eyes and I doubt she'd have been able to spell architect." Her eyes flick between Renée and Parnell. "Me and Maryanne didn't know this, *I swear,* but Mackie's crew were grabbing the most vulnerable ones when they left the flat, the ones feeling a bit down, hormones all over the place, you know? They'd offer them drugs, get them hooked and well, you know where that leads . . ."

"Are you still using now?" asks Parnell.

I know what he's thinking. "*If you are, you look well on it.*"

"No, I got clean six years ago. Hardly even drink now. But I keep doing what I do because the money's good and in another few years I'll have saved enough to start again somewhere. Far away from here. New Zealand, maybe."

Yeah, maybe, after you've served your time at Her Majesty's Pleasure, of course. A twin-center break, you could call it—two years in HMP Bronzefield and then on to New Zealand.

"And you pay what to who?" asks Renée.

"Forty percent of my earnings to Gina. More than if I worked for an agency, but I get the run of the flat too. I get to choose who I work with these days."

Renée raises an eyebrow. "So Gina Hicks isn't your landlady, she's your pimp?"

A nervous dry laugh. "I suppose so. I'd like to be a fly on a wall when you put that to her though. Gina likes to think of it as 'rent.' She went all up-herself years ago. I think ever since her old man fled the country, she's tried to live a semi straight-ish life—as much as you can when all your wealth's come from misery—so she doesn't like to think of it as taking a prostitute's earnings."

"She wouldn't have liked Maryanne turning up again," says Parnell before adding, "When did she turn up, Saskia? When did she get back in contact with you?"

"Beginning of the month. I hadn't heard a thing from her since the day she left. I nearly died when I opened the door. So did she, actually— she said she was just chancing it, she didn't actually think I'd still be here. She looked really different, that shocked me too—still pretty but sort of plain, and she'd lost her accent, pretty much. It's like she'd completely erased her past. Can't say I blame her."

"And what did she want?" asks Renée.

"She didn't really say at first, just asked if she could come in. So I said 'yeah, why not' and I went to make us a coffee, but then as I was walking back to the living room, I saw her standing in the spare room"—she pulls a perplexed face—"and I thought, 'What the hell is she doing?' Then suddenly she turns around and says, '*This is where I had him. This is the only place I ever held him.*' And I swear, I know this makes me sound like an idiot, but for a minute, I was like, 'Who? What are you talking about?' and she said 'Daniel' and then burst into tears. Jesus, she'd even given him a name."

"Her baby." confirms Renée. "So she'd regretted giving him away?"

Saskia nods. "Although she certainly didn't at the time. All she ever used to talk about was the money she'd made, what a great option it'd been. I don't think I even knew she'd had a boy."

"Regret's not always an instant thing," says Parnell. "Time does the opposite of heal sometimes."

"Time, and not being able to have kids," replies Saskia, matter-of-fact. "It all came pouring out over three cups of coffee. She was married now, see, and they'd been having IVF and it hadn't worked. And she thought her husband was having an affair to cap it all off. She just kept saying that she couldn't stop thinking about him—Daniel—whether he was happy, what he looked like now, that sort of thing." She gives a small shudder. "It was weird. I mean, I felt sorry for her and everything but I hadn't seen her for so long, it felt awkward."

"So how did she end up staying at the flat?"

"She just came out and asked me. She might have lost her accent and that gorgeous black hair but she definitely hadn't lost her front. She said she'd left her husband and she was running low on money and she didn't know what to do now. I felt like I couldn't say no. But it was OK for a few days though, we chatted about old times, how mad it all was, and I was starting to think, not that she could stay with me permanently or anything, but just that we could be friends. Then all of a sudden she starts getting intense again."

"Intense?" asks Renée.

"Hassling me to put her in contact with Gina so she could ask her about Daniel. 'Ask what?' I said. She says, 'Gina might know where the parents are now, where *he* is.' She reckoned she wasn't out to make trouble, she just wanted to know he was OK." Her face darkens. "Well, of course, I knew Gina would flip so I tried to put her off. I said I didn't know where Gina lived and that we hardly spoke, I just direct-debited the 'rent' to her. But then she starts saying, 'Can't you pretend there's a problem with the flat, the plumbing or something, and then maybe she'll come here?' I was like, 'Yeah right, Maryanne, like Gina's going to turn up here with her toolbox.' I think she'd almost forgotten what they were like, how dangerous they could be. Anyway, we had an argument about it, I said she'd have to leave and so she piped down after that, said she'd drop it. And she did as well, until about a week later when she tells me she's run into someone and found out where Gina lives. She was fucking elated."

"Who?" says Parnell, elbows on the table, leaning in. "Who had she run into?"

My heart quickens and I move closer to the screen. This is it. This is the moment where my life could literally be pulverized. After all, how do I know she can be trusted? How do I know she meant what she said back at the house? It could all be a game. An elaborate ruse to undermine any case we try to bring against her favorite-landlady-cum-pimp.

Gina Hicks' voice floods my head.

"Saskia knows she's on to a good thing . . ."

"I don't know who she'd run into," she says firmly, subject closed. "Just *someone*. I didn't ask because I didn't want to know." In that moment she looks straight at the camera, eyes lasering mine. "She didn't have the exact number of the house but she went over there a few times, reckoned she saw Gina pulling into her road once but she ignored her. And so she kept going back, almost staking out the place, it was nuts. Anyway, after a few visits, I get this 'what-the-fuck?' call from Gina, asking if Maryanne's been in touch with me. So I say she has, and that she's probably not going to let things go until she gets some sort of answer, so can she just meet her, fob her off with something? Eventually she says, 'OK,' and we go to the house a few days later."

"We?" says Parnell, sensing something concrete.

"You bet. I was worried for Maryanne but I won't lie, I was worried about my position with Gina too. I thought if I was there, I'd be able to . . ."—she takes a moment to think of the word—". . . mediate, keep things civil. I thought Gina would appreciate that. Guess I shouldn't give up my day job, eh?"

"What happened?"

"It was Gina's fault it all turned nasty. Maryanne was fairly calm to begin with, just asking questions, you know? But Gina was in a funny mood, I could see it the minute she let us in. She could have just said, '*I don't know where the parents are, sorry. But I know they were great people, they'd have given him a great life.*' End of story—well hopefully, anyway. But she didn't, she told her the truth."

Parnell pulls in closer. "The truth?"

She drags her fingers down the side of her face. "There were no *parents*. They were just acting, people paid by Mackie to make the girls feel better about handing their babies over. The vast majority were sold on to traffickers, global setups, for seriously *big* money too so God knows what happened to them. Nothing good, I'd say. And Gina told this to Maryanne."

"Did you know this?" asks Renée.

A small movement, pitiful. "Not at the time. I'd have never gone along with it if I'd known. I mean, I was greedy, I've admitted that, but I'm not a monster. I honestly thought those babies were going to safe homes."

"And why did Gina tell Maryanne this?" says Parnell, confused. "Why not, as you say, just fob her off?"

Saskia looks around the room for an answer. Time doesn't appear to have made sense of it. "Honestly? I don't know. Gina was edgy from the minute we got there, which I understood to a point, but if she'd just played nicely, I reckon Maryanne would have trotted off eventually. Instead she tells us to go up to the first floor, to the utility room, for fuck's sake, like she didn't want us dirtying her good rooms. Then she says Maryanne's got two minutes max before she wants her out of her fucking house. But Maryanne keeps going with *all these bloody questions* and Gina just sort of flips, says she hasn't got a clue where Maryanne's baby is, or anyone else's for that matter. Tells her they were all sold off to traffickers within minutes of leaving the flat. Maryanne went for her, sort of pushed her out onto the landing, there was a struggle."

Parnell's head is slightly bowed. "Are you saying you saw Gina Hicks kill Maryanne?"

"No."

Renée's pen stops in mid-air, Parnell's eyebrows hit the strip lighting.

"I saw them argue and Gina pushed her down the stairs, or maybe Maryanne fell down the stairs, I couldn't say for sure from where I was standing." She puts her head in her hands, talks to the table. "Maryanne must have hit her head because there was blood, quite a bit. And I panicked, I legged it. I wasn't thinking straight. I thought Gina would blame me for suggesting she see Maryanne and I just wanted out of there. But Maryanne was definitely moving when I left. I know I shouldn't have run off and I've lived with it ever since, but she was alive, she was trying to sit up." Her voice gets smaller. "The papers said she was strangled though, cuts on her throat and stuff. I don't know anything about that. I promise you, I don't."

Renée jots a few notes down while Parnell digests this, pushing his chair back from the table, giving himself more room to absorb the enormity of what they've just heard. If he's waiting for Saskia to fill the silence though, he's out of luck. She sits patiently waiting for his reaction, waiting for his judgment.

"Two questions," he says eventually. "Firstly, you confirmed to us that you were having a relationship with Nate Hicks but your colleague, Naomi Berry, seemed surprised by this." He pulls out a piece of paper from Renée's stack. "'Incredulous' is the word my officer wrote. So do you still stand by that claim?"

I don't think Ben would have used the word "incredulous." He's more of a *"fucking gobsmacked"* kind of guy.

Saskia flaps a hand. "Oh God, that. No, I don't stand by it. I wouldn't touch him with a barge pole."

"So why did he say it?" asks Parnell.

Completely deadpan. "Because he's an idiot. But a loyal idiot, to Gina *and* Patrick Mackie. He says and does anything to make sure he stays in favor." She rubs her thumb and first two fingers together, symbolizing money. "It pays him to."

"Would that include strangling Maryanne and dumping her body by Leamington Square Gardens?"

Saskia shrugs, doesn't commit. "I don't know. Maybe?" A harsh laugh. "Do you wanna hear something funny? That affair bullshit, that was all his idea, independent of Gina. He didn't know Gina was going to walk into your station and give you a load of crap about IVF forums and what-not. He thought by making up that story about us, he was deflecting the attention away from Gina and putting the spotlight on himself. He called me after you left their house that day to make sure I said the same thing if you asked. He was so fucking pleased with himself. What an absolute tool."

But the question is, would he want to deflect attention onto himself if *he* killed Maryanne? The answer's "quite possibly"—Nate Hicks' life, his lifestyle, probably his whole self-esteem is built on staying in favor with his wife and her father, and while Gina played a great role, casting Nate as man of the house and her the harassed middle-class mummy, it's pretty obvious now who calls the shots in that relationship.

Renée pulls her up. "So you're admitting you lied to us about Nate Hicks? That you obstructed our investigation?"

"Yes." A long hiss like a snake.

Parnell scrapes his chair forward, closes in again. "You see, you've lied about a lot of things, Saskia. Mainly to protect Gina Hicks too, which brings me to my second question—why should we believe you now? Why are you telling us this now?"

A tension grips her whole body and I feel myself stiffen. Sympathy pains. "Because I know I'm a loose end to them. Gina might have been happy sending that little runt around with a threatening message, but Patrick Mackie?" There's a tremor around her mouth but she leaves the rest unsaid.

Parnell tries to throw a crumb of comfort. "I've seen him, Saskia, he weighs less than Renée here. He's not the man you remember, trust me."

She taps her chest. "Doesn't matter if his body's broken, it's what's in his heart—and there's nothing there, trust me, just a black void." Parnell opens his mouth but Saskia's not finished. "But I'm also telling you because a very long time ago, Maryanne was my friend, and she didn't deserve to die. She didn't deserve me running out on her. I didn't help her that day but maybe I can help her now."

Parnell lets out a pained sigh. "We still don't know who killed her though, Saskia. What you've given us isn't quite enough. Ridiculous as it sounds, Gina Hicks could claim Maryanne walked out of her house and straight into the path of a violent stranger. It's called reasonable doubt and it's the good friend of the guilty."

"Then do your job better." Her voices pulses with anger. Anger at herself. At Parnell. At the sheer misfortune of landing the receptionist job that led to this miserable mess. "Find out what happened to Maryanne or we'll both have failed her, won't we?" Her eyes well up again. "And take it from me, Detective Parnell, it's not a nice feeling."

As I slip out of the observation room and into the lift before Parnell catches me, I consider Saskia's words and can't help but agree.

Failing those who've put their trust in you is not a nice feeling at all.

28

"I'll be honest, it's not looking good, Gina."

Silence.

Parnell, king of the understatement, sits across from a rigid Gina Hicks the next morning. Renée simmers gently beside him, ready to jump in with a barbed word or a subtle knife twist as per the interview plan. Felix Whiteley looks like every other extortionate brief I've locked horns with, bloated in speech and bloated in stature, with an air of cool arrogance masking a hawk-eyed hypervigilance.

I'm back in the observation room, this time with Seth and Ben. Flowers sticks his head in occasionally, asks if there's "anything juicy" to report.

The short answer's no. Nothing juicy at all, unless you count Whiteley's fruit smoothie. Smoothies, in fact—plural. One for him and one for Gina. That's what £650 an hour gets you—a radioactive-looking Fibre-Blast and a hairbrush by the looks of Gina's mane. Her smoothie sits untouched though. According to the custody sergeant, nothing more than a few sips of water have passed her lips since he took her through the charge-room process seventeen hours ago.

Same goes for me almost. Just a couple of pints of water and a few tots of rum. The thought of anything solid makes me heave.

"You shouldn't be here," Parnell had said when he'd found me hunched over my desk this morning, researching concert venues in Vienna. *"Seriously, you look worse than yesterday. Do you know what would do you the world of good, Kinsella? A dose of home comforts. Chicken soup, a whole load of daytime TV and a few days' rest."*

Home.

Comfort.

Two words I'd never put in the same sentence. An oxymoron, Seth would say.

"Honestly, it's not looking good Gina," repeats Parnell. "And it's looking worse every minute we sit here. I'm losing my patience and you're losing any chance of getting out of prison before pension age."

It's been an hour already. The gist of Saskia's statement has been outlined to Gina but "no comment" is the order of the day. "No comment" peppered with the odd, "My client declines to answer" from Felix Whiteley, just to mix things up a little. Keep everyone on their toes.

Same from Nate Hicks a little earlier—Seth and Flowers had toiled through that one.

"Come on, Gina, you must realize that 'no comment' makes you look guilty?" says Parnell.

Whiteley objects. "It makes her look nothing of the sort. My client is acting on robust legal advice, nothing more." His voice doesn't quite suit his body—it's twee, almost girlish.

Parnell sighs, crosses his arms. "Mr. Whiteley, I'm no legal expert, but as I understand it, the point of 'no comment' is to prevent yourself from saying anything that might incriminate you. But this clearly incriminates your client." Parnell hands him a photo—a high-resolution crime-scene snap. "As you can see, luminol has been sprayed and blood detected close to the bottom of your client's stairs. The swirling pattern suggests an attempt has been made to clean up this blood."

Whiteley surveys the photo. Gina stares straight ahead.

"I'd say it's rather early to confirm exactly whose blood that is, Detective Inspector. I doubt your forensics team have even started recovering the blood yet, much less testing it for DNA?"

"Correct. But we all know it will turn out to be Maryanne Doyle's, and therefore combined with Saskia French's statement, we'll have irrefutable evidence against your client."

Whiteley offers Parnell a thin-lipped smile. To the likes of a £650 per hour lawyer, "irrefutable" is a challenge laid down. Gloves off, game on.

Parnell appeals to Gina instead. "Are you listening? *Irrefutable.* So there's very little point to this 'no comment' palaver. The best thing you can do is just talk to us."

It isn't actually, it's the worst. Every word she says makes our life easier, not hers. Whiteley's primed his client to perfection.

She lowers her head. "No comment."

Parnell dips down, he's not letting her get out of eye-contact that easily. "Look, we know Maryanne was definitely injured inside your house—science *and* an eyewitness confirm it—but who strangled her, Gina? Who slashed her throat? Was it you, hmm? My money says no. I don't think you've got it in you."

"No comment."

"Did Maryanne fall? If Maryanne fell then that wasn't your fault, and if you tell us who killed her, that will work in your favor."

"No comment."

Renée sharpens her knife. "Shall we talk about the baby-trafficking then? That's not going to go down well in prison, trust me. Tell us what happened to Maryanne and we might be able to help you."

Whiteley's nearly on his feet. "My client does not wish to answer any questions with regards to . . ."

"Where are the twins?" Gina cuts in, surprising us all. "And Amber?"

Renée looks to Parnell. "My God, we have a comment!"

"Actually, it's a question," says Whiteley. I'm not sure if he's being a smart-arse or there's some important legal distinction.

Parnell nods. "And unlike your client, we're happy to answer her questions." To Gina, "I understand your children are in the care of Nate's mother at the moment."

Contradictory emotions flood her face—resentment and relief doing battle.

"Of course we've contacted Social Services to make sure a more long-term plan is formalized," says Renée, almost gleefully, just to get a reaction.

Gina pushes her chair back abruptly, starts pacing the few steps between the table and the wall.

"Where's Leo?" asks Parnell, tightening the screw.

She opens her mouth but Whiteley stops her with an "*I-got-this*" gesture. "I believe my client has already informed you that her son is in Austria."

"But she seems unwilling to give us an exact address and we need to speak with him, now more than ever in light of Saskia French's claim that he threatened her. It would certainly be to his advantage to contact us voluntarily."

She sits down again, legs crossed tightly, right foot twitching. "Can I ask why you're so quick to take Saskia French's word for everything? Or should I say, Sarah Finch." Whiteley tries to silence her again with a pudgy hand on a bony forearm but she shakes him off quickly. "Have you actually checked Sarah Finch's record? She's not exactly known for telling the truth."

We have, as it goes. The three counts of shoplifting we can live with. A caution for giving a false statement to the police back in 1997 could prove sticky.

"Few people are, actually. Makes our job a nightmare." Parnell turns to Renée. "What's that quote again? The one Kinsella says all the time, the funny one." He pretends to think but I know he knows it. "Oh yeah, that's it—'*Only three things tell the truth—small children, drunk people and leggings.*'" He chuckles to himself. "Good, isn't it? It leaves out science, though. Science *almost* always tells the truth."

I *need* Gina Hicks to tell the truth. As bad as things look for her, they don't look too rosy for me if Parnell and Renée can't crack her open.

Because if Gina doesn't come clean, it means a trial.

And a trial means police testimony.

And police testimony means choosing between coming clean—aka career suicide—or taking my chances and lying on the stand.

Committing perjury.

I have to persuade her to tell the truth.

I stand up and walk out. Seth asks where I'm off to so I say "bad stomach" which shuts him down pronto, and I walk down the corridor to the interview room, feeling like it's the longest mile when it actually can't be more than twenty steps. I knock on the door and ask to speak to Parnell. He acts like it's fine and dandy, an almost expected interruption, but when we come face-to-face, his is thunderous, his language distinctly un-Parnell.

"Fuck's sake, Kinsella." The "F" word from Parnell rocks me and I actually feel tears prick the back of my throat. "If you're after permission to go home, you could have just asked Flowers, you know? He is a sergeant. He does have authority. She was just starting to drop the 'no comments' as well. Jesus!"

"I know. I've been watching it in the other room." I square my shoulders, lengthen my spine—try to make myself as big as possible. "Boss, I want to come in. She might have dropped the 'no comments' but she's not responding to you and Renée, you can see it in her body language. I think I might be able to get through to her, though."

"Oh yes? And what makes you Clarice Starling all of a sudden?" He's tetchy, not buying it. "Anyway, we've got enough to charge her without a confession. It's not ideal but we've worked with less."

Here goes.

"Seriously? You've got enough to charge her with assault, possibly, *if* Forensics can come up with something to prove Maryanne was pushed down the stairs, because Saskia's statement alone won't do it, she said she couldn't see properly. And Gina's right about Saskia's character. She'll be torn to pieces if this goes to trial. As for the murder, you've got zilch, and you don't think she's got the stomach for it anyway, nor do I. But we both know she knows who did it. She's just not going to give it up unless she feels she has to."

And she has to. She absolutely has to.

Seth walks past, shooting me a funny look which thankfully Parnell doesn't notice. Parnell's too busy digesting the fact he's being lectured to by a twenty-six-year-old DC.

"Look, Boss, it makes sense," I say, trying to sound levelheaded. "I've spent the most time with her, I know what buttons to press. Think about it, I've been there for every interaction she's had and it was *me* she asked for when she came to the station that day."

"To tell you a pack of lies, which could mean she thinks you're gullible."

His words sting but to be fair, I'm punching below the belt too, implying he and Renée aren't nailing this. "Or it could mean she finds me easy to talk to, compassionate. But, hey, if she thinks I'm gullible, then great. In trying to trick me, she might end up tricking herself. Anything's worth a shot, surely?"

He doesn't answer, just walks back into the room and proposes a fifteen-minute break. I assume it's so he can call the Crime Scene Manager to talk trajectories and get some definitive proof that Maryanne was pushed down the stairs, but it appears I'm wrong.

And it appears I'm in.

While Gina's taken to use the bathroom, Parnell calls me in and explains to Whiteley that I'll be taking Renée's place. Whiteley gives a detached shrug—one inexpensively dressed police officer is much the same as another to him. Renée, completely devoid of any ego, is equally indifferent.

When Gina comes back into the room, she tries to mirror Whiteley's "whatever" stance but there's a tiny shift in her demeanor. Not softer, but less pinched. She obviously sees a friendly face in me. Or maybe a stooge? It doesn't really matter, though, I can work with either.

"Hello again." She sits down, her posture slightly less rigid than before. "Were you out celebrating New Year's last night, you look like you might have been?"

Parnell's eyes flick to the tape. The last thing he wants is some barrister on a six-figure retainer claiming the interview was flawed because one of the officers was hungover. Thankfully I haven't switched it on yet.

I smile. "I'm fine thanks, Gina. Had to rush my makeup this morning, that's all."

"Lucky you. I'm still wearing yesterday's."

I grant her one more smile before the tape goes on and I open up the case-file. I take out a number of the postmortem photos and lay them across the table. Whiteley rests his chin in one hand, casting an expressionless glance over the macabre jigsaw.

"Are these supposed to shock me?" says Gina, flatly. "I don't mean to sound callous but I was a doctor for fifteen years before I had the twins, mainly general practice but a little time in emergency too, so I'm afraid I'm really not that squeamish."

"It's different when you know the person, surely?" I say.

"No comment."

Here we go again.

"It's different when you caused those injuries?"

A look to the ceiling. "No comment."

"But then, which of these injuries did *you* cause, Gina?" I hold up the head shot, point out the deep laceration across the front of Maryanne's hairless head. "I mean, we're pretty sure you—or your stairs—caused this, but what about this?" A chest shot this time, a red-blue bruise, possibly knee-shaped between the ribs. "Or how about this?" Finally, Maryanne's throat—the fingertip bruising, the superficial slashes.

"No comment."

"Was it Nate?" I say, picking up the pace. "Word is, he's a bit of a 'yes' man, but would he kill for you, Gina? Is he that devoted? Or that dependent on you? You and your father's money?"

"Fucking Nate."

It's not the swearing that startles me, it's the pure, unfiltered contempt. I take a second to work out how to use this to our advantage but Parnell's ahead of me, keen to keep prodding the wound while it's still gaping raw.

"You and Maryanne fought," he states. "She fell or you pushed her and then you panicked. You asked Nate to sort it, didn't you?"

"No comment."

He keeps going. "Or maybe you didn't ask him? Maybe Nate got rid of Maryanne of his own accord?"

"No comment."

"Are you scared of Nate, Gina? Of what he's done?"

She sighs. "No comment."

Same old, same old, but there's a weariness creeping in.

"Look," I tell her. "All we need is one fiber or one skin cell to match the trace we've got off Maryanne's body and Nate's going away, Gina. It'll be better for you, *for your children,* if you talk to us—if the truth comes from you."

At the mention of her children, she draws a sharp breath and closes her eyes.

I now know exactly how to play this.

I start clearing away the photos. "You know, you can follow Mr. Whiteley's advice if you want, but my inspector's going to charge you anyway, and then do you know where your 'no comments' will get you?" The threat in my voice forces her eyes open. "The Old Bailey—Court One, maybe. Media speculation. Strangers judging you, calling you a monster and a bitch on Twitter. And not just for your part in Maryanne's death, but for what you did all those years ago, all those babies you sold." She blinks hard, more a twitch than a blink. "Oh yeah, that will all have to come out. Whenever you do finally get out of prison, I don't think you'll need to worry about catering for Christmas drinks again. You'll be a pariah."

Whiteley clears his throat but I don't give him the chance. Not when Gina's looking so horrifically spellbound.

"You're not a bad person, Gina. You've done some really bad things but you're not a bad person, I genuinely believe that." I nod sideways toward Parnell. "My inspector here thinks you're nothing but a liar. He thinks you told me a pack of lies when you came in to see me on Christmas Eve, and in the main he's right, most of it was lies, all that stuff about meeting Maryanne on the IVF forum. But the thing is I've checked your medical records—your IVF struggle wasn't a lie, was it? Nine rounds! Must have been very grueling. I can't imagine how much the twins must mean to you. Well, it's obvious all your kids mean the world to you."

She gives me a long hard stare before leaning over to Whiteley. They whisper back and forth for a few seconds before the confab ends with a solemn nod from Gina and an "on-your-head-be-it" shrug from her brief.

There's a palpable silence before Whiteley says, "My client admits that there was an altercation at her home with the deceased, Maryanne Doyle. Maryanne fell down the stairs and injured herself but she left the house, walking wounded. She has no idea what happened to her after that."

I shake my head, disappointed. Inside I'm screaming.

"I'm afraid that's not good enough, Gina. You've only admitted to what we already know. To quote the popular phrase, 'We'll see you in court.'"

I stand up, willing Parnell to join me. Willing Gina to start panicking and pour forth.

Parnell's knees have barely had time to click before my second wish comes true.

"I offered her money but she just wouldn't go," Gina says, looking up at me. There's amazement in her voice, a twisted wonder at the fact not all problems can be solved with money. "That's all I wanted, for her to go away, to stop talking about the ba—" She cringes, can't say it—"to stop talking about what we'd done, all the things that went on back then. But she just wouldn't shut up so I told her. I told her the truth, that I didn't know where . . ." She can't finish that sentence either. "She went completely berserk. She said she was going to come back the next day and the day after and that she'd tell my children what I'd done with her child." Her lip curls. "She wasn't so worried about her child back then, not when she was earning good money. I pointed that out to her and she went for me, well, we went for each other, really. We were *both* pushing each other."

All the cringes and the half-finished sentences will have to be filled in at some point. Hours of fact-checking and tedious substantiation always follow even the most detailed of confessions, but right now it will do if it moves us on to the main event.

I sit back down. "The fall didn't kill her, Gina. Who did?"

"I don't know."

"Yes you do." I lean in. "Think about this very carefully. What happened with Maryanne happened because you didn't want your kids knowing what you'd done—well, if this goes to trial, they'll know everything. And so will everyone else, all their friends, their friends' parents, their teachers. Every dirty little detail. The baby-factory, the trafficking, the pimping. They'll hear about Kristen too. Your kids will find out about what happened to Kristen."

The look on Gina's face tells me two things—one, that she's unraveling, two, that Kristen's probably dead.

The look on Parnell's face reminds me of another thing. I wasn't supposed to be here last night. I'm not supposed to know about Kristen.

I push on.

"Can you live with your kids hating you, Gina? Thinking you're a monster? Reading every gruesome detail in the papers, online. Can you really run that risk?"

"Don't listen to them," warns Whiteley, although his heart's not really in it. He knows he's lost control. "They're simply trying to intimidate you."

Gina's head shakes continuously, side to side. "But I can't run that risk. And he wouldn't want me to."

"He?" says Parnell. "Nate?"

She looks at me, ignores Parnell. "If he admits to it, there's no trial, no details, no media?"

Not quite.

"If there's guilty pleas all round, it'll move straight to sentencing and a lot less detail will be out there in the public domain. Your kids will definitely be less exposed, I can promise you that."

"He'd want me to do this." She whispers this more to herself, than us. "He wouldn't want the kids suffering, he wouldn't . . ."

"So it was Nate?" I say, my breath coming quickly.

"Fucking Nate." That vicious spit again. "Do you really think he's got the balls to do something like this? I was shaken up after Maryanne fell, I didn't know what else to do. She was moving, sort of, but she'd hit her head badly, there was a lot of blood. I just froze."

"And?"

"And? And who else does a girl turn to when she's in trouble?"

29

"She had a problem, where else would she turn?"

Gina's words verbatim.

Patrick Mackie sits across from us, radiating calm and contentment, as chilled as a man sitting on a deck chair watching the sun rise over the Serengeti. His illness has ravaged him, no doubt—he used to be good-looking in his day, according to Parnell—and close up, under the glare of the single light that hangs over the table, the six-to-twelve months prognosis strikes me as somewhat ambitious. But there's a steeliness to him, a mental strength that seems to prop up his ailing body and it's fair to say he looks like a man who has no trouble sleeping. Maybe that's what happens when you only have a limited number of sleeps left.

Or when you don't have a conscience.

"So were you in the house?" asks Parnell. "Did you see what happened, how things went down?"

He shakes his head. "No, I was out with the twins, minding my own business. I don't go far, obviously, but at the end of the day, who in a kids' playground is gonna recognize me and it was dark by then. You didn't recognize me in broad bloody daylight." He points at Parnell, exploding into a chuckle which inevitably tips over into a dry, violent cough. "Anyway," he says, wiping his mouth, "There I was spinning Max and Mia on the roundabout—loves of my bloody life, them two. Getting to spend time with them was worth all the risk of coming back, even now. They really ground you, little kids, don't they?"

"I wonder if the little kids you sold into God-knows-whatever went to a playground or had a spin on a roundabout. Do you ever wonder about that?" asks Parnell.

I don't know what twisted evil leads him to shrug, "No, not really" but when he clocks my face, he feels the need to explain. "Look, I did what I did, love. No point dwelling on it. Take that as a bit of advice from a dying old man."

The cough starts again. I could offer him more water but I stare at him dispassionately, warmed by the thought of him drawing his last breath in this dark, depressing room.

"So there you were playing dear old grandad in the playground and what?" asks Parnell, once the hacking dies down.

"Gina calls me up, explains what's happened. And I think, *Maryanne Doyle, now there's a blast from the past.* Cocky little Irish mare with a right mouth on her."

This surprises me. "Do you remember every foot soldier you ever employed, Mr. Mackie?"

"Foot soldier? Are you having a laugh? She came up with the plan. She was a right piece of work. And I was hardly likely to forget her, anyway—little bitch did a runner from the flat with a stash of coke and around four grand. I don't forget those sort of things."

"You must have been delighted to hear that same 'little bitch' was currently lying on your daughter's floor, half-conscious."

He waves a hand, bone-thin and veiny. "Oh do me a favor, love. Over ten grams of coke and a few thousand quid? Yeah, maybe if I'd got hold of her at the time, I might have taught her a small lesson in respect. But nearly twenty years later? What I did had nothing to do with all that. I was just helping my daughter, like any good father would. There was no way Gina was going to prison, not over that little tramp."

"But she is going to prison, Patrick." I drop the Mr. Mackie, it's too deferential for this piece of dog shit. "Whether Maryanne's fall was an accident or not, Gina played a key role in a child trafficking operation."

He points a finger at me. "She made sure those babies were born healthy, that's all she did. And she only did that because I told her to. I controlled that girl, I can see that now. I should never have brought her into the business but like I said, no point dwelling on things."

Parnell's voice is low and steady. "Forget what Gina did. Tell us exactly what you did to Maryanne."

He pauses for a few seconds, playing with us, savoring the game. "Oh, what the fuck," he says eventually, smiling broadly. "I suppose I might as well. There's not a lot you can do to me now, is there? I'll be dead by next Christmas."

And the world will be a brighter place for it.

"I knocked her out first," he says, flippantly, looking at me, then Parnell. "Couldn't be bothered with all the kicking and scratching and it's not like she took much knocking, she was barely conscious by the time I got there. Then I got her into the garage. I was going to cut her throat at first—I was knackered, wasn't sure if I'd have the strength to strangle her—but then I didn't want any more blood to deal with, there was enough back in the house." He throws his hands up. "So that's it really, I strangled her. And then I waited a good while—until, God, half-three, four in the morning—and then I headed up to north London, dumped her by her precious fucking gardens. Made sure folk got the message loud and clear."

"Folk?"

"Anyone who'd passed through that flat with even a half a mind to open their mouth."

"A big risk though," I say. "Dumping her in the middle of central London?"

He shrugs. "Not at that time of day, not really, not around there. And when you're dying, nothing feels that risky, love, trust me."

Parnell reads my mind. "Mr. Mackie, no offense, but I'm finding it hard to believe you did this all by yourself. You're dying, you're very weak. How did you get Maryanne into the garage? Into the car, for that matter? Gina?"

"No!" he says, voice raised and pissed off. "As soon as I got back I told her to take the little ones and go to a hotel for the night. She didn't know what I was going to do. Is that absolutely clear? My daughter had nothing to do with this."

"Where were Amber and Leo?" I ask.

"Dunno, love. Gina said she'd take care of all that, make sure they didn't come back to the house."

Parnell's not letting up. "Mr. Mackie, the person on the CCTV footage lifted that body out of the car with considerable ease. You didn't do this by yourself. Was Nate with you?"

"Nate? You're having a fucking laugh." That same smack of contempt. "He ain't got bad brains, that lad, I'll give him that, but he ain't your first port of call when you need a bit of muscle. Big lad, soft as shit though. But I've still got a lot of friends over here, Detectives. Associates. People I can call on if I need a . . . favor."

"And I don't suppose you're going to give us the name of that 'friend,' are you?"

"Be delighted to. Chap called Gavin Eckers. Used to work for me in the nineties, been running the Shakespeare down Nunhead way for the past few years. He was always a good lad, Gavin. Didn't even flinch when I asked him to take me for a spin, help me get rid of something. Fat lot of good his name will do you though—he had a little accident a few days back. I don't like loose ends, you see."

With *this* as a father, had Gina ever stood a chance?

30

The wind-down of most cases is generally tedious and time-consuming but there's an air of collective bounce within MIT4 as we edge toward the end of January. Of course, it could just be the relief of a much-awaited payday on the horizon or maybe the slight shift in temperature from "baltic" to "a bit nippy," but in all probability, it's the sheer unfettered delight of not having to prepare for a trial. Guilty pleas are always seen as a job well done, back slaps all around, and the pints and Prosecco flow every night in the Bell Tavern. Even Steele comes out eventually. It's the first time I've seen her tipsy. We even get her singing one particularly rowdy night—her and Parnell murdering "Islands in the Stream" with not a tuneful note between them. Melodically challenged might be the kindest way to put it.

It makes me laugh though. Then I loathe myself for laughing.

Because while I still have my job and Dad still has his freedom, Maryanne Doyle is still very much dead. Buried in a field in Surrey at the cruel insistence of Thomas Lapaine—a man who can barely speak her name—despite her family's pleas for her to be brought back to Ireland and buried alongside her mam. And probably soon enough, her dad.

The day we clear out the incident room I feel knotty and nauseous. Someone else needs it now, I get it—there's been a fifteen-year-old fatally stabbed just behind St. Pancras, whereas we haven't had anything new in that requires more than a few desks stuck in a corner somewhere—but still, I don't feel quite ready to pack Maryanne away yet and I literally can't bear the thought of Flowers, maybe Ben, tossing her remnants into boxes then kicking the boxes across the floor because they're too hungover to pick them up. I've seen it. Christ, I've probably done it myself once or twice. But Maryanne's different.

Maryanne will always be different.

In the end, I do the only thing I can do and I stay late that night, making sure that everything's done neatly. That Maryanne's last hours in this room are at least orderly and in some way, dignified.

The photo featuring "Uncle" Frank thumps me in the solar plexus one last time. Demented with guilt, I call Dad and ask him to tell me the truth about how big a part his so-called blood-brother played in the operation. Am I shielding a key player or just another hustler? A fully paid-up trafficker, or just a lager-fueled letch? For one laughable, never-gonna-happen second, I swear on everything I hold dear that if Dad implicates Frank in anything more than just enjoying the hospitality in that flat, I'll call Steele right away—or probably Parnell, if I'm honest—and I'll confess everything there and then. To hell with careers and families, they're overrated anyway.

But Dad's cagey. Noncommittal. He says "He wouldn't be surprised" if Frank had put some money up, had some direct links to the top, but he claims he doesn't know for sure, and he certainly doesn't have any proof.

And so the ball falls squarely back in my court. Do I protect Dad or go after Frank? I can't do both. We might not share DNA with "Uncle" Frank but still, our roots are too entwined for any of us to survive the fallout of a formal investigation into Francis "Frank" Clayton.

So I choose Dad. Like I always knew I would, except for one mad, fanciful second.

Good daughter.

Bad cop.

And between all the public backslapping and private self-condemnation, the business of Murder goes on. We're still trying to locate Leo Hicks. Witness intimidation isn't a thing we take lightly, even when it's carried out by public schoolboys with gangster complexes, acting at the behest of their mummies.

In fact, even when the CPS advise it could be tricky to prove, given that Saskia wasn't our witness at the time Leo threatened her.

It turns out the concert performance was true, at least—not that Leo Hicks ever turned up. The Kensington Symphony Orchestra were left to perform with one less violinist at the Wiener Konzerthaus in Vienna, and both his parents still refuse to shed any light on his whereabouts and nothing enlightening has shown up on their phones. The only thing we can be sure of is that he hasn't flown out of Austria, although with the train system providing links to Germany, Italy, Switzerland and Hungary to name just a few, Leo Hicks could be practically anywhere. Sinking a beer in Munich or having an audience with the Pope in Rome.

When I'm not schmoozing with Interpol, I'm trawling through the death records of every Kristen who passed away in late 2000. Assuming her death was actually registered is stupidly optimistic of me, given it's likely she was disposed of in a rather more unofficial fashion, but someone's got to try, you know. A young girl's life has to be worth at least a brief wild-goose chase.

When it proves to be exactly that, I run a search for every Kristen reported missing in the UK and Ireland in the early noughties and there's one that looks interesting—a Kristen McCloud, reported missing by her mother in February 2001, after moving to London in May 2000 from County Kerry. Kristen regularly phoned home, her mother tells me, although she hadn't been back to visit, however the last time she called had been the first week of December 2000 and she recalls her daughter did sound a bit down that day. She never heard from her only child ever again. Saskia French takes a look at her photo, pitifully insists it's not her while her chin wobbles and her eyes bulge with tears. Gina Hicks struggles to even glance at it. Both women haunted in their own way by the reality of what happened to Kristen. Both still wanting to believe that maybe she was out there, living a great life with an army of children and just a couple of faint scars on her wrists to remind her that her life wasn't always so wonderful.

We're still waiting on sentencing. While in theory a guilty plea should be straightforward, there's always a bit of sniping that has to happen between prosecution and defense around what the agreed facts are, and in this case, the point of sending a terminally ill man to prison. With any luck though, Patrick Mackie will die inside. Which means he'll serve a maximum of twelve months for murder.

I can't dwell on that for too long, my insides start to itch.

My guess is Gina will get five years for assault—we now know it was assault, the location of the bloodstains suggests a push, not a fall. I'm not sure they'll bother too much with an assisting an offender charge, not when there's a host of historic trafficking charges gathering pace but we'll see. It's fair to say prison isn't suiting her. In the four weeks since she was charged, her honey-blond hair has gone gray at the roots and stripped of her makeup and all her Wandsworth-set props, she looks ordinary. Almost featureless. She doesn't get many visitors either. All the people who drank her posh wine and ate her Christmas canapés appear to be staying well away. It's only really Felix Whiteley and occasionally me or Parnell who grace her presence, scavenging for more information that she refuses to give. The only time she speaks is to ask after the twins, who she doesn't want visiting, and the occasional abrupt inquiry as to her dad's health. There's not a word about Nate, and poor Amber—*"Leo's mine, Amber's Nate's"*—hardly gets a look in either. When the chips are down, Gina Hicks obviously feels that blood is unequivocally thicker than water.

Something I understand only too well.

In a reversal of fortune that I know she just loves, it's me who stalks Jacqui in the busy weeks that follow. It's me who leaves the voicemails and begs for her time. We finally meet one lunchtime in a café by St. Paul's. I order a panini and a large cappuccino. Jacqui says she doesn't want anything and then bursts into tears.

I've had easier meetings, that's for sure. I've certainly had more truthful meetings.

In an effort to diffuse the bombshell I'd dropped about Maryanne being in the boot of Dad's car, I go big and I go broad, throwing everything but the kitchen sink at Jacqui. First, I claim I was drunk when

I said it. On medication and drunk. Having man trouble. Overtired. Later I hint toward drug use, trying to suggest that I'd entered some kind of hyperreality, brought on by excessive weed use, that genuinely made me believe that Dad had been stashing dead women in the boot of his car. For good measure, I detail a few other crazy hallucinations I'd been having. Some other bonkers accusations that I'd made (*"I've cut the weed out now, honestly . . . learned my lesson there, I promise . . ."*). I even end up confessing that I've been seeing a counselor at work and I now realize that there's a possibility I might have been transferring my feelings toward Alana-Jane's murdering father onto my entirely innocent one. Transference is very common when you're mentally fragile, I say.

I should be offended that she believes it all so easily, but I'm far too busy just being grateful that she forgives me. Not to mention hugely relieved that she never did mention anything to Dad.

Thank the Lord for Jacqui's easy readiness to sweep anything unpleasant under the carpet.

Dad and I haven't met up yet. We're letting the feelings lie fallow, just occasionally speaking on the phone. One night he mentions going to Ireland in the summer, maybe just the two of us. He pitches it as an opportunity to lay flowers on Gran's grave, the least he can do after all this time avoiding the place, but I know he hopes we'll lay some ghosts to rest too. That atonement might be found strolling idly past Duffy's field or walking side by side up the Long Road.

I say I'll think about it to avoid the awkwardness but I know it won't happen. To me, it feels wrong.

It feels right to go back to where Maryanne was found though.

It's a mild day, freakish for January. "Hotter than Madrid!" so I'm told by just about everyone. However, it certainly isn't drier than Madrid. Swollen gray clouds have been spewing torrents of rain for the past hour but if anything, it feels beautiful. Oddly fitting for what I'm about to do.

Near to where Maryanne was found, a few bouquets sit under a plane tree. Small, modest bouquets, laid mainly by the kind residents of Leamington Square.

Goodnight and Godbless, The Okonjos (number six)

We didn't know you but we are very sad you have died, lotz of luv, Lily and Freya Markham (number fourteen) xxx

When the moment feels right I crouch down and to anyone watching—not that anyone is watching as far as I can tell—I probably look like I'm just reading all the messages, soaking up the grief.

What I'm actually doing is plowing hard into the rain-softened dirt with my fingers. It takes a bit longer than I expected but I just keep on digging. And when I've finally made a hiding place a few centimeters deep and then the same measure wide, I take it out of my pocket and place it in the ground, patting the mud back in tightly and covering the area in mulch.

The small shiny Tinkerbell I'd meant Maryanne to keep.

Aiden Doyle and I mosey along nicely—going on dates, staying in bed, delighting each other with every dull fact about ourselves. And yes, I know it's wrong. I know that secrets always kill relationships in the long run but I can't even fathom what "long run" means at the moment, and in any case, according to every self-help book I own, we should be worrying less and living more in the here and now.

So here I am now, sitting on his lumpy settee, waiting for my cheese-and-bean toastie to be served.

"I'm thinking of going to Canada," he shouts from the kitchen, or at least I think that's what he shouts over the pounding thump of the doof-doof music that I've learned he worships.

I stand up, turn the volume down—this gets me a side-eye. "But you've only been here a few months. Christ, you don't let the grass grow."

He leans in the doorway, a cheese grater in one hand, a spatula in the other. God, he's gorgeous.

"Not to live, yer big eejit, although it is supposed to be great there. Aren't Canadians supposed to be the happiest people on earth or something?"

"I think it's the Danes actually."

"The Danes?" he says, unconvinced. "What've they got to be so happy about?"

"Oh I don't know, social democracy, work-life balance, damn sexy women . . ."

"Last one'll do me." He thwacks me on the arse with the spatula. "Anyway, smart-arse, I'm not on about emigrating, I mean for a holiday. See my brother and his kids, you know? We never really got on, me and Kevin. He's a good bit older than me and he's a bit of a square . . ."

"Says the man who wears an 'I Heart Sums' T-shirt?"

I dodge another thwack, take refuge back on the settee.

He grins and carries on. "But after what happened to Maryanne, it makes you think about things, you know?"

I do. It makes you think about family. About the unbreakable bonds that withstand almost everything. Every foible and idiosyncrasy. Every failing and poor life choice.

"So do you fancy it then?" he asks, looking nervous. "A holiday to Canada?"

"I'm not sure. You'll have loads of catching up to do . . . and it . . . it seems a bit full-on." The hurt registers on his face. "For now, anyway," I add quickly. "It's just I'm a hell of a slow mover, Aiden, and it's only been a month. Hey, listen, my last boyfriend didn't get under my top until we were three months in so you should count yourself lucky, sunshine—you'd practically seen my uterus in the time it took him to get near my bra."

Humor. The last line of defense in any awkward situation.

"Just think about it, OK?" he says, not letting up. "I'm not talking tomorrow, maybe over the summer? There's loads of good festivals around then. Escapade's in July, gets all the best DJs."

Maryanne loved dance music too by all accounts, sneaking off to Turnmills whenever she and Saskia felt brave enough. Aiden and his sister could have been sibling ravers.

Coulda. Woulda. Shoulda. The sadness is too much.

"I promise I'll think about it," I say and I honestly mean it. Who knows, I might have won the lottery by the summer, if I actually start playing the lottery, and then I won't need to worry about careers and possible disciplinary panels, charges of gross misconduct and professional suicide.

"'I'll think about it' will do for now," he says, handing me a beer. *Beer with cheese toasties?* "Me mam always used to say she'd 'think about it' right before handing over whatever it was you wanted, so I'm feeling positive, I gotta tell you." He walks over to a sideboard and takes out a small photo album, returning with it with a cheeky smirk on his face. "Here, you should get yourself acquainted with who we'll be visiting, and the rest of me family if you're interested."

I am.

The first few photos are in black and white. A grimacing old man, leaning on a stick in front of a tin bath, and then a similarly morose old woman scowling against the same backdrop.

"Me great nan and grandad," he says, standing behind me. "Kills me how fecked-off they look in front of the camera, suspicious of it, like. Bit different now, eh? Don't know what they'd make of the selfie?" I laugh and flick forward, encounter a slightly younger-looking man holding up a fork of hay like an umbrella, then a tiny woman with a perm and a red buttoned coat, as grim-faced and rigid as one of the Queen's Royal Guards. There's none of Jonjo Doyle, unsurprisingly. Plenty of his mam—a plump pretty woman in an assortment of summer dresses. I feel anxious as I move toward the more recent photos but there's actually only one of Maryanne. Carefree and laughing and sticking her fingers up to the camera.

"That's the only one I have of her. Apart from the one I gave to you guys. Anyway, keep going," he says, prodding me. "You're supposed to be drooling over the Canada ones, whetting your appetite."

And who could blame it for being whetted? There's glaciers and waterfalls, mountain views and Downtown Vancouver at night. There's also two of the cutest lads I've ever seen, growing up before my eyes. Nappy changes and bathtimes give way to senior school photos and ice hockey games, all steadily documented for the uncle they probably never expect to meet. The last few are really recent, there isn't an ounce of puppy fat or a badly chosen outfit left to coo over. Jaws have been strengthened, chests defined and hair styled.

"Good-looking lads, eh?" he says, proudly. "Kian there, the one on the right with the flash hairdo—makes him look like he's been electrocuted—doesn't he look like his aunt Maryanne?"

The smell of burned cheese sends him hurtling into the kitchen in a whirlwind of panic and repeated expletives. Alone, I draw the photo closer. My breath comes quickly and my body feels like it might not withstand all the beams of *"how-the-fuck-didn't-I-see-this-before?"* energy currently chasing through my veins.

Because Kian Doyle does look a bit like his aunt Maryanne, yes.

However, he looks a whole lot more like somebody else.

Somebody his aunt Maryanne never got to know.

31

"There's no point denying it, Gina. We can get his DNA from a hair-brush, a toothbrush, he doesn't have to be here. Leo *is* Maryanne's child." I square my shoulders, ready for the denial but she just looks at me, relaxed and resigned, like she's almost wondering what took us so long.

I'm wondering what took us so long. Now I've seen it, I can't un-see it. The same ocean-blue eyes, the same charcoal black hair. He's a frac-tion different around the mouth maybe. Thinner lips, a slightly more tapered chin—inherited from whoever his father was, I suppose—but overall, the likeness is unmistakable. His cheekbones rival Aiden's.

A Doyle through and through.

"Leo's my child." Her declaration rings out across the empty visiting room. "I raised him. I nurtured him. I'm the one who stayed with him in hospital when he had bronchitis as a baby. I'm the one who sang to him, taught him the days of the week, how to tie his laces. I'm the only mother he's ever known. That *woman*, the one who spat him out into the world, she didn't want him. She chose designer clothes and fancy handbags over him. She doesn't get to turn up years later laying claim to a child she literally held for two minutes." A brittle laugh. "She held on to the brown envelope a lot longer, I can tell you."

"Why did you keep him? Why didn't you sell him on?"

She closes her eyes and breathes in deeply, lungs filling up with air while her head fills with precious memories. "He was just so beautiful. So perfect. I couldn't understand how she could give him up but she did"—she clicks her fingers—"just like that. She just shoved him into my arms like he was a pair of shoes in the wrong size and started counting out the money."

"And your dad let you keep him? That baby was worth a lot of money to him."

She shrugs. "Maryanne had shown her true colors by then, suggesting he turn the whole thing into a production line. He knew there was more to be made so he said 'yes.' I think he felt guilty."

"Guilty?" I'm not sure it's an emotion Patrick Mackie understands but I guess Gina knows him better than me. Even monsters can have hidden depths.

"I'd been working for him for ten years by then. Ten years," she says, reinforcing the point. "I was still only twenty-eight. I think he knew working for him had stripped me of any life. I just wanted something to love, something that wasn't *business*, a hint of a normal life. So I told him straight out that if he loved me, he'd let me take Maryanne's baby."

"But you could have had your own baby?" As soon as I say it, I realize that this might not be true. We know about her fertility issues and was IVF even so prevalent in the 1990s?

"Taking an unwanted child was easier," she says simply. "My life was hectic enough with all the studying and working for Dad. Being pregnant would have been a nightmare—or that's how I saw it then. Anyway, because of who I was, men hardly ever came near me. And zitty Med students weren't really my type either."

"You didn't get your normal life though, did you? You carried on with your dad's *business* long after Leo."

She corrects me quickly. "I carried on working at the flat, supervising the girls, delivering the babies. I stopped being involved in . . . everything else."

"By everything else, you mean the drugs, the prostitution rings, the major frauds?"

The look of pure malice could be for me, or for herself. Odds on, it's the latter.

She shakes her head. "I never wanted to be part of all that. Never. And that's part of the reason why having a child made sense. I knew Dad would let me step away from the more dangerous aspects if I was a mother." She leans forward onto the table, exhausted, broken. "Deep down, all I'd ever wanted was a proper career, a family, decent friends. And I finally got it when I met Nate. He was respectable."

"So Nate could have been anyone really? He was just your passport to a normal life."

She doesn't look offended by the suggestion. "You could put it like that, I suppose. He had a young child so it was certainly a passport to a ready-made nuclear family. Leo. Amber. One boy. One girl. It was perfect. And I think I did love him, in a way. I liked that he'd been brought up well. He knew all the best restaurants, all the best schools, where to ski, what wine to pair with what meal. He was part of the scene that I wanted to be part of so I made myself love him. But it turns out he wanted to be part of my dad's scene even more."

"Not so respectable."

"He was corruptible." Her eyes bore into mine. "Most people are, given the right set of circumstances."

There's no way Gina Hicks knows anything about me or Dad—*how could she?*—and yet her words sound heavy and loaded.

She carries on, chin propped on one hand. "I recognized Nate's greed the first time I met him, but that was good, I knew it meant he'd accept who my dad was, where I'd come from."

I nod. "Nate fronts some of your dad's businesses, we know that."

She doesn't argue. "I was OK with that. Listen, I said I wanted more of a normal life, not that I wanted to completely disown my previous one." She shrugs again. "Whatever Dad and Nate got up to was fine with me, I just didn't want to hear about it. And then when Dad fled the UK, it got easier anyway. We were happy. Things were good."

"Until Maryanne came back, asking about her baby."

Her voice is hot. "Until my dad came back and got his claws into Leo. Filling his head with all this talk of succession, about taking over the family business. And Leo idolizes him, that's the worst part! Thinks he's this great big legend and wants to be just like him. He'd do anything to impress him. It kills me to watch."

I try a theory out for size. It's been bubbling and forming since two this morning.

"Was Leo at the house, Gina? Did he see you push Maryanne? Is that why you wanted him out of the country, to keep him out of all of this?"

She sits up, says nothing for a while. There isn't a sound in the room but I wait out the silence, determined she'll break first.

She does after a huge sigh.

"Not bad, but not a hundred percent. He wasn't there at the time. He didn't see what happened. He came home shortly afterward, though, while I was waiting for Dad. He wasn't supposed to, he was supposed to be at rugby practice but it was raining and he was already getting over a nasty cough. He had the Vienna performance to think of."

"And he saw Maryanne."

"*She* saw *him*, that was the problem." She pauses, rolls her eyes. "Oh for heaven's sake, do you honestly think Leo had any idea who she was? He's a teenage boy, Detective. He doesn't register anyone unless they're half-naked or carrying some sort of sports equipment. But *she* knew though. She knew straightaway." Her face sours. "Touching, isn't it?"

I picture Leo Hicks walking into that house. His hair blackened a shade darker by the rain, the sculpted spikes dampening into curls. And those telltale blue eyes staring straight into the eyes of the woman on the floor. The woman who gave birth to him.

Of course Maryanne knew and it was the reason she had to die.

If Gina didn't have the balls to do it, daddy dearest would, and she knew this. She as good as killed Maryanne when she called Patrick Mackie, asking for his help.

"I tried to do everything right by Leo. He was my perfect boy. Private school, extracurricular *everything*, educational holidays, piano lessons." Even now, she can't help but puff up with pride. "He's so incredibly gifted, you know? He was playing Chopin by his tenth birthday."

I'm not sure what I'm supposed to say so I say nothing. I feel a quiver of something though. Things quickly falling into place.

"And it was all fine until my dad came back." She looks straight at me, defiant. "You have no idea how it feels to be scared of your father." I blink away something. A laugh? A tear? "To feel like he defines you and that no matter what you do and how hard you try, you'll never escape what he is. That maybe you're as bad as he is, deep down. I didn't want that for Leo. I had to get him away, out of the country, away from my dad's poison."

I don't have the heart to tell her I think it's too late. That Leo is no longer Maryanne's baby or her perfect boy.

Leo Hicks is Patrick Mackie's boy now.

He was the second he helped his grandad dispose of Maryanne's body.

Maybe even helped murder her?

The shallow slash marks to her throat—hesitation marks, Vickery suggested. Someone trying to work up the courage. An inexperienced killer, the whole team had agreed. Not the shaky work of one of the UK's most wanted criminals.

But can we prove it?

Will we ever be able to prove that Leo Hicks unwittingly killed his own birth mother?

From the car park I call Richard Little—the piano teacher whose car was stolen and used to dispose of Maryanne's body. He confirms he has a pupil called Leo Hicks. He's been rather worried about him, in fact. He was supposed to be back in lessons from 17th January and he hasn't heard from anyone, neither Leo nor his parents. No one appears to want to take his calls.

He also unwittingly confirms that Leo knew he'd be in Malta at the time his car was stolen. He explains they'd talked about Malta in their last lesson, a few weeks before Christmas. Leo had been to Valetta with his parents when he was younger and he told him it was a beautiful place. Such a cultured young man, he gushes. So talented.

I let the gushing praise burn out then thank him for his time, tell him he's been very helpful.

Which he has, I suppose.

His confirmation is hardly cast-iron evidence but at least it's something. Something to build a case from if Leo Hicks is ever caught.

With a heavy heart and the rumblings of a migraine, I call HQ and ask for Forensics to be sent back over to the Hickses' to seize all of Leo's shoes. You never know, we might get lucky with a footprint, although we haven't been too big on luck lately, and I strongly suspect Leo's clothes would have been destroyed within minutes anyway.

Patrick Mackie doesn't like loose ends, you see.

32

"I hear you're considering a secondment."

For once Dr. Allen isn't bang on the money. I'm not considering a secondment, I'm going on secondment. On "attachment" anyway, which isn't pure semantics or fart-arsey Met-speak, it's actually the main reason I agreed.

On "attachment," while I might be learning new stuff in a new building with new people, I essentially stay under the wing of my Operational Command Unit. Or in simpler non-Met speak, I stay tethered to Steele's apron strings.

Still very much part of Murder, in spirit if not in body.

"I've decided to take it," I tell Dr. Allen, who looks pleasantly surprised. "Well, it is only for five months and it's '*very prestigious*,'" I add, mimicking Steele's mantra.

She allows herself a smidge of a smile. "So where are you off to?"

"The mayor's office, no less. Working on the final draft of the Police and Crime Plan. It's a four-year plan, quite a big project."

Dr. Allen sips her black coffee, nods her approval. "Very prestigious indeed. And high profile. It sounds like a fantastic opportunity, Cat. The content of the work must be hugely appealing."

It is. Sort of. What's more appealing is not having to look Parnell and Steele in the eye for the next five months, although I'm not entirely sure five whole lifetimes will lessen the guilt I feel every time Parnell praises me for playing a blinder with Gina Hicks in the interview room. For going after her confession like my world depended on it.

I'm not entirely sure Parnell's not suspicious about that either, but that could just be my paranoia.

The kind of paranoia five months' distance might go some way to dissolve.

"Sod the content of the work," I say. "The job's based in Southwark which means I can walk to work in half an hour, no public transport. Who in their right mind would turn that down?"

"It's a bonus, yes, I can see that. But I don't believe for a second it's your main reason. It must have been a very hard decision."

It was. I miss Parnell already and I haven't even left yet.

"It's nine-to-five, that's an ever bigger bonus." That's met with a stern stare but I'm only half-joking this time. "Seriously, nine-to-five is good. I've got some stuff going on in my personal life, family stuff. I could do with my work life being a bit more routine." I laugh out loud, stick my fist in my mouth. "Jesus, did I just say 'routine?' Not exactly the maverick rookie cliché I thought I was."

"Really, is that how you see yourself? Mmm, I'd challenge you to think about that, Cat." I lean forward, challenge accepted. Dr. Allen reads my body language perfectly. "Well, it's just that only a few weeks ago, you talked about your obsession with fairness, your need for reassurance that certain rules work. Those aren't generally the concerns of a dyed-in-the-wool maverick. You may be more conformist than you think."

I nod because she's right. It's true there's part of me that has this deep desire to conform. To be like the Emily Becks of this world, breezing through life with a kind of universally alluring blandness that makes everyone look at you, but not too closely.

Neither ignored nor adored.

"So what happens now?" I ask. "Do you tick the 'not batshit crazy' box and send me on my way?"

"Do you think I should?"

"I'm definitely sleeping better."

Of course, it's easier to sleep better when you're being spooned by a sexy Irishman several nights a week, but I gloss over that fact. God knows where "shagging a member of the victim's family" comes on Dr. Allen's over-empathy scale.

"That's encouraging," she says, manufacturing an encouraging smile. "A good night's sleep should be a priority, not a luxury. But it's not the only benchmark of progress."

"Meaning?"

"Meaning you've moved forward in other ways."

But backward in the ways that count. Integrity. Honesty. Trust.

I swallow down the self-loathing and try to sound pleased. "Really, do you think so?"

"You certainly seem more present than in our earlier meetings. I never really had the sense you were 'here' until recently. You were physically here, of course . . ."

"But mentally, about fifty miles south of Botswana?"

I expect a smile but it doesn't come. "You're far too hard on yourself, Cat. You were distracted, that's all I meant. Distant."

"Distant *and* over-empathetic? Is that even possible?"

"Very much so. Most people's personalities are a mess of contradictions. It's rarely a case of being A or B."

Don't I just know it.

"So what's the 'benchmark of progress' on the empathy front, Dr. Allen? Do I have to prove I've become a cold-hearted bitch before you'll sign me off?"

Snarky comments aren't a "benchmark of progress" either but she allows it. One for the road, hey?

"There's nothing wrong with empathy per se, Cat, but it's all about levels. And too much empathy in the job you do can be debilitating. It's very difficult to make rational decisions when you are literally *feeling* somebody else's pain. Now, compassion . . ." She tilts her head the other way. "Compassion is another thing entirely. It's possible to feel compassion for someone without it overwhelming your circuits." She glances at the clock, two minutes and counting. "But I'd say you've made progress there too. DCI Steele tells me you played a key role in your latest case, and I believe that wasn't an easy one either?"

The praise makes me nauseous, I shrug it away quickly. "It was straightforward enough. We got guilty pleas so we're just waiting on sentencing, and the medical reports for the old guy. He should get sent down though. Fuck him and his illness. Very few people deserve lung cancer, Dr. Allen, but he's definitely one of them . . ."

Dr. Allen gives me her Mona Lisa smile. The elusive one. The one that's annoyingly impartial. I think about practicing it in the mirror tonight, I reckon it must come in handy.

"Well, that's about it," she says eventually, not quite standing up but bracing herself to. "We'll have follow-up sessions every six weeks and of course you know where I am in the meantime." A slight pause. "But is there anything else you wanted to say, or ask, today?"

I think about this. "I suppose there is one thing." She picks up the humor in my voice, responds with a preemptive smile. "If it's rarely a case that you're either A or B, does that mean I can be a spontaneous sexy maverick *and* a slave to routine?"

She laughs. "Absolutely. Although, don't judge routine too harshly, Cat. It gets a bad press in today's adrenaline-fueled society, but it provides a level of safety, a level of reassurance. It's OK to crave routine. Most people do, if they're honest."

"I don't crave it," I say, a little snarky again. *Two for the road.* "I just need some personal time and Murder doesn't leave room for much else."

The routine for the foreseeable future, as stipulated by Jacqui, self-appointed chief mediator, is for me to have dinner at her house, *"Six p.m. sharp, not a minute later"* a couple of times a week.

With Dad there.

Although no Noel, thank God. Noel's back in Fuengirola, pulling pints in low-rent strip clubs again and paying off whatever gambling or drug debt Dad bailed him out of.

We've only had two summits so far but Jacqui's been in her element, presiding over anodyne conversations about loft extensions and Finn's prowess on the football field, while feeding us home-cooked stews and hearty roast dinners. The kind of food that's supposed to say "family," I think.

Restorative food.

Healing straight out of a packet.

Truth is, the healing tends to start when Jacqui's not there, when she's clearing up in the kitchen or holding sleep-time negotiations with Finn. That's when Dad and I sit in silence—a strained but strangely peaceful silence—watching the TV, laughing or tutting at the same things.

Always the same things.

And in any case, Jacqui needn't worry. Dad and I are bonded for life now in a way we weren't before.

Because I'm not just the keeper of his secrets anymore. He's the keeper of mine.

ACKNOWLEDGMENTS

It takes a large number of people to make the largest of dreams come true so here goes . . .

To my agent, Eugenie Furniss, for believing in me so passionately from the outset. Your enthusiasm for my writing knocked me sideways! Huge, huge, heartfelt thanks.

To Katherine Armstrong, editor extraordinaire—thanks for loving Cat, Parnell et al as much as I do, and for applying your shrewd eye and big heart to *Sweet Little Lies* and making it all the better for it. Thanks also to Bec Farrell who first championed my book, and to all at Bonnier Zaffre—you've made me feel so welcome during what has been a slightly out-of-body experience! Thanks also to Jon Appleton for his eagle-eyed copy edits.

To Richard and Judy and WHSmith for choosing *Sweet Little Lies* as the winner of the "Search for a Bestseller" competition. It's rare I'm rendered speechless but well done, you managed it.

To Erin Kelly, Anna Davis and Rufus Purdy at Curtis Brown Creative. Can't believe it's nearly three years since I walked into the boardroom with a hint of an idea and a whole load of self-doubt. I owe you a huge debt for helping me flip that around the other way!

To Alan Howarth for his invaluable insight into police procedure. A "couple of quick questions" turned into months of daily badgering but please know how appreciated it was. Any remaining errors are entirely mine, not Alan's.

The list of cheerleaders is endless. To anyone who ever listened to me constantly banging on about writing a book and managed to stay interested, thank you. Special shouts to Helen Powell, Carla Todd, Cat

Sweatman, Fiona Kirrane, Alison and Garry Naughton, the Frear family and Jenny Quintana (and indeed all my CBC cohorts!).

To Mum, whose love and faith in my ability is as constant as the sun, and to Dad, a first-class storyteller and presumably where I got the gene. I hope I've made you both proud.

To Neil, for absolutely everything. For tea, plot suggestions, keeping me sane and making me feel like the only girl in the world. You're a prince among men, baby. This book wouldn't be what it is, and I wouldn't be where I am without you. I love you, always.

And finally. Thank you, lovely reader, for buying my book.

xx

CAZ FREAR grew up in Coventry, England, and spent her teenage years dreaming of moving to London and writing a novel. After fulfilling her first dream, it wasn't until she moved back to Coventry thirteen years later that the second finally came true. She has a degree in history and politics, and when she's not agonizing over snappy dialogue or incisive prose, she can be found shouting at Arsenal football matches or holding court in the pub on topics she knows nothing about. *Sweet Little Lies* is her first novel.

READ ON FOR AN EXCERPT FROM
STONE COLD HEART
BY CAZ FREAR.

AVAILABLE IN HARDCOVER,
E-BOOK, AND DIGITAL AUDIO
IN JULY 2019 FROM HARPERCOLLINS
PUBLISHERS.

@MadLou wishes I'd been choked with my own placenta at birth.

@daveholby2 wonders how I can live with myself.

I won't dignify Mad Lou with a response but Dave makes a fair point. You see, I always knew I had it in me to kill someone. Whether I could live with it afterwards, now there was the real question.

Because you can kid yourself that you know who you are. You can declare yourself to be a strong person, a weak person, or maybe one of life's middle-grounders, ricocheting between warrior and wimp depending on which side of the bed you got out of. But, trust me, until you've seen the light fade from someone's eyes, knowing it was you who flicked the switch, you who crushed their last seconds of hope, then you've got no clue about what strength or weakness means. You've got no idea about the horrors you can learn to live with.

See, ultimately, *life* makes you live with it. Its routines. Its regimes. Its way of pulling you on to the next thing before you've properly evaluated the last.

And fundamentally, nothing changes anyway. The world still turns. Night still follows day. You still stand in supermarket queues, wondering how you always manage to pick the slowest one. You still whine about train fares, phone bills, non-dispensing cash machines.

You still *live*.

And she'd have lived too, if only she'd calmed the fuck down.

1
AUGUST 2017

'Cat, wait . . .'

He knows my name. *How the hell does he know my name?*

I keep moving forward, pretending I haven't heard him over the incessant gurgle of the coffee machines and the insipid soft jazz. I'm nearly at the door now. Just a few more strides and I'll be safely outside, away from Casanova's attention and basking in the scents of a grimy London summer.

Warm beer. Bus diesel. Raindrops hitting hot pavements. Bliss

'Hey, Cat, wait a second . . .'

This moment's been looming and I could kick myself for not listening to my gut and taking my custom elsewhere. Actually, I could kick DC Ben Swaines. Swaines has become the worst kind of coffee snob since he starting dating a barista from Sydney, and now it's all 'earthy' this and 'resinous' that, because why use one adjective when you can use three or four?

I don't even drink the damn stuff.

Casanova, owner of The Grindhouse, has been using this as a ruse to flirt with me over the past few weeks, suggesting he whisk me off to Vienna – first class, of course – where the traditional Fiaker is bound to convert me, and declaring that 'Only sex and a round of golf at Gleneagles' can match the thrill of finding a new single-source coffee bean.

It takes all sorts to make a world, as my mum used to say.

'Please . . . hang on . . .'

He's louder this time. Insistent. It doesn't help that it's late afternoon and The Grindhouse is in the dead zone. There's only me and one end-of-tether granny shovelling radio-active looking goo into a squirming toddler's mouth, so frankly, there's no way I can ignore him again without appearing rude or stone deaf. With no other option, I put my game face on and swing around, smiling. He's already walked out from behind the counter and I'm momentarily thrown by the full length of him as he's been half a human the entire time I've been coming here. Just a floating buff torso in a Ralph Lauren shirt, doling out la-di-da come-ons and caffè macchiatos.

'Oh God, don't tell me.' I slap my hand to my forehead. 'I've left my card in the machine again, haven't I?'

Could this be my fault? Maybe I've led him on? Maybe he's mistaken forgetfulness for a convoluted form of foreplay?

'No, no, you're fine,' he stutters, which in itself is a bit odd. 'I just wanted to ask you something. It's rather delicate, really. Can we sit down?'

It's an instruction rather than an invitation and I should absolutely say no. I should have said it weeks ago, in fact. I should have said, 'No, I don't want to go to Vienna. I don't want to go anywhere with you. I have a boyfriend who makes my insides flutter' instead of laughing it off with some crack about having lost my passport. But then, I've never been good at out-and-out rejection. It's the people-pleaser in me. It's the same reason I do the coffee run when I don't even drink coffee.

And for that same reason, I reluctantly sit down, giving him a quick aesthetic sweep as I do. I don't know why, but from the other side of the counter, I'd never quite appreciated just how striking he is. Coal-black hair. Eyes the colour of aged whiskey. Lashes I'd gladly swap mine for. Around early forties, I'd say, with that killer combination of boyish good-looks and older-guy knowingness. I doubt he sleeps alone too often. I'd say he's rejected even less.

'So, what can I do for you?' I sound like an overgrown Girl Guide. 'Although you'll have to be quick. I can't have the troops' coffee going cold. I've seen people fired for less.'

He pauses, clearing his throat. 'Well, it's all a bit awkward, and honestly, I'm so sorry to trouble you with it, but it's about my wife, you see. She's been acting rather . . . well, *odd*, I suppose, saying really quite disturbing things. It's completely out of character and, if I'm honest, I'm starting to worry.'

His wife?

The toddler screams and I quickly feign interest, buying myself a few seconds to recalibrate where we're headed now that it appears I'm not about to be hit on. Unfortunately, though, there's only so long you can feign interest in the confiscation of a stuffed giraffe and so, reluctantly, I turn back, pasting on a sympathetic smile.

'I'm sorry to hear that. Not sure how I can help though?'

'Well, I'd have thought that's obvious,' he says, looking perplexed. 'You're the police.'

'And how do you know that?'

'Know what?'

'That I'm a police officer.' I can wave bye-bye to any future undercover work if my institutionalisation's *that* blatant.

'You walk by with that fat chap most days – and he's definitely one. Believe me, if you work near a major police station for the best part of ten years, you get to know the signs. The badly fitting suits, the air of importance. They're dead giveaways.' His face softens. 'Not you, though.'

Moving on. 'I still don't understand – how does me being a police officer help you with your wife?'

'I need advice, of course.'

Instantly I relax, knowing I'll be laughing about this in ten minutes. Cracking jokes with the team about the guy who mistook the Metropolitan Police for Marriage Guidance. It's on a par with the fool who asked Parnell – said 'fat chap' – to arrest his neighbours because their tree was blocking his Sky dish and he couldn't watch the wrestling.

Still, I'm a professional and so I rustle up an appropriately solemn tone. 'Look, I'm sorry you're having problems, I really am, but this isn't a police matter. Surely there's a friend or a family member you can talk to? Or if you're genuinely worried about her mental health, maybe a doctor might . . .'

'A doctor! Worried about *her*?' His laugh is hale and hearty and shot through with malice. 'You don't understand. It's not *her* I'm worried about. It's me. She's unstable. She's made threats against me, several times.'

This changes things. I won't be dining out on this any time soon.

'OK, well, threats *are* a police matter. Has she physically threatened you? Because if she has, we take that kind of thing *very* seriously. But you need to go to your local station and make an official complaint. That's my advice.'

He circles his thumbs, agitated. 'They aren't physical threats. She's too clever for that. She's subtle, you see. Sly. People underestimate her.'

'Can you be more specific?'

'Specific?'

I'm cautious of putting words in his mouth but time's ticking on and I've got a tower of witness statements to slog through – a chip shop stabbing on the Caledonian Road where, would you believe it, everyone was too busy buying haddock to notice a murder happening two feet in front of them.

'Well, has she blackmailed you? Damaged your belongings?'

'No, no, nothing like that.' His tone says he's frustrated with me. Christ, *I'm* frustrated with me. I feel like I'm missing the subtext here. 'It's more that . . . well, she keeps saying she's going to make me suffer, she's going to make me pay. And it's almost every day now. The mood swings. The threats. Is that specific enough for you?'

Specific, yes. Criminal, no – although it's a grey area and it's getting greyer. Words still aren't quite weapons in the eyes of the law, but with new legislation coming through, making someone's life intolerable isn't as tolerated as it once was and Amen to that.

'So what have you got to pay for? Sorry to ask but context is really important with these kind of complaints.'

He suppresses a smirk that says *'take a good guess.'* 'What can I say? None of us are perfect, Cat. I never claimed to be the world's most honourable husband.'

A claim only ever made by the bottom 10 per cent.

In that moment, I make a decision: throw him a bone and get the hell out of here. Back to the chaotic safety of Murder Investigation Team 4's MIT4 squad room. I'll even buy Swaines one of those fancy-pants coffee machines if it means never having to set foot in here again.

'Look, all I can say is that if it's becoming a daily thing, you might – and I stress *might* have a case for Controlling and Coercive Behaviour.' He leans in closer, enthralled – a bit too close and enthralled for my liking; this guy isn't big on personal space. 'It's a fairly new offence that addresses emotional abuse within relationships. There isn't much precedent, though, and I'll warn you now, it's very *very* hard to prove.'

'Controlling and Coercive Behaviour,' he repeats, eyes glinting as he tries the term out for size. 'Thank you.'

I stand, picking up the now lukewarm coffees. 'As I say, I'm not even sure it applies here without knowing more, and it's not my area of expertise, I'm afraid. But speak to someone at your local station, see what they think.'

He shakes his head. 'No. No, I don't need to speak to anyone else. You've been more than helpful.' I'm not sure I have. I'm even less sure I want to be. 'And besides, I'm not actually going to make a complaint. I'm not even going to tell her that I've spoken to you. That isn't what this is about.' His grin makes my organs shiver. 'I'm just safeguarding my position, that's all. Working out what I can threaten her with further down the line if her behaviour gets worse.'

This is madness. I only came in for three Café Cubanos and an apricot flapjack.

He walks me to the door, positioning himself in front of the handle. 'So what is your area, Cat? Let me guess – I'm thinking murder?'

'Got it in one.'

This amuses him. 'Really? I was actually joking. You look far too . . . well, too sweet to be dealing with murder. It must be the curls – and those freckles, of course.' He taps the bridge of my nose, a movement so quick and light that I barely have time to flinch, never mind knee him in the bollocks. 'So tell me, how long have you been a police officer?'

'It was my five-year anniversary last week.' I tip my head towards the door. 'And if I want to make it to six, I really need to get back.'

'Wow, five years and you're still doing the coffee run?' He smiles knowingly, although I'm damned if I know what he thinks he knows. 'You must be very keen.'

And there it is. That posh-bloke entitlement. That ego-driven reflex that assumes I do it because of him.

'You should take this then – in fact, I insist you do – as a thank you.' He reaches behind me to a carved wooden ornament – a black and red devil mask, wizened and grotesque. 'Wood's the traditional five-year anniversary gift and I've been meaning to get rid of it anyway. It scares the customers, especially the children. It's antique, though, worth plenty.' He holds it in front of his face, amber eyes glinting through the narrow, jagged slits. 'I picked it up on a work trip to Huehuetenango – that's in Guatemala, if you're not familiar. It's supposed to be El Conductor, otherwise known as Lucifer's principal assistant.'

I offer a tight smile, dredging my manners up from somewhere. 'Thanks, that's really kind of you but I'm can't take it, I'm afraid. It's against the rules to accept gifts from the public and I'm a real stickler for the rules.'

Which is a statement beyond parody, given the lies I've told. The lines I've crossed.

But hey, I never claimed to be the world's most honourable police officer.

Another claim only ever made by the bottom 10 per cent.

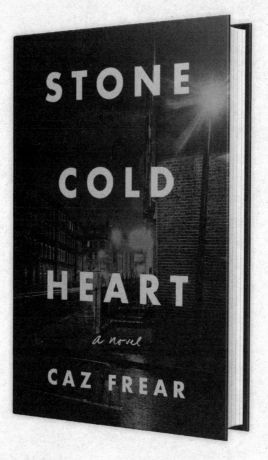